P R A I S E   F O R

EARTH SONG, SKY SPIRIT

"A remarkable collection of stories by some of the best
American Indian writers today."

—DAVID WHITEHORSE (LAKOTA/COMANCHE),
professor, California State University, San Marcos

"These stories offer a chance to enter the lives and communities
of diverse native peoples . . . a wondrous work."

—LARRY MYERS (POMO),
executive secretary, Native American Heritage Commission

"EARTH SONG, SKY SPIRIT brings together stories that speak of the
experiences of Native American peoples, recounting grim struggles
to survive in worlds not of their own making. They also reveal
the determination, resilience, and small victories that allow
Native Americans to endure."

—REBECCA KUGEL (OJIBWE),
professor, Department of History, University of California, Riverside

Earth Song, sky Spirit

EDITED WITH AN INTRODUCTION BY

Clifford E. Trafzer

Short Stories
of the
Contemporary
Native American
Experience

ANCHOR BOOKS
Doubleday

NEW YORK   LONDON   TORONTO   SYDNEY   AUCKLAND

AN ANCHOR BOOK

PUBLISHED BY DOUBLEDAY
a division of
Bantam Doubleday Dell Publishing Group, Inc.
1540 Broadway, New York, New York 10036

ANCHOR BOOKS, DOUBLEDAY, and the portrayal of an anchor
are trademarks of Doubleday, a division of
Bantam Doubleday Dell Publishing Group, Inc.

Book design by Terry Karydes

Library of Congress Cataloging-in-Publication Data

Earth song, sky spirit : short stories of the contemporary native American experience / edited with an
introduction by Clifford E. Trafzer. — 1st ed.
p.   cm.
1. Indians of North America—Fiction.   2. American fiction—Indian authors.   3. American fiction—
20th century.   4. Short stories, American.   I. Trafzer, Clifford E.
[PS508.I5E25   1993b]
813'.01083520397—dc20   92-44297
CIP

ISBN 0-385-46960-8
Copyright © 1992 by Clifford E. Trafzer

All Rights Reserved
Printed in the United States of America
First Anchor Books Edition: August 1993

1   3   5   7   9   10   8   6   4   2

ACKNOWLEDGMENTS

The following selections in this anthology are reproduced by permission of the authors, their publishers, or their agents:

"From Aboard the Night Train" by Kimberly M. Blaeser © Kimberly M. Blaeser. Reprinted by permission of the author.

"The Moccasin Game" by Gerald Vizenor © Gerald Vizenor. Reprinted by permission of the author.

"Prisoner of Haiku" by Gordon D. Henry, Jr. © Gordon D. Henry, Jr. Reprinted by permission of the author.

"The Day the Crows Stopped Talking" by Harvest Moon Eyes © Harvest Moon Eyes. Reprinted by permission of the author.

"The Well" from *Ramparts*, Volume 2, Number 1, May 1963, by N. Scott Momaday © 1963 by N. Scott Momaday. Reprinted by permission of the author.

"Lost in the Land of Ishtaboli" by Don L. Birchfield © Don L. Birchfield. Reprinted by permission of the author.

"Faces" by Julia Lowry Russell © Julia Lowry Russell. Reprinted by permission of the author.

"Adventures of an Indian Princess" by Patricia Riley © Patricia Riley. Reprinted by permission of the author.

Acknowledgments

"Lucy, Oklahoma, 1911" by Craig Womack © Craig Womack. Reprinted by permission of the author.

"Fear and Recourse" by Maurice Kenny © Maurice Kenny. Reprinted by permission of the author.

"Earl Yellow Calf" is reprinted from *The Indian Lawyer* by James Welch with the permission of the author and W. W. Norton & Company, Inc. Copyright © 1990 by James Welch.

"Grandpa Kashpaw's Ghost" from *Love Medicine*, by Louise Erdrich © 1984 by Louise Erdrich. Reprinted by permission of Henry Holt & Co., Inc.

"Sun Offering" by Annie Hansen © Annie Hansen. Reprinted by permission of the author.

"Lead Horse" by Diane Glancy © Diane Glancy. Reprinted by permission of the author.

"Bone Girl" by Joe Bruchac © Joe Bruchac. Reprinted by permission of the author.

"Spirit Woman" from *The Woman Who Owned the Shadows*, by Paula Gunn Allen © 1983 by Paula Gunn Allen. Reprinted by permission of Aunt Lute Books (415-558-8116).

"The Cave" by Jack D. Forbes © Jack D. Forbes. Reprinted by permission of the author.

"Akun, Jiki Walu: Grandfather Magician" by Darryl Babe Wilson © Darryl Babe Wilson. Reprinted by permission of the author.

"Marlene's Adventures" by Anita Endrezze © Anita Endrezze. Reprinted by permission of the author.

"The Approximate Size of My Favorite Tumor" by Sherman Alexie © Sherman Alexie. Reprinted by permission of the author.

"Shadows and Sleepwalkers" by Cait Featherstone © Cait Featherstone. Reprinted by permission of the author.

"For Her with No Regrets" from *Shantih* 4, #2, Summer–Fall, 1979, by Duane Niatum © Duane Niatum. Reprinted by permission of the author.

"Avian Messiah and Mistress Media" by Andrew Connors © Andrew Connors. Reprinted by permission of the author.

"Slaughterhouse" by Greg Sarris © Greg Sarris. Reprinted by permission of the author.

Acknowledgments

"Joseph's Rainbow" by Inez Petersen © Inez Petersen. Reprinted by permission of the author.

"The Dream" by Penny Olson © Penny Olson. Reprinted by permission of the author.

"Silver Bass and Alligator Gar" by Ralph Salisbury © Ralph Salisbury. Reprinted by permission of the author.

"Danse d'Amour, Danse de Mort" by LeAnne Howe © LeAnne Howe. Reprinted by permission of the author.

"Clara's Gift" from *A Yellow Raft in Blue Water*, by Michael Dorris. Copyright © 1986 by Michael Dorris. Reprinted by permission of Henry Holt & Co., Inc.

"The Return of the Buffalo" from *Almanac of the Dead*, by Leslie Marmon Silko. Copyright © 1991 by Leslie Marmon Silko. Reprinted by permission of Simon & Schuster, Inc.

SONG OF THE EARTH

It is lovely indeed
It is lovely indeed
I am the spirit within the earth
The feet of the earth are my feet
The legs of the earth are my legs
The bodily strength of the earth is my bodily strength
The thoughts of the earth are my thoughts
The voice of the earth is my voice
The feather of the earth is my feather
All that belongs to the earth belongs to me
All that surrounds the earth surrounds me
I am the sacred words of the earth
It is lovely indeed
It is lovely indeed

FROM THE NAVAJO ORIGIN STORY
AS TOLD BY CURLY MUSTACHE

For the
Woman
with
Blue
Hands

CONTENTS

Contents

Contents

Contents

Contents

Contents

INTRODUCTION

Clifford E. Trafzer

In a dream I first met an old Indian elder. He had long white hair that fell neatly down his back to his waist. The old man walked with me on the north bank of Snake River, pointing out places he thought important for me to know. He took me to the site of Palus Village where he had been born, and he showed me the petrified heart of the Giant Beaver that had been slain by four Palouse warriors during the early years of creation. The elder told me where on the river the people had crossed the Snake, and he showed me the trail the Palouse had used to enter and leave the black basalt canyon. As we walked along the old man spotted a leafy green plant growing between us and the riverbank.

"Oh, you will like this," he exclaimed. "This is a good root, and it's delicious."

With that, the elder got down on his knees facing the plant and me. He began to unearth the root with his hands, and as he did, he sang his song, a song of thanksgiving to the earth and to the plant. He sang a song praising the Creator and extolling the virtues of the root itself. Then, as dreams often do, the entire scene changed. I was whisked away upriver, carried by the wind to the Nez Perce Reservation. I sat at a large round table with several Nez Perce women, and we talked about children and families. We sat together talking about Nez Perce families living in Idaho who were related by blood to the Palouse Indians. The women laughed as they explained to me the familial and sexual relations of their people with the Palouse.

Then as quickly as it had begun, the vision ended. But in the morning I remembered it clearly and could get on with my writing. In the fall of that year I was invited to give a presentation on the Yakima Reservation, discussing the importance of oral literature and history in the research and writing of formal histories of Indian people. The topic was an easy one for me, and the audience understood my views, since most of them were Native Americans. When I finished my talk, several Indians from the Yakima Reservation suggested that I visit a Palouse Indian doctor named Andrew George.

Now, I had heard of Andrew George before, when I was on the Umatilla Reservation of Oregon, Nez Perce Reservation of Idaho, and Colville Reservation of Washington. In fact, many times I had heard about the old Palouse medicine man who was born at Palus Village and grew up in the "old way" along Snake River. Many times I had heard of Andrew George, but I had never been able to track him down. Andrew George, it seemed, was always on the move, his services much in demand. To me, he was an Indian phantom, a spirit, a stick person from the Northwest. Sometimes I wondered if he existed at all.

The people had assured me that Andrew George was on the Yakima Reservation that day and that he was staying with his daughter. Since his daughter had no telephone, the only way for me to find Andrew George was to drive to her home. And so I did, with my future wife, Lee Ann, and my friend Richard Scheuerman. We followed the directions to take the county road down this way until the pavement ended, turn right at the yellow sign, and travel down the dirt road along the canal to the red pump house. We followed the directions as best as we could until we came to three houses built by the tribal housing authority.

We walked to the front door of a house that we thought was that of Andrew George's daughter. I knocked and waited. Two little girls opened the door, and I asked, "Does Andrew George live here?" Neither girl answered. They both giggled and ran off down a hall to the left. The door stood wide open, allowing the cold wind to swirl around the tidy living room. A few moments later an old man with long white hair emerged from the dark hallway. This was the man from my dream, the one who had taught me so much along Snake River, the one who had sung his song of thanksgiving while bending down and digging out the root.

Before I could say anything, he stepped through the open door, reached out his hands, and brought us inside. We entered his home in silence, and followed him to the kitchen table. Yes, I told myself, this is the old man of my dream. I recognized him and he knew me. I knew that he had called me to his place to listen and learn. For the next three hours Andrew George told us about his people. Through the stories, he told us how Turtle had created the Palouse Hills before his great race with Coyote. He told us how Salmon Chief had taken some power from Rattlesnake. He told us of his mother's and father's exile to *Eekish Pah*, the Hot Country, Oklahoma. Andrew George said they always used to cry when they thought about those days. That was the time when the government removed some of the Palouse after the Nez Perce War of 1877.

Most important, he told us of the spirits within the earth through his words and stories. "You come from that university over there, don't you?" he asked in a blunt but considerate manner. We answered yes, and then he said, "You have those people over there who spend their lives studying the plants and animals. I feel sorry for those people, because they don't really know the plants and animals. They have never talked to them, never heard them speak, never heard their songs. I have seen things they have never seen, heard things they will never hear."

I learned only a small portion of Andrew George's story, but I learned something of his life and that of his family. "That's the way it is," my mother used to say. "You only get to know part of the story, but one day you might get to know more, but maybe not." My mother was right. It all depends on the story and the storyteller. And so it is with this collection of short stories by Native American writers. The storytellers will open your hearts to parts of their worlds, and like Andrew George, they will do so through their words and stories.

Storytelling has always been a Native American art that was practiced communally, and although there were some "specialists" in the field, nearly everyone engaged in the art. Mothers, grandmothers, aunts, and sisters told stories to the children of creation, power, and medicine, particularly during the winter when people huddled around a fire to hear the words. Fathers, grandfathers, uncles, and brothers told stories of love, hunts, and heroes who had saved the people, emphasizing that an individual was not set apart from the whole but was part of a community that required the assistance of those who could contribute most to the well-being of the family, band, or tribe. Unlike the heroes in Western literature who exemplify rugged individualism, the culture heroes in Native American literature act to benefit the larger community by bringing power to the people, slaying monsters that have terrorized villages, or bringing a lasting contribution to the people, such as corn, tobacco, or salmon.

Until the late nineteenth and early twentieth centuries, nearly all American Indian literature was oral, since most native peoples did not have a written tradition. A few notable exceptions stand out, including the first American Indian novelist, Elias Boudinot, a Cherokee who in 1823 published *Poor Sarah,* and John Rollin Ridge, a Cherokee who in 1854 published *Life and Adventures of Joaquin Murieta* and in 1868 a volume of poetry.

During this period, a few Native American writers emerged, such as Sioux authors Gertrude Bonnin and Charles Eastman and Yavapai writer Dr. Carlos Montezuma. Their works reflected their strong sense of being American Indian, and they demanded a reform of the Bureau of Indian Affairs—that agency of the United States government that ruled native peoples. Their writings focused on government policies and thus were largely political. This tradition of political writing and social protest has continued today through the writings of Sioux author Vine Deloria, Jr.

The first Native American writers lived during that era in which the government of the United States kidnapped small children from their families and forcefully removed them to Indian boarding schools. The teachers and administrators of the Indian schools carried out the instructions of the Bureau of Indian Affairs to destroy that which was American Indian and replace it with that which was white, Anglo-Saxon, and Protestant. The government attempted to stamp out Native American languages by punishing children for speaking their own languages. Children were taught to speak English and to write the conquerer's language. Many children learned their first English in this way, which did not endear many native children to the written word of white America. In such a climate as this, it is a wonder that any Indian children at all wanted to nurture the English language and the written word. This is one of the major reasons that there were few notable Native American writers during the first half of the twentieth century, with a few exceptions. Will Rogers (who was part Cherokee), WaWa Chalachaw Bonita Nunez, E. Pauline Johnson, D'Arcy McNickle, and other Native Americans produced some short stories and longer narratives discussing elements of Native American life. They also used their talents to comment on the relationship of Indians to the rest of America. During this era, two remarkable writers emerged who produced the modern Native American novel. One was a woman who is considered to be one of the first Native American women to write a novel.

Humishuma, or Mourning Dove (Christine Quintasket), was a full-blood raised on the Colville Indian Reservation of north-central Washington. Although she collected, preserved, and published some of the original stories of her people, she is best known for her novel *Co-ge-we-a, the Half-Blood: A Depiction of the Great Montana Cattle Range*, published in 1927 by Four Seas of Boston, Massachusetts. Drawing on her traditional background, Mourning Dove used the ancient oral stories of the Okanogan Indians to produce a novel that permitted her characters to act out the tales of Chipmunk and the lessons learned during the age of the Animal People. Mourning Dove employed characters to weave a novel that dealt with the culture, history, religion, and stories of her native people. In this way, she wrote from and into and out of her own oral literary experience as an American Indian.

This is a technique used consciously and unconsciously by most Native American writers, and it produces literature that reflects the community of the person. Just as Mourning Dove used community as the basis for her novel, so did D'Arcy McNickle in 1936, when he wrote *Surrounded*, published by Dodd, Mead of New York. Better crafted than Mourning Dove's novel, McNickle's drew on his own tradition to deal with a young man named Archild who returns from boarding school to visit his family but not to stay on the reservation. He is drawn into his community through a complicated plot that involves his mother, who commits a hatchet murder, and his father, a successful individual who wants Archild to develop his musical talents. Within the novel are the struggles for identity between traditional beliefs and Christianity, the constructive and destructive elements of Catholicism, and the issue of mixed-bloods among full-bloods. In the end Archild is sought by authorities who want to charge him with a murder he did not commit, while the Indian agent assures the Indians that they all have been given every chance in the world. The people understand that they have been given no chance whatsoever, since they are surrounded by non-

Indians who destroy rather than nurture American Indian cultures.

The community concept addressed in the works of Mourning Dove, McNickle, and other authors is much more than the writer's people. It is the community of the plants, animals, mountains, trees, rivers, and rocks of their homes. It is connected closely with spirit and place. It is the relationship that A-Juma-We writer Darryl Babe Wilson argues was first established before "time," when the creation set the world into motion with light, breath, motion, and story. It is the creation of yesterday and today, a timeless process that gives birth and life to contemporary Native American literature. Community is the center of the universe for these writers, and their writing reflects the relationship of their community with place—including animate and inanimate life. "Native Writers write out of tribal traditions, and into them," Paula Gunn Allen has written. "They, like oral storytellers, work within the literary tradition that is at base connected to ritual and beyond that to tribal metaphysics or mysticism." Allen's story in *Earth Song, Sky Spirit* deals with a vision experienced by Ephanie, who learns many truths from a spirit woman, a teacher who emphasizes the significance of women in the ancient stories and contemporary lives of native peoples.

Due to their grounding in the oral tradition of their people, Native American writers do not follow the literary canon of the dominant society in their approach to short stories. Rather than focusing on one theme or character in a brief time frame, or using one geographical area, they often use multiple themes and characters with few boundaries of time or place. Their stories do not always follow a linear and clear path, and frequently the past and present, real and mythic, and conscious and unconscious are not distinguishable. Multidimensional characters are common, and involved stories usually lack absolute conclusions. Native American writers may also play tricks with language, deliberately misusing grammar, syntax, and spelling—sometimes in defiance of the dominant culture—in order to make English reflect the languages of their peoples.

In *The Way to Rainy Mountain*, Kiowa author N. Scott Momaday stated that "a word has power in and of itself. It comes from nothing into sound and meaning; it gives origin to all things. By means of words a man can deal with the world on equal terms. And the word is sacred." The power of language is evident in Momaday's story in *Earth Song, Sky Spirit*, entitled "The Well." Momaday masterfully maneuvers his characters so that the reader empathizes with a drunken old woman named Muñoz, who convinces a young man that not far off is a well filled with "whisky." The story reads like an oral account, since Momaday and other Native American writers are gifted storytellers in the oral and written word. Native Americans have used their words well to tell their stories, preserving their traditions, rituals, songs, and history. Contemporary Native American writers draw on this tradition to tell new tales that mirror their survival and continued presence in this country today.

In 1969 Momaday won the Pulitzer Prize for literature, becoming the first Native American to be awarded this honor. His book *House Made of Dawn* is a classic, and it has been reviewed, analyzed, and interpreted by scholars the world over. The book and the prize were important for Momaday, but they were more important to the larger Native American community, particularly Indian writers who saw in Momaday's accomplishments an opportunity to publish their own stories, poems, and novels. A few years after *House Made of Dawn* appeared, the Blackfeet and Gros Ventre writer James Welch produced *Winter in the Blood*, a novel that Welch titled *The Only Good Indian*—referring to General William Tecumseh Sherman's remark that an only good Indian was a dead Indian. Without a name, Welch's character is spiritually dead but tries to find his identity through his family and community.

These are themes common in Welch's other novels, *The Death of Jim Looney*, *Fools Crow*, and *The Indian Lawyer*. The issue of identity is also found in Welch's story in *Earth Song, Sky Spirit* as

Sylvester Yellow Calf reevaluates his life immediately after his grandfather's death. Welch, Momaday, and other Native Americans writers address what it means to be Indian in the late twentieth century. No longer are Indians mounted bareback on swift ponies with feathers flying as they chase over the prairies in pursuit of bluecoats and unsuspecting settlers. These two writers and their predecessors emphasized that Native Americans were real people with real problems, living in American society yet separated from it. Their works examine the role Native Americans play in the larger fabric of the American scene.

Leslie Marmon Silko stirred the literary world in 1977 with the publication of her novel *Ceremony*, which drew heavily on her own community of Laguna Pueblo. Tayo, her main character, is a mixed-blood who returns home after facing the horrors of war, imprisonment, and alienation. Silko skillfully employed dreams, visions, and songs in her work, which focused on identity, health, and life's journey. Through ceremony Tayo tries to find meaning within himself and his community. Silko followed *Ceremony* with *Storyteller*, an autobiographical journey of her own life through stories, prose, pictures, and poems. Recently she has published *Almanac of the Dead*, which ties the contemporary Native American experience with the past and looks beyond to the future. Her story in *Earth Song, Sky Spirit*, entitled "The Return of the Buffalo," carefully ties the Ghost Dance of the nineteenth century to that of today. Indeed, Silko offers the reader an insight into contemporary Native American life in which the Ghost Dance of old is danced and sung to hasten the day when the world turns upside down and life returns to those days before the arrival of the white man. Silko is considered one of the foremost Native American writers today, as is Paula Gunn Allen, who is also from Laguna Pueblo. Allen is primarily a poet, but she is known for her short stories, criticism, and novel—*The Woman Who Owned the Shadows*. Both of these Laguna women have worked hard to share the rich cultural traditions of their community and show how it influences the lives of Indian people today. Allen is best known for feminist literature that demonstrates the power of women within the traditional and contemporary Native American world. Her book *The Sacred Hoop*, illustrates the traditional stature of women within several American Indian communities.

Central to the works of both Silko and Allen is the importance of family, and this theme is also expressed in the works of Louise Erdrich, a Turtle Mountain Chippewa from North Dakota who is a talented novelist and poet. The role of family is a central part of her life, and it is found in her many works, including her story "Grandpa Kashpaw's Ghost," found in this volume. Family is at the heart of her writings, just as it is for her husband, Michael Dorris. Both authors add realism about the Native American community, exposing the beauty and the beast—the positive and the negative—in contemporary life. Suicide, hatred, and jealousy stand side by side with birth, love, and giving. Still, through it all their characters have an inner strength, spirit, and power that are much a part of Indian people and override the ogres within the community. Erdrich is best known for her books *Love Medicine*, *The Beet Queen*, and *Tracks*. Her works weave stories of several characters who are tied together through blood, marriage, friendships, and feuds. Dorris's *A Yellow Raft in Blue Water* offers three stories in one, all by women of varying ages who tell more of the story with each generation. His story in *Earth Song, Sky Spirit* is "Clara's Gift," a gripping account of two sisters who represent opposites. One is self-centered and having a baby that she wants to give to nuns for adoption. The other wants to keep the baby in the family and raise it as her own. The works by Dorris and Erdrich offer a generational approach to literature, whereby the experienced elders end up teaching us a good deal about life. Through it all, the family is central to an understanding of the contemporary life of the people portrayed in their books.

Gerald Vizenor often writes about family as well, but his stories and novels are a product of his strong sense and understanding of the oral tradition. Vizenor, who is Anishinaabe (also known as Chippewa and Ojibway), is a master writer who often composes in the oral tradition on a level that requires the reader to think and reflect. In his story for this volume, "The Moccasin Game," he introduces Native American Silent People from one woodland tribe who think and communicate through hand signs. Two of the central characters are Naiwina and Baapi, who represent male and female personalities. They paddle to a special magical island filled with medicine poles and powerful spirit people. On the island the Silent People play a moccasin game with Wiindigoo, an evil cannibal who has taken the sacred copper circle that had been stolen from a sacred mound. He is greedy and clever, and he keeps winning the game. If he wins all the points, he will take the children of the people, but the people sing and pray and invite the ice woman to help them. She freezes the ogre and puts him in her ice cave, where he can do the people no harm.

Vizenor's story offers readers a chance to enter the complex world of traditional literature with contemporary implications. Voice is all-important to Vizenor, as it is to Gordon D. Henry, Jr., another Anishinaabe writer who emphasizes voice. In his story "The Prisoner of Haiku," Henry shares a part of American Indian history with his readers, telling them of the unspeakable crime of one boarding school run by the Bureau of Indian Affairs. Historically, the schools were established for many reasons, including the desire of the United States to destroy that which was most native, Indian languages. In this story, the teachers and administrators destroy the ability of Henry's character to speak, but they do not destroy his voice. When the prisoner is released from boarding school, he begins his career in subversive activities against the government. He is ultimately placed in prison. While in captivity, he learns the art of haiku, a form of poetry, which he adapts and uses to voice his thoughts and understandings.

Harvest Moon Eyes, a Cherokee writer, presents a character named Sky who receives a vision about change, business, and airplanes that will come to the reservation and transform it. The spirit people have given her this dream so that she will tell others, but it is a dream that tribal leaders want to be silenced, since they plan to sell out their people, dispossess them of their land, and have them removed from their homes so that business and commerce will flourish where cattle once roamed. It is a story entitled "The Day the Crows Stopped Talking," which reflects the day Sky is murdered and the disquieting prospect of an insidious plot to destroy the native estate and humble home of a small tribe of poor people.

Like Harvest Moon Eyes, N. Scott Momaday deals with a killing and the unfortunate side of reservation life in his story "The Well." He introduces Hobson, a young Indian celebrating at the Jicarilla fiesta in northern New Mexico. Hobson first encounters a blow hole that emits cool wind, the breath found deep within the earth. Hobson then meets an elderly woman named Muñoz, who is drunk. Amid the dancing and singing some of the young men have fun abusing the elder woman, particularly one fellow who nearly kills her. She is saved by Hobson. Afterward the young man and elder woman share a fire until the old one wants more "whisky." She claims that there is more whisky in the Well, and they travel off to find it. Along the way, the elder meets a tragic fate.

Momaday provides a setting that is central to the story, since place is a significant subject in Native American writings. This is a point skillfully presented by Kimberly M. Blaeser, an Anishinaabe writer, in her story "From Aboard the Night Train." By train and thought she travels from Minneapolis to France and beyond. Continually her character thinks back to her place on the White Earth Reservation of Minnesota. In her mind she sees the new gambling center, where her former teachers, friends, and family play their games of chance. She watches an elderly lady use her love medicines to beat the odds and bring herself luck. Blaeser creates a sense of place, community, and continuance of cultural identity. This is also true of Choctaw writer Don L. Birchfield, whose story "Lost in the Land of Ishtaboli" examines a futuristic world of the Choctaws who have had to travel underneath the earth in order to survive. Yet, although the movement of the people underground took place many years before, the people are adamant about preserving the language, philosophy, and story of their people.

Thus, community arises as a major component of most of the stories found in this volume. "Faces," by Julia Lowry Russell, a Lumbee Indian from North Carolina, has much to say about one's place within the community. Unhappy with the face that peers back at Janis in the mirror one day, Russell's character sculpts a new face out of cleansing cream. Janis creates a face with no background, no roots, and no life. Tired of seeing her own mother in her face, she creates a face with no mother, family, or community. With her eyes, she looks beyond her mask, peers deep within herself to see the spirit. She connects with her mother and family and learns to tie herself in a positive way to her mother, aunts, grandmothers, and all the grandmothers before her. Russell is able to do this within the story, but in real life it is not always the case, since one does not have complete control over one's fate.

In her story "Adventures of an Indian Princess," Patricia Riley, a Cherokee author, introduces a foster child who is an American Indian living with a white family named Rapier. On a trip they visit Cherokee country, where young Arletta spots a man in a buckskin outfit with Plains beads, Maidu abalone shell necklace, Chippewa floral beaded moccasins, and Sioux headdress (turkey feathers). She is repulsed by the man, but the Rapiers insist on taking Arletta's picture with a "real" Indian. After providing Arletta with fake tomahawk, necklace, and headdress, they snap her picture and race on home without understanding the Indian girl's humiliation. One's Indian identity is often muddled, particularly if the person is of mixed-blood ancestry. This is the case with Lucille in Craig Womack's "Lucy, Oklahoma, 1911," a story that focuses on a family with a Creek mother and white father. Womack, who is himself a Creek Indian, creates a story that revolves around an abusive father who exploits his charge, a Creek boy who has oil money.

Like other authors, LeAnne Howe, a Choctaw writer, examines death as part of her story. She offers "Danse d'Amour, Danse de Mort," which introduces the Bone Picker, a specialist who scrapes the flesh off the bones of the dead and wraps the remains for preservation. She depicts some of the mortuary practices of her people through traditional eyes as well as those of the foreigners—the French priest and invaders who are repulsed by Choctaw traditions. The outsiders sit in judgment of the native people, a circumstance that has not changed since the first invasion of this land. Throughout history Native Americans have had to contend with the invaders, deciding for themselves if they should accommodate the whites, move into the interior, or stand and fight. Maurice Kenny, the noted Mohawk author, offers a view of the Southern Cheyenne chief Black Kettle's situation during those days just prior to Colonel George Armstrong Custer's surprise attack on the Cheyenne and Arapaho on the Washita River. In his story "Fear and Recourse," Kenny explores factions among the tribe, the pro-war and pro-peace people, and he offers Black Kettle's vision that whites wanted to exterminate Indian people.

Kenny understands that the life cycle ends with death, however tragic the loss might be, and James Welch examines this topic in his story "Earl Yellow Calf." Sylvester Yellow Calf attends the funeral of his grandfather Earl. Sitting with his family and appreciating the large number of people who have come to pay their respect to his grandfather and family, Sylvester is honored that his grandparents have been important as part of the community, and he is pleased to see his grandmother smile when the priest commends Earl Yellow Calf's soul to heaven. Louise Erdrich, an Anishinaabe writer from Turtle Mountain, addresses a similar theme in her "Grandpa Kashpaw's Ghost." This is a moving tale about one of the "took-in" children, named Lipsha, and his thoughts as he watches Grandpa Kashpaw die from eating love medicine that had been ill-conceived, improperly constituted, and incorrectly blessed. The old man's death forces Lipsha to remember happier days fishing with his grandfather. Life is fragile, he learns, and death offers the living a perspective. When they return home, Lipsha's grandmother tells him that Grandpa's ghost lingers, first in his favorite chair and then in bed with her. Lipsha orders the ghost to retreat and it does, meaning no harm but carrying a message of love and concern. Another ghost lingers in Lenape writer Annie Hansen's story "Sun Offering." When Jimmy's uncle dies, his spirit takes three or twelve days to reach the land of the dead. There is confusion over this point, since his uncle is part Salish—people who believe that it takes three days to arrive in the land of the dead—and part Lenape— people who believe that it takes twelve days. The family hears scraping, rock against rock, and they are convinced that the uncle's ghost is close by. Like the story by Erdrich, Hansen's story circles about the family that faces good times and bad times together.

Spirit teachers dance across the pages of many of these stories. This is true of "Lead Horse," written by Cherokee author Diane Glancy. In a unique style, Glancy flashes the story to the reader, requiring concentration and thought about the words, their meaning, and their connection to the story. Nattie is the Lead Horse who experiences more than one visitation during a thundering storm that drives the spirits onto the house and yard. She sees and hears many things during the storm, including Joes, who comes in a dream and outside through the window. In her vision she sees Dorothy in red moccasins and Toto too. Nattie has helped her family in the naming of their lives, and she has received the ultimate blessing, a round table where she can face her family. The spirits come and go in Glancy's story, but the reader is left believing that something of the spirit remains within.

Abnaki writer Joe Bruchac agrees, since his story "Bone Girl" explores a tribal tale about an alluring woman who appears late at night by the light of the moon. Within the story, the main character takes a creative writing class from a white instructor who cannot understand why Indian stories have no point and why Indian writers cannot fit their work into a "model" that would make sense to those in tune with Western writing. The skull face of the ghost found in "Bone Girl" carries the message of survival, since it has appeared again and again for hundreds of years. While this ghost has no voice, the phantom found in "Spirit Woman," by Paula Gunn Allen, speaks to Ephanie, a confused Native American who is trying to understand her life. The spirit woman brings meaning and understanding to Ephanie by sharing a traditional story about the creative power of Spider Woman. Ephanie discovers a pattern of life that is filled with birth and death, flowering and withering, and many other dualities. She gains a sense of herself in relationship to community through tribal traditions. In the end Ephanie can dance, sing, and experience the beauty of the creation.

Through the spirit, the characters of many stories find life, and so it is in "The Cave," by the Powhatan, Saponi, and Lenape writer Jack D. Forbes. In his story, a nameless character is kidnapped and pursued by agents of the United States government in an attempt to kill him—just as the government had attempted to exterminate all Indians. The character escapes but survives by establishing a relationship with the earth around him. He seeks sanctuary in a cave, the womb of the earth, where he finds refreshment, life, and knowledge. He prays and the power comes to him. He survives and reconnects with his community, where he makes offerings and prayers though Father Peyote. John Wildcat returns to the area again and again, but he cannot find the cave that holds historical treasures about the American Indian past. The cyclical return of Wildcat to the cave where he renewed his life and found a spirit is a theme also found in Darryl Babe Wilson's "Akun, Jiki Walu: Grandfather Magician." Wilson's father was A-Juma-We, while his mother was Atsuge-We, both from the Pit River country of northern California. The characters in his story play out their lives in this region, in the green forests and beside the rushing rivers.

Wilson's story tells of the relationship that develops between Akun, the grandfather, and two boys. It is also one in which the boys learn to work together. It revolves around Akun's making a magical bow with mysterious arrows that are taken by the boys. The arrows become lost—or, rather, stuck—in the North Star, falling to earth and creating a lush forest and a special spring that emerges from a basket. The boys are sent to trap a woodpecker, a bird sacred to these native peoples, and they take a hero's journey through mountains and rivers. When the boys, Akun, and their father return home, Akun makes bows and arrows, but most important, he puts spirit into them. The boys are taught the strength of working together to accomplish things. They are taught to unite like a quiver full of stout arrows.

Anita Endrezze, a Yaqui writer, provides a story entitled "Marlene's Adventures," which also focuses on family and community. Marlene is aging and growing tired of the people around her. She finds life dull, mundane, and monotonous and wishes for youth and excitement. This is when she learns that her husband has been hospitalized and rushes to the hospital to discover that he has a tumor. In the process, she realizes that she prefers a life without such excitement. A medical problem is also the subject of Sherman Alexie's "The Approximate Size of My Favorite Tumor," a story filled with dark humor. The Spokane Indian writer introduces Jimmy Many Horses III, who is married to Norma, who, like Marlene, gets bored with life, leaving her husband and children to seek adventure with Jimmy's favorite Flathead cousin. The story is set on the Spokane Indian Reservation in northeastern Washington, where Many Horses remembers stories about friends and family, the day he met Norma, and the day he told his cousin he had 755 cancerous tumors in his body. During one of his checkups he asks his doctor for his prognosis. When the doctor replies that he is dying, Many Horses replies, "Not again." Norma returns to reenter a relationship of accommodation and resignation with her husband and children. The reader may wonder if all will be well, but the ambiguity is life.

The uncertainty of living and loving is also the theme found in "Shadows and Sleepwalkers," by Arapaho writer Cait Featherstone. In her story, a woman is attracted to a man who apparently has returned from the Vietnam War. Her attraction to him seems positive enough, but with time the relationship falls apart. The war brought a void to Michael's life and an inability to cope. Life, we learn, is filled with expectations and hope, disappointment and sorrow. In a much different style, Klallum author Duane Niatum offers "For Her with No Regrets." This is a love story between an Indian and a Jewish woman named Suzanne. She is married, a situation that gets them "into more corners than a chess game." They find that their grand encounter is marked with remarkable lovemaking and that their bed becomes their "El Dorado." The secret relationship is on and off, but in the end Suzanne returns to her husband. Still, they both remember and have no regrets for the love they shared.

Andrew Connors, an Ojibwe writer from Bad River, Wisconsin, presents "Avian Messiah and Mistress Media," a story about police harassment of Indians and a well-meaning Indian named Cloud, who inadvertently begins the Avian Dreamers movement to save the birds. Cloud becomes a reluctant hero of common people and college students, but his role in the entire affair is overshadowed by Janice Sebline of WMTJ News, who turns Cloud's situation into a media event. While others jockey for recognition, Cloud concerns himself with a small sparrow, praying that it will survive without guilt. Cloud is an urban Indian, living out his life away from his community. Still, he is not a typical hero in the Western sense. This is true of most "heroes" found within the stories, including the boy found in "Slaughterhouse," written by the Pomo-Coast Miwok author Greg Sarris.

Frankie is the main character in Sarris's story, but he is immediately cast as part of the larger community. His grandmother, Old Julia, and a gang of boys form the nucleus of his family, while his drunken father and other family members remain on the periphery of his life. The narrative is filled with boyhood adventure, including a friendship and young love that develops between Frankie and Caroline. As in the ancient stories of Native Americans, Frankie journeys to a place where he is not supposed to be and learns something from his transgression. This is a moving story, reflecting the tragedy that has always been a part of the Native American experience. While Sarris plays out the drama through one central character, Inez Petersen, a Quinault writer, uses an entire family. In "Joseph's Rainbow," she focuses on an abusive mother who drinks and beats her children. Ultimately her neglect leads to the death of eight-year-old Bobby. The children are led by the oldest one, Joseph, who tries his best to put a positive spin on the situation. However, Joseph must report his own mother to the Children's Service Division after she beats baby Teena. This is an emotional story, particularly in light of child abuse today. Such abuse once led government authorities to take Indian children from their homes, communities, and people to be raised by non-Indians away from their reservations. Today, Indian people struggle to resolve their own family problems and child custody issues without the intervention of non-Indians. Still, these problems are part of everyday life of reservation and urban Indians everywhere.

Child abuse is also the subject of Penny Olson's "The Dream." This is a haunting tale by an Ojibway writer whose main character wakes up terrified, remembering a close neighbor named Mr. Walker, who sexually assaulted her as a little girl. Now an adult, Anne suffers from a recurring dream, experiencing again the horror of the abuse. Like other stories, the events described occur throughout contemporary society, demonstrating that Native Americans are part of the world today and not quaint remnants of a "vanishing race." The interacting of families and family members—including children—is important in contemporary Native American literature. Indeed, children are often found in the stories written by American Indian authors, individuals who were greatly influenced by the positive and negative actions of their own childhood—their parents, grandparents, and relatives.

In "Silver Bass and Alligator Gar," the Cherokee writer Ralph Salisbury presents a captivating story that moves in and out and through such topics as siblings, parents, mixed-bloods, and storytellers. The story moves toward a tragic boat accident in which the boat slowly sinks and three fishermen are nearly killed. Still, they survive, including a father with a bad heart condition, which takes his life a year after the boat accident. The drama is a metaphor for Indian people who have been greatly injured but who cling to life for their own survival and that of their people. Like Native Americans, the characters in Salisbury's story are determined to keep the circle alive, in spite of tragedy and death. Native Americans act as a community to do this, even when individual members of the community refuse to cooperate in the maintenance of the people. This is the case in "Clara's Gift," a story by Michael Dorris. His story emphasizes the extended family, as two sisters are confronted with a dilemma—what to do with Clara's child.

Pregnant out of wedlock, Clara goes to live with nuns who are eager to give the child up for adoption by a good Catholic family. Her sister, Ida, does not share the enthusiasm for this plan and decides to take the child back to her Montana reservation and raise her as her own. In doing so, Ida follows an old custom among many American Indians to adopt children unceremoniously and keep them as part of the family and community. Dorris shows the duality between the selfish Clara and the giving Ida, and he explores the immediate and warm bonding between Ida and the baby, Christine. Like all infants, Christine faces an uncertain future among Indians who have weathered many storms and will surely continue to do so in the future.

It is this uncertain future that becomes the subject of Leslie Marmon Silko's "The Return of the Buffalo," a story that ties the past to the present. In a speech, Wilson Weasel Tail offers the words of Pontiac, the great Ottawa leader. Then he reads a letter to President Ulysses S. Grant by the Paiute prophet Wovoka. In the letter and subsequent narrative, the reader learns something of the Ghost Dance movement of the late nineteenth century. Silko suggests that a noted anthropologist provided incorrect information when he wrote that the Ghost Dance died with the senseless killing of Chief Bigfoot and the Lakota men, women, and children at Wounded Knee, South

Dakota, in 1890. Silko is correct, for the Ghost Dance is still alive among many diverse Native American people over one hundred years after the murderous attack by the Seventh Cavalry. Native Americans still dance and sing and pray for the death and rebirth of the earth.

Silko writes that the spirit people are still outraged over the past and that American Indians are still tied closely to the "Spirit of the Earth." In accordance with old prophecies, white people too often lack the spirit within, and they will self-destruct unless they learn to understand the songs of the earth. Silko's story captures the beliefs of many contemporary Native Americans who understand clearly that they are part of today's world but that their tribal traditions, languages, ceremonies, and stories create a relationship to this land that is unmatched by others. Their relationship is with each other as a community and with places, plants, and animals. Their relationship forms a legacy, and they have a future that is based on this past experience. Story is the magic that ties all of these themes and ideas together. Leslie Marmon Silko once said that it is "story that makes this into community," that Native Americans must have stories, since that is how "you know; that's how you belong; that's how you know you belong." The stories brought together here are all written by Native American authors who understand the power of stories, the strength they bring into and out of their particular communities. Most of these stories are original to this collection, and they represent the best in contemporary Native American short fiction. *Earth Song, Sky Spirit* offers readers an opportunity to understand elements of our rich, diverse, and vibrant Native American cultures.

A few years back Andrew George died. Members of the larger Native American community of the Pacific Northwest sang over his body all night, raising their eagle and white swan fans, sending their prayers skyward. They concluded the last song just before dawn and raised their right hands to the sky with their palms spread wide to send and receive the power. Although he is dead, Andrew George visits me still, telling me stories of Coyote, Chewana, and Tahtah Kleyah. I sit and listen with both ears, hear those stories again and again, and marvel at those tales. I wonder at his words.

IMBERLEY M. BLAESER is of mixed ancestry, Anishinaabe and German. An enrolled member of the Minnesota Chippewa Tribe, she grew up on White Earth Reservation in northwestern Minnesota. Currently an assistant professor of English at the University of Wisconsin—Milwaukee, Blaeser teaches twentieth-century American literature, including courses in Native American literature and American nature writing. Her work, which includes personal essays, poetry, short fiction, journalism, reviews, and scholarly articles, has appeared in various journals and collections, including *World Literature Today*, *American Indian Quarterly*, *Akwe-kon*, *The Notre Dame Magazine*, *Cream City Review*, *Northeast Indian Quarterly*, *Loonfeather*, and *Narrative Chance: Postmodern Discourse on Native American Indian Literature*. Blaeser's study of a fellow White Earth writer, *Gerald Vizenor—Writing in the Oral Tradition*, will be published by the University of Oklahoma Press in 1993.

FROM ABOARD THE NIGHT TRAIN

Kimberly M. Blaeser

The moon gives some light and I can make out the contours of the land, see the faint reflection in the lakes and ponds we pass. Several times I see or imagine I see glowing eyes staring back at me from a patch of woods beside the track. When we pass through the tiny towns, I try to read their signs, catch their names from their water towers or grain elevators. Occasionally the train stops at . . . Portage . . . Winona . . . Red Wing.

Once, traveling on the Fourth of July, I sat aboard the Amtrak and watched one Mississippi river town at its annual fireworks. Balls of light burst over the water, illuminating the bank, the families gathered together on blankets, the lovers sitting with hands, arms, or legs entwined, the jubilant children exploding in motion like the rockets overhead. I knew I had the best seat in the house—and the loneliest.

Watching that scene, I remembered one summer in France. By

chance I had landed at a lovely village called Anncey during a local festival. I checked in to a hotel just across the street from the festival grounds and went to enjoy the activities. But it was all happening in another language. I didn't even know what they were celebrating. Wandering into a carnival area, I stood back and tried to figure out the games they were playing. Everywhere I went, I could have been behind the glass of an Amtrak train, I was just a gawker. I walked two miles that night in order to have dinner at a hotel away from the festivities. Then, back in my own lodgings, I tried to block out the sounds from the crowded streets below. Although the next night I returned to the festivities with some locals and had as fine a time as anyone there, I never forgot that first night, when the whole world was happening without me.

In my sleeping compartment, watching the night countryside, I feel that same way now. So much world rolls by my window. Like a voyeur I watch the various reunion scenes. The little dark-haired boy in a leather jacket sits, legs dangling, on the hood of a car waiting for someone to arrive, scoop him up, and give him a present from the trip. I imagine myself stepping off the train onto the depot platform and reaching out to tousle his pollen-soft hair. I'd like to hear him sing the songs they teach in his school. But instead I watch the woman in the terrible plaid pants take his hand and I can't help but imagine that someday that little boy will be a golfer with ugly plaid pants of his own. The night continues on that way scene after scene. Vast opportunities. My great distance from them. And yet I feel these scenes add up to something, some meaning or lesson about all life, and I try to put it into words for myself but find I can't. I finally give up, roll over, go to sleep, and dream.

At first, I am back in France sitting on a stone wall, holding an open bottle of wine and watching my companions do the cancan in slow motion. Then the director of my dream abruptly cuts that scene and begins to loudly berate the camera crew. The scene goes dark, I jump off the wall and land in another dream I know very well: I am lost in urban America.

The basic plot of the recurring nightmare has remained the same for years. Sometimes I am the wrong color in some neighborhood or another, trying not to draw attention to myself. Sometimes I have taken a walk on a lonely day and suddenly realize, in Hansel-and-Gretel fashion, that the markers to my safe haven have all disappeared and night is descending. Always I am without the resources I need to find a way out, to escape, to return to my friends or family who are somewhere at a picnic, or gathered for a holiday celebration, or fast asleep (early to bed, early to rise). I don't know where I am—except in the wrong, wrong place. I have no map. I'm dressed differently than everyone around me and they are beginning to stare at me or point or mumble loudly about the intruder. Either public transportation is not available, or I don't know how to use it. Either it's after bus and train hours, or I have somehow been stranded without any money. In one dream I actually had a friend with me and we had a car, but all the streets were one way going the wrong way, in the direction where something dreadful was about to erupt. We abandoned the car and ran on and on through streets we didn't recognize, feeling ourselves pursued and about to become the victim of someone's violent behavior. The closest I ever came to escaping was in that dream when we jumped aboard a boat that would take us away, we didn't know to where, but away from that particular urban nightmare. I awoke from that dream just as I was reaching into my pocket for the forty dollars we would need to pay our way. I don't know if I found it, but at least we had a chance that time. Most of the nightmares end when I thrash myself awake and lay sweating and reassuring myself that I am safe and vowing that never, never will I venture into the heart of any city alone.

Tonight, as usual, I struggle violently to escape. I cry out as I wake and then sit up, listening, wondering if anyone has heard. Finally I relax, lie back, feel the rhythmic rocking of the train beneath me, and turn on my side to be comforted by the farm fields and woodlands we pass.

Through the years I've gotten used to these nightmares, I

understand why noisy crowded streets—whether indifferent or threatening or simultaneously both—should frighten me. The daily Chicago news is of gang violence, random beatings, and drive-by killings. Over the years I've read hundreds of remembrances of families whose child or mother or sibling has been abducted and presumed or found dead. I've read of the families' usually belated realization that someone is missing and their futile searches for the lost or stolen member. And at night I dream the part of the abducted, the innocent who wanders into the wrong neighborhood, who asks direction from the wrong silver-haired gentleman, who gets into the wrong cab. It makes sense that I should have these nightmares, I who come from a five-block-main-street kind of midwestern town.

But now I am awake, keeping my vigil over the Midwest's pastoral kingdom. Chicago, even Minneapolis seems a long way away. A few hours later, still in the deep night hours, the train arrives at my stop, Detroit Lakes, the closest I can get to my destination.

Suddenly, as I descend the two steps from the train, the porter hands me into one of the reunion scenes. "Hi, honey, how was the trip? Did you get any sleep?" "A little. Been waiting long? How are the roads?" "Long enough to beat your dad in two games of cribbage . . ." Hugging and kissing, we carry on the usual end-of-the-trip conversation. Glancing back at the train windows, I get an uneasy feeling. I imagine I am looking into eyes hidden behind mirrored sunglasses.

Rumors about the coupons surface in nearly every conversation about town. The paper will carry coupons for five dollars in free chips. The shopper will have the coupons. People have been wearing disguises in order to cash in more than one coupon a day. Folks set their alarms for two, three or four A.M. and arrive bleary-eyed to cash in the midnight-to-five A.M. coupons. They skip lunch and run out on their noon hours to cash in the day coupons. This week the *Fargo Forum* will have coupons. Someone ordered forty papers. The papers last week were all sold out.

Someone has been following behind the shopper truck when it makes its night deliveries stealing the papers from the mailboxes.

We decide to stay up late just to see. We sit in the porch with the lights out. Night scenes begin to unfold again. I think of how we used to sleep in the porch in the summer and then slip out in our pajamas to run about the yard and sometimes all the way to the other end of town. Giggling, sshssshing and sneaking our way through the alleys, we waked dogs, dropped to the ground at the first sight of car lights, and swiped carrots to nibble along the way.

I remember the winter night that big dog came and ran off with our car's extension cord and we all watched thinking it must be mad and the summer night that skunk wandered into town and, barefooted, we followed it around the neighborhood—at a safe distance—trying to figure out what it was doing there. And I remember that night the tornado hit Bejou and we all stood at the dining-room window watching the storm and never realizing the danger and terror a few miles away. And the time that stranger was around town in the blue car and we were all wary of him but afraid to tell our parents because they might want us to stay in when we wanted to play chase or walk down to the park and swing in the dark.

Tonight, watching out the window with a lone mosquito buzzing about my ear, I feel my past alive on the other side of the screen, hiding in the shadows of the bushes, about to jump out. With that hope or expectation pressing against all my organs, pressing against my very skin, I reenter the present night.

Not much happens now as we watch. Two people go by on bikes. We spot a couple of cats. We haven't seen a car for ten minutes, just the lights when they U-turn in the filling station on Main Street. One by one everyone wanders back into the house, forgetting about the intrigue of the shopper thefts. We go back to the real world of cut-throat and widow whist. After an hour of card play, I no longer watch us as from the window.

·   ·   ·

I have gone out for my first look at the casino. It's not at all like Las Vegas or Reno and yet it is. I mean, there are a bunch of shinabes dressed in white shirts and bow ties! These are people whose first name is always placed in quotation marks in print as if to say "Honest, this is the real name." Now they all wear these pins bearing names like "Frogman" Joe Brown, "K-Girl" Wanda Clark, or "Blackduck" Frances Wadena. I wonder if the casino management complained at all about the extra expense. I mean, these pins have to be really big to accommodate some of the names, like "Catbird" Sylvester Littlewolf or "Sailor" Rodney LaDue Be-she-Ke. There are all kinds of people I know whizzing about looking like dressed-up paper-doll images of themselves. Remember using the fold-over tabs to attach a new hairstyle to the dolls and it always looked a little like George Washington's wig? Or how a tab would slip and the hair would assume some wild angle? I keep waiting for someone's tab to slip, the transformation seems just too unreal.

In Las Vegas or Reno there are a bunch of strangers whizzing about and lots of lights blinking and noise everywhere and smoke and you don't expect it to make sense or be familiar. But here I see people I've known my whole life, looking like little mechanical parts in one of those machines where you put the coin in and everything moves until the money runs out or the time or however they count it. I want it to stop for a minute so I can get my bearings, but someone keeps putting money in. My former high school psychology teacher wanders by carrying a notebook. I see my old 4-H leader having breakfast in the dining area and I swear I see her checking the muffins for tunnels like she used to each year at the county fair. The town's best piano teacher is playing nickel slot machines, one with each hand. I get stamped and collect my tokens and begin feeding the poker machines. I'm laughing and talking to my machine and I feed almost all my money but then I hit a straight flush and win fifty dollars. I cash in my money and walk around to see the other machines. I notice something happening at the blackjack tables and I wander over. I'm standing back a little and it's a good thing because I gasp when I get a good look at the dealer. He's probably in his late forties, a good-looking man, very Indian with prominent cheekbones and long graying braids wound with colored cloth. Not that unusual, but I recognize him. Only I remember him as a young man with black, black hair, a great laugh, and eyes I could never meet straight on. He was an apprentice medicine man.

Before the full absurdity of it can sink in, I take in the rest of the scene. A crowd has gathered round because one player is on a winning streak. She too is Indian. Seventy years old, I guess, a slight woman, yellow-gray hair, some age spots on her face. Nothing physically striking about her. Her voice is unpleasantly shrill, the sound of a killdeer. I've watched craps players before for the sheer joy of hearing their chanting and romancing of the dice, but her call and response is too nervous, too thin to bring pleasure. Yet she speaks constantly to the dealer or to her audience. "Come on, dealer. Deal me blackjack." "Okay, dealer, let's go, I need an ace." "Call for your card, call for your card." "Okay, bust dealer, bust." And she gets her blackjack. Or the dealer busts. I watch several hands, inching my way forward, and then I see what I knew I would see and yet what surprises me just the same because it's here in a casino at a blackjack table. Sage, cedar, twigs of a kind I do not recognize, spirit stones, feathers, a beaded leather pouch—the entire space in front and to the right of her playing space is covered with Indian charms and, I imagine, love medicines. But there's more, a whole menagerie of dime-store variety good luck charms: rabbit's foot, horseshoe, four-leaf clover in a key ring, flowers, little statues, everything but a chia pet! Piled among these charms, piled high in twenty or more stacks are her winnings, stacks of one-, five-, ten-, and twenty-dollar chips.

I watch until there's a change in the dealer and the apprentice medicine man goes off on break. I watch while the new dealer comes under her spell and she continues to pile up chips. Then I feel someone at my elbow and turn. It's another old friend who is another employee here who tells me the charm lady was in yesterday too and did the same thing then. We shake our heads and laugh together in a companionable little gesture but I leave feeling uncertain of what either of us meant by it.

But I have won myself and I go off thinking about how the first computer was funded partly by gambling, by the horse racing industry (the better to figure the odds, my dear), which had, as it turned out, a more farsighted vision than many people in the federal government, who didn't think the idea of the computer would ever amount to much. This is the same government, of course, that worked so diligently to wipe out the "savage" Indian.

I think about progress a lot in the next few days and about what passes for progress. We drive out into the country to look at some land and find lots of roads I think would make wonderful access roads in the winter because a person could easily get stranded with any reasonable snowfall. I think of Aldo Leopold and how he loved to be stranded by high water in the spring. I think of the story of my cousin's birth at the grade school where his mother got stranded when a blizzard blew in while she was hemming towels with the ladies' aid and the story of the baby's first appearance at their farm: wrapped in swaddling towels (neatly hemmed), he arrived by horse and sleigh because the access road was impassable by car.

Nightly we walk about town, talk marriages and funerals and DWI tickets, then sit on the newly installed benches on Main Street. Together we assemble from our memories the town as it was twenty or twenty-five years ago. We remember the little Model Meat Market and the old Pioneer office. We rebuild the Landmark Hotel, take down the vinyl fronts from the grocery store, bring back the old Red Owl, change the light posts, the awnings, the names of the current businesses. I put back the old depot, you the corner funeral home. But soon we are distracted and leave things half constructed when we begin to add the people, what's-his-name, the square dance caller; Ed, the fire chief; and Lydia, the town's best gossip. On the walk back home, we have begun to list very specific things, which is the closest we get to the intangibles: the rental meat lockers, the four-digit telephone numbers, the free ice cream during dairy month.

Late at night in my old bed, I listen to the night sounds of the house and fall asleep counting the changes that have come to my little hometown: The park is off limits after dark now, the football field is fenced in, one-hour photo has come to town along with a tanning salon and a pizza parlor. The dry goods store is gone, the dairy, long gone. People lock their houses now more than the once a year when the carnival comes to town. But all of these changes pale in comparison to what has replaced the bait shop, the used car lot, and Mr. Morton's small farm, what has sprung up on Highway 59 at the edge of town: Las Vegas–style gambling.

When the weekend comes, the casino parking lot is packed and cars line the adjacent street and highway. We go there one more time before I leave and lose some money and time. I think about the jobs and see lots of people working who have never held a steady job before and who I imagine look very proud in their uniforms. I see Elvis having lunch and the rumor is he's going to sing later. Everybody really knows it's not him, but just here and now it's as easy to believe it as not. So he signs autographs and eats a Northern Lights special. A few people in suits get a tour. One lady, who according to rumors didn't want to come and play, wins a progressive jackpot of $32,812.43. I wonder if they give her the pennies too. I ask a few people about the protesters and if that was all settled, but nobody here wants to talk much about that. They also either don't want to talk about or don't know anything about how the profits will be spent. "Big payments . . . spendoolicks every month!" jokes one of the cocktail servers. "Maybe they're gonna educate us again," another says with a laugh. I ask one of the ladies at the change booth, one of the money changers, about handling all that cash and she says after a while it just seems like Monopoly money.

I say I think I know what she means. I cash in my few remaining chips, wave at Elvis on my way out, and reenter the sunlit world.

Around town, everyone admits to eating at the casino because they have good specials, but not too many folks admit to spending any money there. Even those I ran into in the casino itself were all there they said for the first time and just came to cash their coupons, but they all knew of other people who were there all the time and had lost a lot of money and . . . hadn't I seen the Gamblers' Anonymous meeting notice in the *Mahnomen Pioneer?*

Taking the train back, I decide to put on pajamas and crawl under the sheets, hoping to trick myself into a good night's sleep. It seems to work. I have slept soundly for several hours, but then the dreams start. I fall in and out of them. But they are not the usual nightmares. I am in a place where folks know you ten, fifteen, twenty years after you've left and still see in your face that of your grandfather or aunt or cousin. I know I am home and I feel safe.

But soon strange, strange things begin to happen. I arrive to find all the quiet of my little town gone. People are very busy, too busy to notice my return. They have a schedule that can't be disrupted for conversation over the alley hedge or coffee at the local cafe. I feel a little like the returning-from-the-dead Emily in *Our Town*, who can't get anyone's real attention. Something has happened here to wind these folks up too tight, to make them over like some kind of diseased Stepford wives who have seen the error of their midwestern ways.

I wander around trying to discover someone or someplace that hasn't been transformed; instead I find a drive-up bank, a health club, and a thirty-minute oil change. Still these seem such small tokens of the yuppie life that I don't believe they could transform an entire town. Then while I stand there in front of the Ben Franklin store, everything begins spinning around me. Cars battle for the angle parking spots on Main Street, drivers honk and shout angrily at one another, shoppers push and shove and toss sale merchandise carelessly about, people line up to buy newspapers and then begin madly clipping coupons. Just as quickly as it began, the action is over. The store clerks are clucking their tongues about the silliness of all the people. I feel implicated but I don't know why. I wonder what plague has descended on my hometown and if somehow I am responsible. I take my vague sense of guilt home only to find my own parents buzzing about getting ready to go out for spinach quiche. Through the remainder of the night, these lost-pastoral dreams return in different variations: people sitting around watching the 200 stations they can get with their satellite TV, eating microwave dinners in dim artificial light, staying out of the sun because they don't want to freckle or burn. I come in from ice fishing and see dainty little shoes with heels lined up on rugs by people's entryway doors. When I sit down to play cards everyone is dealing bridge instead of whist or poker. I have faithfully dieted before coming, but no one offers me homemade pie or real mashed potatoes made with butter. I have a flat tire on Highway 59. Cars slow down, but no one stops to help me. Instead, they click their door locks or call out to me to get a name tag. Just before first light, I abandon hope of restful sleep, dress, and then watch the sun rise over all the lakes and towns we pass.

I have an early breakfast with a would-be journalist and some ski vacationers who want to talk about election prospects and the politicians who have written bad checks. Although I too believe the bad checks phenomenon makes a wonderful metaphor for the state of the world, I merely feign attention. I nod or laugh on cue, while I try to read upside-down a story in the would-be journalist's newspaper that has caught my eye. It is about the Russian space station and the cosmonaut who has been up in orbit during the takeover attempt and ultimate dissolution of the Soviet Union. After sixteen long months, they are bringing the capsule back. While the train carries me back to my current home and away from my former, I keep thinking about that poor cosmonaut coming back to find his whole world changed, to find himself a man without a country—at least without the country he left behind.

I watch the ten o'clock national news broadcast. I see him emerge from the capsule. I see him try to stand and have his knees buckle. I know they said it was because he hadn't been able to exercise for such a long time, but I wonder if his weak-kneed feeling might not have more to do with what he saw out the window of the space station and with how the world was happening around without him.

*g*ERALD VIZENOR is professor of Native American Indian literature in the Ethnic Studies Department at the University of California, Berkeley. He is a member of the Minnesota Chippewa Tribe. Vizenor is the author of more than twenty books of literature, history, and poetry. His most recent books are *The Heirs of Columbus*, a novel, and *Landfill Meditation*, a collection of stories. *Interior Landscapes: Autobiographical Myths and Metaphors* was published two years ago by the University of Minnesota Press. *Griever: An American Monkey King in China*, his second novel, won the American Book Award. *Dead Voices: Natural Agonies in the New World*, his fifth novel, was published in 1992 in the series "American Indian Literature and Critical Studies" by the University of Oklahoma Press. Vizenor lives with his wife, Laura Hall, in Berkeley, California.

THE MOCCASIN GAME

Gerald Vizenor

The moccasin games are played by the Anishinaabe, or Chippewa, and many other woodland tribal cultures near the northern woodland lakes of the United States. Cowrie shells and other marked objects were hidden under one of several moccasins. Drum music, singing, and stories were part of the communal temptations of the gamblers and were used to disguise the actual location of the marked cowrie. To lose at the game was to own bad moccasins.*

The Native American Silent People cannot hear, and they come from many tribes on the earth. They travel in the summer with their rich memories and show their remembered stories with their hands. The Silent People show trickster stories with their hands and leave their tribal handprints around the world.

Nawina was a member of a woodland lakes tribe. Late that night she sat with her relatives and others in silence near a fire circle. The heat of the coals warmed the cool mist that rose over the great lake. The moon on the water was silent too, as silent as the hand talkers at the shoreline.

Nawina turned two wooden figures in her hands. There were narrow red bands painted on her cheeks. The moon burned on their bodies as she bound the spirit figures together with leather, and then she returned them to a medicine pouch.

Baapi, the tribal elder, could not hear. He was Anishinaabe and his tribal name means "he laughs." Baapi laughed in silence and told his best stories with his hands. The tribal women smoked their black pipes in silence.

The Silent People could not hear and they talked with their hands that night close to the fire. Nawina means the "one who cannot reach." She was one who could hear. She told what the others said with their hands in silence.

"Baapi is our granduncle, one of the silent tribal people, one of the great wanderers," said Nawina. "The hand talkers lost their ears to the tribal trickster. The trickster, who could become a bear or a human in stories, won their ears in a moccasin game many, many generations ago. The old men loved to play the game of objects hidden under their old moccasins and never thought the trickster could win, but he did and that was the end of their ears for many generations. He hid the ears in a cedar tree. Since then the bears might have eaten the ears, or the crows might have laid them bare in the winter birch trees."

Nawina watched their hands and told their stories. The moon brushed their hands in silence. "The Silent People come to the woodland lakes each summer to tell their stories with their hands," she said. "The loons, and the toads, the snakes, and evil winds never learned to hear their hand stories."

Baapi laughed in silence and moved his hands near the fire. "Baapi said the trickster created silence, and the wind, and the ice woman to remember the winter in the summer," said Nawina. "The earth was wild, and sometimes we told each other that the silent water spirit released the hand talkers from sound."

The silent women smoked their black pipes and warned the

old man about the stories about the ice woman. He warned them right back with his hands and told his silent stories about Mikwam, a name that means "ice" in the language of the Anishinaabe.

Baapi laughed and moved his hands. Others repeated his stories with their hands, natural harmonies near the fire that night. Some men braided their hair on the side and laughed with their hands.

"Mikwam is the ice woman, a cold healer, and one of the silent hand talkers," said Nawina. "She lives in a cave on aazihibik, a rock cliff island. Baapi said the men shouted at the ice woman not to torment them, to leave them alone with their dreams and visions. So, the ice woman leaned over their sweat lodge, cooled their sacred rocks, and turned their breath to snow in the summer. Baapi said the trickster turned the world of men cold when it should have been hot."

Silence.

Nawina paddled at the bow of a birchbark canoe. Baapi was at the stern and he laughed with his hands as he paddled on the calm water toward the islands in the lake. There were leather bundles in the back of the canoe. They came closer to the red paintings of animals, spirits, and hands on the rocks.

Aazhibik Island was covered with medicine poles. Thunderbirds and bears were mounted on the masts, and huge spirit catchers were near the rock cliffs. The many trees were packed with bird nests.

"Baapi is a bear dreamer," said Nawina. "He argues with the animals, and birds, the shamans, and even the bone monsters, but he never disagrees with the rock spirits or the ice woman who lives in a cold cave on the other side of the island."

Baapi shouted with his hands near the island. His gestures were wild. Nawina paddled closer, and the water churned the closer they came to the rocks. She threw sacred tobacco over the side of the canoe to calm the water spirits.

Baapi pressed his hands over the red hand prints on the rocks. His small hands turned red. The spirit of the handprint entered his hands. The red moved on his arms and reached his neck and cheeks, but the canoe pitched on the water and he lost his hold on the rocks.

Nawina pushed back from the rocks to protect the canoe. Baapi turned his red hands over and over and laughed. His hands turned lighter and then the color was gone.

"Baapi tries to trick the rock spirits," said Nawina. "The hand talkers are wanderers from many tribes on the earth, and they are the first to press their hands on these rocks. The red hands on the painted rocks are the stories of the elders, the first hand talkers who lost their ears to the trickster."

Ogin, the one child who lived on the island with her mother, stood on a rock and watched the canoe. The child wore golden ribbons in her hair and an owl head tied to her waist. Baapi laughed with his hands. He waved to the child and then talked to her with his hands. Ogin means "rosehip" in the language of the Anishinaabe.

"Ogin was born with dreams," said Nawina. "She remembers the stories of the ancient blue people, the trickster beads, and she sings medicine songs that she has never heard. The Silent People could not hear her clear haunting voice over the lake that summer."

Ogin raised her arms and danced on the rocks to the canoe. Baapi stood in the canoe. He laughed and his hands danced. The child moved her hands as she danced in silence, and then she danced out of reach over the rocks.

Booch, her mother, stood high on the rocks over the water. She stood between the medicine poles. She was a shaman and wore a loose blue collar around her neck. Booch means "it is certain" in the language of the Anishinaabe.

"Ogin found a golden ribbon in the ice and her mother worried too much about death," said Nawina. "Booch shouted to the bears, she tattooed her shoulders, and she covered the island with medicine poles to protect her child from evil spirits."

Silence.

Nawina and Baapi paddled past several reed houses that were

floating near the shore of another island. Each reed float was decorated to represent a terminal vision of men who had broken visions. Men who had dreamed too much were transformed with only parts of birds and animals. Maang, the loon, had no more than the feet of a loon. Diindiisi, the bluejay, had the head and wing feathers of a bluejay. Migizi, the eagle, was no more than the head of the bald eagle and he screeched his words.

"Migizi pretends to be human because he tried so hard to be an eagle," said Nawina. "He shouts that the men who dream too much, the men who try so hard to escape their human bodies, are the men with weak visions. The humans with unbroken visions hold the bear and eagle in their hearts. Baapi and the hand talkers are the ones with visions, and they do not wear feathers and claws as a disguise."

Silence.

Wiindigoo, the handsome evil sorcerer and cannibal, came out of the cedar woods to be with the others around a birchbark canoe frame on the shore of the island. Nawina, Baapi, the hand talkers, children, and mongrels were watching the canoe maker.

Wiindigoo could not be seen as evil by those who had not heard an unbroken vision, and so, when the handsome sorcerer came over to the canoe, the hand talkers were troubled and held their escape distance, but some of the tribal people on the shore were touched by his manners and unaware of his disguise that summer.

Nikan, the honored canoe maker, was a bony, toothless, and ugly tribal man who wheezed as he spread his arms to measure the cedar ribs of the new canoe. He wore a birchbark waist band with an unusual circular design. He could hear and teased the children and mongrels. The mongrels were shied and turned over, but the wiser children mocked his sounds as those of an evil demon from the underworld. The children pretended and would not see the real evil sorcerer until it was almost too late.

Ogin was persuaded to stand with the other children in the bow of the canoe to hold down the new ribs. Nikan moved slower and slower and told stories as he spread the pitch that sealed the bark. His stories tested the trust of the children. Nikan means "my bone" in the language of the Anishinaabe. He never failed to begin a sentence with the word "true," even though what he said may not have true. The word was his conversational signature.

"True," said Nikan, "the trickster created birchbark and canoes to deliver the first women on the earth to the bears, and the bears have never been the same since."

"The bears get the women, you get the birchbark, and we get nothing but your true stories," said an old man who could hear. The women laughed and the hand talkers whistled with their hands.

"True," said Nikan, "the first woman was blown in a canoe over the ocean, over the mountains, and down to this place. The birds brought her food, bears loved her, and we got the bark to remember."

"Baapi said, is that why you wear birchbark?" asked Nawina.

Nikan unrolled a sheet of birchbark and held it out for the hand talkers and children to see. There were several red handprints on the scroll. The children measured their hands with those on the birchbark. Ogin placed her right hand on the bark and a small blue handprint remained beside the larger red ones. Baapi was sure the hand talkers had been warned that the evil sorcerer would menace the tribe.

"Would you gamble the birchbark on a woman?" asked Wiindigoo. He smiled, and his voice was warm and generous. So warm that some of the tribal women were taken in by his charm. There was nothing evil in his words or gestures.

Nawina moved her hands and warned her granduncle, but there was no reason to repeat the obvious to the Silent People. Even without a vision to sense the presence of evil, the hand talkers could read the mongrels. The canoe maker shied the mongrels, but they crouched, growled, and backed away from the handsome sorcerer.

"Would you gamble?" repeated Wiindigoo.

"True, men are so much better at canoes than women, but show me now what it is that you would gamble," said Nikan.

"This sacred tribal history," said Wiindigoo. The sorcerer uncovered a copper circle with seventeen tribal figures carved on the wide rim.

Wiindigoo held the copper circle over his head. The summer sun blazed on the figures. The cannibal said he would play the moccasins for the birchbark canoe, and if he loses, the copper circle would be returned to the Silent People. The hand talkers and children circled the evil sorcerer to see if the sacred copper was true.

"True," said Nikan, "you would eat women and the birchbark."

"Coward, you might win at the moccasin games," said Wiindigoo.

Baapi moved his hands close to his chest. He argued in silence with the handsome cannibal. Wiindigoo smiled and taunted the old man and the canoe maker with the sacred copper circle.

"Baapi said the trickster told the Silent People to wander and hold their memories on the copper circle," said Nawina. "The circle has never been taken from the sacred mound on the island."

"Baapi is a coward," said Wiindigoo. "There, you can see, the first moccasin game is marked on the circle, the first Silent People who played the game and won."

Wiindigoo turned the copper circle to catch the sun. The hand talkers were blinded for a moment by the bright light that bounced on the circle. Baapi moved his hands and the others rushed at the evil sorcerer to claim their sacred circle, but in an instant the light and the cannibal had vanished. The children searched for his footprints, but they found nothing on the shore.

Silence.

Wiindigoo returned later for the moccasin games.

Baapi and Wiindigoo took their sides in the game. The worn beaded moccasins were turned over on the leather. The hand talkers, hand singers, drummers, and others moved closer to one side of the moccasin game that summer. Four moccasins, cowrie shells, drums, rattles, striking and score sticks, and the sacred copper circle were on the leather ground cover laid near the canoe.

Baapi crouched over the moccasins. The drummer sang a moccasin game song, and the sound was an invitation to the tribal people on the islands. Many, many people gathered at the shore. Wiindigoo inspected the cowries to be sure only one was marked.

Ogin stood at the end of the leather cover with a golden ribbon in her black hair. She wore an owl head tied at her waist as a charm. Traces of blue light moved with her hands in the bright air.

Wiindigoo turned the four cowries in his cold hands and placed them under the moccasins. One of the cowries was marked. The object of the game was to choose the moccasin that held the marked cowrie shell. The sorcerer was alone on his side of the leather cover. No one would drum or sing on his side of the game.

Baapi moved his hands over the moccasins. The drummers and hand singers taunted the evil sorcerer. The hand talkers on one side of the game searched for a certain manner or gesture of the sorcerer on the other side, a short take of breath, a sudden turn of the head or shoulders, a sign that might reveal the location of the marked cowrie under the moccasins. The singers in other games tried to disguise and tempt the players to choose or reveal a bad moccasin and lose the game.

Migizi posed as an eagle over the game. He screeched his words. Mitig, an older stout woman, leaned over and studied the moccasins in such a way that the sorcerer might reveal the location of the cowrie. Mitig means "tree" in the language of the Anishinaabe.

"Wiindigoo is a cannibal, he eats clean children," said Mitig.

"He is sure to eat me if we lose the cowrie, and even the

weather has turned against me this summer," screeched Migizi. The warm wind ruffled the feathers on his neck.

"You have nothing to fear," said Mitig. "No cannibal would eat half a man with an eagle head, not even over a moccasin game."

"Baapi said the cannibal has no taste for silence," said Nawina.

"He never moves his hands," screeched Migizi.

Wiindigoo laughed at the mongrels and two curious children moved closer to his side. The hand talkers chanted in silence to distract the sorcerer, but his attention could not be turned from the children or the four moccasins. The mongrels held their escape distance.

"The trickster gave us the moccasin game," said Mitig. "We play to please the rock spirits, so why must we play with mister cannibal?"

"To win the children and the circle," said Wiindigoo.

"Shoot that monster with the trickster stone," screeched Migizi. "He waited too long over the third moccasin."

"Shoot him with your eagle neck," said Mitig.

Booch aimed a blue medicine pouch at the cannibal. She hissed and wild voices came from the pouch. Ogin touched the owl head at her waist and danced around the monster. The owls sounded in the distance.

"Baapi said cannibals never eat children who hold stones that have been stuck by lightning," said Nawina. She handed stones to the children and the sorcerer laughed over the moccasins. He paused over the last moccasin.

"When did he say that?" screeched Migizi.

"True, my grandmother made me swallow two blue lightning stones and no one has ever eaten me," said Nikan. The sorcerer and the hand talkers laughed over the moccasins.

"No stones here," said Mitig. "Come eat me, cannibal."

Mitig, the older woman, laughed so hard she doubled over and held her stomach with both hands. The drums sounded and the hand talkers laughed. Baapi moved his hands over the moccasins and searched for a sign that would reveal the cowrie.

"Baapi said, shoot him with our spirit," said Nawina.

Nawina opened her medicine pouch and loosened the leather on the two wooden spirit figures. She turned the spirits toward her granduncle and chanted the names she heard in a vision. The hand talkers crouched and posed as shamans. Rattles sounded in the cedar trees. The old hand talker was shot with spirit and he waited to hear the marked cowrie.

Baapi reached over the leather and pretended to turn the first and the third moccasin but the cannibal revealed nothing. The marked cowrie would not be there. Wiindigoo laughed and reached for the children. Baapi moved his hands over the moccasins once more.

"Baapi could lose the circle and our best canoe," screeched Migizi.

"True, but we have the best chance," said Nikan.

"Baapi, throw the last moccasin, the last one," said Mitig.

"No, turn the second," screeched Migizi.

"Turn the last moccasin and win the circle back," said Wiindigoo.

"The cannibal is right," said Mitig.

"Mitig is right, she can see inside shoes," said Nikan.

"Baapi said she hears the cowries," said Nawina. Baapi turned the last moccasin and lost the game. Mitig heard the sorcerer, the marked cowrie was not under the last moccasin. Nikan lost his new canoe. Wiindigoo won and would not return the sacred copper circle to the Silent People.

Silence.

Migizi, the eagle man, told the hand talkers at last that he was the one who had stolen the circle from the mound. He wanted an unbroken vision, to be either a man or an eagle, but not a man with an eagle head. Wiindigoo told him he could win back his vision in a moccasin game if he stole the circle from the sacred mound. Migizi played with the cannibal. He lost the circle and remained the broken vision of an eagle.

Baapi lost the chance to return the circle and lost the new canoe at the same time. The cannibal vanished once more but the hand talkers knew that he could not stay away from the tribe very long. Soon he would come for the children.

Silence.

The Midewigaan, or Grand Medicine Lodge of the Anishinaabe, was held that summer to restore the spirit of the people. The lodge was made with white birch saplings bound in an arch. The lower part of the structure was covered with pine boughs.

Nawina and Mitig, the first two tribal women, and many others were candidates that afternoon for initiation into the Midewiwin, or the Grand Medicine Society.

One red band was painted on the faces of the candidates for initiation into the first degree of the Grand Medicine Society. The faces of the others in the lodge are painted green, some with red spots, to indicate the rank and degrees of the members. There were older men with medicine pouches made from weasel, mink skins, and bear paws.

Baapi, the first hand talker to reach the fourth degree, lead the two women and the other candidates to their initiation. There were bear tracks leading to the entrance of the sacred lodge.

Nikan, who was a third-degree member, waited at the entrance to taunt the candidates. Those who came to be initiated into the lodge had to endure human temptations, the menace of mongrel names, and the treacherous powers of nature.

Wiindigoo returned and waited to tease and torment the women at the entrance to the lodge. The two women were called "animosh," and the names of other animals as a test of their resolve to be initiated into the lodge. The word animosh means "dog or mongrel" in the language of the Anishinaabe.

"True, back to the bush with the animosh," said Nikan.

"No, not back to the animosh," wailed Wiindigoo. "These fat women are too lusty to be wasted on secret old men and wild herbs, these must be my women of the winter."

Nawina and Mitig had followed the bear tracks and remained

silent at the entrance to the lodge. They looked into the lodge at the painted medicine poles and would not be distracted by the canoe maker or the sound of the evil sorcerer. Mitig said later that the initiation at the entrance was no more trouble than one night with a covetous man.

"True, grand medicine is the road to death, turn back, save your heart and shadows from the demons of the unknown," said Nikan.

"Grand medicine has no power but the flesh," said Wiindigoo. "There is nothing to be gained from sweat and secrets in dead skins, nothing."

"True, the old men wait to catch your breath and waste your thighs."

"Show me your lusty eyes, one glance to please your heart before you touch the death stone and never return," said Wiindigoo.

Nawina turned toward the sun but she did not raise her head or show her eyes to the cannibal. Mitig heard the sound of death. She closed her eyes and spread her fingers out to hold her balance.

"One last chance to save your heart," moaned Wiindigoo. "One last chance to hear the sound of lust before those old men shoot you with their poison from dead skins."

Baapi moved his hands and invited the candidates into the medicine lodge. The sound of water drums beat in their hearts. Ogin, the spirit child, translated the sacred processional songs for those who waited on the outside of the birchbark lodge: "The ground trembles . . . my heart fails me as I am about to enter the spirit lodge."

The fire cracks near the entrance. There are gifts near the medicine poles decorated with red and blue bands. Ogin listened close to the lodge and said to the others that "four old men, fourth-degree members, are giving advice to the candidates."

Baapi laughed and moved his hands over his head. Those on the outside of the lodge began to taunt the candidates on the inside. Nawina and Mitig heard so many voices from the elders and those outside that they were not sure how to move or re-member the course of their initiation.

"Baapi said there are many forces and voices in the world, and the medicine society teaches how to hear and balance the good and evil that lives in everything," said Nawina.

"Balance the voices outside the lodge," said First Man.

"Baapi said we must hold our ears to our heart," said Nawina.

"Concentrate on the songs and sacred pole," said Second Man.

"Follow the bears on the medicine path," said the blind sha-man.

"Rise over the seven temptations on the medicine path from your youth to your old age, and you will be blessed with the balance of grand medicine," said Fourth Man.

Baapi moved his hands and laughed over the candidates. With his fingers he drew the path of life on the earth. The old men moved their thin shoulders. They had heard this many times before but waited for the voice translation.

"Baapi said the last temptation, the evil spirit that waits to catch old people, is the hardest one to avoid," said Nawina. "He said evil catches us sometimes when we laugh too much, and when we least expect to hear from evil."

Baapi laughed with his hands. The other men laughed and then covered their mouths. The candidates were nervous and held back their laughter. This was their time to hear but not to be heard. Bezhigo, the blind shaman, moved with the bears in the lodge.

Many, many people had gathered outside the medicine lodge. The hand talkers and many children were there, playing with bear paw sticks and other games. The people talked and threw their taunts, humor, and insults over the pine boughs at the candidates. The candidates must endure the distraction or they would never be able to balance the world as members of the medicine society.

Booch wore her blue collar, and her face was painted blue and red. She leaned over the pine boughs and shouted to the candidates inside. Her eyes were wild, and there were strange medicine tattoos on her shoulders and arms. Ogin stood close to her mother and translated the songs. No one has ever explained how she could understand the sacred songs of the medicine society. She said the songs came in a vision and she heard the songs echo over the lakes in the late summer. The owls and bears heard the same songs.

"Watch out in there, those old men stole their power from women, and now they pretend that the trickster taught them their secrets," shouted Booch.

The hand talkers waited at the treeline near the medicine lodge and moved their hands in silent songs. The water drums and rattles sounded in the cedar. The initiation songs echoed over the water to the islands. The grand medicine songs were heard forever.

Silence.

Wiindigoo returned to haunt the medicine society. Later he teased the hand talkers to try their luck once more at the moccasin games. The sorcerer won a new canoe and the hand talkers lost their copper circle that had been stolen from a sacred mound. The children were curious that afternoon and the first to notice the cannibal at the site of the moccasin games.

Wiindigoo crouched over the moccasins on the leather ground cover. He turned the moccasins over and over and then tumbled the cowries from hand to hand. The birds were silent in the cedar, and the mere presence of the cannibal weakened the rich light that played through the trees near the shoreline.

Baapi laughed and moved his hands at the end of the medicine society ceremonies. The hand talkers and the mongrels held their escape distance from the cannibal.

"Baapi said the hand talkers need an advantage," said Nawina. "We need a new spirit to outwit the sorcerer and return the circle."

"So, where are those big tricksters when we need them," said Mitig, "the tricksters who gave us birchbark, mongrels, and the rest?"

"True, the old man lost my canoe and we thought he was a trickster," said Nikan. "Now the cannibal is back and looking for more."

Wiindigoo hunched over on the leather and placed the four cowries in his mouth. He pretended to swallow the cowries, but later he turned them one by one in his hands. The cowries were stained with dark shadows. The hand talkers watched from a distance and then laughed in silence.

"Trickster games created the animals and the tribes," said Wiindigoo. "So, are the hand talkers all talk and no play?"

"Why bother with more games?" screeched Migizi. "We know what you want, and we know how you stole the sacred circle."

"Migizi is a liar, not a gambler," said Wiindigoo. "No one listens to a coward with a broken vision, no one but the dead."

"Play with the cannibal and you lose your soul," screeched Migizi.

"Migizi is right about that, but he had nothing to lose," said Booch.

"Migizi is the one who stole the copper circle and lost his shadow on the mound," said Wiindigoo. "Listen to him and your past is gone forever."

Wiindigoo smiled and turned the cowries in his hands. He held out the marked cowrie and pretended to place it under a moccasin. His hands were bloodless. The hand talkers threw their moccasins on the leather cover and taunted the cannibal. Mongrels moved closer to the moccasins and barked at the children.

Baapi laughed and moved his hands. The hand talkers repeated what he said and then sneered at the cannibal. Ogin beat the drum, a slow beat that reached the islands. She danced around the moccasins.

"Baapi said he lost the canoe," said Nawina. "Now he wonders what the cannibal wants from the hand talkers."

"Your children, nothing more than your children," hissed Wiindigoo. "Wager the children for the copper circle in one more moccasin game."

Baapi moved his hands and frowned for the first time in many years. The Silent People moved their hands in wild circles and then turned their back on the cannibal. The hand talkers huddled so the cannibal could not hear their conversation. They talked about the ice woman who lived on the island. Wiindigoo could not see their hands or hear the translation.

"Baapi said the ice woman could win the game," whispered Nawina.

"True, but she could never win at moccasins," said Nikan.

"Baapi said he wagers his bear skin that the ice woman could win any moccasin game and return the sacred circle," said Nawina.

"You need more than a bear skin to be around her," screeched Migizi.

"True, my new canoe against your bear skin," said Nikan, "that the ice woman loses the moccasin game."

"Canoes, bear skins, but not a word about our children," said Booch.

"Baapi said never bet against the ice woman," said Nawina.

"Never, if you count on summer," said Booch.

"Baapi said the ice woman never loses because she has nothing to fear, and nothing to worry about in the winter," said Nawina.

"True, but we need trickster stories in the winter," said Nikan.

"Baapi said the children should decide," said Nawina.

"How could we win without our sacred circle?" asked Ogin.

"Baapi said the ice woman can win," said Nawina.

"The ice woman lives alone in a cold cave on the island," said Booch.

"She never heard of the moccasin game or the circle," said Mitig.

"Baapi said the ice woman is on the circle," said Nawina.

"True, but who cares, she turns cannibals into ice," said Nikan.

"Play for the stories on the circle," said Ogin.

"Baapi agrees, he said we wager our children on the return of the canoe and the stolen circle," said Nawina. "Four more games each in two rounds and the hand talkers might never be the same."

Baapi laughed and the hand talkers cursed the cannibal in silence. The mongrels circled the moccasins and barked at the children. Ogin beat on a water drum and many birds landed in the trees over the game.

"Choose your moccasins," said Wiindigoo.

"Baapi said the hand talkers want the eagle man to turn over the first moccasin in the game," said Nawina.

"No, no, not on the first turn, not for the children," screeched Migizi.

"Migizi is a loser," said Wiindigoo.

"Baapi said no one is a loser," said Nawina.

"The hand talkers lost their past on half an eagle," said Wiindigoo.

Bezhigo, the shaman, leaned closer to the cannibal and moved his wild hands in silence. The shaman was a hand talker and lost his vision as a child in a thunderstorm. He was struck by lightning and recovered with a vision that healed lost shadows. Bezhigo, a nickname, means "he is alone" in the language of the Anishinaabe.

"Bezhigo said he would dream the eagles back if the eagle man loses the first turn of the moccasins," said Nawina.

"Not the eagles, not more half eagles," screeched Migizi.

"So, you stole the circle and lost a head to the eagles?" asked Mitig.

"Migizi, your choice is death or more feathers," said Wiindigoo.

"True, death is not so bad, but eagle heads never die," said Nikan.

Wiindigoo turned the cowries in his hands and then raised each of the moccasins. He beat the moccasins with a stick and then placed a cowrie under each. The hand talkers and children moved closer to watch the cowries. The mongrels barked at each moccasin. The cannibal smiled and then touched the eagle man on the head with the stick.

"Migizi, this is your last chance to be a whole man," said Wiindigoo.

"Migizi, the wise eagle man," the children shouted, and pushed him toward the moccasins. "Find the cowrie and win back our circle, win back the tricksters and our lives."

The eagle man watched the cannibal and then leaned closer in silence. He searched for a way to escape from the game, but then with a sudden rush he turned the third moccasin. The hand talkers moved back from the leather. The birds in the cedar were silent, and the mongrels stopped panting. The marked cowrie was not there. Migizi had lost the first game.

Migizi turned and ran toward the lake to escape from the cannibal and the hand talkers. Bezhigo waited for him near the shore. The blind shaman shivered and waved a huge eagle wing in his direction. Thunder sounded on the water. The eagle man pulled feathers from his head and neck and swam out to the island where the ice woman lived. Migizi screeched from a great distance, "The circle is lost, the eagle is dead, the ice woman is the end of summer."

"Three more games and the children are mine," said Wiindigoo.

Baapi laughed with his hands and the singers tried to distract the cannibal with moccasin game songs. The children circled the moccasins and the cannibal reached out with his dark hands to touch them as they danced.

Nawina shook a rattle over the moccasins, and then she touched each moccasin with a beaver stick. She turned the second moccasin. The marked cowrie was not there either. The drums were silent. Nawina had lost the second game.

"Two more and the children are mine," said Wiindigoo.

"Baapi said you would be too lonesome without the hand talkers, he said even cannibals must have a game to be remembered," said Nawina.

"Never be lonesome with these children," said Wiindigoo.

Booch placed blue medicine poles in a circle around the leather ground cover. She aimed a medicine pouch at the cannibal and then touched the moccasins. Ogin sounded the water drum and the birds soared closer to the game.

"The cowrie is under the first moccasin," shouted Booch.

"Yes, yes, or under the last moccasin," teased Wiindigoo.

"You turn the moccasin, turn the first one for me," shouted Booch.

"Wait, consider the last moccasin," said the cannibal. He leaned closer and touched the first and then the last moccasin with his dark fingers. He tried to confuse the hand talkers and the children. Wiindigoo pretended to be interested in the first moccasin, but his manner was a countertension.

"Remember the silent past and your blue child before you choose the first moccasin, because the cowrie might be under the last," said Wiindigoo.

"Wiindigoo is afraid to turn the first moccasin," shouted Booch.

"Fear is the game, nothing more," hissed Wiindigoo.

"Nothing more?" shouted Booch. "Loneliness must scare you the most, but how can you be sure of anything human if you have no fear of death and games?"

"The best moccasin games are lost to fear," said Wiindigoo.

"Wiindigoo, would you cut your hair and crossdress as a woman if the marked cowrie is under the first moccasin?" asked Booch.

"Make your choice, and when the cowrie is not there, you must cut your hair and stand naked for the rest of the game," said Wiindigoo.

Baapi laughed and moved his hands over his head. The hand talkers turned from the moccasins to consider their choices. Nawina whispered a tribal secret to Booch.

"Baapi said he tried to avoid the last moccasin, so the cowrie must be under the last one," said Nawina.

Wiindigoo was silent. He smiled, touched the children as they danced around the moccasins. He touched the first moccasin and waited. The Silent People moved their hands in a chorus.

"This is the last chance to win the first round, my hair, or your body, but you must turn the moccasin," said Wiindigoo.

Booch studied the handsome cannibal once more and turned the first moccasin with a stick. The marked cowrie was there. The hand talkers waved, the birds bounced in the cedar, and the mongrels barked over the turned moccasins. Ogin beat the water drum, a rapid sound. Mitig and the canoe maker danced on the leather. Booch won the first round of the game.

"Wiindigoo lost his hair, mark that on the sacred circle," said Mitig.

"Booch won the first round on the third turn," said Nawina. "So, the cannibal must now uncover the marked cowrie on the first or second turn of the second round to win the moccasin game."

Wiindigoo waited in silence. He smiled and tried to charm the women over the moccasins. Booch cut his black hair down to the cold bone. Mitig shared a leather dress trimmed with cowrie shells. The cannibal wore the oversized dress for the second round of the moccasin game. The hand talkers covered their mouths in silent laughter.

Silence.

Baapi laughed and moved his hands. He polished four new cowrie shells on the leather ground cover, and then he marked one cowrie. The cowries were much brighter than the ones the cannibal used in the first round.

"Baapi said the hand talkers trace the migis cowrie, the sacred cowrie of our creation stories, from the water in the east to this game," said Nawina.

Baapi moved his hands. He beat the four moccasins on the ground and then placed them in an even row on the leather. The hand talkers considered the right moccasin for the marked cowrie.

"Baapi is worried because the ice woman is not here, and we

could lose the game without her power of winter," whispered Nawina.

Wiindigoo was bald and wore leather for the second round of the moccasin games. Booch won in the third turn. The cannibal must win in the first or second turn to hold the canoe and circle and win the children.

Ogin beat the water drum, an invitation to the second round of the moccasin games. The children danced closer to the cannibal and taunted him with their hand moves. He was no longer a menace with a bald head.

Wiindigoo laughed at the children and moved his head to their music, but he was nervous. He did not notice that a child had placed the marked cowrie under a moccasin.

Booch shouted at the cannibal to turn the first moccasin. He teased the moccasins with the back of his hands. When he touched the second moccasin the children danced around the medicine poles. The sound of a drum rushed over the water.

"Cannibal, cannibal, turn the second moccasin," chanted Booch.

"The second, the third, no one tricks me with the cowries, not even the trickster," said the cannibal. He watched the hand talkers and the children and then turned the first moccasin. The marked cowrie was not there.

Wiindigoo lost the first turn of the second round. The children danced and shouted around the medicine poles. Ogin beat the drums and the mongrels bounced on the leather. No one could hear the cannibal over the moccasins. Wiindigoo hissed, "Wiindigoo never loses in the end."

Silence.

Migizi screeched that the ice woman was on the water in a canoe, but no one believed him. Nikan, the canoe maker, was seen on the water near the island. He wore his winter clothes and shivered that summer.

Mikwam, the ice woman, rode high in the bow of the canoe. She was narrow and transparent, blue at the bone, and she waved the birds out of summer. The birchbark was frozen hard, and a cold mist trailed in the water from the island. The ice woman landed and froze the path from the shore to the moccasin games. The hand talkers and children shivered and rubbed their arms to stay warm. "True, the cannibal never loses," said Nikan.

"Baapi said the ice woman never loses either," said Nawina. She reached out to touch the ice woman and shivered in the iced air.

Booch tried to touch the ice woman, to show her trust, but she could not stand close for more than a minute or two. Ogin reached out and the ice woman embraced her, the two touched in a blue light. She was the only one who was not cold near the ice woman.

Silence.

Wiindigoo waited near the moccasins in his iced leather dress. His bald head was frosted. The cannibal smiled and moved his hands to mock the ice woman and the Silent People.

Mikwam never turned a smile. Her lean face was cold and blue with thin lines. She had no summer memories. Later she crouched on the leather close to the moccasins.

"The ice woman said she would hide the cowries," said Ogin.

"The other moccasins remain," said Wiindigoo.

"Baapi said the ice woman will turn him to winter," said Nawina. The hand talkers and the children waited near the shore to avoid the cold near the moccasins.

Nikan dressed for winter and moved closer to the game than the others. He smoked his pipe, shivered from time to time, and laughed at the bald cannibal.

"True, this is the last round," said Nikan.

"That cannibal could still eat our children," shouted Booch.

"True, but not at one meal," said Nikan.

"Baapi said watch your mouth because the ice woman might freeze your tongues," said Nawina.

Baapi laughed with his hands and then started a fire on the shore. The hand talkers said the leaves had turned, the stones were iced, and the winter in the summer bewildered the birds.

Ogin waited beside the ice woman and beat the water drum, but the water had frozen. The afternoon light turned blue between them. Booch sounded a gourd rattle.

Wiindigoo was distracted by the ice woman. The moccasins were blue and the air turned colder and colder around the game. The cannibal moved slower and slower. His hands turned blue and stiffened.

"Baapi said the cannibal is too cold to hold the circle," said Nawina.

"Too cold to eat our children," shouted Booch.

"True, the colder a cannibal the better," said Nikan.

Wiindigoo moved one hand to turn a moccasin. He moved slower and slower, and then the cannibal was frozen solid over the game. His bald head and smile were frozen as he reached to turn the moccasin that would have won the game. The ice woman froze the cannibal solid as he reached to win the children and end the stories of the hand talkers.

Nikan pounded the cannibal on the head with his pipe. The children and the hand talkers touched the frozen arms and bald head of the cannibal. The mongrels licked his blue hands and bare arms. No one feared a frozen cannibal in the least.

"True, the cannibal is frozen solid, too much winter in the heart," said Nikan. "Winter in the summer and we won my canoe, your circle, and the children back."

"He's bald and frozen," shouted Booch. "What did we fear in him?"

"His smile was always frozen," said Mitig.

"So, what should we do with him now?" asked Booch.

"Feed the cannibal to the mongrels," said Mitig.

"No, no, the mongrels would be cannibals," said the blind shaman.

"Push him into the lake," said Mitig.

"True, but he might float back," said Nikan.

"Worse, he might thaw out in the water," shouted Booch.

"Baapi said the sacred circle and our silent past has been returned, and the ice woman won back our new canoe," said

Nawina. "We must remember in our stories, the winter in the summer, and the ice woman who saved our children."

Baapi laughed and moved his hands. Mikwam talked with her hands, and everyone was surprised. Booch gathered the medicine poles, and the mongrels ran off with the cold moccasins. Baapi and the ice woman talked and talked with their hands.

"True, but what about the frozen cannibal?" asked Nikan.

"Baapi said the ice woman would hold the frozen cannibal in her ice cave on the island," said Nawina. "Wiindigoo would live in winter forever."

"Good idea, no one could thaw him out there," said Mitig.

"Maybe so, but what happens when the ice woman turns lonesome one winter and the rest is one long summer?" asked Booch.

"Mikwam would never be that lonesome," said Mitig.

"Stranger things have happened to the hand talkers," shouted Booch.

"True, but not for a bald cannibal in a cowrie dress," said Nikan.

"Baapi said we owe our stories to the ice woman, and we should never forget the great silent power of winter in the summer," said Nawina.

Silence.

Nikan was dressed for the winter, but the hand talkers shivered as they pushed the frozen cannibal down to the shore. The children laughed when the hand talkers raised the cannibal into the canoe because one arm broke loose and floated in the water. The cannibal was bound to the center of the canoe, and one arm was tied to the back of the frozen cowrie dress.

"Baapi said the trickster created silence," said Nawina.

"True, but no one else said anything," said Nikan.

"Baapi said the hand talkers can tell their best trickster stories in the winter because they are silent," said Nawina.

"True," said Nikan.

g ORDON D. HENRY, JR., is a member of the White Earth Chippewa Tribe of Minnesota. He earned a master's degree in creative writing from Michigan State University and a doctorate from the University of North Dakota. He is currently a professor of languages and literature at Ferris State University in Big Rapids, Michigan. Henry has published widely, including poetry and short fiction, in *Songs From This Earth on Turtle's Back*, *Earth Power Coming*, *Black Warrior Review*, *Racoon*, and *Northeast Indian Quarterly*. In 1986 the Blue Cloud Press published his *Outside White Earth*, a book of poetry.

THE PRISONER OF HAIKU

Gordon D. Henry, Jr.

He never saw himself as a prisoner, at least as far as I can know. And of course he carries another name, but I use the name "the prisoner" as a reference to the years he spent in prison for idealistic crimes. He received ten years for burning down liquor stores, federally funded enterprises, and other imposing white structures, on and around the Fineday reservation. Apparently, he lost his voice many years before that in a distant government boarding school. A few teachers in the school didn't like the way he continuously spoke his own native language in school, so they punished him. Two strong men with the force of God and Jesus who knows what else dragged him outside on a bitter wind-chilled Minnesota day and tied him to an iron post. They left him then without food, without water, through the night. Somehow the men believed the force of the cold, the ice hand of winter would reach out and take the boy by the throat and silence his native language. The other boys looked out the windows of their quarters, but they saw only tree shapes through snow slanting, as far as the light of the building let their eyes reach. Even so, they heard the punished boy screaming in defiance all night, defending the language, calling wind, calling relatives, singing, so he wouldn't forget. The screaming went on all night, and in the morning, on a bright winter day, when the school fathers went out to untie him, the boy could speak no more. No matter how fiercely or how often they beat him, the boy would not, could not speak. The teachers' tactic worked on the boy: He no longer spoke his native language. But the punishment went further, deeper than the imposition of social structure: The boy couldn't speak English either. When he opened his mouth to try, less than a whisper stirred air in an inaudible act of diminished physical volition. Boys who were close to him then said that though they heard nothing, they felt something: a coolness floated out of his mouth and went directly to their ears to the point where—the boys claimed—their hearing was frozen in time. That is, though they walked away from the boy with the frozen words, they felt the breath-held syllables melt in their heads later, in words of the Anishinaabe language, and still later in Native translations of circumstances and relationships that they never would have thought of without remembering the cold in their ears. Moreover, boys who went to the same boarding school, years later, testified to hearing Native words whirling up with every snow from sundown to sunrise in their winters at that place.

I know this: I slept in the ruins of the boarding school last December, waiting four nights for snow, and I heard the voice of the boy. What was spoken is untranslatable, immutable, subject to semantic contexts of pain most people can't fathom in the world in which they hear and speak. Yet the voice had a strength, a powerful resilience.

As for the boy, he drifted back to the reservation where he became a silent man of hands, a sculptor, then a political artist, an invidious communicator of visual forms. He made a living that way until he turned to acts of sabotage, for him another form of art. For the sabotage was never performed without the grace and idealism of an artist. When he burned liquor stores, when he burned federally funded structures, he mixed flammables so magnificently the buildings burned in colors and fireworks that left the reservation and nearby communities gasping "oh [incredulous] mys." One time his fire left a smoke that drifted into the shape of a human face. People who saw it swear the face was of an old one, the first bringer of light, or of one who floated in a stone white canoe. On another occasion his fireworks illuminated the night with the words "The Treaty of 1837." On the night of his greatest political burning, on the night of his seventh fire, on the night in which the flames reached up, exploding bottles, licking the dark with colors and room cracklings, on the night people gathered to see in the flames an old lodge, ancestors within the lodge, throwing melted clocks into the air, burning the country-and-western ambiance, of chairs and wall hangings, pointing to the melting jukebox, singing instead healing songs through that wasting machinery, to tell the people the lodge is still open, on that night the FBI found the silent man and arrested him among his cache of art materials in an abandoned barn near the state game refuge.

What could he do? Speak in his own defense? Nod his head with his hand on the Bible and convey the truth in a series of still-lifes, or antlered sculptures, for a jury who didn't understand his artistic aims? For a jury who had been selected by two lawyers, one of whom would represent him without knowing what he could say? He resorted to one last symbolic act. He made a shirt and painted the words "guilty" and "not guilty" on the front and back. Then just before he entered the courtroom, he put a cigarette in his mouth, gestured to his lawyer and pointed at the tip of the cigarette. When the lawyer gave him a light, however, he took off his shirt and crushed the tobacco of the cigarette onto the shirt and set it on fire with his lawyer's lighter. He went to Deepwater Prison after a one-week trial.

For years prison meant a series of drawings to this artistic warrior. With the permission of prison officials, the man made a series of historical murals on the walls of his cell. After two years and a few changes in the mural, prison officials pushed for inmate education. A lovely white humanist came into the school and taught a class on Oriental poetry. She explained the conceptual foundations of such work, the cultural orientation, the affinities between form and image, between isolation and universal vision. She taught the prisoners how to read and write haiku. The political artist adopted the form and wrote graceful passages that he passed on to the professor one evening before class. The professor carried the works with her on the commuter train the next morning and wept thick silver tears on a brown autumn day as the train passed through smoking urban neighborhoods. She advocated the prisoner's release, based on the beauty of his words. She passed his words on to poets and scholars, lawyers and radical political activists and the prison board. "The unusual nature of the man's crime," she was informed by the prison board, "stems from his unusual methods of producing forms that illustrate his personal conceptions of beauty, and to release him on the basis of his ability to produce beautiful words might reinforce his use of art to commit philosophically grounded crimes." For the final week of class the professor prepared a lesson aimed specifically at the Native prisoner. She introduced the class to translations of tribal dream songs. According to her, these songs carried the same intense brevity of some haikus and Zen koans. She hoped to make a connection for the prisoner: He could write haikus and they could be like dream songs for him; a culturally, politically appropriate act could be generated in a foreign form, from language to language, image to form. Obviously, the professor didn't understand the nature of the Native prisoner's criminal acts. What she hoped the prisoner would understand in the relationship between haikus and dream songs was deeply embedded in the prisoner's history. A partial loss of language, new forms, old forms were part of his existence before the professor gave him a final farewell kiss. This was the last connection she made with the prisoner since she failed to win his release. But the time in the class, the education the professor had given him, inspired the prisoner to write haikus and dream songs. And he wrote only in those forms, as he understood those forms. When he wrote letters home he wrote haiku letters; when he wrote prison officials he wrote in the language of dream songs; when he wrote editorials in Indian newspapers he wrote haikus; when he wrote old girlfriends he wrote in one form or the other. This went on for two years and became the prisoner's only form of communication. Still, he could not speak.

Then, through a cultural coup, a group of Native advocates for religious freedom convinced state prison authorities to allow Native spiritual leaders to come into the prison and conduct traditional ceremonies. Since the education program had been scrapped, the officials agreed. For over a year, spiritual leaders came into Deepwater to discuss Native culture and perform ceremonies. One elder spoke about oral history and prophecy; another discussed dancing and drumming; one talked of prayer and the sacred pipe. A fourth elder brought the sweat lodge into the prison. In time, the elders and one or two helpers from the outside conducted monthly sweat lodge ceremonies for the prisoners.

The Native prisoner participated in the ceremonies from the beginning. But in the first lodge when it came his turn to speak, another inmate had to explain to the elder, Samuel Little Boy, that the man could not speak, that he would pray in silence and pour water on the rocks, then pass the water bucket to signify the end of his personal prayer. At the end of that first sweat lodge ceremony, Little Boy spoke to the group, outside the sweat lodge. "This man," he said, nodding toward the prisoner of haiku, "he had to pray in silence here. And I know his story, why he doesn't speak, why he's in here, in this prison. A little while ago after we came out he handed me a note and he gave me tobacco. He wants to speak again. So in one month we will begin healing sweats for this man. Offer prayers for him until that time."

When Little Boy returned a month later, the sweat went on as planned, but the voice didn't come back then. So the group went on with Little Boy sponsoring one sweat a month, and each time they prayed for healing for the prisoner who could not speak. After three more ceremonies, he spoke, but the words were brief and breath soft.

> The earth embraces
> in song the blue sky
> moves one face after another.

Apparently the healing wasn't complete. And for four more healing sweats nothing changed. The prisoner spoke, but briefly, softly, always with the same syllabic rhythm, always in strange poetic words. Finally, another prisoner who had been in the poetry class remembered the haikus and the dream songs, and he realized those were the forms the man spoke in. When one of the Indian prisoners informed Little Boy about the ways and reasons for the political artist's speech, Little Boy suggested that the healing sweats continue until the prisoner could speak freely, beyond the limits of the literary forms he'd learned. Four more sweats produced nothing more, and Little Boy never came back to the prison. A Native newspaper ran Little Boy's obituary in January. He died on New Year's Day bringing wood into his home on the Fineday reservation.

No other elder picked up the spiritual traditions program for Deepwater Prison, and the Native prisoner spoke only in haikus and dream songs.

I made a point to find the man, to read his words, to hear his voice. Four years after he was granted parole, I met him on the reservation, at the Strawberry Inn bar. It took some time for me to adjust my vision when I entered the bar, but when I did my first glances stopped just short of amazement at the Indian artifacts and artwork in the place. Old photographic prints and drawings hung on the walls above booths at the rear end of the room. A variety of red pipestone pipes hung above the bar, reflected in a wide mirror behind a stand of hard liquor. Some pipes were carved into animal shapes of eagles and buffalo; some had plain red bowls with carved twisted stems; some stems were ornamented with feathers and beadwork. On both sides of the mirror simulated treaty documents covered the wall in glass cases. Human clay figures, about a foot tall—each unique, in facial features and physique, each marked with an engraved pictograph on the forehead—lined shelves above the treaties. Except for the bartender, there was only one other person in the place. He sat drinking at a stool, a few feet from a murmuring jukebox, examining the positions of balls on a pool table.

I spoke first. "I know you," I said. He looked my way for a moment, then lifted the bottle between his legs. "I'm here to see your writings, your drawings. I want to put them into a book," I went on. "I've talked to your brother, he said he would let you know that I was coming to see you."

> When the church bells ring
> the road to Rush Lake breaks off
> one cold crow calls there.

That was all he said before he got up from his stool and walked away. I didn't understand the meaning of it until later, when I watched the smoke gliding away from an introspective cigarette. I met him the next morning on the road to Rush Lake. He handed me a birchbark bundle and walked away on the road to the old grave houses.

HAIKUS AND DREAM SONGS
OF ELIJAH COLD CROW

> The red horse eats
> from blowing weeds in human
> indulgence at dusk.

The river with a
missionary's name wears an
ice face at dawn.

Walls leave no company:
a man's shadow grows solitary
moon songs in a cell

So many sundown dogs
improvise on a bark fugue
running for machines

Names travel autumn
wind under the formation
of white cranes passing

Flammables in air
sculpted moment to moment
a heart hungry for home

A sky full of shapes
animals of days above
animals below

A dried flower lifts
then you too are gone away
wind over concrete

The Prisoner of Haiku

Let the girls sleep deep
in dandelion grass, let boys
explode from their skin

An old woman cries son
under uniformed photographs
the red hawk keens out

A leader mouths peace
on the bright road from Yellowhead
one thousand trees fall

Who will sing for whom
when he who sings for no one
must die singing

An old dancer whirls
on his bustle feathers shake
surrounding a cracked mirror

What has fallen to earth
this time has fallen to earth
in a whole fog.

Deer measures silence
between words and guns going off
again and again

The road to eternity
is closed by x's and y's
a roof between the eye and cloud

Prison guards sleepwalk
in a cancerous vista
of domestic quarrels

Travelers come out
of sun looking for Indian-
made real crafts real cheap

This one-eared woman
whose father slept with crow once
saw him turn to steel

The sweet upside-down
cake the radical's wife made
changes the dialogue

Anger comes and goes
one fire ant walking the tongue
to the back of the head

Tired of windows
the dull dead dream of cities
Santa Claus lights go out

Eagles nest in the refuge
uncle returns from Vietnam
a drunken shortstop misses a pop fly

A museum with two doors
one door out into the rain
a dark full bus leaves

He of the golden hand
metallurgical carnivore,
carnival god of grease

and meat grows great
until trickster finds
his racing heart.

Oh, you must agree
the words will hold to the end
meaning what they must

Save the fish with beer
one can funds anti-Indian
underprivileged drunks

Now the blue heron moves
striding twice over wet stones
lifting, twisting snakes

Two old ones in this
doorway of light calling come
down come down come down
from that high wall

Two crows rise from a
squashed possum breakfast
cawing in sun bands

Lips to skin under
squash-blossom necklace the day
holds no more for us

Bezhig, neezh, Andaykug
Awkeewanzee neeba, gee
weesinnin wabun

Church women speak out
Flower drives a new galaxy
to her father's funeral

Under the iron tracks
through dwindling space of closing eyes
(a bridge of panted names and years)

Then mother reaches out
picks up the golden cross on
the red Formica table

Winter comes for her
sings her death in the guild hall
a boy receives a blanket

In the moon of the
frozen doorknob, what looks good
takes part of your tongue

With many fathers
I leave my voice of the past
not speaking is not knowing

Hands gesture open
the space around the stone form
man, woman, child

Descended from stone
before the merging of clans
into treaty bands

In black and white, words
coordinates, rivers, lakes, mark
lines over red earth

Signatures, names, the
undersigned, with marks and lines
anglicized in print

Clan leaders, head men
scripted identities so
many with an x.

Andayk, Flatmouth, Sweet,
Minogeshig, Broken Tooth,
an x by the name.

On 59 a moose
lopes through wisps of prairie snow
lost but not afraid

Tracks of birds in dirt
hieroglyphs around stumps are
filling with warm rain

An oar in water
a hand lit by moonlight
journeys holding sky

The dream x of man
the woman in the chromosome
shadow into light

Smell of autumn smoke
trachoma drags away a child
in a fevered village

Name energy repose
before the blue gun reports
death on a distant hill

Winter lasts and kills
and graves can't be dug
by ordinary hands
with ordinary shovels

The heart runs on from an
essential terror, the news is
there is always news

Days are numbered
like numbered suns
sunlight gestures
into dust to a picture
near a radio

The dream x, old man
an immigrant at a station
waiting for his wounded son
an American shadow

Bear ascends the stairs
one golden glass from oblivious
to women problems

A boy painted himself
white and ran into a river

A boy painted himself black
and fasted out in the sun

A boy painted himself
yellow and rolled in the mud

A boy painted himself
red and white and black and yellow

Crossing Wind's stick is
invisible at the Megis Lake drum

Abetunge he who
inhabits his X mark
in the presence of_____.

The dream x draws us on. I cannot speak for Cold Crow, but his words have forced me from the page. I see how he returns to old forms, and in my references to documents, I hammer away at myself for thinking of myself, and an old drunken shadow builds another wall. In the dark I look for my hands and find windows beyond the fringes of light around my fingers. On the road a few memories wander away singing, their tracks filling with falling snow. This is who I am, a few photographs taken for a moment of truth, a few belongings wrapped in brittle paper, a few dead relatives away from my own road into the sun. And I don't want to think of Cold Crow anymore. He died where we all die, on the way to death, run down by a vehicle out of control. I went to find him on the road where he gave me his haiku manuscripts, and I found him there, frozen in a ditch, beyond wild wheel tracks. He was the subject of his own name, covered with winter crows feasting on his body. Of course they whirled away when I discovered him; of course I discovered him when they whirled away in great numbers. He had no eyes then. What I had to ask him ran wild with tears from my own eyes. "Cold Crow," I said to the dead body, "I understand now your name. I understand the dream songs, the haiku attempts. I understand this frozen road; the words will come back. They will return from the air and re-form on distant lips." But Cold Crow had no lips; these too were taken by the voracious birds in a thousand bloody painful kisses. So I looked to the rest of the body. Everything was there. One hand rested on one breast, the fingers of that hand pinched at the tips, near an opening in his long black coat, as if Cold Crow stopped in oratory, gesturing to his heart as he referred to some deep truth without words. But there under his hand, inside the coat, were words on yellow notepaper.

A FINAL DREAMSONG

a note to hold
the eyes open a hole
in the Fineday earth

make an x in the snow
where you saw me standing last

I am on this road
to town to find a gun
for my lips

make a circle in the snow
a prayer offering of tobacco
make this place
a prayer place

to each of the four directions
put flags of different colors
when the wind turns warm.

ᕼARVEST MOON EYES is Cherokee and lives in Chula Vista, California. For the last five years she has worked in the field of American Indian education. She is currently working on her first novel, from which "The Day the Crows Stopped Talking" is an excerpt. She has published in *Fiction International* and plans a full-time career as a writer.

THE DAY THE CROWS
STOPPED TALKING

Harvest Moon Eyes

I remember the day they found Sky dead. I was thirty-eight and I had already lived a lifetime. It was Smitty and Gray Buck that found her over by the tribal hall. Shrouded in a protective fence of oak trees, her neck had been broken and she lay crumpled. Like the oak trees, she'd never been able to bend with the wind.

Many big, black crows live in those oak trees. They talk throughout the day. Sometimes they gossip about us with visiting crows from other reservations. It is wise never to talk under the oak trees. One never knows to whom they tell our secrets. The crows cannot be trusted.

When they're not gossiping, they warn us of approaching visitors. As annoying as they can be with their constant chatter, we know that when the crows stop talking, something is very, very wrong here. The day they found Sky dead, the crows stopped talking.

· · ·

Sky slowly made her way across the pasture toward the oak trees that were clustered around the tribal hall. Her long black hair was clasped tightly in a bun at the nape of her neck. Haunted by memories of too many nights in too many different beds, dark circles had become a permanent fixture under her intense blue eyes. But last night's dream had been different.

"For once it's nice to dream about someone other than myself," Sky mused as she made her way carefully around the cow dung scattered throughout the pasture. Earlier in the day, Sky had met with her friend Maggie under the oak trees to tell her about the dream. It was Maggie who had told her to go see Aunt Lil, the reservation's resident dream interpreter. Her conversation with Aunt Lil had left her tired and confused; and now she was making her way to the hill that overlooked the reservation. For years, everyone on the reservation had watched Sky make her way to the top of that hill every time she had a problem.

Sky didn't belong to this reservation. Actually, Sky didn't belong anywhere. She was an unenrolled mixed-blood, an outsider, who years ago roamed onto the reservation in a cloud of drugs and alcohol. She ended up staying. No one seemed to mind. She was harmless and she was pretty; so she always seemed to have a bed for the night and a free meal. Everyone on the reservation knew Sky; and though she was liked, she always knew she was an outsider. Some things were just never talked about in front of her, but she didn't mind. Sky was used to it. Her entire life she had felt like an outsider—not really white, but not really Indian; and like a stray bullet looking for a place to land, she had often become wedged into places and things where she did not belong.

Standing on the hill at the lookout point above Aunt Lil's place, Sky could see the wind weaving its way throughout the reservation. Miniature dust balls of grit and loose ends of reservation life merged with the wind. Choking on the fragments, the wind split the dust across the valley. Settling down among the cacti, Sky's eyes rested on Aunt Lil and Maggie far below. While

Lil and Maggie chattered on Lil's porch, dusk stealthily slid its way across them creating two shadows cackling in the dark.

Sky's thoughts darted back and forth like flickering shadows; dancing separately and together, they whirled around and pressed themselves against each other.

Tired from the day, Sky pulled her knees tight to her chest, wrapped her arms around her legs, and rested her chin between her knees. While she braced herself against the oncoming night, her conversation with Lil and Maggie was temporarily abandoned.

"I wonder what dusk and day do in the dark," mused Sky. Her left hand removed a strand of hair the wind had wedged between her pressed lips. She reached her hands back to the nape of her neck and checked the clasp that held her bun.

The wind reached down and slowly, steadily began to pull and tug at the roots of Sky's hairline. The wind pulled in one direction while her clasp braced itself against the onslaught.

Sky's hands moved to the nape of her neck again. Gnarled hands, hands too old for the rest of her body, held onto her bun in an attempt to keep her thoughts from escaping. But the wind would have its own way.

Sky watched her thoughts escape and she was afraid. She was afraid that her thoughts might break loose from the wind's grasp and settle in someone's mind below. Her thoughts would no longer be her own. Sky knew that the wind could sprinkle her thoughts like dust particles throughout the reservation. People would begin to talk. Secrets would come out. Sky knew she would be the one to blame.

A woman is a powerful thing, thought Sky as she tucked some loose strands of hair back into the clasp. Her eyes wandered down the length of her blue jeans, across the tips of her worn boots, and onto the particles of sand that reached out toward the horizon and the reservation far below. In the daytime, the reservation seemed so peaceful and serene. Children played among the abandoned junk cars and cows grazed lazily in the pastures. But with the night, despair whored its way throughout the reservation—

seldom resting until dawn. Sun brings temporary relief and rest from the nightmares of reality. But then comes the night again, and the circle remains unbroken.

After reaching for a handful of sand, Sky watched it trickle through her fingers. The sand faded from view and in its place she saw her dream from the night before. Rising up from the faded sand, the apparition appeared cloudlike, haunting, until it came into clarity.

Sky saw silver hair braided with alternating pieces of silver and feathers. Then she saw long, dark hair moving like fingers scaling a piano. Lightly the dark hair entwined itself with the silver hair. Tears fell through the clouds to the valley below.

Maggie's spirit stood by Lil on the porch. She no longer wore peach lipstick. Her eyes no longer beckoned to the men on the reservation. She watched as Lil moved through emotional quicksand across the shadowed porch.

Lil moved toward the picture hanging crooked on the wall. The picture that captured Lil and Maggie before they both became old was placed softly across the quilt. The binoculars, Lil's eyes for so many years, hung loosely from around Lil's neck. Maggie spoke to Lil, but Lil could not hear her. Maggie was not there for Lil.

As Lil bent to lift the rocking chair into her arms, her eyes rested on the small airplanes lined up on the airfield below. The runway stretched itself tightly over the land that was once occupied by tribal buildings like tights across a whore's thighs.

The houses that once dotted the hillside had been moved. Loose dirt, dirt darker than the dirt that surrounded the empty lots, was all that remained to mark what was once reservation life.

Lil's house was still there. Her house was the last home to be moved, the last life to be uprooted. Only one slice of the past stood untouched. The lookout point with its cacti garden remained. Beyond the hill, where once there were empty valleys, estates sprawled, border to border, electric fence to electric fence, touching each other yet separate from each other. Sky wondered if something was being locked in or if something was being locked out. Maybe both.

The oak trees were gone along with the crows. Unable to compete with the airplanes, the crows moved to somewhere unknown. The crows' chatter was replaced by the high-pitched whine of dirt bikes racing along the hillside. Cows that once wandered lazily across the dirt roads were replaced by fast cars whizzing to and from the small airfield.

Sky trembled from the chill left by the dream. Stretching her bare arms forward, she pushed the dream away; and hearing a noise behind her, she turned and stood up. Struggling against the darkness that grasped her, she crumpled against its force.

It was the next morning that Smitty and Gray Buck found Sky among the oak trees next to the tribal hall.

The reservation was the only real family that Sky had, so most of the people showed up for the burning the following evening. There wasn't much to burn: a pair of blue jeans, an old flannel shirt, and a worn Bible were all that marked the passing of her life. The wake that followed was quiet: There were only a few tears, but a lot of eating; and by morning, Sky was quietly buried on top of the hill that she loved so much.

No one ever notified Les McCann, the sheriff out of Smateren Creek, about the murder. It was just one of those many tacit agreements found in reservation life. Death had long ago become an everyday matter on the reservation; and after all, why involve an outsider about someone's death if the person wasn't going to be missed? Besides, Sky's death was of little importance compared to the larger issue that was being debated down at the tribal hall.

Tom Crow sat with his back to the open windows that faced the oak trees. Wiping sweat from his forehead, he tried again to adjust the electric fan so that the cross breeze would cool him down without blowing his papers all over the tribal council chambers. It had proven to be hotter than usual during the meeting he'd had with Aunt Lil and her Council of Elders, the Gray Panthers of the reservation.

Through years of negotiations as tribal chairman, Tom Crow had learned to affect an easygoing manner. Wearing Western clothes, chomping on a toothpick, he'd lean back in his black swivel chair, his arms and legs open for any discussion. But these theatrics had, as usual, no effect on Aunt Lil and the Council of Elders.

"They've become a collective thorn in my ass," Tom grumbled as he spit out what was left of his chewed-up toothpick. After reaching for the phone, he dialed George Brent's number. Wiping a trickle of sweat from the back of his neck, he cradled the receiver while he tried to adjust the fan again.

"Hello, George? Tom Crow here. Listen, we've got a little problem out here. We need to talk before the vote tonight. Got a few minutes?

"Yeah, George, I know I told you everything looked good for the land purchase, but some of the elders have doubts. They're capable of influencing a vote either way," said Tom as he tapped the end of his pencil on his empty coffee cup.

"Well, what they're concerned about is selling part of our land. It seems they've changed their minds; and now all they want the tribe to do is lease the land to your people on a hundred-year lease," Tom continued. "Yeah, I know I told you we were all for selling part of our land, but ever since a white girl died out here, the elders have been acting strange.

"It seems this girl told a couple of the elders about some dream she'd had, and now the elders think they're going to lose the reservation," Tom said nervously.

"You don't understand, George—wait, hold on a second," said Tom as he froze in midsentence.

"Sorry, I thought I heard something—anyway, as I was saying, there's still a lot of superstition out here. People put a lot of weight into Lil Pachuca's dream interpretations. No, I'm not saying I believe or I don't believe her, it's just that I've never known her to be wrong, that's all," Tom said as he adjusted the fan again.

"Listen, all I'm trying to say is that I can't openly go against the elders. It would show disrespect and I could just kiss my career good-bye as tribal chairman. But I've got an idea—hold on again, George." After putting down the phone, Tom quietly crossed over to the open windows. Looking out, he saw some cows grazing near the oak trees.

"Sorry about the interruptions, George, but I thought I heard someone outside my window.

"Okay, George, I'll see you out here in about an hour and we'll go over things before the vote tonight.

"Worried—no, I think we can work something out. Yeah, see ya later," said Tom. Hanging up the phone, he turned toward the open windows and watched a shadow pass out of sight among the oak trees.

Sitting in a rocking chair on her porch with an old red-and-white patchwork quilt thrown across her lap, Aunt Lil waved as Indian Joe flew by in his jeep. Long silver hair waved back at her.

Joe is still a good-lookin' man after all these years. It's too bad that his emotions are as reckless as his driving, thought Lil as she reached for the binoculars that were hidden beneath her rocking chair.

Scanning the reservation with her binoculars, she focused in on the Mercedes Benz parked outside the tribal hall. Other than George Brent's car, things seemed pretty much as usual: The tribal hall looked stark against the backdrop of grazing cattle and junk cars. But it wasn't always this empty. Anyone could rent the tribal hall for fifty dollars a night. Lil had heard whispered that the tribal council, like a high-class call girl, went for even higher stakes than the hall. But no one had ever proven any of the talk was true.

Lil lowered the binoculars and thought about the meeting that had occurred earlier in the day between the elders and Tom Crow.

When Lil, acting as spokesperson for the Council of Elders, told Tom about Sky's dream, he had seemed genuinely interested in hearing her interpretation. This had surprised Lil and some of the other elders. Ever since Tom had graduated from college, he had seemed more white than Indian: He seldom showed up at any of the pow-wows; and he rarely consulted with the elders about tribal affairs. Although he seemed interested in what Lil had to say, when she told him the dream meant that they were going to lose their land to outsiders, Tom had patiently reminded her that Sky was white, and not one of their people. How could she have a dream about their future? This, she was at a loss to explain. But until she could adequately explain away Sky's dream, she and the other elders had vowed to Tom Crow that they would vote against the selling of the land to George Brent for the building of his casino.

But, as it turned out, Lil and the other elders lost the fight that ensued later at the tribal meeting. They were outvoted by the younger ones; and so George Brent was allowed to purchase land for his casino. In return for the vote of support, George agreed to hire only Indians to work the casino. The reservation's guaranteed 40 percent profit margin would be divided into equal shares among the heads of each family on the reservation. Everyone was happy. Everyone except the elders.

Lil never knew for sure why the elders lost the fight, but she did know that within two months of the casino's completion, some people on the reservation were driving new cars and wearing new clothes. At first she, and some of the elders, thought that Tom Crow had sold the reservation out, but his lifestyle never changed, and so once again he was voted in for another term as tribal chairman.

It's hard to believe it's been two years now since Sky was killed and the casino was built. I'm forty now, and lately I've been feeling more like fifty.

No one ever found out who killed Sky or why. It was too bad about Sky, but that silly dream of hers caused a lot of unnecessary trouble and nearly disrupted plans for a casino.

The reservation still hasn't seen its 40 percent profit, but my money's safe in a Keogh plan and my oldest boy is at Stanford. I really didn't want to kill Sky, but she never could keep her mouth shut about anything. I had to do it. I'd feel better about it, though, if the crows would start talking again.

Swiveling in his chair, Tom Crow turned his back to the open windows and the oak trees beyond.

n. Scott Momaday received the Native American Lifetime Achievement Award in 1992. He won the Pulitzer Prize for literature in 1969 for his book *House Made of Dawn*. Momaday is an artist, poet, and novelist who is also well known for his short fiction. His many books include *The Way to Rainy Mountain*, *The Ancient Child*, *The Names*, *The Gourd Dancer*, and *Angle of Geese and Other Poems*. Momaday is Kiowa and lives in New Mexico. He is a professor of English at the University of Arizona.

THE WELL

N . S c o t t M o m a d a y

She was there on the day of his homecoming. She passed along the road in front of the trading post, not walking, but pitching her little crooked steps in the ambiguous motion of the old and lame. He watched her through the window. She was unchanged. The years of his absence—in which he had become a man—had done nothing to her.

She was old the first time he had seen her, and drunk. She had screamed at him some unintelligible curse from the doorway of her shack when, as a child, he had herded the sheep nearby. And he had run away, hard, until he came to a clump of mesquite on the bank of an arroyo. There he caught his breath and waited for the part-fox dog to close the flock and follow. Later, when the sheep had filed into the arroyo and from the bank he could see them all, he dropped a piece of dried meat to the part-fox dog. But the dog had quivered and laid back its ears. Slowly it backed away and crouched, not looking at Hobson, not looking at anything, but listening. Then Hobson heard. He knew even then that it was only the wind, but it was a stranger sound than any he had ever known. And at the same time he saw the hole in the ground where the wind dipped, struck, and rose. It was larger than a rabbit hole and partly concealed by the choke cherry which grew beside it. The moan of the wind grew loud. It filled him with dread. For the rest of his life it would be for him the particular sound of anguish.

He had returned on a Tuesday. On the following Monday the Jicarilla fiesta began at Stone Lake. The tents, pitched on the near hills, were white as wool in the sunlight. Riders in bright shirts and hats, their boots spurred and taped white around the insteps, rode among them, along the edge of the water, to and from the corrals: slim Utes and Apaches, Navajos in denim and velveteen. The barterers clustered about the dance ground drap-ing bright rugs, exchanging baskets and pottery, flashing the sil-ver on their wrists and fingers. The children milled around the refreshment stalls or raced among the tourists, laughing and yell-ing. The timbered slopes to the north were russet and, beyond them, the dark peaks towered, sheer and shining.

Hobson had drunk heavily and gone the morning without food. When he arrived at the lake nausea began to overcome him. He walked across the road and up the hill to the Quintana tent. He sat at the table and Josie Quintana gave him posole and coffee. They did not talk. When he had eaten he became sleepy, and he went outside and lay down under a wagon. He tried to remember how Josie had looked twelve years before. He no longer knew her. He no longer knew anything of these people. For a time he fixed his eyes on the landscape, but it too had changed. His homeland lay dim and dark in his memory, and there only. He slept.

He awoke to the cold and the sound of the drums. It was dark. He could see the gray shapes of people moving about. Below him and across the road, the dancers circled the fires slowly, their feet shuffling almost imperceptibly. The chant of the singers was low, rolling, and monotonous. He wedged himself into one of the rings and tried to take up the chant. Deeper than the drone of waterfall, and as incessant, it made pure sound of the dark. He closed his eyes, and shapes almost familiar to him took form against the lids. He was a long time in the dance.

Startled by the hand on his shoulder, he whirled, blinking.

"Hey, c'mon. I show you something," Levi said. He was dead drunk, and he enunciated slowly, carefully, laboring with his tongue. "C'mon," he repeated and pulled at Hobson's arm. His eyes were glazed and half-closed in the firelight. Minute beads of sweat glistened on his nose, and spittle oozed from the corner of his mouth. His lower lip hung wet and purple, even as he spoke.

Hobson supported him as they made their way from the dance ground. It was painfully cold away from the fires. There was a moon and the night was bright, but a bank of black clouds was rising in the west. As they neared the corrals Hobson could hear voices. He asked who was there.

"C'mon, I show you damn funny something," said Levi. He began to laugh. He pulled Hobson in and out among the wagons and along the fence. They turned a corner and Hobson saw the outline of two men standing close together and weaving as they made exaggerated gestures and shouted. Lying on the ground at their feet was the old woman Muñoz, writhing and screaming. She struggled to free her skirts from their boot heels. Her head jerked and her little arms flailed against their legs. The men were convulsed with laughter.

"Wheee Ha! See? See?" Levi squirmed in his glee. "See? I told you, no? We got ol' wooman Muñoz. She been to her wheesky well!" He stumbled and fell against the fence. Leaning there too weak to move, he wheezed and watched. Hobson gaped. He recognized Ruben Vicenti. The other man was a Ute whom he had never seen before. He was short and thick, without a neck, and his arms reached barely to the hips. He held a bottle and wore a rodeo harness to which there was affixed a numeral 4.

The old woman Muñoz gasped. Hobson suddenly wanted to retch. He had never seen her at close quarters. Her dress was torn from one shoulder. It hung loose from the other, exposing half of her chest. The sallow skin of her arms sagged from bones which bore no flesh. The little hands were gnarled and hideous, grown curved into claws. Thrashing like a thong, the exposed breast was shrivelled and elongated. Her legs, kicking against and ripping her ancient dress, were incredibly thin and huge-jointed. The little humped back, angular and grotesque, heaved and twisted in spasms. The long white hair was matted with damp and dirt. It swung round her head in a blur of motion until it fell in a pale tangle at the old woman's face. And she was suddenly still and silent. They looked at her. Their laughter stopped. *Dead. She is dead,* Hobson thought. *Oh God they have killed her.* He wanted to walk or run, move, but his limbs were leaden. Slowly the old woman Muñoz turned on her side and raised her head. One of the claws parted the hair from her face and she peered at him. Even under the mask of white dust the little face was deeply furrowed about the toothless mouth and along the hollow jowls. Thin streams of blood trickled from either corner of the mouth, giving the chin the appearance of a hinge. There were no lips. The eyes were the centers of round shadows, large and black as the sockets of a skull. But the ugliness of the eyes rent the shadows with the wild gleam of the old woman's hatred.

"Bastards," she rasped. "You will be in hell." It was little more than a whisper. Still she looked only at him. They watched as she struggled to sit up. At last she was upright, and only then did she look away from him.

"Give me a drink, huh?" The hatred was spent of its sound, and the voice was pitiful.

Number 4 saw his chance to restore the scene, which, when the old woman stopped fighting, had given way to fear and perplexity. He moved over her and shouted: "Ha! You want some wheesky, huh? Here!" He tilted the bottle above her. It spilled over her face. She reached for it, but he held it beyond her reach, spilling it again. The whisky fell in her hair and eyes, and her tongue wagged to take it in. He continued to shout, "Ol' wooman, why don't you go to the wheesky well? Huh?" She began to sob softly, almost inaudibly. It was not the response he wanted. He began to feel himself betrayed. "WHEESKY WELL, OL' WOOMAN!" The whisky was gone. "Aw, c'mon, ol' wooman. Call me names, huh?" She only sobbed. He looked at the others. Their faces were blank. "Gotdammit!" he said, and his chin began to quiver. He stepped back and wedged his boot into the dirt. He kicked with all the might of the short and massive leg. The earth flew against the old woman and she cringed.

Number 4's fall was entire. He seemed for a long moment horizontal in the air. The impact was unbroken; it was absorbed by the whole of his back surface. Throughout, the pudgy arms were outspread and the stricken face expressed a kind of over-stated amazement. He grunted like a pig. The old woman Muñoz blinked. She raised her hand and pointed a finger at him. Then, in a satire of decorum, she placed the hand over her mouth and cackled, "Eeeee heh heh heh heh." There was no mirth in it, only derision.

Number 4 rose. There was pure rage in his red eyes, and the certain vision of having been made a particular fool.

"You weech," he said. "You gotdamned weech!"

"Leave her alone. She is sick," Hobson said.

Number 4 looked at him.

"She is sick," Hobson repeated. "Old and sick."

The old woman Muñoz lay still for a long time after the three men had gone. Hobson watched her. Her back swelled and fell with breathing, but she made no sound. She had stopped crying.

"Old woman," he said after a time, "wait for me. I will be back."

She did not move or answer. He went to the Quintana tent and got a blanket. He made a fire near where the old woman lay and put the blanket over her.

"It is cold," he said.

"It is cold," she repeated, and she sat up.

He sat beside her and opened his hands to the fire. For a time they were silent, listening to the chant and the drums. The moon moved upward in the sky and shone in a long bright line on the lake, but half of the sky was black now. He could see her without looking at her, out of the corner of his eye. She smelt of liquor and old age.

The chanting grew faint and no one came to their fire. It began to grow light on the line of the hills. He had dozed. The old woman Muñoz was looking at him. The fire had burned away and only the embers remained.

"Are you cold, grandmother?"

"Whisky," she said softly. "I want whisky."

"You must go home, old woman. You will be sick."

"Whisky. You gimme whisky, huh?"

"I have no whisky," he said.

"Hey, we go to the whisky well, okay?"

"No," he said. "There is no whisky well. It was a lie. They were making fun of you."

"Those bastards don't know nothing! You come with me. I will show you where is the whisky well."

He watched her as she made ready to stand. His throat was dry and he was numb with cold. His mind had begun to turn on him. He got to his feet and helped her.

"Yes, old woman," he said. "Yes, the well. Take me to the whisky well."

They walked along the corrals. The chanting had died away. The narrow horizon before them had become a pale and brilliant rose, and it began to rain.

As they were about to turn the last corral, Number 4 stepped in front of them. Hobson saw the low gray arc as the blade flashed across the old woman's middle. The blow spun her into the fence. He caught her before she could fall and heard the footsteps fade in the distance. His eyes were wide and he saw the poles of the fence. They were gray and smooth where the bark had been stripped away and the sun had dried and burned them. He laid the old woman down.

He walked south until he came to the arroyo. He stood on the edge and looked at the sky. The bright jagged line between the hills and the dark clouds was almost gone, but he could see one patch of pure color where there was a saddle on the skyline. There, like a small pool of water, was eternity. As he looked at it he thought he heard the first wind of the morning. But it was only the ruse of the silence. There was no wind. There was only the windless rain.

D on L. Birchfield, a member of the Choctaw Nation of Oklahoma, is of mixed Choctaw and Chickasaw blood. He is a former editor of *Camp Crier*, published by the Oklahoma City Native American Center. His history of *Camp Crier*, 1974 to 1980, appeared in the Summer 1988 issue of the *Native Press Research Journal*. A freelance writer since selling his first magazine article as a college sophomore in 1968 to *Collegiate Scene Magazine*, he is a 1975 graduate of the University of Oklahoma College of Law.

LOST IN THE LAND
OF ISHTABOLI

Don L. Birchfield

As soon as McDaniel was alone in his room, he went to the air vent beside his bed. Deftly, with the practiced hand of doing something for the third time, he removed the screws in the grille plate, hid them beneath his bed, placed the grille within easy reach of the air tube, wriggled into the tube feet first, on his stomach, reached out, picked up the grille, and fitted it snugly into place behind him.

He wriggled backward up the small tube until it emptied into the familiar comfort of K42. This time, however, he moved quickly down K42 in the direction he had not taken on his two previous trips, thankful that K42 was large enough that he could move through it on his hands and knees.

He had formulated a theory for the designation schemes of the air tubes, and if he was right he might find a way out of Ishtaboli.

He passed up several small side tubes, confident that he

was still in the area of the Academy of the Little Choctaws, but as he neared a large, arterial tube, where he would be able to walk upright, he crawled down a small side tube to get his bearings.

Long before he had crawled to the grille plate he could hear the music, and he knew he would find children rehearsing for the children's festival.

At the grille he could see a room that was all dance floor, with full-length mirrors along one wall. A troupe of boys were singing:

> Gonna swim a lake till it runs out of shore
> Gonna follow a river till it ain't a river no more
> Gonna climb a tall tree and shout at the sea
> You got it all, but you ain't gettin' me!

All the while the boys were dancing, whirling, dividing into groups, re-forming in various patterns.

But now the pace quickened, and they entered into a tap dance routine. They danced faster and faster, taking turns taking center stage. McDaniel found himself keeping time with the music.

They finished the routine with a frenzied flurry and burst into song:

> Gonna shout at the sun
> Go sleep in the sea!
> But come back tomorrow
> And shine on me!

When the music ended and the boys sat down to rest, it became quiet enough that McDaniel could hear clearly, through an adjoining tube too small to enter, a plaintive female voice singing a slow-paced song with emotion and grace.

Sunshine, shine a smile at me
Bounce it off a distant star
Let it search the heavens far
Prancing, dancing star to star
All the way from where you are
To where I wait to see
The smile you smile at me.

McDaniel crawled back to K42. He hurried on the arterial tube. If he had guessed correctly about the destination scheme, he expected to find it identified as 00, and from it he would be able to find his way to MM again, but by a much shorter route.

But it was not 00. It was a kind of destination he had not seen before. Its sign read THEATER BYPASS B.

Perhaps this theater might be the one where Little Elroy and Little Ejay were supposed to be in dress rehearsal for tomorrow night's presentation of a children's theater production. If so, he thought he might better check it out because those two kids were practically the only ones who ever visited him in his room, something they did often, and at all hours, and it would be good to know that they were not on the loose while he was in the air tubes.

The first small side tube he tried brought him to a grille plate near the center of the theater, high on the wall near the ceiling. He had a clear view of the stage.

The stage was dark, the theater itself dim, with people scurrying about in the area in front of the stage. Presently a loud voice shouted, "Places, everyone! Let's try it again from the top, and this time let's have some fog!"

There was a drum roll, and a voice boomed, "Ladies and Gentlemen, the Theater of the Little Choctaws presents *The Legend of the Little Bitty Bragger.*" Fog billowed across the stage, which was eerily and selectively lighted, showing a swamp. Wind howled and shrieked, dissipating the fog, revealing the outline of a large person sitting in shadows beneath a canopy of spider-webs.

The voice of a narrator intoned:

There was an old woman who lived way back in what our people call the sticks. Everyone said she was a witch. Her sister said so, and so did the Head Doctor, at his death, to the One-Next-In-Line.

How old the old woman was, nobody knows, but she was so old that the oldest old man could recall as a child being told not to go where the old woman was.

As McDaniel listened, he pondered whether to leave immediately or wait until Little Elroy and Little Ejay had shown up on stage so he could be sure they were going to be occupied here for the evening. He decided to wait.

The narrator launched into an explanation of how the old woman had become a witch, explaining that sometimes there was not enough food in the winter for everyone to survive, and at those times some of the old people would be asked to die so the little Choctaws might live. But these old people did not want the little Choctaws to cry for them, so an elaborate ruse had been created in which the Head Doctor would accuse some old woman of being a witch, and the entire village would chase her down and kill her.

The narrator intoned:

Never in the history of our people was there an old woman so chosen whose eyes did not fill with tears as her eyes spoke the words she knew she could not say: 'Oh, Head Doctor, you chose me to die for the little Choctaws! Please give me the strength to do what I know I now must do,' which was, before lighting out for the woods, to crouch down, and look all around and cackle.

They say that that old woman in the swamp outran
everyone who chased her. They say that from then on
they could hear her, that many were the times, on the
darkest of nights, when the moon was gone and the
wind was just right, from the depths of a swamp no
eye ever saw, there came the ear-piercing peal of her
skin-crawling squall . . .

McDaniel was mildly startled when the stage lights came on
full, but it was nothing compared to the way the hairs on the
back of his neck stood straight up as an incredibly fat, skinny-
necked, tortoise-headed old woman, sitting at center stage,
jumped up and screamed, "Sai hoke Chahta!"
The narrator intoned:

The old woman lived fat and good, stealing from
the snakes and the spiders. The spiderwebs were so
tightly strung from cane to cane above her head, that
they were like a dinner bell telling her whenever a fat
bug became entangled in them. And whenever the
old woman heard that dinner bell ring . . .
At center stage, the old woman jumped up and
said, You be as fat and juicy as me, and I'll be the very
last thing you see!

The narrator intoned:

Then one day the old woman heard something
new, something she had not heard for a long, long
time, the incredibly loud screaming and squalling of a
baby newly born.
On stage the old woman jumped up and said,
Wooooo, weeee! If there ain't a set of lungs on that
honey, then I better go see what it is.
On stage the lights dimmed away to darkness.

The narrator intoned:

> The old woman found a little baby boy. She took him in and taught him what he needed to know, but she had a mean streak in the way she went about it. For pure spite, so he would grow up ugly, she did not force his head between the boards, did not flatten his little skull, did not allow the top of his head to slope steeply downward to his little eyes. She made him a little hatchet and pretty much left him alone. The old woman raised him good, and then she died. He was still so little when the old woman died that for a long time he didn't know what to do. Somehow, he became a little dreamer, dreamed he was a great warrior. Many were the times his mighty war cry burst across the canebrake . . .

On stage the lights came up, and McDaniel saw Little Elroy standing there holding a little hatchet, naked as the day he was born. In a voice so loud and booming it took McDaniel by surprise, Little Elroy screamed: "I have no mother! I have no father! There was an old woman here, but she smelled so bad I ate her! By the bugs above, I am now the biggest, meanest warrior in this whole, damn place!"

As the narrator launched into a recitation of how the Choctaws cringed in their villages, hearing this mighty war cry, fearing the great warrior who had eaten the old woman in the swamp, McDaniel crawled back into Theater Bypass B. He followed it until it intersected a large arterial tube marked THEATER BYPASS A. This he followed until it led him to THEATER BYPASS D. At some distance down this tube he crawled into a small side tube. At the grille plate he found himself almost exactly across the theater from where he had been, still high on the wall, near the ceiling.

Little Ejay was not yet on stage. The narrator intoned:

There were many such sweet little girls among the Chahta, and at the flower festival each spring, the Head Doctor would honor the sweetest little girl of all by carrying her to the top of the mound, there to perform a clitoridectomy with his teeth. Never in the history of our people was there a little girl so chosen whose eyes did not fill with tears as she said, 'Oh, Head Doctor, you chose me to be an Honored Woman among our people,' except for one little girl, who, when the Head Doctor leveled his finger squarely between her rapidly developing, naked little breasts, stamped her foot on the ground and said, 'Damn! If the Pawnees don't get you, the Head Doctor does!' That little girl became a legend among our people, and they say that the little girl chosen to confront the great menace in the swamp was of her clan.

The stage, which had been dark, now brightened. And there, knee deep in swamp water, holding the hand of the Head Doctor, was Little Ejay, wearing only a short skirt made of reeds.

The Head Doctor said, "Fear not, little one, for when you confront the great menace, I will be not far behind. Together we will get rid of him."

Little Ejay said, "Oh, Head Doctor, it is not fear of the great menace in the swamp that causes my knees to knock, and my voice to quiver, and my body to be wet with sweat. I am afraid if I let go your hand I will fall down and drown."

McDaniel backed out of the tube and made his way to Theater Bypass C. There he negotiated his way to a grille plate, only to find himself on the wall of the backstage where curtains blocked his view.

He heard Little Elroy shout, "I have no mother! I have no father! There was an old woman here, but she smelled so bad I ate her! By the bugs above, are you an old woman too?"

And he heard Little Ejay answer, "Oh no, great warrior, I am just a little girl."

McDaniel backed out of the tube, back to Theater Bypass C. He followed it away from the theater, away from his room, confident now that both Little Elroy and Little Ejay would be occupied on stage for quite some time.

He decided that the only way ever to find the edge of Ishtaboli was to follow one of the arterial tubes until it ended. He had thought he could find MM again, where he had learned the things on his first two trips through the tubes that left no doubt that he would not be allowed to survive the national championship game. He would die in that game, he was certain, in the dark, chasing the glowing ball. He had to find a way out.

He could return to his home tube and then find MM by going in the other direction. But that would take too much time.

Theater Bypass C soon dumped him into RR. It seemed as good an arterial tube as any, so he followed it, passing up dozens of opportunities to enter smaller tubes.

Finally, when he was absolutely certain that he was far from the Academy of the Little Choctaws, he entered a small side tube.

From the grille plate he could see a lecture podium and a blackboard where an old woman was speaking. "Another aspect of classical Choctaw grammar concerns its complete lack of any equivalent of European punctuation marks. We might consider the case of an aborted attempt to create a Choctaw semicolon, which the Okla Falaya facetiously claim was an invention of Moshulatubbee's Tuskahoma, Aiahokatubi. Whether that may or may not be the case, the example does date from the early nineteenth century.

"This Choctaw word for semicolon was 'kosh u ibichilu bakapa okhoata apokfopa atoshba nutakhish achafa.' A literal English translation renders it as 'a lopsided, uncircled, one-whiskered, one-half hog nose.' Its pictograph representation was like this . . ."

McDaniel watched as the old woman wrote on the blackboard:

HOG NOSE	LOP-SIDED HOG NOSE	LOP-SIDED, UNCIRCLED, HOG NOSE	LOP-SIDED, UNCIRCLED, ONE-HALF HOG NOSE	LOP-SIDED, UNCIRCLED, ONE-WHISKERED ONE-HALF HOG NOSE

McDaniel backed out of the small tube, but before returning to RR, he crawled into another small tube nearby.

To his surprise, the room was a small office where a man sat at a desk listening intently to the dress rehearsal of *The Legend of the Little Bitty Bragger*, which was being piped in over an intercom. The grille plate was near floor level. McDaniel could not see the man's head and shoulders. But he could see that he wore the tunic of a Lighthorseman.

The Head Doctor was beginning to holler his plea. "Oh, great warrior, we are a miserable people, for we have lost the knowledge of how to find our Sacred Hidden Valley Where Rocks Are Born. If I tell you how to find an old woman who lives far, far away, who might still be alive, and who might still remember how to find our sacred valley, will you undertake this great quest for us? Will you find our sacred valley?"

McDaniel could picture in his mind Little Elroy standing on stage, shouting "If it's rocks you want, it's rocks I'll get. If they're hidden and sacred that's better yet. It's a great warrior you need, so let's not dally. The whole thing sounds right down my alley. But before I go, there's one thing I must know, and then it is forth I shall sally, but not until you tell me now—what in the hell is a valley?"

McDaniel returned to RR. He set off down the tube, walking briskly, passing up many side tubes. When he had traveled a considerable distance and there still seemed to be no end to RR, he crawled into three successive small tubes, trying to get his bearings, but found only dark, silent rooms at the grille plates.

Finally, in the fourth side tube, he heard the harsh, commanding voice of Colonel McGee, and at the grille plate found the colonel boldly instructing a room filled wall to wall with elders. McDaniel could see the most venerated old men and old women in Ishtaboli, among them many members of the Council of Doctors.

The colonel was saying "But what did it mean when he said 'First I scare my enemy, then I kill him?' "

"I'll tell you what it meant in the gray dawn of an autumn morning in the year 1808. It meant that he divided his three hundred Choctaw warriors into three groups, holding the third group in reserve under his command.

"Just at dawn, when a village of the Fast-Dancing People was just coming alive, the first wave charged, filling the air with the sound of one hundred lusty throats . . ."

Having already heard "Sai hoke Chahta" that evening, McDaniel was nevertheless ill prepared to hear it as he heard it now. Inadvertently he had slithered some distance backward in the tube before he realized what he was doing.

The charge caught the village completely by surprise, and the light Choctaw war axes split many skulls before the Fast-Dancing People could marshal to meet the attack. But once they did, they threw it back, joyous to see how they so greatly outnumbered their attackers.

"At that critical psychological moment, the second wave launched its attack upon the flank of the Fast-Dancing People. Imagine what went through the minds of those people as they could not help but wonder how many more Choctaws were yet to attack, as they heard for the second time that morning . . ."

McDaniel was prepared for it this time, but still the scream curdled his blood.

"The Fast-Dancing People met the second charge as stoutly as the first. They also got all of their old people, and all their women and children, moved to the rear, so their warriors could beat back the two-pronged attack.

"Their hearts must have been soaring. They saw that they would repulse the smaller Choctaw forces. Then, from behind them, they heard the voice of Pushmataha and one hundred others . . ."

McDaniel clamped his hands over his ears as tightly as he could, but still the scream turned his knees to jelly.

"The third Choctaw wave hacked the women and children and the old people to pieces, right before the eyes of the Fast-Dancing warriors. Horrified at what they were seeing, they turned to try to make their way to their helpless loved ones, and as they did, they were hacked down from behind by the Choctaws in the first and second waves.

"The helpless loved ones pushed toward their warriors, trying to flee from the third Choctaw wave, blocking their own warriors from reaching it. In those moments those Fast-Dancing People knew nothing but terror, and in those moments the Choctaw warriors slaughtered them all, every man, woman, and child."

McDaniel crawled backward out of the side tube, back to RR. When he found he could stand upright, something beyond his control seized him, and he began to run. He ran and ran and ran.

Finally he could run no more, but he was determined not to stop again until he came to the end of the tube.

It was a long walk, but finally RR ended. It ended at a hatch, a curious hatch indeed. It would have looked more at home in a submarine.

It opened easily enough, and he stepped through it into a huge tube that curved out of sight in each direction. A sign said NORTHWEST HANGING WALL BELOW. SECTOR 12 POWER CONDUITS ABOVE.

He had taken a few steps out into the tube, toward the center, when he heard a sound in the distance. The sound was so eerie, so frightening, that he had turned to dart back through the hatch when a recessed trapdoor slammed shut on it. He clawed at it, but it had no handle.

He was still clawing at it when a roaring, howling wind lifted him off his feet and sent him tumbling head over heels down the tube.

The tube was heavily padded, which was all that saved him. He tumbled and tumbled and tumbled. The howling and roaring continued for what seemed like forever. Finally he managed to pull his knees up under his chin and lock his arms around his legs. Tucked up like a ball, he rolled like one, on and on and on.

The wind died away as quickly as it had begun. He found himself sprawled in the tube, not knowing which way was up. He lay with his eyes closed until his head stopped spinning. He heard the lid of a side tube spring open, heard it slap back into its recessed holding.

He staggered toward it, wondering how he would ever find his way back to his room, knowing that he had failed miserably at trying to figure out the designation schemes for the tubes, knowing that he could wander around for days until he stumbled upon some tube that he had been in before, some tube from which he knew how to get back to his room.

The side tube was MM. He could barely contain his joy. He was so relieved that a fit of nervous anxiety washed out of him, leaving him trembling so that he could barely open the hatch.

Inside MM he took the first side tube he came to, hoping and anticipating that it would take him to the Northwest Hanging Wall, a hope that grew as it angled downward before it leveled out again.

At the grille plate he lay staring into the gloom at some sort of vehicle. It was mounted on railroad tracks and looked like a rocket laying on its side. It had an entry hatch on top, and what appeared to be a windshield, and looked capable of great speed.

He heard footsteps. Soon a man appeared carrying a clipboard. He stopped at the vehicle, raised the hatch, and peered inside. He began writing on the clipboard.

McDaniel heard other footsteps.

"Schedule that one for maintenance."

"The command car?"

"Right. Get Engineering and Development on it as soon as they open. It's got some wires crossed somewhere. The central computer can't shut it down."

"It's entirely manual?"

"It's a loose cannon. Fire it up now and none of the engagement blocks would stop it. It would override the switch signals. The buffers wouldn't even. . . ."

The voices trailed off as the men walked away.

McDaniel stared through the grille. He was staring at his ticket out.

He waited until he had heard nothing for a long time, then he tried pushing against the grille. It wouldn't budge. He crawled backward up the slope of the tube to where it widened enough for him to turn around, and then he crawled backward back down the tube to the grille plate.

He placed his feet on each side of the grille and pushed. It popped out.

It seemed to McDaniel that it made a terrible racket clattering around on the ground. But no one came to investigate.

He scrambled out of the tube and replaced the grille. The screws had pulled out of their holes, leaving them no purchase, but the plate did not need them to remain firmly in place.

He raised the hatch and climbed into the vehicle. He lowered the hatch and sat staring at the console. There was room for only one person, and that was a tight fit. Gauges, levers, buttons, and dials were spread out before him in a bewildering display. There was no steering wheel, and there were no foot pedals. He could not see through the windshield.

He sat staring at the gauges and dials for a long time. He finally decided the vehicle probably was controlled by the stick that thrust up from the floor between his knees.

He found a button marked START and pushed it. The machine roared to life, and as it did, the windshield came alive.

He sat staring at an electronic display that he guessed to be a map of all of Ishtaboli. It was a maze of tracks and tunnels and switches. Pinpoints of light filled the display, and, at intervals, flashing lights of various colors competed for his attention.

Above the display a message flashed at him: "Proceed with caution when leaving the maintenance yard."

He studied the display, finding the maintenance yard. He saw a flashing orange dot there, bigger and brighter than the others, which seemed to mark his position. It was along the Northwest Hanging Wall.

The nearest way out seemed to be a direct shot down the curve of the hanging wall to a point marked WEST PORTAL.

He was studying the display when the cockpit was suddenly filled with a female voice. "Good evening, Commander. One Switch has no record of your flight plan. Please enter your destination codes."

McDaniel stared at the console. He looked up at the display. He looked back and forth between the two. Finally he took the stick in both hands and pulled it all the way back.

With a thundering roar the vehicle leaped forward. As it did, the display changed. The map disappeared, reappearing almost instantly, much smaller, at the far left side of the screen. In the center of the windshield, dominating the display, was a large, three-dimensional image of the track and tunnel ahead, with objects at the side of the tunnel already beginning to fly by. At the far right was a smaller two-dimensional map showing the layout of switches and tunnels and tracks immediately ahead.

McDaniel was thrown backward in his chair by the thrust of the takeoff. As he roared down the tunnel he saw the image of a man standing in the middle of the tracks waving his arms frantically. The man barely was able to dive out of the way as McDaniel went flying by.

"Commander, Computer Central shows that your vehicle has been logged for maintenance. Automatic shutdown will follow immediately."

But there was no shutdown.

"Commander, Computer Central shows that your vehicle is defective. Automatic derailment will follow immediately."

But there was no derailment.

The vehicle picked up speed and nearly began to fly. Objects at the sides of the track appeared and disappeared so swiftly McDaniel could not identify them.

"Commander, the maintenance defect in your vehicle is such that Computer Central cannot engage safety override. Initiate manual shutdown immediately."

McDaniel ignored the voice, concentrating all his attention on the screen.

"Commander, your mission has been tentatively logged as an emergency errand of mercy, possibly a runaway. One Switch is attempting to clear the tracks ahead. Please enter your emergency responder identification authorization codes."

McDaniel watched the objects fly past him on the screen. He watched the flashing orange dot racing along the map, racing along the curve of the hanging wall.

On the display to the right he saw a vehicle, which had been coming toward him, turn into a side tunnel. As it did, he saw a red light far ahead turn green.

Out of curiosity, to see what might happen, as the next side track approached, McDaniel jerked the stick to the right.

The succession of things that followed happened in such rapid order, with only fleeting portions of milliseconds between them, that McDaniel was not certain how much of it actually happened and how much he imagined.

He was barely aware that a bright orange light had flooded the cockpit when straps shot around his body from out of nowhere, just as a huge balloon instantly appeared in front of his face, blocking his view of the screen, all barely having time to take place before the vehicle braked so sharply and suddenly, with McDaniel thrust forward so powerfully that strapped as he was, and with his face buried in the big balloon, only those parts of his body inside his skin could respond.

The feeling of having all of his insides crowded into one small place lasted until he thought he was going to pass out, and then the feeling, and the straps, and the balloon, and the bright orange light were gone as suddenly as they had appeared, replaced by a thrusting of his body to the left as the screen showed his vehicle making a hard, fast turn out of the hanging wall and into the tunnel to the right.

"Yeeeeeee haaaaaaa!" yelled McDaniel. What a car! He could go anywhere in this car! Was it not, after all, the command car? And their computers could not control it.

On the screen, far ahead down the track, flashed a bright red light. He found his position on the map.

DEAD END AHEAD said the sign. There was one chance to get out before the dead end, and he took it, a turn to the left.

A short distance farther he took another turn to the left. Soon he was coming up to the Northwest Hanging Wall again, and a sharp turn to the right put him back on it.

With glee he jerked back on the stick, loving the roar of the great thundering machine as it leaped forward. He pulled the stick as far back as he could pull it and held it there.

He ignored the blurred shapes and fleeting images on the three-dimensional screen, ignored the smaller map of the layout of tracks and tunnels in his immediate vicinity, and concentrated solely on the flashing orange dot on the Ishtaboli map as it rocketed down the hanging wall toward the long sweeping curve into the west portal.

In no time at all he felt the machine leaning, fighting to stay on the tracks as it entered the curve.

"Commander, your mission has been officially logged as a runaway. Initiate manual shutdown immediately."

McDaniel watched the walls of the tunnel fly by. He glanced frantically at the maps. There was no side tracks, no side tunnels, no way out.

He pushed the stick forward, to slow the craft, but nothing happened. The vehicle did not slow.

"Commander, decelerate immediately. Collision will occur in T-minus fifteen seconds."

McDaniel jerked the stick every way he could jerk it, but the vehicle continued to fly toward the wall.

"Commander, disengage automatic thrust modulator. Initiate manual shutdown immediately. Collision will occur in T-minus ten seconds."

Frantically McDaniel searched the console, trying to find the thrust modulator.

"T-minus nine, T-minus eight, T-minus seven . . ."

He began throwing switches, flipping levers, pushing buttons.

"T-minus six, T-minus five, T-minus four . . ."

He pushed everything he could see to push. Then he saw a red button off to the side marked STOP.

"T-minus three, T-minus two . . ."

McDaniel hit the stop button.

The release of pressurized air hissed and hissed and hissed. There was a mechanical shuddering in the vehicle, a rocking back and forth and a distinct feeling of settling downward maybe two or three feet, and then stillness and quiet.

The video display went blank. It was replaced by a message: "Your score 519. Previous high score 286,882 by Little Elroy. If you wish your score recorded, enter your name now."

McDaniel sat staring at the screen. He sat staring at it for a long time.

Finally he raised the hatch and climbed out of the machine. He walked all the way around it. He got down on his hands and knees and looked underneath it. He stepped back several paces and saw a sign standing above it: ROCKET POWERED ROLLER-COASTER COMMAND CAR RIDE.

He looked all around him. In the dimness he could barely make out a few other objects. They were amusement park rides.

A weary hour later, an hour of many twisting, crawling turns, he was crawling out of the air tubes through the grille plate into his room. Replacing the grille, replacing the screws that no longer bit into anything, and which had not been necessary to hold the grille tightly in place, he found himself wondering, idly, why the two grille plates he had opened and fitted back into place had had screws they did not need.

He lay down thinking about it. Screws were universally understood to be reversible, a rhetorical sort of door, a symbol of invitation. If there had been no screws in the grille plate in his room, would it have occurred to him to open it, enter it?

What sort of person places symbols of invitation so strategically in such a place as this, and to what purpose? And if his trips through the tubes might have been invited, might they have also been monitored? He fell asleep thinking about it.

J ULIA LOWRY RUSSELL is one of the approximately forty thousand Lumbee Indians who reside in and around the small town of Pembroke, North Carolina. Educated in the all-Indian schools of her hometown, Russell holds bachelor's and master's degrees in English. She has been a public school teacher in North Carolina for twenty-three years and is currently English Department chairperson at Purnell Swett High School in Pembroke.

FACES

Julia Lowry Russell

Looking into the mirror, Janis saw at a glance everything she hated about her face: She looked just like her mother. The round face that refused to be anything but round; the short pug nose; and the beginnings of a double chin. Ugh! She hated it when anyone said (and someone always did) "Oh, she looks just like you, Margery," and then grinned as if he or she had found the perfect way to flatter both of them. Janis usually just *grinned* back. Who wants to look like her mother!

Taking a jar of cleansing cream out of the medicine cabinet, she lost her reflection for an instant only to have it reappear when she closed the door again. After opening the jar and balancing the lid on the rim of the sink, Janis began slowly and methodically to cover her face and throat with cream.

"You really get to me." Janis cursed her mother's reflection. Her feelings for her mother were a mixture of bitterness and admiration. "Nothing I've ever done in my entire thirty-two years has ever truly satisfied you," she told her. "So why was I surprised tonight when you really liked the blouse I got you for your birthday. 'But pink? You know I never wear pink, Janis. Didn't they have any other colors? A nice blue, perhaps?'" She mimicked her mother's oh-you-shouldn't-have-but-since-you-did-why-didn't-you-do-it-right voice.

"Take that!" Janis playfully slapped a bit of cleansing cream on her mother's rounded cheeks. "And that!" She added a dollop to her pug nose. "Not bad." As she played with the cream and her mother's reflection, she became fascinated by the transformation of their shared visage. The more cream she put on, the more the reflection did not look like her mother and the more mesmerized Janis became. Soon she found herself reaching deep into the jar and scooping out big globs of white cream, putting it thicker and thicker all over her face, creating a new face, a more pleasing mask for her mirror-mother. Soon nothing was left but two big, dark eyes. Janis's brown eyes had never looked like her mother's green, critical orbs. "Green eyes that don't like pink blouses," Janis complained to the two eyes in the mirror.

The dark eyes followed her movements as Janis set the jar in the sink and wiped her hands on the washcloth that she took from the bar beside the basin. She looked up, met the eyes staring out of the cream, and winked. When one of them winked back, she felt a delicious wickedness.

After dropping the cloth into the sink beside the empty jar of cream, she slowly smoothed the prints her fingers had made. Carefully Janis planed the layered cleanser on her mother's face, for it seemed extremely important that not a single line be left. She worked diligently until, even under close scrutiny, she couldn't detect a single trace, just a smooth, white, blank expanse. Still the dark eyes glittered in the mirror, beckoning Janis into deeper mysteries, for, like any mask, the white, molded cream made its revelations and suggested its secrets.

Janis looked at the eyes peering out from the mask. She studied them with some satisfaction. They were definitely hers! She smiled and they smiled in reply, encouraging her. To what? For a long moment they watched each other, Janis and the eyes-that-were-not-her-mother's. Then she knew. She would create the face she had always wanted. "Sculpture in Cold Cream," by Janis Davis.

She lost her mother's reflection once again as she rummaged in the medicine cabinet. There she spotted an old orange stick that had become lost, separated from the manicure set. Perfect. "If cleansing cream can be the clay, then certainly an orange stick can be the awl," she announced out loud, pleased with her ingenuity. After closing the cabinet door, she looked at those eyes and nodded in conspiracy. Janis began another transformation.

Working with increased concentration, Janis moved the top layers of white cream up from the right side of her face, leaving a slightly thinner white covering behind. She mounded the newly moved cream into a thick line that ran a couple of inches under the right eye, starting from the middle of the socket and extending up and around the corner. Here she smoothed it out until it blended back into the rest of the cream that lay along the side and ran only slightly into the edges of her hair. This she accomplished with her finger. But this new mask needed more definition, more refinement. "I *need* an *awl*," she intoned in her best Boris Karloff voice.

With the orange stick she removed some of the roundness from the top of the mound. Carefully she wiped the stick on the washcloth. Then she carved a hollow under the angular mound, a shadow almost. Taking great care, she worked the cream so that no lines or prints appeared on the smooth surface. Surveying her work, Janis liked her artistic endeavors and felt the power of genesis. What is the mystery? Vague shadows flitted through her thoughts, but the eyes smiled their inscrutable insistence and the face with two histories drew her attendance.

Janis acknowledged the duality before her and continued the metamorphosis. First she moved some of the cream from the left lower portion of her mother's mask, creating an angular cheekbone. She made sure the shallow hollow was perfectly formed underneath. Checking to remove any signs of fingerprints pressed into the mask like those left in clay by the ancients, she looked at the reflection. "These cheekbones don't look a thing like my mother's," Janis noted with satisfaction. The eyes in the mirror urged her to complete the creation.

She moved to the nose, feeling an odd thrill of urgency and giddiness. Quickly she rummaged in the cabinet to secure a second jar of cold cream and immediately set to work. Holding the orange stick close to its tip and drawing a line from the inside corner of her right eye down, swerving out a little before she stopped to indicate the nostril opening, Janis watched it emerge. She repeated it on the left side of her face. Good. After putting the stick down, she took both index fingers and smoothed the indentations made by the stick so that her newly defined nose blended gradually into her beautiful high cheekbones. Then, dipping into the sink and into the second jar for more cream, she molded with her fingers a wonderful Roman nose. It seemed to Janis an elegant nose, glorious in its length and flowing lines. Definitely not pug, she thought.

Janis knew that the chin was the next step. Gingerly she molded the cream into a firmly squared jawline and watched the small double chin fade out of prominence.

Janis stopped to admire her work. For a while she reveled in the sharp angles and dramatic shadows, and decided that she was right to hate roundness. The eyes in the mirror smiled their approval, but Janis became irritated with her mother's reflection.

The irritation grew. The more she looked, the more disgruntled she became. Something was wrong with her new face.

It was too smooth. That was it. There were no lines. "Lines reveal character," Janis had heard her mother recite countless times when they discussed their family's ancestry. According to her mother, one could read a person's history in the lines on his face. It was one's ancestors' way of "etching themselves into the future." Janis usually yawned through her mother's family lectures and rarely bothered to credit them with much wisdom. But maybe she was right. For once. (Janis wasn't about to relinquish any more cherished grudges than she had to.) The face etched in cold cream and reflected in the mirror was no longer hers or her mother's. It had no history, no heritage. "This face has no *Mother*, no family, no community."

She removed the washcloth and jars from the bottom of the sink and turned on the taps. One fantasy down the drain, she thought, amused at her own pun. She looked again at the face without a past. "No past means no future," she warned the reflection while she waited for the water to get hot.

Janis stopped her idle movements, arrested by the dark eyes in the mirror that seemed eerie and detached. She peered at the white, grotesque mask. She wasn't smiling anymore, but somehow Janis felt as if the eyes were. She tried consciously to change the expression in her eyes, but nothing seemed to affect them. She shivered. She was uneasy, and a little afraid of those eyes that were watching her, that had teased her and tempted her to mask her mother's face. It dawned on her as they stood facing each other that the game wasn't over.

Bending over the sink, Janis rinsed off the cream and scrubbed her hands, slowly at first and then with more vigor. She wanted to make sure it was all off before she dared look. Groping for a towel, she pressed one hand over her eyes so she wouldn't meet those other reflected orbs. She buried her face into the folds of the towel and waited. One minute. Two. She had to look.

Janis ran her fingers down the length of her nose. It felt right, familiar, not the nose she had created in the mirror. With her right hand she traced the lines of her nose while her left hand followed the cold, elongated beak that extended out and overshadowed the mouth in the looking glass. The dark eyes in the mirror were filled with horror. Hers? Or theirs?

"No," she murmured quietly. "No . . . no . . ." She cupped both hands around her face frantically feeling the round full surfaces that signaled her cheeks, her face. But all the while she saw heinous angles and dark recesses punctuating the mask. In the mirror she saw a severe, sharp jaw that seemed to sever the face from the rest of the body. Eyes glittered and watched in silence.

She panicked. Desperately she ravaged the contours of her face seeking that which the mirror refused to reflect. Where was her face? Where was she in the mirror? Mentally Janis conjured up an old childhood ritual chant: Come out! Come out! Wherever you are! She knew she was somewhere in that mirror, behind that distorted visage. She sought to find herself in the mask, somewhere deep in the creation. She found the face within her hands, but those hideous eyes refused to reflect the truth.

"Come out!" she commanded as her hands began pressing her face with furious motions, trying to gain control of the image. "Come out. Come out. I know where you are," Janis demanded, her hands formed into fists. She pounded her cheeks with heavy blows. "I will come out," she cried with determination to eyes that glared back defiantly and danced with madness to a contrary song. "Please . . ." she pleaded in a whisper.

Then through the beating of fists and the breaking of glass came the old image. It bounced off the fragmented shards and reverberated from the porcelain. Janis, looking deep within those eyes, saw her mother, aunts, grandmothers, and all the grandmothers before her. She saw that which was within, hidden in the names and faces. Hers and theirs, there in the mirror, reflected again and again and again.

*P*ATRICIA RILEY was born in Mobile, Alabama, of Cherokee and Irish ancestry, and raised mostly in Fort Worth, Texas. She is a doctoral candidate in the Ethnic Studies Department at the University of California, Berkeley, with a specialization in contemporary Native American literature. She has recently published a critical essay analyzing James Welch's novel *The Death of Jim Loney* in *Fiction International* and is currently at work on a dissertation on Louise Erdrich's novels. The mother of two children, she writes as much as possible.

ADVENTURES
OF AN INDIAN PRINCESS

Patricia Riley

The dingy blue station wagon lumbered off the road and into the parking lot as soon as its driver spotted the garish wooden sign with the words INDIAN TRADING POST written in three-foot-high red, white, and blue letters. Beneath the towering letters was the greeting WELCOME TO CHEROKEE COUNTRY, accompanied by a faded and rather tacky reproduction of someone's idea of a Cherokee chief complete with a Sioux war bonnet. A smaller sign stood next to the large one and attested to the authenticity of the "genuine" Indian goods that the store had to offer.

The driver, Jackson Rapier, foster parent extraordinaire, assisted by his wife and two teenage daughters, had decided, at first seeing the aforementioned sign from a distance, that coming upon this place must indeed have been an act of providence. Only yesterday they had received their newest addition in a long chain of foster children, a young Cherokee girl, eleven or twelve

years old, called Arletta. The social worker had told them that it
was important for the girl to maintain some kind of contact with
her native culture. When they saw the sign, they were all agreed
that this trading post was just the ticket. It would be good for
Arletta and they would all have a good time.

Mrs. Rapier twisted around in the front seat and looked at the
dark girl wedged between her pale and freckled daughters, the
youngest of whom was absorbed in the task of peeling away what
remained of a large bubble of chewing gum from around her
nostrils. Mrs. Rapier sighed, then tried to smile encouragingly at
Arletta as she pushed bobby pins into her wispy red hair. "You're
gonna love this place, honey. I just know you will."

"Yeah, Arletta," the eldest daughter said, making faces at her
sister over Arletta's head. "You ought to feel right at home in a
place like this. This looks like just your style."

"Just your style," the sister echoed and resumed picking the
gum off her face.

Arletta looked around her, assessed the situation, and decided
she was outnumbered. She knew they wouldn't hear her even if
she voiced her objections. They never listened when she talked.
When she had arrived at their home, they had seemed to be full
of curiosity about what it was like to be Indian. But all the
questions they fired at her, they eventually answered themselves,
armed as they were with a sophisticated knowledge of Indian
people gleaned from old John Wayne movies and TV reruns of
The Lone Ranger.

Arletta imagined she could survive this experience. She had
survived a great many things these last two years. Her father's
death. Her mother's illness. An endless series of foster homes.
She was getting tired of being shuffled around like a worn-out
deck of cards. All she wanted right now was to be able to stay in
one place long enough for her mother to track her down and take
her home. She knew her mother must be well by now and probably getting the run-around from the welfare office as to her
daughter's whereabouts. For the time being, staying with the

Rapiers' was the only game in town, and she felt compelled to play along. She arranged what she hoped would pass for a smile on her face and said nothing. Behind the silent mask, she ground her teeth together.

The midsummer sun blazed off the shiny chrome hubcaps someone had nailed above the trading post door and reflected sharply into their eyes, making the transition from air-conditioned car to parking lot momentarily unbearable. Mr. Rapier was the first to brave the thick, heated air. He wiped a yellowed handkerchief across his balding head, which had begun to sweat almost immediately upon leaving the car. He adjusted the strap that held his camera around his neck and waited while his wife and daughters quickly climbed out of the car and made their way with swift steps to a battered red Coke machine that stood beside the trading post's open door.

Arletta hung back, squinting her eyes against the brightness. She had no interest in the trading post and was determined to stay outside. Off to the left of the Coke machine, she saw a tall, dark man suddenly walk around the side of the building leading a fleabitten pinto pony with a blanket draped awkwardly across its back. Arletta had to laugh at the way he looked because a Cherokee, or any other kind of respectable Indian, wouldn't dress like that on his worst day. Before her mother's illness, Arletta had traveled with her throughout the United States, dancing at one powwow or another all summer long. She knew how the people dressed, and she learned to recognize other tribes by the things they wore as well. This man had his tribes all mixed up. He wore a fringed buckskin outfit, with Plains-style geometric beaded designs, a Maidu abalone shell choker, and moccasins with Chippewa floral designs beaded on the toes. On his head was a huge, drooping feather headdress, almost identical to the one pictured in the sign beside the road. Arletta noticed that there was something else not quite right about the way he looked. His skin looked funny, all dark and light, almost striped in places. As he came closer, she could see that the dark color of his skin had

been painted on with makeup and that the stripes had been made
by the sweat running down his skin and spoiling the paint job.
Arletta had never in all her life known an Indian who looked the
way this man did.

After buying everything they wanted, the Rapier family came
spilling out of the trading post just in time to be impressed by the
cut-and-paste "Indian."

"Oh, Arletta," Mrs. Rapier said. "Look what you found. A real
live Indian! Go on over there like a good girl, and I'll have
Jackson take a nice picture of the two of you together. It's so
seldom you ever see one of your own people."

Arletta froze. She couldn't believe Mrs. Rapier was serious,
but then she knew she was. Mrs. Rapier and her entire family
actually believed that the man they saw before them was a bona-
fide Cherokee chief. What is wrong with these people? she
thought. Can't they see this guy's a fake?

Mr. Rapier walked behind Arletta and put his sweaty hands
on both her shoulders. For a moment, she thought he was going
to give her a reprieve, to tell her that she didn't have to do this,
that it was all just a joke. Instead, he pushed her forward, propel-
ling her toward the man with the rapidly melting face. She knew
then that they were giving her no choice.

Mr. Rapier arranged the girl and the costumed man in what he
thought was a suitable pose and stepped back for a look through
his camera. Dissatisfied with what he saw, he turned and walked
back into the trading post to return minutes later with an enor-
mous rubber tomahawk, a bedraggled turkey feather war bonnet,
a smaller version of the one worn by the costumed man, and a
shabbily worked beaded medallion necklace with a purple and
yellow thunderbird design. He thrust the tomahawk into
Arletta's hand, plunked the headdress on her head sideways, and
arranged the necklace around her neck with the quickness of a
ferret. Surveying his creation, he smiled and returned to his previous position to adjust his camera lens.

"Smile real big for me, honey," he said. "And say the magic
word. Say Cherokee!"

Mr. Rapier grinned, his pale beady eyes twinkled at his clever remark. Arletta felt her mouth go sour and a strange contortion of pain began to move around in the bottom of her belly.

The costumed man took her hand and squeezed it. "Come on now, honey. Smile fer the pitcher," he said. His breath was stale rye whiskey and chewing tobacco. Standing next to him, Arletta could smell the pungent sweat that rolled off of him in waves, making his paint job look even worse that it had when she first saw him. Her stomach felt as if she'd swallowed an electric mixer, and she bit her lips to keep the burning in the back of her eyes from sliding down her face. Through her humiliation, Arletta glared defiantly at the man behind the camera and stubbornly refused to utter Mr. Rapier's magic word, no matter how much he coaxed and cajoled. Finally the camera whirred once like a demented bumblebee and it was done.

Mrs. Rapier dabbed at the perspiration that puddled in her cleavage with a crumpled tissue and praised her husband's photographic genius. "That was perfect, Jackson," she said. "You got her real good. Why, she looks just like an Indian princess."

Appeased by his wife's esteem, Mr. Rapier bought everyone a round of cold drinks and then shepherded Arletta and his rapidly wilting family back into the dilapidated station wagon for the long ride home. The superheated air inside the closed-up car was stifling. Arletta suddenly felt as if she were being walled up alive in some kind of tomb. The syrupy soda that had been so cold when she drank it boiled now as it pitched and rolled inside her stomach. She took off the hideous turkey feather headdress and dropped it, along with the phony rubber tomahawk, onto the floor of the car. Slowly, deliberately, Arletta removed the cheap beaded medallion with its crude rendering of a thunderbird from around her neck. Her fingers trembled as she ran them across the tops of the large, ugly, and uneven beads. Turning the medallion over, she read the tiny words printed faintly on the shiny vinyl backing while the painful turbulence inside her stomach increased.

"Mr. Rapier, could you stop the car?" she said. "Mr. Rapier, I don't feel so good."

Mr. Rapier adjusted the knob on the air conditioner's control panel to high and drove on without acknowledging that Arletta had ever spoken. He was already envisioning how her picture would look in the photo album where he and his wife kept the captured images of all of the foster children they had cared for over the years. He hoped she hadn't spoiled the shot with that stubborn expression of hers. He wanted to put it next to the one of the little black girl they had last year. She sure had looked cute all dressed up in those African clothes standing next to that papier-mâché lion at Jungle World.

Mrs. Rapier pulled down the sun visor and began to pull at her perspiration-soaked hair with jerky, irritated movements. She looked at Arletta in the visor's mirror and frowned.

"Arletta," she said, "you need to hush. You've just worn yourself out from the heat and playing Indian. You'll be just fine as soon as the car cools off."

For an instant, Arletta pleaded with her eyes. Then she threw up all over the genuine Indian goods: "Made in Japan."

"Arletta!" Mrs. Rapier screamed. "Look what you've done! You've ruined all those lovely things we bought. Aren't you ashamed of yourself?"

Arletta flashed a genuine smile for the first time that day. "No, ma'am," she said. "No, ma'am, I'm not."

CRAIG WOMACK is a Creek Indian from Oklahoma. He received his master's degree at South Dakota State University and is completing a doctorate in Native American literature at the University of Oklahoma. His works have appeared in the *American Indian Quarterly* and the *Native American Culture and Research Journal*. His short stories have appeared in *Evergreen Chronicle* and *Windmill*, and he is currently writing his first novel, which will deal with the Creek people.

LUCY, OKLAHOMA, 1911

Craig Womack

"Lucille, wake up!" he had said, standing over my bed that morning, shaking me until I rattled.

"Daddy," I answered, acting like I just come out of a deep sleep.

"Why did you turn those pups loose," he demanded, and hit me hard across the mouth and then turned so red I thought he'd catch a-fire.

Well, what if I did see something when I woke up after hitting my head on one of the beams in the pole barn? I don't rightly know if what I told Daddy was lying, but I didn't turn them loose. I might walk around a little at night in my sleep, but I didn't wander out to that pen. Anyway, I might have told him the truth if he wouldn't a-yelled at me so early in the morning.

Now, I ain't *exactly* saying that I might or might not know who unlatched that gate, pulled apart the hogwire, and shooed those cubs out. Fact is, I ain't saying.

"Where's my snuff can?" Daddy screamed before breakfast that same morning as he grabbed one of the mule harnesses hanging off the post on the front porch. He threw it at Mama and said, "Rachel, have that boy, Dave, hitch up the one-eyed mule."

Mama only said, "Ihi," bent back over the cornbread, and turned it over quickly, so the yellow cake slid out steaming from the iron skillet.

The thing I like about early dawn, just before daylight, is the birds. I sit on the porch, and I can't see them in the dark, but I hear them. They make those little flapping explosions of air, flitting away on rounded wings like the puff of a large brown moth. They break the silence as they light out from the ground beneath the stand of oaks next to the field where Daddy plowed. The whippoorwills. Listen to them close and you'll hear it too. They say "whippoorwill's a widow, whippoorwill's a widow." Now, don't go asking me how those poor whippoorwills could all be widows, but that's what they say before daybreak.

"Lucy, stop daydreaming and get in here and help with breakfast," Mama hollered out to the front porch. I hopped up, got inside, and washed the drift off the potatoes and sliced them; I watched them plop, hissing, into the lard. I set them on the table next to the pitcher of buttermilk and said, "Hompaks cey," to get everybody gathered up to eat. I heard all my brothers, the whole den, come into motion, and they commenced to wiggling out of their beds, slithering into their overalls, their bare feet thumping the floor.

But that's not what I was fixing to tell you. All this trouble started when I had the dream, just a few hours before daylight when Daddy woke me up, stood over my bed and carried on, shaking all the stuffing out of me. I have the same one over and over. At night I dream the devil's shadow. Satan is sitting on top of me, straddling my chest, burning me into a deep sleep, a heavy weight that presses down. He wants to slip inside me through any one of my seven natural openings. He ain't picky. I fight him with everything I have. I claw at his eyes, bite his cold white arm, kick him in that one place, but he has me pinned. He smells of coal oil and smoke. I try to find the flames, and I look up and see a kerosene can in his hand with fire licking the top and spilling down the sides. I hack and cough for want of air; I rub my eyes from all the smoke. I notice his eyes. Look white and blank, like he's got a lot of nothing in his head. I almost think I recognize him, someone real familiar, but I can't quite say who. It's a face I've seen before, almost within reach, a passing blur, blank and without form. None of my fighting does any good, and I know, in order to get him off me, I have to say the right words, throw off the dream, come wide awake with the fluttering of my eyelids. I quote all the scriptures they learned me over at the Sunday School Daddy makes me go to at Willow Creek. I start in a-working on him: for God so loved the world, then I hit him with the wages of sin is death, and get in a little for all have sinned and come short of the glory of God and keep shouting them verses, *I mean just a-getting it,* until I finally dry up my supply of Bible. I wake up in a sweat and hollering, but that particular evening I woke up unable to scream, and when I come out of it, I was plumb over to the pole barn!

Well, what could I do but make my way back into the cabin and try to get what little sleep I could before sunup when Daddy would wake me for my chores?

That's when I saw Dave crouched in the dark by the wolf pen. Daddy was guardian for a little Creek Indian boy who come into a bunch of oil money the year after statehood. An orphan. You know, like Daddy said, them full-bloods ain't got enough sense to take care of their money when they get a heap of it, so they need white people to watch over them. Daddy didn't like him much 'cause when Dave and Mama talked that Creek, he didn't understand all of it. Sometimes Daddy said he never would a-married an Indian woman if he'd of known she'd be whispering secrets all the time. One time he said to me, "Lucille, what does that boy tell you about being over at his grandmother's? What are they messing with over there?" I just told him, "Aw, he just goes to help that old woman chop wood. She's too old to do it herself." Letting on like I didn't know much. He said, "Lucille, don't turn your back on that boy 'cause you can't trust him. You know him and that old woman are wolf clan. Way out there away from everybody, don't even come out of that hole in the woods of theirs to go to church. We try to help him when all the time I reckon he's over by the spring with that old woman, where no one can see them, making medicine against me."

Course, I may have forgotten now and then to tell Daddy one or two things I overheard Dave and Mama saying. Like this one time I heard Dave telling her about a couple of men he seen over at the stomp dance. These two men live together way back in the sand hills, away from everybody, without any women. Dave said, "Poosi," he called my mama Grandmother, "Poosi, those two men come down to the stomp dances and strap on the turtle shell leggings. They lead the morning dance dressed up as women, and they stagger around drunklike, clowning and flirting with the male dancers. Sometimes they call it the drunken dance, but I don't understand how come they do that. The young boys giggle when those men take to joining in with the womenfolk, but the old ones always frown and tell them to show respect."

Mama said, "Dave, those two are men of power, the ones blessed when the spirits gave them vision from both worlds, the male world and the female world. That is why they put on the leg rattles and dance like women. You must show respect for them; the old ones are right. Respect those who are different. They have been touched by the spirit world."

Now, Mama is always going on like that—talking about taking care to not offend any living thing and how everything, even animals, has their own spirit. When Daddy kills squirrels, Mama cleans them. She waits until he ain't around and takes some of the hair from the right feet of them squirrels and buries it out yonder in the front yard beneath the willow tree, saying a little prayer to them, explaining that we are sorry for having to kill them, and we mean no disrespect. Just that we need them for our family to eat. Now, like I was fixing to tell you, at the store where we trade in Weleetka, where we go of a Saturday, where the menfolk gather, where they chew and whittle, where they stand around and swap their stories, Daddy throws in right there with them. He knows about them men Dave was asking Mama about because he's heard the white men at the store whispering and talking about them. Sometimes Daddy grabs up Mama's broom and pretends to be those fellers doing women's work around the house. When he takes to prancing about and making fun of them like that, Mama gets real scared and says, "Ihi, show some respect. You do not know what you are doing." After Daddy goes out of the house, she burns cedar and prays that those fellers won't get offended. Sometimes I get confused and don't know who to believe, what with Daddy saying one thing and Mama saying another.

Like this one time Daddy had an old mule named Sally, and she was pretty nearly worn out. She'd get in the harness and lolly-gag right in the middle of the field. Come noon, Dave used to wait for Daddy with a bucketful of cool well water on the edge of the field in one of the cotton end rows. Well, Daddy could see he was just about to get to the end of the row and get his dipper of that sweet, cold water when the old mule Sally lay clean down in the middle of the row. Daddy threw a terrible fit kicking that mule and hitting her with the reins. He shouted himself hoarse. "You old whorish Jezebel, get yourself up out of that furrow." Finally he lifted up the end of that old moldboard plow and dropped it on her haunches. Sally just layed there a-bellering and all the time Dave hollering in Creek for Daddy to leave that mule alone. Finally Daddy stomped off to the shed and come back carrying a can of kerosene and Dave grabbed a-holt fast of Daddy and screamed, "*Manks, manks,*" and Daddy drug him behind in tow and dumped that kerosene all over Sally and Dave run off into the woods crazylike and crying and Daddy lit that poor old mule on fire and I never heard the like what with Dave running through those sand hills howling and Sally bellering and the smell of burning hair and flesh, my God.

Later that evening, Dave come out of the woods and took to mulling about in the front yard over by the well while Mama give Daddy a haircut on the front porch. My little brothers was all lined up behind Daddy, making faces and pulling on each others' suspenders, fighting over who had to get shorn next. Daddy had just got in from plowing, and Dave kind of just stood around and eyed him while Mama tried to clip Daddy's hair. Daddy screamed, "Boy, ain't you got no work to do?" Dave didn't say anything; he just held up some harnesses he'd been trying to piece back together. Mama forgot to sweep up the hair clippings. She didn't remember till after supper, and when she went out to the front porch, all the hair was missing. No one had seen Dave that evening, but at bedtime when we all got bedded down on our pallets, he slipped in and told me he had been to his grandmother's. Daddy don't like Dave leaving anywhere off the place where he can't keep at least one eye on his whereabouts.

Anyway, did I tell you here I was clean out to the pole barn in the middle of the night half asleep and still shivering from that dream I'd had? I could barely make out someone in the darkness. It was Dave sticking his hand through the hog panel and petting one of those wolf pups. Now, I wouldn't a-seen him a-tall, but the moonlight shined on the farmyard that night, and I could see all the way to the edge of the fence where the cow pasture ended and the woods started up. The cows had bedded down along the fenceline. I recognized Dave right away 'cause he had on that old throw-away pair of overalls Daddy give him, and he was hunkered down on his haunches like he always did around that wolf pen. Everybody else just stood against the fence to look at them pups, but you'd think Dave was down on the floor playing with his baby cousins or some of his kinfolks.

Daddy got them pups out hunting last winter. Not many wolves left in these parts; we hear of a few that have run deep into the hills and up into the Quachita Mountains. Even though a bounty's out for the handful of 'em left, Daddy just enjoyed chasing them; he didn't kill them. Just liked to run his hounds after them. He'd get out there in the woods and lay his head down of a log and listen to them all night long. He could tell who was a-leading and who was a-bringing up the rear. If it's a hot trail or a cold trail, he could tell you. He found him some baby cub wolves, and he brought them home and built a little pen out here where we live at the edge of Weleetka. Daddy loved them wolves more than anything else on the farm, and he spent more time in that pen chasing and playing and working out his meanness than he did in the field.

So, I'm out there that night fixing to step out of the barn and say to Dave "What are you up to?" and I open my mouth to say it when I go thinking. Daddy told me that if I didn't stop sleepwalking, he was liable to make me start sleeping down in the cellar with the door locked. Maybe it's better if I leave well enough alone and keep quiet, I said to myself. Nobody needed to know I'd been out there.

Of course, now I'm wide awake what with this new development, and I decide to stay put and see what Dave's up to for my own curiosity's sake.

And what do I see but Dave talking to those wolves? I always suspicioned he wasn't quite right and with the moonlight kinda shining on the pen, and those pups at that awkward, half-growed, gangly-legged age, loping up and down the length of that hogwire growling and snuffling a little at Dave's hand, and him speaking like he's talking to someone across the table, I start to get a little spooked like maybe I shouldn't be watching this after all. Dave starts in and lifts his face up, and suddenly I can see him there in the half-light, his boyish face with those sad, deep eyes wet way back against his near-black skin. I think, my God, him looking up like that, surely he'll see me, but he didn't. I can't quite get the words right to tell you how it all sounded with his voice rising in the moonlight, but it went like this here:

> *Yaha tecakkeyet*
> *poca*
> *omalka atekes*
> *cen-ro-co-pe-ya-res*
> *esponwikas*

matafopke hue-re tan ce-yacet
ometat pohossatos
ne-re ha-re se-homen-cen
haken aka wapas

Cen-ro co-pa-re
momis ra-la-ketskares
he-ya hote tokon
hatam ce-he ca-res
nere anrawan wakayof cen hanken pohayof

Now, I'm just telling you what I heard in the middle of the
night out there after I woke up from my dream. Something in his
words, some meaning of sorrow within them, saddened me, and I
felt like I shouldn't a-been watching, much less spying. It went
something like him calling them brothers and grandfather and
kinfolk the way I understood it. He said he felt sorry for them.
Or, I guess I should say, he was apologizing for them being all
locked up and for everyone forgetting how much they like to
stand on the edge of the woods and lift their voices in the moonlight. He ended, I reckon, by promising them that he would see
them sometime again. Then Dave turned the wolves a-loose. He
got in amongst them and chased them out of that pen of Daddy's.
The pups were loping around the yard, running up to Dave and
crouching before him, sniffing at his overalls, but, at the same
time, they kinda looked at him like even *they* wondered what he
was up to. They even loped around the yard for a spell like they
wasn't quite sure whether they hadn't oughta stay. I just knew
they'd get in the chicken coop or scare up the cows or come
sniffing around me and wake everybody up, and then I'd be in for
what's for. Bounding over to where the fenceline walled out the
woods, they jumped clean over the top strand, then they stood at
the edge of the oak trees for a while before trotting off. I stood

there and watched them disappear into the shadows. Dave snuck back in the house and got up in there where the rest of the brood was all laying around on those pallets sleeping. Morning was coming on; the first of the whippoorwills started to call out like I told you they do before daybreak, so I gave Dave time to fall asleep and snuck back in.

After that morning when Daddy woke me up screaming about those pups a-missing, I kept away from him for a long time. Anytime he come around me after that, I bounded off like a skittish cat. I need to tell you something I ain't let anyone in on yet. Until now I couldn't speak of it, and I'm still a-studying it. About two weeks after Dave run them pups back into the hills—I remember 'cause a hard freeze had come and Daddy had waited for weeks for the ground to thaw a little so he could get the corn in. He was laid up so sickly that he couldn't get out in the field nohow, nice weather or not. There had come an influenza with the cold weather, and so many of them that lived around us got it. No one took ill at our house but Daddy. I went in to his room to change them drenched bed covers, and there Daddy laid white and pale, looking no more than a little dried-up branch in the middle of those sweaty, yellowed sheets. Sweat dripped off the end of his chin, and he motioned for me to come close. Just kind of rasping out "Lucy" seemed to drain all his energy. He looked too weak to even talk, and he wanted me to change the wet washcloth from his forehead.

I noticed something funny about his eyes—they glowed like coal embers. Out of his head with the fever, I reckoned. So, I started to take off the washcloth, but when my fingers brushed that flaming skin, I jerked my hand back like I had burnt it on the stove. Before I even knowed it, he raised up and grabbed a-holt of my arm with a grip like a snapping turtle. With strength I would a-never expected in his condition, he pulled me up against him. I shuddered at the feel of his clammy flesh and wet shirt and tried to wiggle free from his arms, but he had me pinned. His lips brushed against the back of my neck, and then I felt his hot breath in my ear. At first my mind went blank, the words slipped away from me, the words that would break his grip, get him to turn me loose to leave me alone. Finally, gritting my teeth and throwing off my speechlessness, I sputtered, gasping for breath, "Turn loose you old devil or I'm a-telling Mama." Then I leaned over and bit him as hard as I could on his shoulder. He bit his lip, until I thought it would bleed, to keep from shouting out, and I dropped the washcloth. Here I run my legs just a-hooking them out of that house.

Mama said, "Oh, Lord. What in the world's got into that girl now? If she ain't wailing in her sleep, she's running around like a wild animal." I stood trembling like a wet cat behind the outhouse: crouching, listening, wide-eyed, and rigid. After Mama hollered from the front porch, "Lucy, go off into the woods and look for some hoyanica," I gathered myself up and hurried out toward the trees.

The shadows of dusk coming on and me out looking for willow roots for Daddy's fever. From the edge of the woods, I could see Mama out in the front yard, bent over the log section, beating her last root as hard as she could with a wooden mallet. I headed down toward the flat place by the creek where the cows go to drink, next to where the woods start up and the fence ends, 'cause I knew about a stand of willows over yonder. We've had a little dry spell, and I had a lot of trouble digging up those roots, but, as I pulled them from the ground and put them in my apron, I got to studying the situation. I thought maybe I could use a little medicine of my own. Dave first give me the idea. Whenever we seen Daddy off out of earshot, Dave and I used to talk. He kind of explained my dreams to me when I took a notion to tell him about them. Dave said, "Lucy, I think you have a bad case of *Lokha.*" *Lokha* is spirit animals that lives in a person. It goes out of the person's mouth at night and changes into the form of a chicken. Shifts back and forth between a chicken and a person. It practices witchcraft and steals and eats people's hearts. Dave said to me, "You can tell if a person has *Lokha* by the way they breathe 'cause the *Lokha* sounds just like a chicken clucking. You know when the *Lokha* are around and trying to get inside people because you'll see a chicken go out into the hot sun, stretch its wings out, and lie down." Dave said them *Lokha* is having a fever when they do that. That's a real bad sign when them chickens have a fever spell like that.

Dave up and decided that *Lokha* was probably the problem and said I could take care of their bad medicine by burning some cedar leaves and cudfoot on the fireplace coals, burning them together on top of the woodstove, burning the mixture and breathing the smoke, burning and breathing to ward them off. "If anyone comes in your room and leaves signs of their presence," he said, "use those herbs. Let the smoke rise and hold your hands above it like you do when you warm them over a fire. Smoke them real good, rub the smoke all over yourself. Then lean over and breathe it in four times, so you get some inside you too." Now, when he first told me that, I thought, what with those clannish full-blood ways of his and what they told me over to the church about Indians making idolatry out of weeds and dumb animals, I just figured not to think too seriously on it. Not to mention all the times Daddy warned me about staying away from Dave. But out there by the willows I got to recollecting on the advantages of having a little medicine of my own, and smoking myself and the room where we all slept to keep anything bad from happening. I hadn't had too hard a time finding them willow roots, and I knew if I looked hard enough, surely I could scare up a mess of cedar leaves and cudfoot too.

It ended up not as easy as I suspicioned; like I told you we had kind of a drought-like, and I found myself getting deeper into them woods and further away from the cabin. I looked behind every rock, tree, and bush for that medicine, but I found none, and it kept getting darker. Now, I ain't afraid of the dark, at least not while I'm awake, but I couldn't see very well to hunt for those plants. I seen both cedar and cudfoot plenty of times 'cause Dave had pointed it out to me on our trips when Mama sent us off to hunt kindling. Dave always taught me things like that, you know, how to use plants and such. He knows the woods, he knows where roots and leaves are to be found, sumac, wild grapes, gum trees, and which plants set things right with the animals. Well, anyway, I'm clean over to the spring by Dave's grandmother's, and I knew with all this dryness that I might have a little better luck over there. Sure enough, I spotted a cedar stand, and I got up amongst them trees, and, Lord, that cedar smell got to kind of calming me and making me feel better. Some real dry leaves lay about that I thought would burn particular well, and I even managed to find some cudfoot growing closer to the spring. From down by the spring where the path started up that led to the cabin, I heard some voices when I was just fixing to leave. Sounded like some older men talking in Creek and discussing something important like at a meeting. I ain't so sure about these stomp-dance kind of Indians, the ones Daddy always warns me about, ones like Dave's grandma, the ones who don't go to church and all. So, I decided to kind of sneak up there where I could have a look and they couldn't see me. Next to the path that led up to the house grows some tall cattail reeds, and I got up in there amongst them and hunkered down just enough so I could see to where I had heard the voices coming from.

Four men were standing around. The oldest one was directing the others, and he kept gesturing, instructing them how to build a fire, pointing here and there while they picked up things and placed them where he wanted, telling the others where to set the logs. I recognized him—he was one of those two men who live together who Dave had asked Mama about. The man who lives with him was one of them helping out. I had seen them come into the store together in Weleetka, so I kinda knowed what they looked like. A bundle hung around the older man's neck from a rawhide shoulder strap, and in one hand he held a turtle-shell rattle. He didn't have them build it just any old way; he had them men to place the logs so each one pointed in a different direction—north, south, east, and west—like four opposite wagon wheel spokes. They left a little space in the middle of the logs. It beat anything I ever seen. Dave and his grandmother sat, kind of watching all the goings-on, on a felled log behind the fire the old ones got started up. The blaze looked kind of puny, but it burned real steadylike. The eldest man nodded at Dave, and Dave got up quickly without saying anything and headed toward the shack like he knew exactly what the man wanted. Before I hardly even knew he had left, Dave come back, and I liked to jump out of them cattails. Dave had a-holt of something Mama had been hunting for months—Daddy's razor strap.

I strained to hear what the old one and the fire builders was saying to one another, but I only caught the sound of the men all beginning to chant together at once. Their voices, soft, rhythmic, rose up with the smoke of the fire, and Dave and his grandmother, their eyes screwed shut tight, took up the chant with the menfolk. The men directed their words toward the fire as they stood in a circle around it. The old one lifted the razor strap high above his head, and Dave and his grandmother stood up in front of the log where they had been sitting, and he throwed Daddy's razor strap into those flames. I heard a *whoosh!* and a suck of air, and they all leaped back a little as that fire blazed up until I thought it would catch one of those old men a-fire, but it didn't. Those blackjack logs just a-blazing. Now, I know about blackjack 'cause it burns with a hot, even flame. Mama always has me hunting it for the stove. Next thing, Dave's grandma asked the man in charge to excuse her; he nodded his head in agreement; she headed off for the shack. I watched her disappear down the path, and I figured she must of got too hot around the fire. But she emerged back into the light of the circle in less than a minute. She faced the old man and opened her fists, and this time I did jump and gritted my teeth from screaming. She had handfuls of blond hair, and I knew it couldn't of come from none of them around there. Then it hit me. That haircut of Daddy's out on the front porch. As the three men looked on, Dave's grandmother handed the hair over to the old one. Then she untied her apron and commenced to pulling out bits and pieces of what-have-you: an old pocket watch that had stopped working, a piece of busted plow line, fingernail clippings, and they all belonged to Daddy!

The old one begin to throw the stuff in one at a time; with

each handful he took to shaking that turtle rattle a little faster, and them little pieces hissed and made black smoke when they hit the flames. Every time he turned loose of a fistful of them knickknacks, the fire got higher until the flames leaped so far above them menfolks' heads that I could see the shadows dancing off the cedar stand where I had gathered the leaves. I thought, My God, how can those little pieces of personal belongings make a fire jump like that? Turning, all at the same time, they face Dave's grandmother standing, by then, before the log seat. She nodded, turned around, and lifted from behind the log something in a tow sack. They started to chant even louder; their voices rose to a high-pitched tremolo when she raised off the burlap. There stood a crude human doll, made out of clay, about a foot in height, and they had stuck some of that blond hair on top of its head.

Each of the four men positioned himself around the fire so that he stood in one of the four directions facing the logs, seated himself on the ground facing inward, and the oldest one sat at the west. From the edge of the fire, he scooped up a glowing red coal and raised it to the bowl of a small clay pipe and lit it after having stuffed it with some tobacco from his pouch. He passed the pipe and each man blew smoke toward his direction—north, south, east, or west. Dave's grandmother got up and placed the doll between the men, and they all gazed upon it. The eldest announced the purpose of the ceremony: They had gathered to punish a murderer. They all nodded in agreement. I strained to hear their words—something about a relative of theirs being killed. Dave's grandmother came forward, picked up the doll by the neck, and heaved it in the middle of them flames. That doll landed perfectly upright and stood in the middle of the blaze in the space between the logs. As the men stared at the doll, the fire burned brighter and brighter, and the flames crawled up the side of that little clay man. I smelt burning hair and watched the blackened blond wisps catch on the wind and light from the little feller's head, slowly floating up over the cattails. The clay doll turned a fiery red until I thought he would melt or blow up. I tried with all my strength not to stare at the doll, but I could feel him pulling my eyes toward him.

The more I gawked at that fire, the less sure I was of what I saw. The logs started to look like barns or outbuildings with flames shooting out the sides. I thought I could hear voices screaming and hooves pounding and wood crashing and splitting. That doll in the middle looked like someone in one of those buildings trying to fight his way out of the flames. The man in the fire seemed to be moving yet, at the same time, standing still. The burning barn glowed in the background. As if to beckon me toward the flames, its roof, a collection of many swelling orange-red claws, reached out and clutched and motioned me inside. Everything happening: voices shouting, feet running, embers crackling, the barn beckoning, everyone in a desperate hurry yet blindly stumbling about, all of it making me want to see more. The whole picture, as I stood and gazed, seemed unreal, yet more real than the cattails around me. I could of sworn the little man tried to jump out of the fire, and the men watching looked frightened for a second like maybe they thought he could get out. They wanted to back up, but the oldest one motioned for them to stay put where he had seated them.

I could see so much, so many faces, such great motion, like no other fire I'd seen before, and the picture got bigger as those oak logs cracked and popped. I might as well have been standing in front of it instead of out in the cattails; I felt as though I'd have to back up from the heat. In the fire I could see some people trying to help put it out—looked like they had just got there—running back and forth between the well and the barn, which had flames a-climbing up the sides of it like wild grape vines creeping up a fence. I gasped and stood still as a fencepost, watching the fire from out there in the cattails. The flames shot out the roof of the barn and cast a hazy glow that lit up the ground all around, so I could see it framed brightly, like a painting, against the dark woods, and Lord, it was beautiful. I remembered Dave saying that his people purified everything by starting a new fire at the beginning of the year. They kept the fire sacred and rekindled it before eating the corn harvest. They done that at their Green Corn Ceremony. Daddy never let us go to any, but Mama had told me plenty about it. All that church stuff commenced to running through my head like weeping and gnashing of teeth and unquenchable fire where the worm perisheth not, but I felt peacefullike as I stared into the flames and listened to the cicadas singing off in the trees.

Then I finally laid a-holt of the picture dancing beyond reach in the flames. My mind kinda turned loose of something and let it all come flooding in upon me. That clay man flickering in the fire was Daddy. His white thin frame looked as scraggly as the young peach tree he leaned up against in the front yard, and, like the tree, he was fixing to fall. Mama had throwed a comforter over his bare shoulders, and she tried to hold him back. Somehow, I heard their voices swirling around in the flames as I stood watching. She begged, "Ihi, you're too sickly to go into that fire. Let the neighbors work on it; you can't do anything." But Daddy's meanness was limitless and so was his strength, so he cursed Mama and throwed her down into the dirt and run into the barn before any of the neighbors knowed what happened. He got in there and started opening them stalls. He grabbed up a driving whip and beat those mules silly to get them out, but they just bunched up in the corner and started kicking the sides of that barn until old one-eye finally kicked a hole clean through. Mrs. Fixico, our neighbor from the next section over, screamed, "Throw a tow sack over their heads so they can't see." Daddy hollered back, "Damn your hide woman," and took to beating them mules harder while they threw themselves furiously against the barn wall. I saw one of the main beams give away and heard it crash as it hit the floor. The near side of the roof sagged and the barn sloped like a little hill. Daddy got in that stall with those plunging mules, and Mr. and Mrs. Fixico had to hold Mama down to keep her from lighting out and dragging him out of there. Daddy laid a-holt of old one-eye by the halter and had got him dragged out of the stall, but he stood and balked at the barn door with that burning beam laying in front of it. Daddy tried to coax him over and one-eye kind of bunched and squared himself up like a horse does just before he gets ready to hop a creek. One-eye cleared the beam easy enough, but he caught his rear hoof and landed off balance and rolled with Daddy underneath him still holding on to his halter. That old mule got back up like nothing ever happened and run out of the barn over to where the cows were mooing and running the length of the fence at the edge of the woods. When the rest of the mules seen one-eye take the lead, they all followed suit and charged out like a battalion of soldiers, all hopping over Daddy, pretty as you please. Daddy kept flickering and dancing in and out of the shadows of the fire, and one minute I thought it was him laying in that barn, and the next I could of sworn I was looking at that little clay man standing upright in the center of them burning logs.

Suddenly it got so bright that I felt like it might hurt my eyes to look any more, like staring at the sun, but I still couldn't turn away. I heard something almost like a gunshot, and that little clay man blew apart into pieces and collapsed in the flames. The blackjack logs popped loudly, sparks flew and rose up into the night air; a rising column of burning embers and molten clay floated out over the spring.

I seen about all I could bare to look at, but I couldn't hardly force myself to leave. The darkness had completely swallowed up those cattails until I could barely make out the grandmother's cabin down the path in the distance. Keeping in sight the cedar stand for my bearings, I pushed them reeds back and headed for the trees. The quarter moon dipped like a hook over the treetops, and I felt a stinging slap when I run into a willow branch. From back toward the fire floated a little smoke and some dying embers, but the voices had fallen silent. They had all gone on, I reckon. The sound of cicadas humming filled the air, and I walked faster toward home to avoid the strong pull of the blaze behind me.

I reached the end of the woods where our grass pasture starts, held apart the bobwire strands, and pulled myself through the fence. The willow roots spilled out of my apron, and I was fixing to pick them up when I heard voices from the farmyard—what sounded to me like neighbors. I knew nobody come to visit us much. Daddy didn't allow none of Mama's people over to the house. I pulled my apron back together and hurried on when I felt something. For a minute there, I thought it had come a little rain. It had started falling before I reached up with my hand and touched my hair, and like a rain, it continued to fall as I pulled back my fingers, covered with black, dusty soot. I thought, well, I didn't notice that back at the fire at the spring. The barn set in a low spot, so I could never see it until I got real close, but I could hear those voices getting louder and the sound of running footsteps around the farmyard. It felt far too hot for a spring evening. When I noticed a column of burning fragments rising, small pieces of glowing wood splinters slithering up the night sky, I began running; I had to see. The house appeared before me, then the pump, the tree, the yard, the barn. The whole bunch stood around him, my little brothers out there in their overalls, shifting from one foot to the other with their hands in their pockets. Mama was sitting down on the ground coughing and I reckon she must have busted loose and pulled him out of that fire by his feet. They stared down at Daddy who looked so small and white against the orange fire swallowing the rest of the fallen barn. One of my sisters tried to put his work shirt on him, but he lay motionless as she pulled his arms through the sleeves and buttoned it up. Mr. Fixico climbed on his mare to go fetch the doctor. Behind them the barn gave a final groaning sag and caved in on itself, sending sparks that shot up over the front yard.

I turned my back on the whole brood of kin and neighbors and looked toward the woods.

I heard no more voices from the front yard because they had carried Daddy into the house, only the sound of the crackling of the last barn embers. Everything else had gone silent except for the woods. I looked at the fence where our pasture ended and the woods began. The fenceline had become alive with motion. The cows, running back and forth from one corner to the next, confused and looking for a place to get out, threw themselves, again and again, against the wire strands until they finally found a weak spot where they charged through the bobwire. I heard them crashing through bushes until their bellowing grew fainter as they ran deeper into the woods. Old one-eye didn't even bother to go through the cow's hole; he got a running start and cleared the top strand without even touching it. He sailed over the fence, mane and tail flying, back feet extended, forelegs ready to land and light out toward the woods, and all the while that quarter moon shining directly above him. From the trees, the humming of the cicadas grew louder until I thought my ears would split. I saw those wolf cubs on the other side of the fence at the edge of the woods, near the hole where the cows had jumped through. Looked like they had been encouraging them cows on as they busted through.

The last couple of weeks the cubs had come up at the edge of the trees, and Daddy had left food in their pen every day to try to lure them back into the farmyard. The pups stood together in a circle facing each other, and I could see their upturned muzzles and gray necks as they started their long wails into the night air. Their voices rose higher and higher until I thought they would burst if they didn't stop, separate notes, rising sharply together; their chorus echoed from the hills and filled the woods. Then their howl began to taper down into a quiet, steady tremolo that grew softer and softer until I could barely hear it—no more than a purr from a cat. From over toward the direction of the spring, I heard an answer—a steady yelping, a high squeaking yip-yip-yip, almost playfullike. Then she spoke for all of them, and I strained to hear it right this time, listening with everything I had, as she called me. I told you I listen to her in the morning singing "Whippoorwill's a widow" except now I swear I hear her saying "Whippoorwill's Lucille," and I know she's speaking to me. I laid on my back in the cow pasture and soaked up the call of that widowed bird, a voice from the night woods.

MAURICE KENNY, a Mohawk from New York State, is the author of eighteen collections of verse and fiction, most recently *Between Two Rivers: Poems 1956–1984*, *Humors and/or So Humorous*, *Lost Mornings in Brooklyn*, and *Greyhounding This America*. His work has appeared in more than seventy-five magazines and thirty anthologies and has been honored with an American Book Award, the Hodson Award, and two Pulitzer nominations. He has served as poet-in-residence at several institutions, including the University of Oklahoma and the University of Wisconsin—Oneida, and has been cited by St. Lawrence University for his distinguished service to literature.

FEAR AND RECOURSE

Maurice Kenny

The freezing moon hung over the village.

Ash and willow were bare. Cottonwoods held but few leaves, starched leaves that a week past had ribboned the winding creek golden and orange, leaves now rattled by heavy winds.

A mile off from the village ponies grazed under watchful eyes of young herders, boys too young for hunt or war. The near-skeletal frames of thin ponies were coated with thick fur. Even the herders' half-wolf camp dogs wore heavy coats and nestled as close to the fires as allowed.

Snow would fall early. The narrow river where the camp had been pitched was freezing. The women would soon need to chop holes in the ice to draw water.

Monahsetah dreaded this cold weather. It meant she would need to go out on the plains and pull roots for the pot as again food was in short supply. It was not only her duty, but the belly would grow very angry. Would there be no end ever to this hunger; would the buffalo return to their lands; would the pony soldiers and the whites leave the country; would it ever be easier to endure, survive; would the war end? If she lived to be a hundred she would never forget the horrors at Ponoeche, the slaughter of her sisters and brothers, the screaming women in the village, the fury and hate of the white soldiers as they thrust sabers into the pregnant bellies of the young women, her own terror in trying to escape, eluding the guns and knives of those butchers. It was survival as now pulling roots from the frozen earth was equally a matter of survival. Her people could never be out of danger as long as the white man remained. Their villages grew larger as her own village grew smaller. She couldn't count the dead at Ponoeche but they were in staggering numbers. Some people left the village to go north and never returned to the leadership of her father and Black Kettle. She truly mourned the deaths, and especially of White Antelope. He was a good man, kind and thoughtful, gentle and loving, and wise. She would even miss Jack Smith with all his brute and sardonic sullenness. "White Eyes" . . . that's what they called him. Half-breeds were never to be trusted. They had grown up together. They lived in two worlds, half-breeds . . . never a real part of either, and were considered as much a cur, mongrel as any half-wolf camp dog. Jack's mother's milk must have been bitter when he sucked. But the Bents were also half-breeds, and the chiefs of the band trusted George. Charlie was wild, certainly, untamed, irresponsible . . . and he always would be. It was the white blood. His father was greatly respected and he was a man of courage and had tender moments, a tenderness not passed down to Charlie, who was a ball of fire streaking across the horizon.

She looked up from her thoughts. Day was approaching. Light filled the morning sky. The sun was rising. She watched as men prepared to go to the creek, the Washita.

Though the air was bitter, there were those daring men who

clung to the old custom of bathing immediately upon waking. Black Kettle was one such man. He walked along the edge of the stiffening stream prompting those too timid to take the plunge, encouraging the bathers.

A child, naked but for moccasins, leaned against a gray chinaberry tree. The boy was crying. The old man stopped and inquired the reason. The boy pointed to the ice forming in the brittle grass that hugged the shore. The chief reared back startled. The boy's whimpering and his naked flesh awoke painful memories. He placed his blanket about the child's shoulders and with a pat and half a shove sent him on to his mother.

The shouts of the shivering bathers reached his ears and he stared at their frolic. Yet his glance shot back to the jagged ice teething the banks and the trickle of the boy's blood soaking through the hard winter. The child had attempted to follow his older brothers into the stream, slipped, fell, and cut his leg. Now blood stained the river. The Washita ran red as had Sand Creek, Ponoeche, four years before.

Apprehensive, weary, the old sachem returned to his lodge. Chilled by the short excursion into the morning cold, he took the horn of broth his wife, Woman-here-after, offered. He sipped slowly, first blowing upon the steaming liquid. He pulled an old robe about his head and tied it around his waist. He thought of the boy, his wound, his blood on the river . . . only a spot, a trickle. He thought of his young men laughing and sporting in the freezing stream. His thoughts clouded. He saw these same young men floating on that river, their faces down, their backs riddled with black holes from which blood seeped in profusion. The Washita ran red.

Shuddering, he spilled the broth on the floor. Woman-here-after came quickly and covered his eyes with the robe, and she too then turned to the wall of the lodge. For a brief moment they remained quiet and shielded. The dust spilled by the fallen broth disturbed might well cause blindness. The old rituals were still observed. It was necessary to cover the eyes until the dangerous dust settled once again on the dirt floor. The old woman hobbled off to the rear of the tipi and left the man once more with his thoughts. He dragged the blanket off his head. He recalled that this same blanket, now more brown with age and dirt than purple with dye, had belonged to his older brother, White Antelope. He closed his eyes to honor his brother's spirit. Upon opening, his gaze was blurred. White Antelope had been shot before him while standing in front of his lodge. He visualized the thin ribbon of blood weaving out upon the sluggish current and how it stained the forming ice. He watched as his brother slumped into the freezing water, his arms still folded across his chest, his face showing less pain than utter shock, surprise not that he was dying but that his white brothers had betrayed his people. Now there was the child's blood on the Washita.

He called to Woman-here-after, and sent her to fetch the holy men.

Though the village lodges were warm with burning twigs and buffalo chips, the pots were nearly depleted of root. Provisions the Tall Chief Wynkoop, their newly appointed agent, had dispersed in the summer were nearly consumed. The hunt was poor. Hunters returned with only a few rabbits. Buffalo and deer had wandered into distant mountain canyons to escape the fierce winter settling upon the land. The mountains were too far for the weakened ponies to travel, ponies already eating little more than bark stripped from the cottonwoods at the river edge. The hunters themselves were too weak from lack of proper nourishment to make that long trek to those mountain preserves.

He would again send runners to the Tall Chief emphatically imploring for provisions.

With her mother and other women and children, Monahsetah went daily to the hills to dig and pull roots, but the stacks of withered turnips grew thinner. They gathered dried sage leaves and made a drinkable tea. They beat the bush to frighten whatever fowl still sitting, though most had gone south. The women looked to the dogs. One by one, the old dogs no longer strong enough to pull a travois or young enough to bear spring pups lost their lives to the empty pots. A woman called her cur, perhaps first gave him a handful of cold bear grease, and, then, as he nuzzled to her skirt for warmth and affection, she would take its neck between her strong fingers and wrench out the little whine of life. Or she would bash its head with a husky club.

There in the Washita valley between the northern Antelope Hills and the southern Washita Mountains, the Cheyenne awaited winter's toll . . . even though their agent, Tall Chief Wynkoop, had advised them to move out and away from this valley. There was danger though he could not be sure just what the danger was or where it would descend from, but he sensed an ominous presence of wrong, perhaps evil. The vibrations of this pronouncement stirred within the depths of the encampment, yet the headmen would not move the village. It was warmer here in this valley of the Washita, the earth's depression and the woods along the shore provided some succor from the cold, surely more protection than the open vast plains to the south where, yes, they could hide, perhaps escape, whatever evil that Tall Chief spoke of which pursued them. Whatever should happen, winter with its cold and hunger would claim its due. Children and old men would die of exposure or from the lack of nourishment. An old grandmother who had no young son to care for or feed her would inconspicuously wander, stumbling, out into the snowy plains and search for a place to drop her bundle near a small pile of rocks. She knew in reality that her people would share what hot broth or dog bone in the pot with her, but she didn't wish to be an extra burden on the food supply . . . there were hungry children. She knew in the spring when the encampment broke up and moved on they would pass the pile of rocks and perhaps find her special and curious beadwork and know it to be hers. They would call out her name as they passed either north or south, hail her spirit and, because probably that's all that the wolves would have left, her spirit. But should there be a bone, a friend might place it on a small scaffold of a nearby cottonwood and leave some vestige of food for her spirit's journey into the world of shadows. She would then be at peace.

These many fears weighed heavily upon the chiefs and hunters of the band, the Hairy Rope people. Yet they had known hardships and hunger before. The people would survive.

Now, however, the village felt the teeth of hunger sink into the very tissues of the belly. Game was scarce. Not a covey of quail could be routed out of the bush, or turkey found, not even frozen in the snows. Young boys managed to dig out the burrowed homes of chipmunks and climbed trees for birds trapped north by the weather, and proudly ran to their mothers to present the trophies skinned and cleaned for the pot. While the fires cooked the thin stew an older brother, or perhaps, an uncle, angry, grumbled in the rear of the lodge. Once the chipmunk had been boiled with a few herbs and some frozen roots, the mother called her friends to the feast and praised her young men's prowess, and spat ridicule upon the men of the lodge, calling out if they were women they should dress as such, then perhaps she could find them husband-hunters to care for them.

Any and all excuses were taken to celebrate when there was provider, and the feast, no matter how small on such insignificant game, produced an important support to morale. At such times, good feelings were necessary.

Yet in the time of the freezing moon there was little to eat and less to celebrate at a foolish feast. Hunger was so great that it was known that some women had taken rawhide straps and boiled them down to a nourishing soup. Dogs became very scarce in the village and even a boy's pet raccoon was sacrificed to the stew pot. Snakes, when found, were prized, and twigs of certain trees boiled.

Black Kettle expected Major Wynkoop would arrive in the camp with a little flour, a side of bacon, some sugar, a sack of coffee. Perhaps General Hazen at Fort Cobb would have some head of cattle driven to his hungry people. He had sent a small party of young men to Hazen to inform him of the starvation. Once more he would implore Wynkoop to send seeds and implements for spring farming; to bring men who could teach them how to plow and raise cattle. The buffalo herds had thinned, depleted by both Indian and the newly arrived white settlers.

The people would all die of hunger. Twenty years before, Chief Yellow Wolf had begged the government to send the instruments of farming knowing bad days for the Wi-ta-pi-u would come. Still the government had not answered the old chief's request. But the white man had greens on the plains, berries in jars and beef hanging from rafters. The white man had . . . he had pushed the buffaloes away and brought hunger to their bellies. The young men would grow angry again, dissatisfied, when they saw their children and their wives starving. When they bury the first child who dies of hunger they no longer will tolerate this ugly predicament. In spring when the ponies are fat on sweet grass, they will paint the face and belly that had been full of hunger and burn those very barns and probably murder the ranchers. It would be out of his power to stop them. He wasn't even sure if he truly wanted to hold up his hand. There is no way to counsel with ravaging hunger . . . it does not parley, only cry out pain in the belly.

In the time of the freezing moon, the moon of the mean face framed in hoarfrost when leaves crisp on the rocklike ground and ice forms teeth along the banks of the leaden streams, there was more than just hunger of the village that troubled the minds and the hearts of the Cheyenne chiefs. Rumor spread that the pony soldiers would ride to destroy the village . . . the same as they had ridden four years earlier when they came peacefully under the protection of Fort Lyon at Ponoeche, Sand Creek. Perhaps the headmen should give ears to the Tall Child who warned of bad omens.

Runners appeared in the village reporting that a great party of bluecoats was assembling and readying for war. Hunters found pony soldiers' scouts on the plains. Traveling warriors returning to camps farther down the Washita entered the village to seek the chiefs with information. There was thunder to the north and the rumbles were heard in the south . . . the safe campgrounds between the Antelope Hills and the Wichita Mountains.

Men called out to form a war party and go upon the plains to meet the bluecoats. Black Kettle knew how ridiculous this was.

In his village there were a few warriors young enough to battle;
and their ponies were weak. Most of the warrior-age men were
out hunting. A few of Tall Bull's Dog soldiers were at his fire, and
it was these young men who called to make a war party, to paint
and call it was a good day to die. The old sachem knew this was
foolish. You do not war in the cold and snow on weak ponies and
empty stomachs.

All grew uneasy. All knew some of the young warriors were
still out on war parties in the north, and would return only when
their ponies were exhausted in the freezing weather and stumbled
from hunger as the grasses were stubbled beneath blankets of
snow. Black Shield, Red Nose, and Crow Neck were still out.
When they return they would bring many scalps, perhaps, a cap-
tive and they would hold a great victory dance. The chiefs knew
those young warriors would also bring the long dark shadow of
the bluecoats and their guns in pursuit. The chiefs sent messages
to these men with word to cease all warring and to return to their
home village. They warned that they must travel peacefully
through the lands held by the whites and make no depredation.
The moon of freezing had risen and still no sign of Crow Neck or
Black Shield, no sign of Tall Wolf or Red Nose or Porcupine Deer
. . . only persisting rumors of the gathering of bluecoats in anger:

> We pitched our tents on the banks of the Arkansas on
> the 21st of October, 1868, there to remain usefully
> employed until the 12th of the following month,
> when we mounted our horses, bade adieu to the luxu-
> ries of civilization, and turned our faces toward the
> Wichita Mountains in the endeavour to drive from
> their winter hiding places the savages . . .

> To decide upon making a winter campaign against the
> Indian was certainly in accordance with the maxim in
> the art of war which directs one to do that which the
> enemy neither expects nor desires to be done.

His [General Phil Sheridan] first greeting was to ask
what I thought about the snow and the storm, to
which I replied that nothing could be more to our
purpose. We could move and the Indian villages
could not. If the snow only remained on the ground
one week, I promised to bring the General satisfactory
evidence that my command had met the Indians.

. . . I consoled myself with the reflection that to us it
was an unpleasant remedy for the removal of a still
more unpleasant disease. If the storm seemed terrible
to us, I believed it would prove to be ever more terrible to our enemies, the Indians.

I would, in the absence of any reports from him [Ma-
jor Joel Eliot sent ahead as scout], march up the bluffs
forming Antelope Hills and strike nearly due south,
aiming to encamp that night on some one of the
small streams forming the headwaters of the Washita
River . . .

One of them [Osage scout] could speak broken English and in answer to my question as to "What is the
matter?" he replied, "Me don't know, but me smell
fire."

. . . the battle of the Washita commenced. The bu-
gles sounded the charge and the entire command
dashed rapidly into the village. The Indians were
caught napping . . .

Wrote a disillusioned Army officer: There was no
confidence to be placed in any of those Indians. They
were a bad lot. They all needed killing, and the more

they were fed and taken care of the worse they became.

The plan of [Generals] Sherman and Sheridan was to launch an extensive and carefully prepared campaign to drive the tribes into the reservations set aside at Medicine Lodge, and to pursue and kill those who refused to go. The drive would come at the approach of winter so as to place the Indian at the greatest possible disadvantage.

And a footnote to this excerpt of William N. Leckie:

It is worthy to note that at the time this decision was made, no preparations of any kind had been made for receiving the Indians at the reservations . . .

Bitter winds snaked across the valley driving before it a thin veil of snow. Here and there in the darkening hours of oncoming twilight whirls cyclone to the steel-blue sky. Five silent men turned up furs against the blustering winds that nipped the ear or muddy cheek or rankled in the stiffening joints. Drifts covered the trail. There was still light in that gray sky to show signs south.

The old chief rode at the rear of the party. Chilled and worried, he slouched over the pony's mane, his knees barely clinging to the only warm spot of the night: the animal's sweaty flesh. His cold fingers, naked to the winds, loosely held the stiff reins.

Before him rode Little Robe, huddled in fur, one hand touching the iced metal of a carbine. Beyond, Big Mouth, Little Rock, and Spotted Wolf of the Arapaho clucked their ponies on through the blizzard. A mile behind a few young men followed.

As the party traveled on into the night, the snow ceased and the winds calmed somewhat, leaving only the icy sting of winter. The blue night was quiet and cold beyond endurance, yet the five men did not halt the march to build a warming fire.

It was so cold that leather reins snapped; it was so cold the earth cracked as if a blistering sun of summer had baked the earth and seamed the soil. Frost appeared on the fur of their robes, and tiny icicles hung in the shaggy hair about their ponies' bits.

The old chief stayed at the rear of the party in the hope of saving the strength of his pony, which wouldn't be able to lead in a charge. Forty miles stretched before them, and the animals would exhaust themselves easily too early in the ferocious weather. The old man talked to the beast as it lumbered across the hard ground. In the crust of snow its unshod hoofs beat out a soft squashing crunch and the bell tied to the bridle jingled solitarily, echoing over the quiet of the plains like the soddened and sad sounds of a drum.

To the left and right, in the distance, on the ridges beyond came the baying of coyotes. He heard their cries and knew their hunger. This night not a rabbit scurried across the trail, nor prairie dog darted from its earthen burrow. Not even the flaming tail of a red fox thrust up like a sleek feather from behind a snow-covered bush. Tonight his brother, the coyote, would go hungry like many of his people in the village. There had always been a brotherhood between the Cheyenne and the coyote. Coyote brought the people from dark into the light of this world. Had Sweet Medicine not bundled the Scared Arrows in his furs? The Great Spirit had sent this cunning little fellow to traverse the whole of the known world and to talk to the Cheyenne, as the ancient stories told. A warrior society had taken the coyote's name and gave him much respect. Tonight he was hungry and not a berry on the bramble nor mouse beneath a sage leaf. As with brother Cheyenne, brother coyote was hunted down and slaughtered by ranchers and bluecoats alike. He too was despised; he too was an unpleasant disease deserving of removal, meaning of course death and extinction. Coyote was also being driven from his winter hiding place; like the wolf, the beaver in the streams, eagle of the skies. Why was it the white man found these creatures so despicable? And the Indian, the Cheyenne. Yes, even the earth that they plowed up, tore up, crisscrossed with iron roads. Was there nothing that pleases the white man except the sight of Indian blood on the snow? He destroyed all he touched.

Again the male coyote called out to his female on an opposite hilltop. No food in sight. Only a party of humans stumbling on their horses through the darkness. They were friends. No danger.

Stars appeared in the crystal sky and shimmered in hard blue coldness. Slowly moon rose and bathed the night with a pale ghostly sheen. Beneath this not quite full moon, the snow spar-kled, icy twinkling in the flow of a fast river. Once more coyote howled and his cry was followed by the deep whine of a wolf who also was out in the darkness on the hunt. The wolf smelled death.

The chiefs moved on the same steady but slow, determined gait. None spoke, nor looked back, nor made motion that he recognized his trusted friend and worn companion. They barely noticed the ponies' lowering heads and the snorting spurts of steam jetting from their nostrils.

Little Robe silently chewed a hunk of cold greasy pemmican; Big Mouth, Little Rock, and Spotted Wolf stared straight ahead while warming their tingling fingers within their furs; the older chief, Black Kettle, bent lower over the neck of his pony. The other young men following behind had stopped to build a fire.

He was weary. The great Moke-to-ve-to, head chief of all the Arkansas Cheyenne, the Hairy Rope people, the Wi-ti-pi-u, was indeed weary. It was a tremendous effort to stay saddled; it was an effort to hold the reins; it was painful to keep his fur robe from slipping off the shoulders, to urge his pony onward down the long trail, this same trail he had ridden hundreds of times since young manhood, ridden in war parties, horse raids, the hunting party, hurriedly ridden in escape, joyfully ridden to new spring camp-grounds where buffalo grazed and the pronghorn stared down the mountain and elk bellowed through canyons; ridden to offer, make peace. Once more, perhaps the last time, he would ride the trail south for his people.

The five exhausted, worried men rode to Fort Cobb. There they would appeal to their friend, General William B. Hazen, commander of the fort. They would beseech him for military protection. Knowing the bluecoats were marching on a winter campaign directed against Cheyenne, Black Kettle could only presume out of past experience. His peaceful village was vulnerable and consequently would be attacked. His people were so weak they would not stand to the cavalry's barrage for long. Sand Creek was never far from his thoughts. After a long council it was decided that these five chiefs would journey across the night to Fort Cobb. Once more, if necessary, he would place his mark upon paper to save his people. He would prove to General Hazen that he was friendly, and wanted peace.

The pony stumbled on the slippery crust of hardening snow. It jolted the aging man; he nearly lost his balance. He pulled his furs tightly about his shoulders and stared ahead, down the cold trail. The wind whipped again in fury. Angry with the night the five tired humans had to endure it. The wind drove against them.

For a time, he attempted to put fear of attack out of mind. He tried to recall the faces of old friends, friends he had known when first coming south from the Pa Sapa territory. There had been Yellow Wolf to greet him, make a place at the campfire for his small band, to welcome the young brave eager to prove himself in raids against the Kiowa and Comanche. Probably Yellow Wolf had more to do with his intellectual growth than any other man. When young, he had often sat at the older man's feet in council and listened in rapt attention. Yellow Wolf was aging but wise. Peace was always his first thought, peace and trade with the white man. There had been those, Indians and whites alike, who had laughed at the old chief when he implored the Indian agents to bring them farming equipment and seeds and to hire a white man to build them a wooden village and to instruct them how to raise cattle. Yes, many had laughed. And no implements had ever arrived in the wagons crossing the plains. As Yellow Wolf fled north, now Black Kettle fled south for protection from the bluecoats and the Great White Father who could never understand the Indian nor his way of life. Yellow Wolf was finished. A soldier's bullet took him down at Sand Creek, took him as it had his friends, War Bonnet, and Standing Water, and White Antelope. These were bad thoughts to keep alive like burning coals in his mind. Think only of the people still living, hungry and waiting. And yet how fully and frighteningly he realized the white man thought them a bad lot and needed killing, and that they were presently pursued not to be placed on a reservation, but pursued, hunted like game to be slaughtered and nailed to the wooden village walls like the stuffed heads of deer and buffalo trophies. Did not some bluecoat carry in his pocket White Antelope's scrotum used as a tobacco pouch? His anger commenced warming his body. The sting of the wind was not cutting as rawly into his cheek that now burned.

Moke-to-ve-to had been hostile once. He had painted and rolled his pony's tail for the warpath. He had even placed his knife below skin and tore away scalps of enemies. He had fought the Ute after they captured his first wife, Vo-ish-tah (White Buffalo Woman) and taken her to their village never to return to the young warrior-husband; taken her away from him as though they had ripped a rib from his chest, the loin of his thigh. He had raided Pawnee and Crow for ponies, he had attacked the ancient enemy, and it was true, he had at times led depredations against the white settlers and the pony soldiers. They had advanced too far into Cheyenne lands. They drove off the buffalo when their bullets did not stop him in his roaming tracks. They had carried their diseases under their blankets and shook those same blankets of disease out upon the people. They gave his young men rot-gut whiskey that made them mean and lazy, weak; some young men and women went to the white man's coffeepot and never returned to their village fires. Perhaps even worse than these atrocities, they had brought the bluecoats and their guns who found it sport to kill innocent children, women pregnant with the Nation's young; who smashed the heads of infants, raped young girls, sliced off the manhood of his warriors and dignified old chiefs. These were cruel men, men whose hearts were not sweet, but bitter like the gall of their oxen. These were vicious men who wished only for the extermination of the Wi-ta-pi-u. Oh! the Cheyenne had been so wrong, so thoughtless to open their robes to those men. So he had danced in the firelight of the darkness, thrust the point of his lance into the earth, and rode off to battle, calling hookahey to his followers. Yes, it was a good day to die for your principles, for your blood, for your Nation and Creator and Mother Earth. Hookahey. And so he would return to his village, his face painted black for victory, his hands already vermilion with blood, and dance the great victory celebration with the white scalps dangling from the tip of his lance, blood still fresh on his war club.

The hunger revenge that had once driven him to war now again, on this night of the freezing moon of the hard face, blew upon the old ashes protecting the coals smoldering in his heart. He took warmth from this fire and urged his pony on into the darkness.

One day amid the thick of battle it came to him that he and his people were to be exterminated by the white man. He saw, as in a vision, that all the people had fallen down, and all the horses had fallen down. The war club throbbed, the arrow quivered, the carbine smoked, but all the people had fallen down. All that remained standing was the white man's fence post, his singing trees along the roads, and the steam of the iron horse. He turned immediately and rode among his warriors calling to cease fire, to end the killing. He Moke-to-ve-to, Black Kettle, head chief to the Hairy Robe people, would war no more. He would bundle his lance in the skins of coyotes, he would dismantle his carbine. He would break his arrows. He would raise a white flag above his lodge. Not because he loved and trusted the white man more and his peace treaties, which benefitted only the white man. He had watched for many summers the death struggles of all the creatures of the plains and the mountains. He watched the sharp ax fell the cottonwoods. He listened when women called out that the hackberry bushes were plowed under and that the turnip had been crushed by the pony soldiers. He had seen the lands, loaned to them by Mother Earth, grow smaller and smaller until they were insignificant islands in the middle of the white man's sea of grass. He had heard the bluecoats' gunfire and watched their guns kill his strongest men, his most powerful braves and his wisest chiefs. He had watched pregnant girls die, bellies cut open, and the spawn of his people's blood smashed.

He had watched as hundreds died with the blanket disease and observed those great holes, gashes in the faces of those who had survived the blanket's weight. He learned you could not fight the soldiers that the Great White Father had sent into his lands. The soldiers fell upon them like rain with the strength of a blizzard and the power of lightning. Their flood could not be stopped nor driven back to their lands by the eastern shores. They sprang up like a new grass after spring rains. Peace must be made. The lance must be put down for the plow, the war club for the hoe. They must learn new ways, a new Cheyenne way. They must plant seed of a garden, raise cattle to graze. The voices of the shadows came to him. Yellow Wolf spoke. Tobacco spoke, even the traitor, One Eye, spoke. The people must survive. They must grow strong hearts, strong bodies, strong minds. His young must firm up every muscle of their being, throwing off the bad gifts they had accepted from the white man.

This is why this great warrior when proclaimed chief became a man of peace, statesman whom now the young men laughed at, ridiculed, and had cursed. The war lord, Roman Nose, scoffed at this peace chief, and persuaded the old man's young braves to join him and Tall Bull with the Dog Soldiers and the hostile Lakota warriors. Where did it get Roman Nose? Death. Where did it get Tall? Death. His bones bleached at Summit Spring.

The big soldier chief, General Sheridan, had called him a worn-out and worthless old cipher. Others of his own Nation named him a fool. At the signing of the Medicine Lodge Creek treaty his own men went against him and threatened not only to kill his stock horses but to take his life. None of this mattered.

Nothing was important but the endurance of the Wi-ta-pi-u. Not even his death by assassination would be important.

He gathered his family and relatives about him, he gathered his trusted friends, who, like himself, believed in this peace, and they villaged together. There were those in his camp who sneaked off to raid the whites. One day they would stop thumbing their noses and slapping their buttocks in derision and settle down on the lands of the reservation at peace with the white man.

Moke-to-ve-to had been lied to, tricked, made a pawn in the game of survival, yet he was proud to think he had never lied to his heart, tricked his people, or played games with anyone's life. He had spoken out for war when he thought it was necessary, justifiable; and he had spoken out against war when killing involved innocent people. He finally came to realize that it was impossible to fight the swarms of white men. The "pale eyes" meant to stay in the belief it was their destination, an act of progress in the advancement of their most materialistic civilization. Not only had they built wooden lodges, but they had planted trees in the clearing where there were water holes. Victory could never be achieved. The Indian would never push the white man back to the eastern shores. He fought now bitterly with all his strengths of body and mind for peace.

For sixty-seven years, he had watched the cottonwoods green then orange along the riverbanks, and he lived now to insure that for sixty times sixty years more his people would continue to insure the greening of the timbers and the falling of the rain, and to feel and hear the rising of the winds. He could not imagine a time when the ponies would not grow fat on new spring grass, or the buffaloes not roam the plains, or that wild pea would not flower the bluff, and that the men would not ride into the hunt while women waited on the knoll to skin the game killed, dry out the meat, pound it into pemmican with wild berries, and build lodges with the skins. He could not imagine a time when boys would not go to the sacred hill for their dreams, visions of their future.

The Cheyenne way was good. Why did the white man wish to wipe it out? They had been brothers once, and they must hold hands again. A gust of wind brought him back from the shadows of the past. Once more he found himself heading south to Fort Cobb.

> I will say nothing and do nothing to restrain our troops from doing what they deem proper on the spot, and will allow no more vague general charge of cruelty and inhumanity to tie their hands, but will use all the powers confided to me to the end that these Indians, the enemies of our race and our civilization, shall not again be able to begin and carry out their barbarous warfare on any kind of pretext they may choose to allege.
>
> SHERMAN TO SHERIDAN, OCTOBER 9, 1868

> The more we can kill this year the less will have to be killed next year for the more I see of these Indians more I am convinced that they will have to be killed or be maintained as species of paupers.
>
> SHERMAN

> The only good Indian I ever saw was dead.
>
> SHERMAN

The men rode on through the cold night with younger braves following behind. At last the dark sky was streaking with ribbons of light. In the distance the tent peaks of Fort Cobb were sighted.

Upon arriving at the fort, which was really a supply depot composed of army tents, the chiefs were taken to General William Hazen's quarters and offered food and sugared coffee, which they enjoyed greatly . . . before sitting to council. A pipe was brought out from under a robe and a smoke exchanged before the chiefs spoke.

Little Robe and Spotted Wolf spoke first claiming their rights to the Washita reservation. Black Kettle raised his glance from the cooling ashes of the pipe. He sat cross-legged, his blanket loosely pulled about his shoulders, his expressive hands lightly clenched, folded in his lap. His wise sad face showed heavy signs of fatigue and was shadowed with a mask of fear.

> We only want to be left alone. All that we want is that you yellow faces keep out of our country. We don't want to fight you. This is our country. The Great Spirit gave it to us. Keep out, and we will be friends.

His colleagues nodded heads in agreement.
The chief spoke slowly as always, but almost in pain.

> My camp is now on the Washita, forty miles east of the Antelope Hills, and I have there about 80 lodges. I speak only for my own people.

Why should the bluecoats attack, as rumor had it? The Cheyenne were there on the lands granted by the Medicine Lodge Creek Treaty. Grey Blanket (John B. Smith) and the Little White Chief (William Bent) explained the boundaries. The Tall Chief (Edward Wynkoop) advised against it, but George Bent suggested camp there on the banks of Keaha, the Washita, under the winter protection of woods of cottonwoods and chinaberry.

Black Kettle explained that the white men should be blamed for all the murders in Kansas. They had fired upon the hunters. He admitted that he could not keep a strong hand upon his young men. They could not forget Sand Creek and live in dread that the massacre would be repeated. When fired upon they returned fire. Sadly, tragically, deaths occurred.

Big Mouth, the Arapaho, voiced his fear that the rumors would prove correct that the bluecoats were on the march.

Through interpreters, the general listened quietly, intently.

Clear-eyed and not totally unsympathetic but in full knowledge
of their destiny, his lips parted in a half smile as if to negate the
rumor and pacify the chiefs. His thin fingers crawled along the
weatherbeaten cheek to his mustache, which he stroked nervously. Still a young man, not forty years old, a veteran of the
civil war between the states under Sherman's command and a
seasoned Indian fighter . . . still suffering from a wound received by an Indian . . . he was an intelligent commander, and
cognizant of the fact that the Indian had been dealt an injustice.
He was well aware that the white man, emigrant and soldier
alike, fervently desired the Indian's demise through whatever
means available. The faster the better. He knew there were com-
manders in the field who hungered for glory and game and,
should the extermination of "savages" be the road to this end,
then the road would be traveled gallantly. Under the guise of a
punishment expedition, extermination would commence. New
stars would rise over the plains.

Doubtless Hazen was a good soldier, a firm commander, and a
man of intelligent feelings; a man not totally devoid of insight
into human misery or callousness. Though old grievances rankled
in his memory, he could do nothing but carry out orders. General
George Armstrong Custer was on the prowl for scalps and recognition. General Phil Sheridan, his immediate superior, was on
the march, and his aversion to Indians swept like winter winds
across the plains. Hazen possessed full knowledge of Sheridan's
march into Cheyenne territory and his purpose. This was not a
routine patrol.

He made an attempt of honesty, but fumbled with his words in
explaining that he could not stop the soldiers from attacking
hostile villages. Nor could he promise protection at Fort Cobb.
Black Kettle's band, with the Dog Soldiers of Tall Bull, were
known hostiles.

> I am sent here as a peace chief. All here is to be
> peace, but north of the Arkansas is General Sheridan,
> the great war chief, and I do not control him, and he

has all the soldiers who are fighting the Cheyennes
and Arapahos.

The chiefs grumbled among themselves.

Therefore, you must go back to your country, and if
the soldiers come to fight, you must remember they
are not sent from me, but from a great war chief, and
it is with him you must make your peace . . .

The worried chiefs all seemed to stare at a wisp of smoke still
smoldering in the discarded pipe.

But you must not come unless I send for you, and you
must keep well beyond the friendly Kiowas and Co-
manches . . .

This offered nothing . . . wind in the hand.

Hazen stood as if to dismiss the men and paced the small office
tent. Turning abruptly, he looked directly into Black Kettle's
worn eyes, masking the fear and doubt that was not untouched by
anger and disappointment.

I hope you understand how and why it is that I cannot make peace with you.

He added that he had heard through Comanche chiefs that
the celebrated peace chief, Black Kettle, had lost favor with his
young men and that they no longer listened to his counsel or
were under his command.

He did not dispute this accusation, but Black Kettle reasoned
that under Cheyenne custom he could not speak for all the bands
and all the people, that each person was an individual, and that
as headman he could merely advise and not demand.

To this Hazen offered a frugal smile and concluded their talk.
Before the men left the fort, the general had sugar, coffee,

tobacco, and a little flour given them to take back. Then they were dismissed.

He was positive that he would never set eyes upon the "old cipher" again.

Heap Injuns down there . . . Me heard dog bark.

I was rewarded in a moment by hearing the barking of
a dog in the heavy timber off to the right of the herd,
and soon after I heard the tinkling of a bell . . . I
turned to retrace my steps when another sound was
borne to my ears through the cold, clear atmosphere
of the valley—it was the distant cry of an infant; and
savages though they were and justly outlawed by the
number and atrocity of their recent murders and depredations on the helpless settlers of the frontier, I
could not but regret that in a war such as we were
forced to engage in the mode and circumstances of
battle would possibly prevent discrimination.

On the night of November 26, 1868, the moon of the freezing face, the chiefs when arriving in the village found a small raiding party there under Crow Neck and Black Shield with fresh scalps. Already they had urged the women to build a fire for a victory dance to be held at moon-rise.

During the depredations two Kiowa warriors, just back from a pony raid upon the western Ute, entered the village and spoke with the headmen. They told how their ponies had crossed the heavy trail stamped into the snow by many horses that wore shoes. Ar-no-ho-woh (Woman-here-after) offered these warriors hot broth, and soon they left for the Kiowa village down-stream.

Black Kettle prepared for the eventual attack. He tethered his best pony to the poles of his lodge. He placed a sentinel on guard and arranged in his mind how he would ride out to the soldiers before the attack, and speak with them. He would tell them, his white flag above his head, of the peace in his heart. That he did not want to fight. And that they should go home.

From a safe distance Monahsetah observed, dismayed, the celebration. She knew they were foolish, crazy what with the premonitions of danger all about. She knew some of these youths, hot-tempered young warriors, knew they would do as they wished and that her father, Little Rock, or the other chiefs had no control over them. It was cold. It was time for her to go to sleep. She closed the lodge flap and became the darkness.

The joy of the dancers drummed the night. Shadows cast by the fire fell against lodge walls. Black Shield led a young woman by the hand to the dance, and they joined the celebrants. An old woman broke between the lines and stacked dry buffalo chips on the fire.

Black Kettle stepped out into the lateness of the night, looked up at the waning moon and shivered. He looked off south beyond the camp. There he saw the small fire of the pony herders flicker. He had warned the young men that bluecoats were on the march. They laughed at him. They laughed now and ridiculed him for being a worried old woman. They shouted it was winter, snow littered the ground. Look, now it's falling, they pointed. It was the moon of the hard face. Pony soldiers did not fight in this bad weather.

There was no way Black Kettle could counsel these men; they had already forgotten that Mashan (Chivington) had attacked the village at Sand Creek in the moon of the hard face. They refused to listen. Black Kettle's admonishments fell upon the snow and were scattered by the winds. Peace would come at a heavy cost, and the night's revelry would be paid for with flesh and blood. He hoped, at least, that Double Wolf would not join the celebrants, wear out his energies in the exhilaration of the dance and slip into sleep on guard. This might be the very night the bluecoats were stalking the outlying hills preparing to strike the village.

A dog barked. The tinkle of a pony bell struck the night. The herders were probably asleep. The vigil fires flickered in the distance. He heard the cry of a baby.

Now the burden.

Hearing the baby's cry, he remembered the young child's blood smearing the ice edging the creek. He shuddered and entered his lodge.

j A M E S W E L C H is Blackfeet and Gros Ventre and lives in Missoula, Montana. He is a well-known novelist whose books include *Winter in the Blood*, *The Death of Jim Loney*, *The Indian Lawyer*, and *Fools Crow*, which won the *Los Angeles Times* Book Prize, the American Book Award, and the Pacific Northwest Booksellers Award. His collection of poetry is entitled *Riding the Earthboy 40*. Welch grew up on the Blackfeet and Fort Belknap reservations, and he graduated from the University of Montana, where he teaches.

EARL YELLOW CALF

James Welch

arl Yellow Calf suffered his final stroke in April of the
following year. Sylvester had been living in a kitchenette
unit in Bismarck and commuting down to the Standing
Rock Reservation. The two law students from the University of
North Dakota lived in a more modest motel on the western edge
of town. He would pick them up every morning at eight and they
would drive down the Missouri River through a game preserve,
and he always felt the same sense of peace, no matter what the
weather. And there were always waterfowl, ducks and geese,
sometimes swans and pelicans, cranes and osprey. Deer and antelope watched their car pass with only mild interest. He was
always surprised that an area of North Dakota could be so beautiful, so lush and abundant, even in winter. He had driven across
the state, east and west, and had thought of it as nothing but
wheat fields and prairies. He loved that kind of country and
became very attentive in it, as though a discovery would be made

over the next hill, down in the next swale or wash. But this country, the slow wide river, the bare trees and brush, the battered reeds and cattails, the bright bunches of willows, held every color, every texture, under the sun or in the snow or rain. Sylvester began to think of the hour-and-a-half drive as his dreaming time. He drove down every morning, and even in the two or three blizzards, as he crept along at thirty, his mind was concentrated on both driving and dreaming, and the things he dreamed were minute and ordinary—times when he was growing up, fishing or shooting baskets, listening to the radiators clank in the old grade school, watching a muskrat preening in the reeds of one of the potholes around Browning. Other times he thought of college in Missoula, the evening walk with the sorority girl, the runs up Mount Sentinel in the fall to get himself in shape for basketball, the smell of pizza in the dorm. He dreamed of Palo Alto and Stanford, the dry hills, the long nights in the law library, the warm early-spring evenings he pedaled home on his bicycle. Even Helena was becoming a dream to him but the dreams did not come as easily. When he dreamed the small bakery that served good bread and soup, he saw faces and he did not want to see faces, so he stopped the dreams and concentrated on the small slick blacktop road or the sudden flight of geese lifting from the wetlands.

In the three months he had been there, he had thrown himself into the case and had gotten a circuit court date for a hearing on the issues, a small triumph in itself. He and the tribal attorney and the two law students spent most of their time researching prior decisions, taking depositions, filing informations, rounding up expert witnesses. Indian irrigators and tribal recreation people were protesting the periodic drawdowns of the immense reservoir, the diversion of water to downstream farmers and ranchers and hydropower concerns. The state maintained that the modification of the prior appropriation law did not apply to this particular case because most of the reservation water was unused. As far as Sylvester could see there were no new wrinkles in either side's arguments; it was simply a matter of convincing the circuit

court that the Winters doctrine and later court cases had established that the Indians could protect the amount of water necessary for future as well as current use. But he read all the pertinent
water rights cases affecting Indian property. He knew that each
case had to be argued on its own particular merits, that it would
have to be argued again and again all the way to the Supreme
Court if necessary.

At first he didn't know if he wanted to become so deeply
involved. It could conceivably take years to settle the case, but
the more comfortable he became with the reservation people, the
more he got to know the individuals involved, the more he
realized he would see it through to wherever it ended—even if it
meant giving up his new partnership in Harrington, Lohn and
Associates. Lately, it had begun to seem like a small sacrifice.

The telephone call from the priest reached him at the tribal
offices in Fort Yates. He and the two student lawyers were eating
lunch in the lounge with the recreation specialist. He took the
call in the receptionist's area, then called a travel agency in
Bismarck.

The next morning he boarded a small commuter plane to
Billings, then a Northwest flight to Great Falls. By one o'clock he
had rented a car and driven through Great Falls on I-15 on his
way to U.S. 89 and Browning. It was April 16th, one day after
the tax deadline. His grandfather had died on the 15th. Sylvester
smiled as he thought of the irony of the tax deadline and the fact
that his grandfather had been an accountant all his working life.

As he approached the Rocky Mountain Front, he noticed that
the country was greening up, even the foothills as they rolled
toward the mountains. The fires of last summer had burned
through the Scapegoat and Bob Marshall Wilderness Areas but
there were no visible scars along the Front. He could barely see
the lower slopes of the mountains below the dark clouds. He
headed north and west on 89, passing through squall after squall
of rain, sleet, and pebbly snow. The area along the Front was the
last in Montana to give up winter, forming a natural corridor for
the weather that began in northern Canada and swept south in

massive violent storms. But today the weather consisted of spring squalls, and Sylvester was grateful to be going home in such beauty.

The funeral was in the little Flower Catholic Church in Browning. Although Earl Yellow Calf had not been a church-going man, Mary Bird wanted a church service for him. She had rejected a traditional service because Earl had long ago rejected the traditional way of life. He was a rational man and did not believe in the hocus-pocus, he had once told her.

Sylvester sat in the front row with his grandmother and several of the elders, listening to the organ music, smelling the smoky incense, and staring at the closed casket. Finally, all the shuffling behind him ceased and he glanced back and saw that the church was full. People were standing along the back and side walls. He was both shocked and pleased that his grandfather, his grandparents, had been important in the community they had never left. North Dakota, Bismarck, Standing Rock seemed a long way away, Helena even farther. He had come a long way home to the simplicity and peace of his birthplace.

He wondered if the priest had called his mother in New Mexico. Neither Sylvester nor his grandmother had mentioned her last night, and that seemed to be that. But it was his mother's father lying up there in the casket and she surely would have come if she had known about it. But there had been no late arrival of a strange woman, a woman who might have looked like Sylvester, a woman who might have touched him like a son. He tried to imagine what she would be doing this spring day in New Mexico, but he couldn't, and he realized that he did not want to see her ever because she might want something from him and he had nothing to give her.

The incense lulled him pleasantly and he thought of Patti Ann Harwood and he realized that in his subconscious he had connected her with the fires of the summer and fall before. Even now he smelled the smoke and saw the orange glow against the night sky. There had been smoke in the air that first morning she came to see him, and all that early fall he smelled it when he stepped from his car in front of her apartment.

He had gotten a letter from her in the middle of February. She thanked him for all he had done for her and her husband. He was now in the Maximum Security Unit, having decided he could live there until his discharge or parole if she would stick by him, be there when he got out. And it wasn't so bad, at least he had peace of mind knowing he would be safe until then. Myrna and Phil were together in Billings at long last, and she, Patti Ann, was plugging away at her job, neither happily or unhappily. She thanked him for their chaste New Year's eve, which meant more to her than he would ever know, and she wished him, belatedly, great success in the new year. She closed with "your loving pal."

The priest gave a short talk, mentioning Carlisle School for Indians, the years put in as tribal treasurer, then as accountant for the BIA, the fact that Earl loved to fish, the many loved ones he left, the respect and esteem of the community toward him. Finally he commended Earl Yellow Calf's soul to heaven and led the throng in a final prayer.

Sylvester sneaked a look at his grandmother. She was smiling.

L OUISE ERDRICH is a member of the Turtle Mountain Chippewa Tribe in North Dakota and the author of several novels, poems, and stories. She is best known for her novels, *The Beet Queen*, *Love Medicine* (from which "Grandpa Kapshaw's Ghost" is excerpted), *Tracks*, and *The Crown of Columbus* (coauthored with her husband, Michael Dorris). She has also written two books of poetry, *Jacklight* and *Baptism*. Erdrich has won two major literary awards, the *Los Angeles Times* Book Prize and the National Book Critics Circle Award for fiction. She has recently finished her fifth novel, *The Bingo Palace*.

GRANDPA KASHPAW'S GHOST

Louise Erdrich

You hear a person's life will flash before their eyes when they're in danger. It was him in danger, not me, but it was *his* life come over me. I saw him dying, and it was like someone pulled the shade down in a room. His eyes clouded over and squeezed shut, but just before that I looked in. He was still fishing in the middle of Lake Turcot. Big thoughts was on his line and he had half a case of beer in the boat. He waved at me, grinned, and then the bobber went under.

Grandma had gone out of the room crying for help. I bunched my force up in my hands and I held him. I was so wound up I couldn't even breathe. All the moments he had spent with me, all the times he had hoisted me on his shoulders or pointed into the leaves was concentrated in that moment. Time was flashing back and forth like a pinball machine. Lights blinked and balls hopped and rubber bands chirped, until suddenly I realized the last ball had gone down the drain and there was nothing. I felt his force leaving him, flowing out of Grandpa never to return. I felt his mind weakening. The bobber going under in the lake. And I felt the touch retreat back into the darkness inside my body, from where it came.

One time, long ago, both of us were fishing together. We caught a big old snapper what started towing us around like it was a motor. "This here fishing is pretty damn good," Grandpa said. "Let's keep this turtle on and see where he takes us." So we rode along behind that turtle, watching as from time to time it surfaced. The thing was just about the size of a washtub. It took us all around the lake twice, and as it was traveling, Grandpa said something as a joke. "Lipsha," he said, "we are glad your mother didn't want you because we was always looking for a boy like you who would tow us around the lake."

"I ain't no snapper. Snappers is so stupid they stay alive when their head's chopped off," I said.

"That ain't stupidity," said Grandpa. "Their brain's just in their heart, like yours is."

When I looked up, I knew the fuse had blown between my heart and my mind and that a terrible understanding was to be given.

Grandma got back into the room and I saw her stumble. And then she went down too. It was like a house you can't hardly believe has stood so long, through years of record weather, suddenly goes down in the worst yet. It makes sense, is what I'm saying, but you still can't hardly believe it. You think a person you know has got through death and illness and being broke and living on commodity rice will get through anything. Then they fold and you see how fragile were the stones that underpinned them. You see how instantly the ground can shift you thought was solid. You see the stop signs and the yellow dividing markers of roads you traveled and all the instructions you had played according to vanish. You see how all the everyday things you counted on was just a dream you had been having by which you run your whole life. She had been over me, like a sheer overhang of rock dividing Lipsha Morrissey from outer space. And now she went underneath. It was as though the banks gave way on the shores of Lake Turcot, and where Grandpa's passing was just the bobber swallowed under his biggest thought, her fall was the house and the rock under it sliding after, sending half the lake splashing up to the clouds.

Where there was nothing.

You play them games never knowing what you see. When I fell into the dream alongside of both of them I saw that the dominions I had defended myself from anciently was but delusions of the screen. Blips of light. And I was scot-free now, whistling through space.

I don't know how I come back. I don't know from where. They was slapping my face when I arrived back at Senior Citizens and they was oxygenating her. I saw her chest move, almost unwilling. She sighed the way she would when somebody bothered her in the middle of a row of beads she was counting. I think it irritated her to no end that they brought her back. I knew from the way she looked after they took the mask off, she was not going to forgive them disturbing her restful peace. Nor was she forgiving Lipsha Morrissey. She had been stepping out on the road of death, she told the children later at the funeral. I asked was there any stop signs or dividing markers on that road, but she clamped her lips in a vise the way she always done when she was mad.

Which didn't bother me. I knew when things had cleared out she wouldn't have no choice. I was not going to speculate where the blame was put for Grandpa's death. We was in it together. She had slugged him between the shoulders. My touch had failed him, never to return.

All the blood children and the took-ins, like me, came home from Minneapolis and Chicago, where they had relocated years ago. They stayed with friends on the reservation or with Aurelia or slept on Grandma's floor. They were struck down with grief and bereavement to be sure, every one of them. At the funeral I sat down in the back of the church with Albertine. She had gotten all skinny and ragged haired from cramming all her years of study into two or three. She had decided that to be a nurse was not enough for her so she was going to be a doctor. But the way she was straining her mind didn't look too hopeful. Her eyes were bloodshot from driving and crying. She took my hand. From the back we watched all the children and the mourners as they hunched over their prayers, their hands stuffed full of Kleenex. It was someplace in that long sad service that my vision shifted. I began to see things different, more clear. The family kneeling down turned to rocks in a field. It struck me how strong and reliable grief was, and death. Until the end of time, death would be our rock.

So I had perspective on it all, for death gives you that. All the Kashpaw children had done various things to me in their lives— shared their folks with me, loaned me cash, beat me up in secret —and I decided, because of death, then and there I'd call it quits. If I ever saw King again, I'd shake his hand. Forgiving somebody else made the whole thing easier to bear.

Everybody saw Grandpa off into the next world. And then the Kashpaws had to get back to their jobs, which was numerous and impressive. I had a few beers with them and I went back to Grandma, who had sort of got lost in the shuffle of everybody being sad about Grandpa and glad to see one another.

Zelda had sat beside her the whole time and was sitting with her now. I wanted to talk to Grandma, say how sorry I was, that it wasn't her fault, but only mine. I would have, but Zelda gave me one of her looks of strict warning as if to say, "I'll take care of Grandma. Don't horn in on the women."

If only Zelda knew, I thought, the sad realities would change her. But of course I couldn't tell the dark truth.

It was evening, late. Grandma's light was on underneath a crack in the door. About a week had passed since we buried

Grandpa. I knocked first but there wasn't no answer, so I went right in. The door was unlocked. She was there but she didn't notice me at first. Her hands were tied up in her rosary, and her gaze was fully absorbed in the easy chair opposite her, the one that had always been Grandpa's favorite. I stood there, staring with her, at the little green nubs in the cloth and plastic armrest covers and the sad little hair-tonic stain he had made on the white doily where he laid his head. For the life of me I couldn't figure what she was staring at. Thin space. Then she turned.

"He ain't gone yet," she said.

Remember that chill I luckily didn't get from waiting in the slough? I got it now. I felt it start from the very center of me, where fear hides, waiting to attack. It spiraled outward so that in minutes my fingers and teeth were shaking and clattering. I knew she told the truth. She seen Grandpa. Whether or not he had been there is not the point. She had *seen* him, and that meant anybody else could see him, too. Not only that but, as is usually the case with these here ghosts, he had a certain uneasy reason to come back. And of course Grandma Kashpaw had scanned it out.

I sat down. We sat together on the couch watching his chair out of the corner of our eyes. She had found him sitting in his chair when she walked in the door.

"It's the love medicine, my Lipsha," she said. "It was stronger than we thought. He came back even after death to claim me to his side."

I was afraid. "We shouldn't have tampered with it," I said. She agreed. For a while we sat still. I don't know what she thought, but my head felt screwed on backward. I couldn't accurately consider the situation, so I told Grandma to go to bed, I would sleep on the couch keeping my eye on Grandpa's chair. Maybe he would come back and maybe he wouldn't. I guess I feared the one as much as the other, but I got to thinking, see, as I lay there in darkness, that perhaps even through my terrible mistakes some good might come. If Grandpa did come back, I thought he'd return in his right mind. I could talk with him. I could tell him it was all my fault for playing with power I did not understand. Maybe he'd forgive me and rest in peace. I hoped this. I calmed myself and waited for him all night.

He fooled me though. He knew what I was waiting for, and it wasn't what he was looking to hear. Come dawn I heard a blood-splitting cry from the bedroom and I rushed in there. Grandma turnt the lights on. She was sitting on the edge of the bed and her face looked harsh, pinched-up, gray.

"He was here," she said. "He came and laid down next to me in bed. And he touched me."

Her heart broke down. She cried. His touch was so cold. She laid back in bed after a while, as it was morning, and I went to the couch. As I lay there, falling asleep, I suddenly felt Grandpa's presence and the barrier between us like a swollen river. I felt how I had wronged him. How awful was the place where I had sent him. Behind the wall of death, he'd watched the living eat and cry and get drunk. He was lonesome, but I understood he meant no harm.

"Go back," I said to the dark, afraid and yet full of pity. "You got to be with your own kind now," I said. I felt him retreating, like a sigh, growing less. I felt his spirit as it shrunk back through the walls, the blinds, the brick courtyard of Senior Citizens. "Look up Aunt June," I whispered as he left.

I slept late the next morning, a good hard sleep allowing the sun to rise and warm the earth. It was past noon when I awoke. There is nothing, to my mind, like a long sleep to make those hard decisions that you neglect under stress of wakefulness. Soon as I woke up that morning, I saw exactly what I'd say to Grandma. I had gotten humble in the past week, not just losing the touch but getting jolted into the understanding that would prey on me from here on out. Your life feels different on you, once you greet death and understand your heart's position. You wear your life like a garment from the mission bundle sale ever after—lightly because you realize you never paid nothing for it, cherishing because you know you won't ever come by such a bargain again. Also you have the feeling someone wore it before you and someone will after. I can't explain that, not yet, but I'm putting my mind to it.

"Grandma," I said, "I got to be honest about the love medicine."

She listened. I knew from then on she would be listening to me the way I had listened to her before. I told her about the turkey hearts and how I had them blessed. I told her what I used as love medicine was purely a fake, and then I said to her what my understanding brought me.

"Love medicine ain't what brings him back to you, Grandma. No, it's something else. He loved you over time and distance, but he went off so quick he never got the chance to tell you how he loves you, how he doesn't blame you, how he understands. It's true feeling, not no magic. No supermarket heart could have brung him back."

She looked at me. She was seeing the years and days I had no way of knowing, and she didn't believe me. I could tell this. Yet a look came on her face. It was like the look of mothers drinking sweetness from their children's eyes. It was tenderness.

"Lipsha," she said, "you was always my favorite."

She took the beads off the bedpost, where she kept them to say at night, and she told me to put out my hand. When I did this, she shut the beads inside of my fist and held them there a long minute, tight, so my hand hurt. I almost cried when she did this. I don't really know why. Tears shot up behind my eyelids, and yet it was nothing. I didn't understand, except her hand was so strong, squeezing mine.

The earth was full of life and there were dandelions growing out the window, thick as thieves, already seeded, fat as big yellow plungers. She let my hand go. I got up. "I'll go out and dig a few dandelions," I told her.

Outside, the sun was hot and heavy as a hand on my back. I felt it flow down my arms, out my fingers, arrowing through the ends of the fork into the earth. With every root I prized up there was return, as if I was kin to its secret lesson. The touch got stronger as I worked through the grassy afternoon. Uncurling from me like a seed out of the blackness where I was lost, the touch spread. The spiked leaves full of bitter mother's milk. A buried root. A nuisance people dig up and throw in the sun to wither. A globe of frail seeds that's indestructible.

a NNIE HANSEN is a Lenape, or Delaware, Indian who is completing a novel based on the character Jimmy One Rock. Portions of this work have appeared in *Kenyon Review*, and she has written a collection of short stories. Hansen and her husband live in Indianola, Washington, where they own a book-binding business.

SUN OFFERING

Annie Hansen

Jimmy rolled over, opened his eyes, and squinted into the brilliant September sunlight flooding through the window onto the bed. A freighter had crossed the bay. Huge break- ers were hitting the shore below the cabin, crashing against the pebbles and drift logs.

Jimmy stood up, stretched, and went out the small door next to the bed to stand in the tall wet grass to watch the last of the waves hit the beach. With each crash he could feel the pounding vibration in the cool earth under his bare feet. The waves passed as quickly as they came, leaving only the long echo as they raced down the curve of the beach toward the long sandy spit at the end of the bay. Jimmy was lost for a minute in the sweet-breath- ing rhythm of the tide rising and falling against the pebbles.

Jimmy had come to know that every place has its rhythms, its own music. When Jimmy had first come from his home in Okla- homa to this bay, he found that rhythm in water—the waves, the tides, the flooding streams, the rain in the leaves and dripping on the rusty tin roof of his uncle's cabin.

And coming now from two months of fishing in the Pacific, Jimmy felt the softness of the rhythms in this bay, the beat of water muffled by the shelter of all the lush green. This place, this bay, was as different from the harsh unprotected beat of water and wind and blinding sun out on the ocean as it was from the land of his home in Oklahoma. Jimmy drew in a deep breath of cool salt air and felt a shiver run down his spine.

Listening past the sound of the waves, Jimmy heard the almost-underwaterlike sound of the crowing of the little red bantam rooster and the quieter pleading cries of his five Barred Rock hens coming from the locked interior of the '52 Chevy wagon, where they safely spent their nights. Jimmy knew he had time to slip on his jeans and meet Mary across the field. In the five days since Uncle had died, Jimmy had not touched Mary. From respect. From fear.

Every morning since he'd been back from fishing, Mary got up with the sun and the bantam rooster. She grabbed Jimmy's old red plaid wool shirt off the nail by the door and covered her shoulders and thin white cotton nightgown and slipped out the door.

Most mornings, Jimmy would lie in bed and listen to her pick up the water can, and half asleep, he'd imagine her as she walked down the path through the tall stubble grasses and thistles as it led across the fieldlike yard into the cedars. From there she would follow the cool, dark path of deer fern, maidenhair fern, and vanilla leaf to fill the water can at the small stream flooding out into the bay just below the cabin.

Buttoning his jeans, Jimmy went back out the open door. He moved quietly, hoping not to waken their four sleeping sons. Slipping on his T-shirt, he listened again for the bantam rooster, but heard instead a low scraping sound.

Jimmy froze, his blood running suddenly cold. Even in the light of morning, Jimmy was weary. How to explain this feeling, this fear, but in days; the days counting from death.

Uncle's death, like midday sun on glass shards, lit the fragments of Uncle's cultures. Memories of ghost walkers, of lodges burned, water left, food baskets filled, songs sung, vigils kept, games played, stories told, all to set those ghosts, those spirits free. Death became the sunlight on the shards of Uncle's two ancestries: East Coast Lenape people thrown across mountains and land to Oklahoma, and West Coast Salish people, scattered along the beach by disease and lies and allotments. Each flashed memories and stories, filling Jimmy with fear and aching, both for what he knew and what he did not know. Ghosts of the recently dead with ghosts of memory and of history he knew and history he would never know had been dancing around the cabin.

Aunt Lucy, Uncle's wife, had felt it too. She had seen the light dancing across the bright shards and had remembered what she had not thought she'd ever know. At first she'd cried and wanted to burn the cabin, remembering her grandmother's stories of the dead. Even a Christian burial could not stop the fear for Uncle's wandering spirit, for her own safety from other long-forgotten spirits. And Jimmy and Roy remembered Grandma One Rock's stories. Aunt Ethie remembered her great-grandmother's stories until Jimmy and his brother, Roy, and their twin cousins, Floyd and Lloyd, went to Lucy's house. They took down the door and door frame that Uncle's body had been carried out through and burned it, turning their faces from the flames, and replaced it with a door and frame from the old shed. And a calm came back to Lucy. She sprinkled cedar around the door, and they all cooked salmon and clams on the beach and joked late into the night. Feeling safe then, Jimmy and Aunt Lucy even joked about whether Uncle's spirit would take the Lenape path of twelve days or the Salish path of three days.

But the scrape, scrape made Jimmy know that Grandma One Rock, Uncle's father's sister, told the truth in her stories of twelve days—twelve traveling days for the Lenape spirit to get to the other side. He tried to joke with himself that maybe the west was a little closer, since they needed only three days. Or maybe the Lenape just took their time. But Jimmy couldn't help himself for counting back, checking the number of days since Uncle had died. The scrape, scrape seemed to pierce through Jimmy.

Jimmy had known too much in his life to leave his sons alone in the cabin with that sound of scratching on the earth coming toward them. Some of the old stories told of old spirits that looked for young, strong companions to join them on their final journey. Jimmy could never really believe that. But still, he'd seen too much in his life to leave his sons alone with the scratching seeming to come up to them from under the cabin.

Before Jimmy opened the door to the living room, he put his head against the door to hear their sweet muffled breathing. Even in his fear, he hated to waken them. Opening the door a crack, he saw them together, curled in a warm slumber ball of pillows and blankets and young fresh, sweet brown skin on the horsehair mattress on the floor in the corner of the cabin.

No matter where the boys were, how far apart in the cabin they were when they fell asleep, they seemed to roll like marbles on the slanted floor into that corner of the cabin. The Inseparables, Jimmy called them. His brother, Roy, shortened it to the Rebels. And seeing them there, their young, strong bodies in the darkened corner of the cabin, Jimmy thought of Grandma One Rock and of Uncle Arnie and of how they each had been so shrunken, so small, so old when they died, as if they each had been dried brown puff balls, blowing the life of the next generations out in their last breaths. And here, in this cabin, they grew, these sons of his.

The scratching was broken by a clink, like rock to rock, or metal on rock. George, Jimmy's oldest son heard the sound too, and sat up. He jumped up and, not seeing Jimmy, ran to the sound, and before Jimmy could speak or follow, the three youngest tumbled out and across the room behind the cook stove and under the sink.

Following his sons, Jimmy came around the corner into the kitchen in time to see four small butts in the air, and a longer body sprawled out on the kitchen floor. All the heads seemed to be pulled down under the sink as if they were being eaten by the scrape, scraping sound, which was louder now. Jimmy walked toward the sink and hunched down, almost kicking over a tin can half full of long wriggling worms.

"What the hell . . ." Jimmy said. "What the hell's going on?"

No faces appeared to answer Jimmy. Instead, muffled voices came up from under the sink, echoing in the leaky pipes.

"Worms, Papa."

"Big. Big worms."

"Joey's gathering worms."

"Joey's going fishing, Papa," said George's voice. "This is Joey's best place for worms. Joey said we could get worms here. And he's taking us fishing this morning."

Jimmy remembered the story Mary had told him the night after Uncle died as they lay whispering in bed, waiting for the boys to fall asleep. While Jimmy had been gone fishing for the last two months, there were things that had happened that, since Uncle's death, Mary was only beginning to tell Jimmy.

And Joey's dad being in jail was one. Instead of getting water at the creek, sometimes when he felt lazy, Louie, Joey's dad, used to drive to the vacant cabin at the top of the hill for water. The owners lived in Seattle and only camped at the cabin two or three times each summer, leaving the water on between these summer visits, and shutting it off and draining the pipes for the winter. Louie would fill his water cans with water from the hose.

This particular morning, Mary told Jimmy, Louie had gone to get water at the cabin and found the place pretty well trashed, doors busted in, windows broken, furniture on the lawn. He filled his water cans and, as he went to leave, picked up one of the broken chairs to take home and nail and glue back together for Angie. Louie was handy that way. That night the sheriff came to his house and found the chair, accusing Louie of wrecking the cabin and stealing furniture. But in court, the real proof seemed to be the Rainier beer can the sheriff found in Louie's truck. It seems that the cabin was littered with beer cans, one short of a case. All Rainier. And, as the storekeeper testified, Indians drink Rainier beer. Lots of Rainier beer.

The minute Angie heard Louie had five years to serve, she took off with his cousin, Pete, leaving Joey alone. After the trial, Joey cried and wailed and wouldn't go home with any of his relations. That night, Aunt Ethie walked down to Joey's cabin and asked Joey if he was any good catching fish. He said he was pretty good. So she told him to catch her a good mess of fish in the morning and bring them to her, she'd have the fire in the woodstove going good and hot and the skillet greased. The sun was barely up when Joey got to her house in the morning, and he'd been staying there ever since, fishing for her most every day. He'd get barnacles or mussels or little crabs or worms for bait, depending on where he was fishing, what he was fishing for. Mary just hadn't bothered to tell Jimmy *where* Joey got his worms.

Another handful of moist black dirt mixed with slender chips of rotted wood landed at Jimmy's feet. Three worms were plunked into the waiting can, followed by satisfied sighs of approval. Jimmy patted the four backsides, and then leaned down and gently squeezed one of Joey's ankles.

"Catch a couple extra. I'm pretty hungry. You bring Aunt Ethie down here and we'll fry us up a mess of those fish when you get back," Jimmy called over his shoulder, " 'cause I'm not eating no worms for breakfast."

The bantam rooster took up crowing again. Even without looking toward the '52 Chevy wagon, Jimmy knew that the tap, tap he heard was the bantam rooster pecking frantically at the rolled-up windows. But Jimmy didn't look in the direction of the rooster in his '52 Chevy. He kept his eyes on Mary.

Mary's black hair was loose and long down her shoulders. The red plaid shirt was open and Jimmy watched her as she walked toward the old Buick, and he saw the fullness and motion of her breasts and hips under her thin cotton gown like a vision from some dream. Jimmy felt the fever of desire rise as warm in his blood as the heat of the sun on his skin.

Mary saw Jimmy then. She set the water cans down and waved at him, and then she turned and ran up along the edge of the grass to the Buick. Jimmy followed her and watched her open the trunk and saw the curve of her dark legs and thighs as her gown lifted and as she leaned down into the trunk.

Uncle Arnie's '47 Buick had been long engineless and windowless, a hiding place for boys, a nest for squirrels and mice and swallows. But it still had the best tightest trunk on the reservation, perfect for keeping the chickens' corn dry and mouse-free.

With each of her arms extended, she lifted two coffee cans brimming with sweet yellow corn to the sky, making a perfect sun offering. Mary lifted an elbow and used it to close the Buick's heavy black trunk lid. Jimmy was behind Mary now. He reached with one hand to close the trunk. The other hand slipped slowly up her gown, along the curve of her thighs, feeling her warmth, her hair, the smooth curve of her belly, and following up her breasts, catching a nipple in his fingers as she turned to him.

"Jimmy." Mary held out the rusty cans of yellow corn as Jimmy lifted her gown and began to finger her breasts. "The little banty. Listen to him crow. Listen."

Jimmy pressed against Mary and said, "Yes, listen." And they both laughed even as their breath caught and rose and the yellow corn spilled to the ground in a patch of sunlight around their bare feet.

And as Jimmy spread the red plaid shirt on the damp grass next to the yellow corn and as he lifted Mary's gown over her head, Mary's skin, her smell, her touch, her breath became everything to Jimmy. It was everything and yet an everything that made him crazy for more, wanting more and more as he found her breasts, her open thighs, felt her breath moving with his, her moans rising to meet his.

And Jimmy fell with Mary into a time that might have been years, might have been lightning, until his voice rose into the morning, rising past the bantam, past the waves breaking and washing again and again on the beach. And Jimmy traveled to the very center of his world. And then when he lay next to Mary, glistening sweat, breathing the sweet September smells of dried grasses and overripe berries, he fondled Mary's sun-darkened breast as he might a small sacred feather or a smooth round stone from a medicine bundle, remembering the powerful healing magic of its medicine.

The slam of the screen door cracked the air like a shot, and Mary laughed and pulled Jimmy with her as they rolled to the far side of the Buick where they lay and watched the boys tumble off the porch and down the path to the beach with poles and lines and shining cans of worms.

As Jimmy and Mary dressed, they spoke little, each sensing it was a morning full of a beauty much too sweet and fragile for the weight of words. While Jimmy was buttoning his jeans he felt Mary brush her hand along his arm and thought he heard her whisper a single line of Uncle's Salish prayer of thanks, but watching her scoop up the corn and cross the field to the '52 Chevy wagon he wasn't sure if he heard it or felt it or spoke it himself.

Jimmy carried the water cans and met Mary at the Chevy wagon just as the last of the fat black-and-white Barred Rock hens jumped from the open tailgate window, loose feathers and the hot smell of chicken following her out in the breeze of her flapping wings. The little bantam rooster was surrounded by all his hens, all pecking and scratching and pushing to the center of that sweet yellow corn.

ᴅ ɪᴀɴᴇ Gʟᴀɴᴄʏ, a Cherokee Indian, earned her
master's degree in fine arts at the University of Iowa and
teaches creative writing at Macalester College in St. Paul,
Minnesota. She has published four books of poetry and numerous
short stories. The recipient of the Nilon Minority Fiction Award
for her book *Trigger Dance* and the University of Nebraska Press
Prose Award for her poetry in *Claiming Breath*, Glancy is awaiting
publication of her collection of short stories, *Firesticks*, by the
University of Oklahoma Press.

LEAD HORSE

Diane Glancy

Rain blew through the screen. Nattie stood in the open door. Feeling the spray on her face.

A tree in the backyard slammed its door. Or maybe it was the room upstairs. The windows were still open.

Her backyard bushes beat the ground. Back and forth their fists pounded the grass.

Let the curtains stand straight out. Let the storm stomp-dance through her house. Rattle her plastic dress-bags hanging on the door. Her shawl-fringe and feathers.

She watched the lid to the trash can fly across the yard like a war shield. She watched the leaves buck.

What's the battle out there, Nattie? Joes said. He scratched his ear when Nattie looked at him.

Well, he wasn't what she hoped. But it was seeing all that potential in him.

The wind wheezed through the weatherstripping on the door. The whole yard shook. And it was the day of a family birthday. A relative Nattie only wanted to send a card to, usually, but now she was on her way, and the cousins were going to show up and Nattie had a sink full of dishes and a war in the yard and Joes at the table. And he was starting to hum like electricity on the backyard wire.

It's a lot for one old woman, she thought.

It'll be over soon, Joes comforted.

The relatives or the storm?

The trees raised and bowed their arms in exaggerated motions as if the cousins already pulled in the drive. But the relatives were out there under an underpass in their car. The old green Plymouth tossing a little in the gusts of wind. Chewing them but not yet swallowing. Jerking all the while with pleasure Nattie could only imagine.

She was making her corn chowder and cornbread and corn pudding. She should have said she'd meet them at Benny Bill's Ranchero. They could have a steak and dance. But the cousins didn't like that. She could outdude them any time. In fact, they couldn't dude at all. Yes. What a storm-sash she was.

But Joes could still make her blush. And the cousins were coming and she was supposed to cowtow and lick their flitters. The trees swept their arms. The storm shuttered over the house. Horse hooves running.

Still the rain torpedoed the house. Just like Crouper and Boaz, the cousins, when they were boys, roughhousing upstairs and you wanted to yell at them to stop.

You going to close that door, Nat?

When I'm ready.

She'd seen the highway once from a plane. The one time she flew. She'd felt the invisible cord that jerks a plane into the sky. A pull-toy right up to the clouds where the highway and its cloverleaf looked like cucumber pickles in a jar, the tight highway loops like curls of onions.

Maybe a spirit fell to the yard, flailing, by the looks of it. The arms and legs struggling to get up and disappear before someone could look from her house and say, hey, there's a spirit out there. The splot between the elm and oak, and the bushes beating it away. No, the wisteria didn't want any fallen spirit in their yard. Something was being swept out of the Hunting Grounds. The Great Spirit had his war stick out. The old hammock wind-danced.

Then Joes was at the door with her. Kissing her jaw. Rubbing his fingers across her back. Sometimes his hand went just under the fatty part of her hip.

Keep your hands on your own self, she said.

Lightning cracked so loud Nattie closed the door.

It's too late by the time you hear it, Joes told her.

Closing the door's like trying to get in the canoe once the flood's started. He had his hairy hand on her stomach.

Joes, I got the cousins coming for Wilhelmina's fiftieth birthday, though I think it should be her seventieth. I'm trying to get myself geared for the smell of horehound cough drops, mentholatum, and camphor.

And Fedora who was never anything but a chicken liver from the day they first sat her in the crib next to me.

Chicken livers aren't bad.

There was always some memory of them knocking in her head trying to get out. But she wouldn't tell Joes. ONCE THE WORD WAS SPOKE, THE OBJECT FORMED.

In all, she was a lead horse. Not the dull silver metal, *lead*. But the *LEED*.

She remembered once when she and her former husband were returning from her mother-in-law's house in the country. Nattie figured she was driving her mother-in-law's old car. When they finally had to take it away from her. And Nattie's husband followed her on the narrow road at night in their car. It was harder to drive out front. Yet he let her. Or rather, he waited to get out of the yard so she'd be first. He was teaching her already how to get along. Teaching her already to lead.

As if she didn't know—

What's bothering you, Nattie?

I was thinking—

All of a sudden Nattie gulped. There was someone's face at the side window. Not even knocking. Not even hurrying to get in from the storm. She saw him as she turned to face Joes.

Crouper! She opened the door and jerked him in the house. The kitchen lights blinked off and on.

The others staying in the car until the wind stopped whipping the trees. The cousins got their hair piled on top their heads. They don't want the wind to bring it down.

Nattie could see them poking in the car out under the tree. Boaz's four-door twenty-year-old Plymouth wrapped to the ears with rain and leaves stuck to the windshield. Nothing would get through to them. Nattie'd be hearing about every storm they got caught in for years. The fifty-year rain.

Rain-dogs around the sun.

They held their landing pattern for fifteen minutes.

Now tell them to hang these newspapers over their heads and get in here. WHATEVER YOU DON'T WANT SAID, SAY IT OVER AND OVER UNTIL IT'S SO COMMON NO ONE HEARS IT ANYMORE. That's the white man's way. Maybe Boaz'd just turn the Plymouth around and go back to Durant.

But no. How she was glad she wasn't in the car with them. *Whu clumpta. Ere they cahume.* The women screaming because the wind whizzed the newspapers from their heads. But their hair was still there. Just listing a little to the side. A birchbark canoe hanging over one ear. We brought a bag of pecans fresh out of the freezer. Fresh as if we'd just picked them up.

Crouper and Fedora and Boaz and Wilhelmina. Jumping up and down in the kitchen. Named with dignity and light. Why had they turned up such cocoons full of larvae? *Hey! How you world travelers today? Eoouee!*

Mules. Yessie. But she was the lead horse.

You need seat belts for the run into Nattie's house. Joes whistled without knowing what he was doing. But he had a lead horse by the tail. He would light up and ride. Yezzo.

Well, bless her up with real sunshine. But don't look like it's going to shine today.

Rain's a blessing, Wilhelmina.

I hope this isn't a token for the rest of my life.

Yes, she was a bumpo brain for sure.

The rainstorm sputtered over the house, seeming to let up at times—but it soon roared again.

Nattie's kitchen whummed down through her toes. As if falling from the sky. Here's the roof. Smoke hole—She could see falling into it— The upstairs bedroom throw rugs. The white ceiling of the kitchen. The round table, moonlike, where she had to face her own kind. Which is the richest blessing an Indian can have. *Family.* She reminded herself daily. She should bead it on a deerhide bag and hang it above her stove. Maybe with a wood-land-tribe floral pattern.

It seemed to Nattie her house opened like a flower. The back walk, a stem. The kitchen, dining room, living room, and down-stairs bedroom, the wide, round petals. The upstairs room buzzing like the Great Spirit with an attack of lumbago.

Quietly. Shoo. Shoo. She had helped in the naming their lives.

Want me to close them windows upstairs?

No. Things need rearranged. Cleaned up.

The cousins settled in. Fedora stirring Nattie's chowder. Crouper at the kitchen table with a napkin on his lap. Boaz washing the dishes in the sink. Wilhelmina Kleenexed in the next room. Crying over her fifty years and the list of her hair.

Nattie'd hand them some quietude. Just let them stay at her house long enough.

Joes.

Whadhoney? he asked. The cousins looked at him.

She was knifing him with jamspurts. Keeping him fed. Her toes probably curled in her shoes.

A jet-fine landing. Big gawky wings stuck out like Boaz when he dive-bombed from the dresser to the bed.

If she left Crouper alone in the house, he'd probably go through her underwear.

Come on, Wilhelmina. Get your birthday-self in here.

They sat at the table. Boaz. Fedora. Joes. Crouper. Nattie passing the cornbread and chowder. Wilhelmina dragging her wilted self to her chair. They spread in all six directions. North. South. East. West. Down. Up.

The biggest thing that happens to Fedora's when her button jar gets spilled. Crouper swallowed. Sometimes I go over and give it a nudge just so she'll have buttons to pick up.

You seem touchy, Fedora.

I thought Wilhelmina was the touchy one.

I was out yesterday morning trying to chop wood. Boaz ran the honey across his cornbread. That old dead tree's been lying across my backyard now for two years. I chopped and chopped. But it wouldn't give.

I'm not as touchy as Fedora.

Can't we just eat and be quiet? Nattie asked. Chew our cornbread. Swallow. Open our mouth and put in another bite.

A cord of wood costs more than I can afford. No sense in buying it when I got a whole dead tree in my backyard. Boaz always drank his licorice tea with loud sips. I'm going to hire someone to chop that wood.

The house rattled as they ate. Lightning bolts stroked the sky.

I knew it would rain. I heard the blackbirds talking. But they didn't say we'd be stowed up under the underpass. Or hanging on with our teeth—

Crouper excused himself.

I've always been the youngest cousin. I guess I'm not used to being older. And Mother always insisted on us being nice to you, Nattie, even when you came in the house like a horse—

Of course maybe someone from the church could come and cut that wood for me. Then I wouldn't have to pay. Your tea's always good, Nattie. Boaz took two more gulps. And your cornbread. Some of the men have chain saws. It wouldn't take them long. Better than me with the old ax. Never know how long the cold's setting in for this winter. Back in the old days we had snow-storms! We don't have them so much anymore. I remember days when I was a boy the road would be piled with snow and—

What on earth are you talking about, Boaz?

The rabbits were easy to catch because they couldn't hop in the snow. When you've seen so many winters they all stay together like buttons in the jar. Wilhelmina blew her nose.

Something hit the side of the house with a bang.

Where's Crouper? I don't want him looking in any windows around here.

Just the trash blowing around. Joes went to look.

Now if I saved my money, I could buy a chain saw. Then I'd have firewood on my back porch and I wouldn't have to worry about keeping warm, or cooking. Maybe the Handshys' boy would cut it for me. But everyone's busy. Too bad they can't say, Boaz, could I come and cut that wood for you because we just might have snow or a hard cold spell one of these days and we don't want you to be without firewood or worse that tree could fall on your house and smash it in two or worse—

Boaz! This's my birthday and I say *SHUDUP!*

Drag it all out—like pulling string from the drawer your mother saved until she yelled at us and we had to roll it back into a ball.

What do you want, Boaz? For us to get in the Plymouth right this minute and cut your wood?

No, by shucks I'm just talking.

Then hang it UP, Nattie said.

Empty dress-bags. All of them.

No one'd ever know you carry a TOMAHAWK in your heart. Your WITCHERY sticking straight pins in that pin cushion on Fedora's wrist.

You want blood?

No coup sticks for her. NOsirEEEooo.

If I eat Nattie's supper, Fedora'll have to let out my pants with a guessit.

Gusset.

I don't have words for the things I want to say, and the words I DO have DON'T fit the things I can say with them.

Crouper, get in here!

I think people are wearing their old clothing. Not buying new. Fedora scraped the bowl of corn chowder.

Just think of all the words there are to say whatever you need to say! How I wish I knew more words. I feel sometimes there is an exact word for each tiny detail—if only I knew it. How about that ambivalent feeling when I see you, Nattie? Wilhelmina sup-posed. I'm delighted. Yet some remote, inexplicable dread gnaws in the back of my head.

And I want a word for the last of the afternoon just before it turns into evening.

It's called dusk, Fedora.

Not dusk. No, that's too late. That's a dead afternoon. But I want the name for an old, old afternoon—full of stars just before they shine. But are geared up—

The word for after a storm when it's all wet and dripping and quiet—

The storm ain't over yet. I can still hear rain yawl against the roof.

Let's get it out. Let's pull the string until there's none left in the drawer.

Then who's the man's been looking in windows around Durant? He wears a sock on his head.

A what?

Don't even think it.

Maybe we should listen to the radio—

Wilhelmina won't let us turn it on. Ever since she was jilted by a radio repairman.

Crouper wears garters for his socks. I saw them on his dresser. His socks by his chair had tops so stretched he could have fit them on his head.

How do you get the tops of your socks so big?

There was a sudden rush of wind. Then momentary quiet. The sky's kinda greenish— They looked at one another. It's late in the year for tornados—

Crouper tried to excuse himself again— Thought he'd go out and keep a rightful eye on things.

Sit down, Crouper.

Fedora poked the candles into the corn pudding. Nervous as a crooked seam. Boaz sang *happy birthday*. Wilhelmina blew her nose.

The light bulbs in the kitchen quivered again. There was a louder rush of wind. Wilhelmina screamed. Something upstairs fell over. For a moment there was a pinkish fizz of light like birthday candles. Even Boaz yelled out with a bark. Nattie seemed lifted from the house. Up past the white ceiling. The throw rugs in the upstairs bedroom. The roof. Smoke hole. She was Dorothy in her red moccasins. Even Toto. Barking. No, that was Boaz. She was floating over Oklahoma. Above the cucumber-pickled highways and cloverleafs. Heading north. Speaking different tongues. What the dizz— Out into the great black sky. Spirits flapping like spurts of light to keep her right-side up. The cousins talking anyway—

And we know who the star is.

Wilhelmina. Our birthday girl.

What the fluck's going on? Was Nattie the only one seeing SPIR-ITS? Were the cousins shucking raisins into their corn pudding? Drinking coffee and licorice tea? Had someone hit her in the head with the pan of cornbread when they cleared the table?

I think that was the storm's last gasp— I couldn't sleep otherwise. I have to have silence.

You could never sleep in the room with Nattie. She snores—

They all looked at Joes.

Maybe she had died. Hadn't Nattie passed a line of cars on a curve on old Highway 40 long ago? Traffic was slow and she got impatient and pulled out. The boy she was with drank too much. She was driving. And she didn't have sense to stay in line. But passed. The lead horse out there. She made it—pulling back in with an inch to spare. Why was she saved? Just making it around the cars? Maybe her own death just now caught up with her. Maybe there was someone in that oncoming car the Great Spirit didn't want dead at the moment. So she married, had a child— Drove both of them away. Nattie couldn't say what her life had meant—

No, she hadn't died. The cousins wouldn't come to see her if she wasn't there.

We're searching for truth right here with us in the universe.

I know what I'm doing at any given moment. It's the overall purpose of life that's evaded me.

Right fine.

Was Nattie really there in the room with her cousins?

Who can enjoy their birthday with Crouper sitting there—his face down to his ankles?

Just because we won't let him go outside.

Not without one of us going with him.

After the drive from Durant a man needs to get out and walk.

WHAD? Nattie flummed.

You'd walk straight to someone's back window.

What comes over you, Crouper?

I dunno. I'm taking a walk and before I know it I feel someone's window glass against my nose and they're in their house screaming that someone's at the window.

Nattie felt her hands. She wanted the cousins to be QUIET. She wanted to ask if they could see her. She had heard the HORSE HOOVES of the storm. Maybe she was still out there—over the house— She wanted her cousins to SAY SOMETHING to her so she'd know she was in her kitchen and not lifted off the migration trail of the earth. She looked at Joes and her cousins around the table. She saw she wasn't the lead horse without the others to follow. Yes. Just look at them. Head. Tail. Four feet. It took all six. Yeow. North. South. East. West. Earth. Sky. Nattie was in the SPIRIT— Boaz opened his mouth again to say something about chopping wood or—Nattie shuddered with impatience and SPOKE to her cousins. THE STORM'S A HORSE OVER US. A WREATH OF FLOWERING HOUSES AROUND ITS EARS. A BRAIDED MANE. ITS HOOVES TROMPING THROUGH THE YARD—LEAD HORSE OF LEAD HORSES — Yes. Nattie'd seen a SPIRIT of which they were only part.

The cousins and Joes stared at her.

Nattie'd been proud. Thinking she was the whole show. But now she'd had a VISION FROM THE SPIRIT WORLD. She'd been given the birthday gift. She'd shared it with the others.

Boaz cleared his throat with a horehound cough drop. Crouper and Fedora sat looking at one another around the kitchen table. Wilhelmina still stared at her.

Joes stood at the door. Nattie wanted to feel his hand on her stomach— She got up and went to him. The trees dripped the last of their rain into the grass.

Nothing we can't put back together, he told her. —'Cept maybe the upstairs.

If a spirit had fallen in the yard, by jolly, it'd gotten up and gone on. Maybe it'd been Nattie's pride running from the HORSE.

She felt the damp curtain of the breeze on her face. She looked again to see if the cousins were still staring. But Wilhelmina was recouping. The others were starting to stir from their chairs at the kitchen table. Rising almost as children. After the spirit storm that—yes—left them touched for a moment with some pure likeness.

J OE B RUCHAC lives with his wife, Carol, in the Adirondack Mountains of New York. Much of his writing draws on that land and his Abenaki heritage. Bruchac is of mixed Indian, Slovak, and English blood. His poems, articles, and stories have appeared in over five hundred publications, from *Akwesasne Notes* and *The Eagle* to *National Geographic* and *Parabika*. As a professional storyteller, he has performed in Europe and throughout the United States. His most recent books include a novel, *The Dawn Land*, from Fulcrum Press; *Turtle Meat*, a collection of his short stories from Holy Cow! Press; and *Keepers of the Earth*, Native American stories and environmental activities for children, also produced by Fulcrum.

BONE GIRL

Joseph Bruchac

There is this one old abandoned quarry on the reservation where she is often seen. Always late, late at night when there is a full moon. The kind of moon that is as white as bone.

Are ghosts outsiders? That is the way most white people seem to view them. Spirits who are condemned to wander for eternity. Ectoplasmic remnants of people whose violent deaths left their spirits trapped between the worlds. You know what I mean. I'm sure. I bet we've seen the same movies and TV shows. Vengeful apparitions. Those are real popular. And then there is this one: scary noises in the background, the lights get dim, and a hushed voice saying "But what they didn't know was that the house had been built on an *Indian graveyard!*" And the soundtrack fills with muted tomtoms. Bum-bum-bum-bum, bum-bum-bum-bum.

Indian graveyards. White people seem to love to talk about them. They're this continent's equivalent of King Tut's tomb. On the one hand, I wish some white people in particular really were more afraid of them than they are—those people that some call "pot hunters," though I think the good old English word "ghoul" applies pretty well. There's a big international trade in Indian grave goods dug up and sold. And protecting them and getting back the bones of our ancestors who've been dug up and stolen and taken to museums, that is real important to us. I can tell you more about that, but that is another tale to tell another time. I'd better finish this story first.

Indian graveyards, you see, mean something different to me than places of dread. Maybe it's because I've spent a lot of time around real Indian graveyards, not the ones in the movies. Like the one the kids on our res walk by on their way to school—just like I used to. That cemetery is an old one, placed right in the middle of the town. It's a lot older than the oldest marker stones in it. In the old days, my people used to bury those who died right under the foundation of the lodge. No marker stones then. Just the house and your relatives continued to live there. That was record enough of the life you'd had. It was different from one part of the country to another, I know. Different Indian people have different ways of dealing with death. In a lot of places it still isn't regarded as the right thing to do to say the names of those who've died after their bodies have gone back into the earth. But, even with that, I don't think that Indian ghosts *are* outsiders. They're still with us and part of us. No farther away from us than the other side of a leaf that has fallen. I think Chief Cornplanter of the Seneca people said that. But he wasn't the only one to say it. Indian ghosts are, well, familiar. Family. And when you're family, you care for each other. In a lot of different ways.

Being in my sixties, now, it gives me the right to say a few things. I want to say them better, which is why I have taken this extension course in creative writing. Why I have read the books assigned for this class. But when I put my name on something I have written, when you see the name Russell Painter on it, I would like it to be something I am proud of. I worked building roads for a good many years and I was always proud that I could lay out a road just so. The crest was right and the shoulders were right and that road was even and the turns banked and the drainage good so that ice didn't build up. Roads eventually wear away and have to be resurfaced and all that, but if you make a road right then you can use it to get somewhere. So I would like to write in the same way. I would like any story I tell to get somewhere and not be a dead end or so poorly made that it is full of holes and maybe even throws someone off it into the ditch. This is called an extended metaphor.

You may note that I am not writing in the style which I have begun to call "cute Indian." There is this one Canadian who pretends to be an Indian when he writes and his Indians are very cute and he has a narrator telling his stories who is doing what I am doing, taking a creative writing course. My writing instructor is a good enough guy. My writing instructor would like me to get cuter. That is why he has had me read some books that can furnish me, as he put it, with some good "boilerplate models." But I think I have enough models just by looking at the people around me and trying to understand the lessons they've taught me. Like I said, as I said, being in my sixties and retired gives me the right to say some things. Not that I didn't have the right to say them before. Just that now I may actually be listened to when I start talking.

Like about Indian ghosts. Most of the real ghost stories I have heard from people in the towns around the res don't seem to have a point to them. It's always someone hearing a strange noise or seeing a light or the furniture moving or windows shutting or strange shapes walking down a hallway. Then they may find out later that someone died in that house a long time ago and that the spirit of that person is probably what has been making those weird things happen. Our ghost stories make sense. Or maybe it is more like our ghosts have a sense of purpose. I have a theory about this. I think it is because Indians stay put and white people keep moving around. White people bury their dead in a grave-yard full of people they don't know and then they move away themselves. Get a better job in a city on the West Coast or maybe retire to Florida. And those ghosts—even if they've stayed in the family home—they're surrounded by strangers. I think maybe those ghosts get to be like the homeless people you see wandering around the streets in the big cities these days. Talking to themselves, ignored unless they really get into your face, disconnected and forgotten.

But Indian people stay put—unless they're forced to move. Like the Cherokees being forced out of the south or the way the Abenakis were driven out of western Maine or the Stockbridge people or, to be honest, just about every Indian nation you can name at one time or another. There's still a lot of forcing Indian people to move going on today. I could tell you some stories about our own res. Last year they were planning to put in a big housing development that would have taken a lot of land up on Turkey Hill. That little mountain isn't officially ours anymore, but we hope to get it back one day. And that development would have polluted our water, cut down a lot of trees we care about. Maybe someday I will write a story about how that housing development got stalled and then this "recession-depression" came along and knocked the bottom out of the housing market. So that development went down the tubes. But some folks I know were involved in stopping that development, and they might get in trouble if I told you what they did. And I am digressing, my writing instructor is probably writing in the margin of this story right now. Except he doesn't understand that is how we tell stories. In circles. Circling back to the fact that Indian people like to stay put. And because we stay put, close to the land where we were born (and even though my one-story house may not look like much, I'm the fifth generation of Painters to live in it and it stands on the same earth where a log cabin housed four generations before that and a bark lodge was there when the Puritans were trying to find a stone to stand on), we also stay close to the land where we're buried. Close to our dead. Close to our ghosts—which, I assume, do not feel as abandoned as white ghosts and so tend to be a lot less neurotic. We know them, they know us, and they also know what they can do. Which often is, pardon my French, to scare the shit out of us when we're doing the wrong things!

I've got a nephew named Tommy. Typical junior high. He's been staying with my wife and me the last six months. Him and some of the other kids his age decided to have some fun and so they went one night and hid in the graveyard near the road, behind some of the bigger stones there. They had a piece of white cloth tied onto a stick and a lantern. They waited till they saw people walking home past the graveyard and as soon as they were close they made spooky noises and waved that white cloth and flashed the light. Just about everybody took off! I guess they'd never seen some of those older folks move that fast before! The only one they didn't scare was Grama Big Eel. She just paid no attention to it at all and just kept on walking. She didn't even turn her head.

Next night Tommy was walking home by himself, right past the same graveyard. As soon as he hit that spot a light started flickering in the graveyard and he could see something white.

"Okay, you guys!" he said. "I know you're there. You're not scaring me!" He kept right on going, trying not to speed up too much. He knew it was them, but he also wondered how come the light was a different color tonight and how they were able to make it move so fast through that graveyard.

As soon as he got home, the phone rang. It was one of his friends who'd been with him in the graveyard the night before, scaring people.

"Thought you scared me, didn't you?" Tommy said.

"Huh?" his friend answered. "I don't know what you mean. The guys are all here. They've been here the last two hours playing Nintendo. We were just wondering if you wanted to go back down to the graveyard again tonight and spook people."

After than, you can bet that Tommy stopped goofing around in the graveyard.

There's a lot more stories like that one. The best stories we can tell, though, are always the stories where the jokes are on ourselves. Which brings me to the story I wanted to tell when I started writing this piece.

When I came back home, retired here, I came back alone. My wife and I had some problems and we split up. There were some things I did here that weren't too bad, but I was drinking too much. And when they say there's no fool like an old fool, I guess I ought to know who they was talking about. I'd always liked the young girls too. Especially those ones with the blond hair. Right now if there's any Indian women reading this I bet they are about ready to give up in disgust. They know the type. That was me. Oh honey, sweetie, wait up for Grampa Russell. Lemme buy you another beer, lemme just give you a little hug, honey, sweetie. People were getting pretty disgusted with me. Nobody said anything. That would have been interfering. But when they saw me sleeping it off next to the road with a bottle in my hand, they must have been shaking their heads. I've always been real tough and even now I like to sleep outside, even when it gets cold. I have got me a bed in the field behind our house. But I wasn't sleeping in no bed in those days. I was sleeping in the ditches. Tommy wasn't living with me then or he would have been really ashamed of his Uncle Russell.

One Saturday night, I was coming home real, real late. There's a little bridge that is down about a mile from my house on one of the little winding back roads that makes its way up to the big highway that cuts through the res. I had been at one of those bars they built just a hundred yards past the line. I'd stayed out even later than the younger guys who had the car and so I was walking home. Staggering, more like. The moonlight was good and bright, though, so it was easy to make my way and I was singing something in Indian as I went. That little bridge was ahead of me and I saw her there on the bridge. It was a young woman with long pale hair. Her face was turned away from me. She was wearing a long dress and it showed off her figure real good. She looked like she was maybe in her twenties from her figure and the way she moved. I couldn't see her face. I knew there was some girls visiting from the Cherokees and figured maybe she was one of them. Some of those southern Indian girls have got that long blond hair and you can't tell they're Indian till you see it in their face or the way they carry themselves. And from the way she moved she was sure Indian. And she was out looking for something to do late at night.

"Hey, honey!" I yelled. "Hey, sweetie, wait for me. Wait up."

She paused there on the bridge and let me catch up to her. I came up real close.

"Hi, sweetie," I said. "Is it okay if I walk with you some?"

She didn't say anything, just kept her head turned away from me. I like that. I've always liked the shy ones . . . or at least the ones who pretend to be shy to keep you interested. I put my arm around her shoulders and she didn't take it off, she just kept walking and I walked with her. I kept talking, saying the kind of no sense things that an old fool says when he's trying to romance a young girl. We kept on walking and next thing I knew we were at the old quarry. That was okay by me. There was a place near the road where there's a kind of natural seat in the stones and that's right where she led me and we sat down together.

Oh, was that moon bright! It glistened on her hair and I kept my left arm tight around her. She felt awfully cold and I figured she wouldn't mind my helping her get warm. I still had the bottle in my right hand and I figured that would get her to turn her head and look at me. I still hadn't seen her face under that long pale hair of hers.

"Come on, honey, you want a drink, huh?" But it didn't work. She kept her face turned away. So I decided that a drink wasn't what she wanted at all. "Sweetie," I said, "why don't you turn around and give old Grampa Russell a little kiss?"

And she turned her head.

They say the first time she was seen on the reservation was about two hundred years ago. She was dressed then the way she was that night. Her hair loose and long, wearing an old-fashioned long dress and wearing those tall high-button shoes. I should have recognized those shoes. But no one ever does when they go to that quarry with her. They never recognize who she is until she turns her face to look at them. That skull face of hers that is all bone. Pale and white as the moon.

I dropped the bottle and let go of her. I ran without looking back and I'm pretty sure that she didn't follow me. I ran and I ran and even in my sleep I was still running when I woke up the next morning on the floor inside the house. That day I went and talked to some people and they told me what I had to do if I didn't want the Bone Girl to come and visit me.

That was two years ago and I haven't had a drink since then and with Mary and me having gotten back together and with Tommy living with us, I don't think I'll ever go back to those ways again.

So that is about all I have to say in this story, about ghosts and all. About Indian ghosts in particular and why it is that I say that Indian ghosts aren't outsiders. They're what you might call familiar spirits.

*P*AULA GUNN ALLEN is of mixed Laguna and Lakota blood. A professor of literature at the University of California, Los Angeles, she has written criticism, novels, poetry, and short fiction. In 1990 her anthology, *Spider Woman's Granddaughter*, won the American Book Award. Her most recent work is *Skins and Bones*, a collection of poetry published by West End Press.

SPIRIT WOMAN

Paula Gunn Allen

"Sister. Sister, I am here."

Ephanie opened her eyes. Looked around. Saw some-one, shadowy, at the bottom of her bed.

"I have come to tell you a story. One that you have long wanted to hear."

Ephanie saw that the shadowy form was a woman whose shape slowly focussed out of the swirl of vapor she was cloaked in. She saw that the woman was small. There was something of bird, a hawk perhaps, about her. Her eyes gleamed in a particular way, like no shine Ephanie had ever seen. The woman was dressed in the old way and her hair was cut traditionally, so that it fell in a straight line from crown to jaw. The sides formed perfect square corners on either side. Straight bangs fell over her forehead, almost to her eyebrows in the ancient arrangement that signified the arms of the galaxy, the Spider. It was another arrangement of the four corners that composed the Universe, the four days of sacredness that women remembered in their bodies' blood every month.

The woman wore a white, finely woven manta and shawl, each richly embroidered in fine black wool with geometrical patterns that told the story of the galaxy. Ephanie recognized only the spider among the symbols embroidered there. She saw the woman's thick, snowy buckskin leggings, wrapped perfectly around her calves. She raised herself to a sitting position and with her hand made the sign of sunrise, the gesture of taking a pinch of corn pollen between fingers and thumb, then opening them as though to let the pollen free.

The spirit woman began to speak, chanting her words in a way that seemed so familiar, that brought Ephanie near tears.

"In the beginning time, in the place of Sussistinaku, The Spider, Old Woman, placed the bundles that contained her sisters Uretsete and Naotsete, the women who had come with her from the center of the galaxy to this sun. She sang them into life. She established the patterns of this world. The pattern of the singing, of the painting she made to lay the spirit women upon, the pattern of placing the bundles that contained their forms, of the signs that she made, was the pattern she brought with her, in her mind. It is the pattern of the corners, their turning, their multidimensional arrangings. It is the sign and the order of the power that informs this life and leads back to Shipap. Two face outward, two inward, the sign of doubling, of order and balance, of the two, the twins, the doubleminded world in which you have lived," she chanted.

And in the living shadows that swirled around the spirit woman's face, Ephanie saw moving patterns that imaged what the woman was saying. Saw the corners lying flat like on paper, then taking on dimensions, like in rooms as on the outside of boxes and buildings, then combining and recombining in all of their dimensions, forming the four-armed cross, ancient symbol of the Milky Way, found on rocks and in drawings of every land. Saw the square of glossy, deeply gleaming blackness that was the

door to the place of the Spider. Saw held within it the patterned
stars, the whirling suns, the deep black brilliance of the center of
the sun. Saw the perfect creation space from which earth and her
seven sisters had sprung at the bidding of the Grandmothers,
long ago so far, before time like a clock entered and took hold.

She understood the combinations and recombinations that
had so puzzled her, the One and then the Two, the two and then
the three, the three becoming the fours, the four splitting, becoming two and two, the three of the beginning becoming the
three-in-one. One mother, twin sons; two mothers, two sons; one
mother, two sons. Each. First there was Sussistinaku, Thinking
Woman, then there was She and two more: Uretsete and Naotsete. Then Uretsete became known as the father, Utset, because
Naotsete had become pregnant and a mother, because the Chris-
tians would not understand and killed what they did not know.
And Iyatiku was the name Uretsete was known by, she was
Utset, the brother. The woman who was known as father, the
Sun. And Utset was another name for both Iyatiku and Uretsete,
making three in one. And Naotsete, she with more in her bundle, was the Woman of the Sun, after whom Iyatiku named her
first daughter Sun Clan, alien and so the combinations went on,
forming, dissolving, doubling, splitting, sometimes one sometimes two, sometimes three, sometimes four, then again two,
again one. All of the stories formed those patterns, laid down
long before time, so far.

The One was the unity, the source, Shipap, where Naiya Iyatiku lived. The two was the first splitting of the one, the sign of
the twins, the doublewoman, the clanmother-generation. From
whom came all the forms of spirit and of matter as they appear on
earth and in earth's heavens. Which could only come into being
in time, the counting, pulsating, repetitive, cycling beat, held in
its four coordinating patterns by the power of the three who
become seven in all the tales eventually. The forms of flame. The
dark flame. The gold flame. The flame of white. The Grandmother flame. The sister flame. The flame of the sun. The fire of

flint. The fire of corn. The fire of passion, of desire. The flame of longing. The flame of freedom. The flame of vision, of dream.

In the patterns before her eyes, within her mind, that pulsed and flowed around and through her, Ephanie found what she so long had sought. The patterns flowed like the flowings of her life, the coming out and the going in, the entering and the leaving, the meeting and gathering, the divisions and separations, how her life, like the stories, told the tale of all the enterings, all the turning away. Waxing and waning, growing and shrinking, birthing and dying, flowering and withering. The summer people and the winter people, that ancient division of the tribe. The inside priestess and the outside priest. The mother who was the center of their relationship to each other and to the people, the things of the earth. What was within went without. What was without, went within. As Kochinnenako returning home stepped four times up the ladder, each time calling, "I am here." And on the fourth step, at her words, her sister had cried with relief. And Kochinnenako vanished, could not therefore return. Ephanie understood that Kochinnenako was the name of any woman who, in the events being told, was walking in the ancient manner, tracing the pattern of the ancient design.

Ephanie looked at the face of the spirit woman, eyes drawn there with undeniable force, and saw that powerful, gleaming hawk beaked face changing, changing, growing old, old, until it was older than time. The face of Old Woman, of hawk, of butterfly, of bee. The face of wolf and spider. The face of old woman coyote. The face of rock and wind and star. The face of infinite, aching, powerful, beloved darkness, of midnight. The face of dawn. The face of red red flame. The face of distant distant star.

And from that great distance, the voice was saying. In a whisper that held the echo of starlight in its depth. That a certain time was upon them. That Ephanie would receive a song.

"The time of ending is upon the Indian. So few, so few are there left. So many being killed. So many already dead. But do not weep for this. For it is as it should be.

"My sister, my granddaughter. A door is closing upon a world, the world we knew. The world we guide and protect. We have ever guarded it. We ever will protect it. But the door closes now. It is the end of our time. We go on to another place, the sixth world. For that is our duty, and our work.

"But we will leave behind in this fifth world certain things. We go so that the people will live.

"Each spirit has its time and place. And it is a certain spirit, a great one, which calls to us now. We go on. The others come behind us. As we go, they take our place. And when they are ready for the next step, others will replace them. For that is the law of the universe, of the Grandmother. The work that is left is to pass on what we know to those who come after us. It is an old story. One that is often repeated. One that is true.

"It isn't whether you're here or there. Whether the people are what you call alive or dead. Those are just words. What you call dead isn't dead. It is a different way of being. And in some cases, in many, the new place, the new way of looking at reality and yourself, is far more valid, far more real, far more vital than the old way.

"I am not saying we want to die. Only that one way or another we live. And on another earth, just like this one, in almost the same place as the one you are lying in, talking with me, the world where your room is, where the city you call San Francisco is. I am also in San Francisco. But it is a very different version of the place from the version you inhabit.

"Come. See my city. Visit me. I think you will like it here. I think you will be surprised to see that death is not possible. That life and being are the only truth.

"Long ago, so far, the people knew this. That was when they could see the person leave the flesh, like you can see someone take off their clothes. They could see the change. Then old Coyote said there would be death. The people would no longer see the whole of the transformation in its entirety. They would only see the body, first vital, then still. So that they would want to go on from where they were. So they would have reason to think. About what life is, about what their flesh is. So they would learn other ways to know, to see. The katsina withdrew so that you would know their true being in yourself. Iyatiku withdrew so you would put her thoughts into your own hearts, and live them as was intended by All That Moves.

"The story of the people and the spirits, the story of the earth, is the story of what moves, what moves on, what patterns, what dances, what signs, what balances, so life can be felt and known. The story of life is the story of moving. Of moving on.

"Your place in the great circling spiral is to help in that story, in that work. To pass on to those who can understand what you have learned, what you know.

"It is for this reason you have endured. That you have tried to understand. When you give away what is in your basket, when what you have given takes root, when it dances, it sings on the earth. Give it to your sister, Teresa. The one who waits. She is ready to know.

"The stories of the old ones, of Utset, Iyatiku and Naotsete, of corn sister and sun sister and of the Spider, shadow sister, is just that. Each gives over what she has and goes on.

"Pass it on, little one. Pass it on. That is the lesson of the giveaways that all the people honor. That is the story of life here where we are and where you are. It is all the same. Grow, move, give, move. That is why they are always leaving. And always coming home. Why it is so that every going out is a coming in. Why every giving is a getting. Every particle in creation knows this. And only the human beings grieve about it. Because only the human beings have forgotten how to live.

"Jump.

"Fall.

"Little sister, you have jumped. You have fallen. You have been brave, but you have misunderstood. So you have learned. How to jump. How to jump. How to fall. How to learn. How to understand.

"We are asking you to jump again. To fall into this world like the old one, the one you call Anciena, sky woman, jumped, fell, and began in a world that was new."

And the corners grew endless to fill the room. To surround Ephanie and the woman who sat near her on the bed. They grew larger, somehow brighter but with no more light than before, growing, filled, filling her mind and her eyes, her body and her heart with dreams.

And she dreamed. About the women who had lived, long ago, hame haa. Who had lived near caves, near streams. Who had known magic far beyond the simple charms and spells the moderns knew. Who were the Spider. The Spider Medicine Society. The women who created, the women who directed people upon their true paths. The women who healed. The women who sang.

And she understood. For those women, so long lost to her, whom she had longed and wept for, unknowing, were the double women, the women who never married, who held power like the Clanuncle, like the power of the priests, the medicine men. Who were not mothers, but who were sisters, born of the same mind, the same spirit. They called each other sister. They were called Grandmother by those who called on them for aid, for knowledge, for comfort, for care.

Who never used their power to coerce. Who waited patient, weaving, silent. Who acted when called on. Who disappeared. Who never abused. Who never allowed themselves to be abused. Who sang.

And in the dream she opened her eyes. Hearing a bird sing. She looked out of her window. Believing she was home, in Guadalupe, that the golden sun was in the window, that the tall trees were singing to the birds, that the birds were singing to the trees.

She sat up, gazing at the window. From which foggy light streamed. She brushed back her untamed hair with a strong, thin hand. The turquoise ring on her finger shone, dully it gleamed. She saw a white, hand-woven shawl, heavily embroidered with

black and white designs lying crumpled on the bottom of the bed.
She stared at it for a moment, hearing the birds, hearing a chant
in her mind, feeling it throbbing at her throat, feeling the drum
resonant and deep in her chest. She leaned forward and reached
for the shawl. Wrapped it around her shoulders and chest. She
lay back down on the pillow. Eyes wide open she lay. Remembering her dream.

Re membering all the wakings of her life. All the goings to
sleep. Re membering, humming quietly to herself, in her throat,
in her mind she lay. Understanding at last that everything belonged to the wind.

Knowing that only without interference can the people learn
and grow and become what they had within themselves to be.
For the measure of her life, of all their lives, was discovering what
she, they, were made of. What she, they, could do. And what
consequences their doing created, and what they would create of
these.

And re membered the voice of the woman, who sat in the
shadows and spoke, saying "There are no curses. There are only
descriptions of what creations there will be."

And in the silence and the quieting shadows of her room, in
her bed surrounded by books and notebooks and silence and dust,
she thought. And the spiders in the walls, on the ceiling, in the
corners, beneath the bed and under the chair began to gather.
Their humming, quiet at first, grew louder, filling all of the spaces
of the room. Their presence grew around her. She did not
move.

And around her the room filled with shadows. And the shadows became shapes. And the shapes became women singing.
Singing and dancing in the ancient steps of the women, the
Spider. Singing they stepped, slowly, in careful balance of dignity, of harmony, of respect. They stepped and they sang. And
she began to sing with them. With her shawl wrapped around her
shoulders in the way of the women since time immemorial, she
wrapped her shawl and she joined the dance. She heard the
singing. She entered the song.

Spirit Woman

I am walking   Alive
Where I am   Beautiful

I am still   Alive
In beauty   Walking

I am   Entering
Not alone

JACK D. FORBES is of mixed Powhatan, Lenape, and Saponi heritage. He is widely published as a historian, poet, and fiction writer. His autobiographical essay, "Shouting Back at the Geese," appeared in *I Tell You Now*, published by the University of Nebraska Press. He has published in *Earth Power Coming* and has completed a novel, *Red Blood*. Forbes is director and professor of Native American studies at the University of California, Davis.

THE CAVE

Jack D. Forbes

"Night winds, strong night winds, heavy with sand and dust, winds that an hour before had been sixty miles to the north, winds that screeched past obstacles, protesting any interference, winds that gave animate life to creosote brush, branches thrashing wildly around me, giving the illusion of armies of strange midnight creatures joining my flight, all this is part of what I can remember of that night.

"The consciousness of running in a manner so unusual. You see, I was able in the darkness to sense the existence of a dry desert wash; perhaps I saw it as a lighter band of sand and gravel faintly differentiating itself from the rising land on either side—because of the absence of plants.

"In any case, I started running up the arroyo, slowly at first but in an instant fear took hold, perhaps the survival instinct in me, and I started running as fast as I could. It was like the sensation of flying, yet I knew vaguely that my feet were touching the ground.

"How can I really describe it to you? The wind was tearing at me from one side, my right I believe—yes, on the right and a little behind, so that it both blew me over a little and helped to carry me forward. I remember I had lost my hair tie and the small strands of hair were wrapping themselves around my face, getting in my mouth, and every once in a while I would shake my head to get my face clear.

"It was like the wind was lifting me, helping me too by covering my tracks, I think. My legs were churning but I wasn't even aware of them. I was breathing hard but steady, running like a racehorse that has been training for months and finally is in the real thing—tense at first, but then letting it all go, and just as if it were one's nature, moving without thought at a dead run.

"I had no sense of avoiding obstacles. My eyes were sensing things rather than seeing them. My body was quicker than my mind. I just surrendered control, gave up being master, took a seat as a silent rider being carried forward into an opaque but wildly alive world.

"The strange thing is I felt no exhaustion either. Really it was a rare experience, fear giving way to near exhilaration, sweat pouring off of me, feeling my lungs as I've never felt them before, my heart pounding—but I knew, yes, I knew that I was a well-oiled machine performing just right. You know, roaring along like an engine in good repair. Working hard but at the same time effortlessly like it was always intended that I function that way.

"I don't know how far I ran. My only thought was to get as far away as possible. I guess I went maybe ten miles give or take a few, and that's remarkable for me because my left knee usually gives out after four or five, but not that night. No, that left knee did fine—it didn't signal anything to me so I just kept churning sand until, all of a sudden, I felt that I should rest a little and see where I was.

"I guess I had sensed a change. The wind was different, not so direct, more of a circular, meandering wind, and I figured that hills or rocks or maybe some other obstacles were now on my right.

"Also, the barely visible lightness of the wash had changed, narrowed, I think, and I saw that the smoke trees or mesquites and brush were not dancing so wildly and continuously.

"So I slowed to a trot and then a walk. That's when I began to feel the heat of my own body. What a change! You know the feeling, after a hard race, the heat almost overwhelms you and breathing becomes harder. Anyway, I gradually cooled down and as I did I examined my prospects.

"Up to that point I had wanted only one thing, distance between me and them. That was the sum total of my existence for an hour and a half of my life. But then, with that accomplished to a degree, I turned my mind to other things, water, food, a hiding place—especially water.

"But I guess that's not quite true. My instincts had caused me to follow the wash *up*hill. How I knew that in the darkness, I'll never know. But somehow I had instinctively chosen to go toward the mountains rather than out into the dry desert flats. So I was thinking of water, that is—my body was looking for water even while I was just a helpless, lost passenger worried about hiding.

"I walked up the arroyo as rapidly as I could, keeping to areas where I could feel gravel under my feet—because I was now thinking about hiding my tracks. I began to sense that the banks along the wash were much higher. I could almost *see* a sort of horizon line, but only when I didn't look directly at it.

"I stopped at what turned out to be a mesquite tree and I groped around until I found a bunch of pods, stuffing them into my pockets for future use. I broke one open and put a sweet seed in my mouth. It tasted too sweet—almost bitter—but I sucked on it anyway, figuring the sugar would be good for me.

"My hope was that I could find water higher up in the canyon. Failing that, I banked on locating some cactus with fruit or at least young leaves.

"I don't know how far I walked—several miles—but I began to

get anxious and I started running again, at a slower pace this time. I burned up quite a distance that way even though the sandy bottom slowed me down some.

"Suddenly, without knowing when it happened, I began to realize that I could see high cliffs on either side of me—dark walls with no details visible—set off a little from the sky. The night had already passed, so quickly, and daylight would soon be coming.

"Now I worried more about a hiding place than about food or water. I had to find a place out of the sun, invisible from the air, and, preferably one that would stay cool.

"I began to hurry again, using my eyes to scan every part of the cliff walls and to peer up side canyons.

"I was getting frantic as the sky got lighter and lighter when all of a sudden I realized that there were clouds up there, above the canyon. I hadn't noticed them in the half-light of dawn. Anyway, that gave me a little more time, more of a chance, and, as I was trotting along, I prayed hard for rain, really hard, I wanted that water so bad, even a flash flood would do.

"I also began looking up at the mountains, when I could see them, looking for trees or green, anything to tell me which branch to follow. I watched for indications of which side canyon drained the north side and which had the biggest watershed. I didn't know where the rain fell the hardest but I figured the north side would have the most shade.

"It didn't matter much though, because I was actually guided by the sandy floor and the marks left by the last flash flood.

"I finally reached a little valley or gorge, coiled my way back in the mountain, a very shady place with a few mesquites growing along the edges. Ahead of me was a huge pile of boulders, like part of the mountain had fallen in on top of the canyon. I crawled in under the boulders and began following cracks and fissures, little runways, tunnels, and open breaks, right up the arroyo. I could see where the water surged through these openings but the boulders were too big for the water to move. It just undermined them, slowly causing them to shift.

"It was nice and cool there. I stopped every so often to breathe easily and to plot out my next course. It smelled dark and ancient under there.

"Finally I came to a place where my nose scented a change. I could smell water or dampness. It was clear as a bell, you know. No mistaking it unless you're hallucinating. I hurried on to the base of a sheer, smooth wall. It was wet with little rivulets of water, just little threads of water, running down along continuous paths like fibers in a loosely woven tapestry.

"I put my tongue against that wonderful rock and let the water wet it good. I pressed my whole face against it, and my hair. In fact, I pressed my whole body right tight against that cliff, clothes and all, letting my hair get wet, my face, everything. It felt so cool and good, delicious beyond delicious, exquisite beyond all exquisiteness. I just lay there, on that good rock, pressed there, feeling so good, for a long, long time.

"And I prayed. Oh, did I pray, thanking the Great Spirit and the Water Spirits and the Canyon Spirits, and the Mountain Spirits—all of them. I was there a long time, just praying and drinking, getting wet everywhere.

"After a while I let loose and looked around for a good place to lie down. I found a sandy shelf up a little way above the bottom, a place with several exits so I could climb upward fast if a flash flood came or if I heard any footsteps.

"You know, I thought I would go to sleep right away but it didn't happen. I was still too tense, too worked up. So I lay there and went over everything. As a matter of fact, I wanted to have it all clear in my mind because I needed to make judgments. In other words, my life depended on figuring out my next step.

"One thing was in my favor. They didn't know, they couldn't know, just when I had opened the trunk and jumped out of the car. It was so dark, the road was so bumpy and the car was banging over rocks and ruts. I had let the trunk lid up very gradually and the springs had kept it up by itself. They might have driven for miles without noticing. After all, it was so dark, no moon, and no city lights behind them. If they looked in the mirror or even turned their heads they would see only darkness anyway. So I felt that if luck was with me, they could have driven for many miles.

"Even if they had gone only a little way, they would never know how long I had been gone. Where would they look in all that vast dark desert?"

He stopped and chuckled to himself.

"I threw out their tire tools, their spare tire, and a briefcase—oh, yes, and their spare water can, a mile or two before I jumped out. I was hoping they would have a flat and get stuck out there too."

He laughed again, shaking a little.

"I gradually began to relax a little. I determined I was pretty safe, for a while at least, but just to make sure, I got up and crawled back down to where I could find a dead branch with leaves still on it. I used that to sweep away all of my tracks, around the boulders you see, and I made a fake trail off to one side.

"Just an extra precaution. That's the way I am."

He laughed again, to himself more than to any listener.

"Of course, it wasn't necessary. It started to rain up on the mountain later on and most of my tracks were washed out anyhow.

"I went back to my shelter and lay down again, chewing up a lot of mesquite seeds, worms and all. Full of worms, they were, but I figured it was that much more protein so I ate with gusto.

"Finally I fell asleep and that's how I passed the rest of that day."

He paused for a long while, looking thoughtfully at the now-cool rocks in the sweat lodge. Everybody noticed that he looked older all of a sudden, and very tired. He was thinner than any of them and very brown. His eagle nose was larger, and more noticeable because of his lack of flesh, and his prominent cheekbones stood out much like the rear backbones of a half-starved steer. But he was not weak, rather he was tough and wiry, hardened by exposure to the elements, his skin leathery.

George Elk-Hair noticed how his narrow eyes closed to mere slits as he sat there thinking. Finally he looked up, opened his eyes a notch wider, and went on with his story.

"I had a lot of time to think there in that canyon. A lot of time. I decided that it was a good time to fast and pray. Maybe I had been kidnapped for a deeper reason, not just so I could be killed or whatever they were going to do, but so that I could meet the Creator and learn something. So I took that attitude, keeping my mind on holy thoughts and asking for help. I didn't fast completely because I knew that if I got really weak there wouldn't be any people around with a good thick broth to bring me back, so I just ate little things that I could find, just enough seeds and beans and cactus buds to keep me going.

"I didn't kill anything either, not for a long time. I didn't feel like hunting because I was being hunted and I could really identify with all the living things, even the grasshoppers and moths, there in that desert. I just let them be and I believe they all helped me, each in their own way.

"After a while, when I felt safer, I started exploring that whole mountain area. I would get up just before daylight and hike around and then in the evenings too. During the heat of the day, I would find a big rock to crawl under, or way up on top, a tree or big bush to shade me. I spent many nights on top of the highest point, praying and watching the stars, and that's where I had my vision.

"That was a big mountain up there, very rough and craggy. I know I could recognize it still if ever I could get near it again."

He stopped talking for a time, scratching his cheek with the fingers of his left hand and then wiping moisture from above his mouth.

"I still remember what I said up there. I told the spirits my whole story. I said: My name is John Wildcat. Grandfather and Spirits of the Four Directions, you probably know how I came to be here better than I do, but I will explain it so you will know what I want.

"The FBI kidnapped me, or maybe the CIA too, I don't know.

The government didn't like what I was doing, they didn't like what I was saying to Indian people, what I was writing. They didn't like the documents I had found showing how they had been plotting to destroy all of our movements and cheat us out of our lands and resources.

"They have killed many of our people. I think they were going to kill me but I got away. I thank you for that.

"Why did I get away? Why, Grandfather, am I up here on this mountain, praying? I believe that there must be a reason for my life, why I am still alive. What is it? I am here to find that out.

"More than that, Grandfather, I am here to get your help. What am I to do? How can I help my people better? We are so few, so outnumbered, so oppressed. What can we do?

"I don't want anything for myself. I am glad to be alive. I want to see the people I love again, that's true. I can't help that. I'm human, that way. I don't want to hide out forever, that's true too.

"But I don't want any riches, or fame or that kind of thing.

"What can I do, Grandfather?"

He looked around at the circle of Indian faces, all intent upon him.

"You know, it's funny. When those FBI men, or whoever they were, grabbed me, I was getting a good salary, a college professor, I had a nice home and all of that. Now look at me. Now I am an exile, a hideaway, flat broke, no way to make a living; yet the truth is I am richer than ever because I have my life and I have seen great things.

"The Spirits came to me on that mountain. They tempted me too. Coyote asked if I wanted lots of gold or fame, or to win the love of any woman I wanted. He asked me if I wanted great power to rule events, to get whatever I desired.

"And I could see all of those things. A beautiful woman I once loved and couldn't have, all kinds of things like that."

John Wildcat laughed to himself and everybody smiled.

"Oh, she was very alluring, calling to me so sweetly. But I said no, I already was satisfied with what I had. Besides, no love is worthwhile unless it is genuine, that is to say, voluntary, given freely.

"So anyway, I turned all that down. Eagle came and asked if I wanted wisdom. I said yes if it could be used for the good of the people. The eagle said wisdom would not be wisdom if it could be used otherwise. He then flew around me and landed on my right shoulder, asking me if I was willing to suffer still more to get the wisdom. I said yes.

"Then Eagle said, 'Do not cry out. Do not be afraid. I am going to mark you for other eagles to see.' Then he flew up and came down just back of me, sort of hovering in the air, flapping his big wings so that I could feel the breeze he made. Then he took his talons and drew them down my back, making two sets of lines on my back, cutting the skin."

At this point, John turned and showed the others his back briefly. They all could clearly see the marks of Eagle, long scars running parallel to each other, three lines on each side.

"It really hurt me, but I held my mouth tight and then I must have fallen asleep. I dreamed after that and in my dream I saw a cave on the side of the mountain and I went inside. A fire was burning and old Indians took me in and made me welcome. They said, 'Here in this cave, hidden now for more than four hundred years, are the great books of the Indian race. Here in this cave, sealed off from the white invaders, is the library of that great Nezahualcoyotl of Texcoco, a library so vast that it includes books from both the North and the South, both the East and the West, books of all directions, and from the Center, which is *Anahuac*.'

"The old Indians, who were holy men or priests, showed me how to read the books. They were in many languages but all had been translated also into the Mexican language so I could read them all once I learned that tongue, which I did. All this happened in my dream.

"I woke up days later it seems and immediately I went searching for that cave. Since I had already been there in my dream it was easy to find, although no one else could have spotted it, it was hidden so well.

"I lived in that cave for a long time, day after day, week after week, losing track of time. I studied those old books and lived off of pine nuts and dried beans and dried corn I found there. It was waiting for me, it seems.

"Someday I will tell you what was in those books, but it would make such a long story. Now I will just say that they were full of wonderful things that, if known, would make every Indian so proud and change the whole history of the world.

"It makes me so happy to sit here and know that those books which the white people thought they had destroyed still exist, there in that mountain, and that no white people will ever own them.

"There were books about astronomy, about all of the happenings in the sky for thousands of years. There were books about great explorations by Indians and about how Indian colonies went off to the Pacific and over to North Africa where they became known as Egyptians or, I should say, intermarried with the Egyptians and taught them about mummification, astronomy, and pyramids.

"Oh, I tell you! You can be so proud of what our books have in them. The history of five thousand years or more."

He stopped and let out a deep sigh. Then, smiling, he said:

"As you can see, it is hard for me to stop but I must not say too much about the books. That will all come out someday, but for the Indians only. I say that because I was given instructions that those books can be printed only in Indian languages, never in European tongues. And no white man can ever go into that cave, that is an absolute rule!

"Anyway, I had a good time as you can see. For months I didn't notice the passage of time. I was in another world. But finally I knew I would have to leave, in order to find a way to get the knowledge in those books out to Indian people. I knew that would be a big job, keeping it all a secret from the whites.

"Hah, if they found out they would rush in and build a mu-

seum and bring in tourists and white professors would get everything. Indian people would be the last in line to learn about their
own history, and most likely the white governments would suppress it all; or the Christian churches and the Mormons.

"I also started getting lonely! Suddenly I knew I had to leave,
but in what direction should I go? I had to stay hidden. I didn't
want to die, can't you see, with all of this knowledge in my head,
knowledge worth so much to our people.

"If you can imagine it, knowledge enough in those books to
overthrow the entire white version of history!

"Anyhow, I knew I had to stay hidden, I couldn't be captured
by the government, to die or sit around and rot in some prison.
With that frame of mind I packed up as much food as I could
carry and left the cave, closing it up as it was before.

"I filled a skin bag with water and set out to the south, traveling by night always. My body was lean, free of all excess flesh, so I
could travel great distances, eating a little wet posole every so
often and living off the land. Several places I find magueyes ready
for cooking, so I made pits and baked them under the ground. At
those times I just lay around for a day or two, eating as much of
the sweet root as I wanted. Then too I found seeds of many kinds
and cactus buds. I also ate grasshoppers when I could catch them,
apologizing for hurting them.

"In that way I reached the Rio Grande, crossing its broad
sandy expanse during the night. Along one side I found a pool of
tepid water and, after drinking, I took a bath, my first in many,
many months.

"I had hoped to find some Indians in Mexico but the desert
there was all empty of people. As the days passed, I became more
and more desperate, cutting across country in a southeasterly
direction. My feet were tough by then, hard as nails on the
bottom, and my skin had turned to leather but I began growing
weaker. I couldn't find any water and that broad desert was almost empty of life. When I saw a grasshopper I would try to sneak
up on it but if it jumped I was the loser. I didn't have the strength
to chase it.

"I saw a kangaroo rat once and that little creature almost killed me, but then it saved me too. I started running after it, in sheer desperation, like a starving lion chasing a fleet-footed deer. I almost caught it at first but it kept zigging and zagging, just beyond my reach. I chased it for a long ways, losing my sense of direction, losing my mind really. Finally I just reeled around and around, sick all over, shaking, losing my vision.

"I thought I was dead I guess, because I heard singing, many voices singing. It was dark all around, but the moon was out and I could see little bumps on the ground, like round rocks, all about the same shape, and the songs were coming from them. I just lay there in a trance looking and listening, my mouth so dry I couldn't hardly move it.

"As my senses slowly crept back into awareness I felt something right under my left arm. I knew a song was coming from there, muffled by my arm. I looked closely and saw it was peyote plant, singing to me to eat it. So I took out my knife and, praying to Father Peyote in thanks, I cut off a little and started chewing it.

"In that way, don't you see, that little kangaroo rat saved my life. So many wonders in this, our world of magic! That little creature took me right to where the peyote was. It knew that I could be saved that way.

"So it is that the Creator cares for us!

"I stayed in that area for many days and nights, eating peyote and praying. My plan had been to go to the Kickapoo people who live in Caohuila and I prayed now to be guided to them.

"And that was what happened! A few days to the east I met a Mexican family, really they were Julime Indians, out gathering peyote. I really scared them at first! I looked so terrible! And I didn't know what language I was even talking, just rambling in Creek, English, Mexican, or Spanish, I don't know which. Finally, though, they saw my peyote strung around my neck, and gave me some water to drink, water mixed with peyote juice, like in a tea.

"After calming down I was able to explain to them that I

wanted to go see the Kickapoos. They were wonderful people, very, very poor you know, but good-hearted. After a few days they guided me to a highway and showed me how to go to the Kickapoo settlement, going right along with me to see that I got there safely.

"The Kickapoo elders were glad to hear my story. I stayed with them until they were ready to go up to Oklahoma to visit their relatives. Then they took me along, smuggling me across the border without the government knowing about it.

"You know the rest of the story. I have been meeting in peyote lodges, in sweat ceremonies, in long houses, with medicine people and elders all over this part of the country. I have been hiding by day and traveling by night, seeking a way to safely do what I have to do.

"I have even gone back to Mexico several times, traveling in the desert to see little groups of Indians here and there, and down to Texcoco to see where that great library once was.

"It has been hard. I have been lost many times, but each one could make a separate story. My life seems to hang by a thread but the Creator keeps that thread so strong that it does not break."

George Elk-Hair took advantage of a pause to ask: "Don't you feel the need of a rest? You have been hiding so long. You need to put flesh back on your bones, and see your loved ones. Why don't you stay here with us for a time and we will find a way to let your relations know you are still alive."

Wildcat narrowed his eyes and looked far-off, toward the south.

"Ah yes, that would be so very good. But there is one thing I didn't tell you."

Wildcat paused and breathed heavily for a few moments.

"The cave is there, far to the south, and in that place are things so wonderful as to be beyond all understanding. My life, the thread of my life, now runs only in that direction, all else is gone.

"The government thinks that I am safely dead. I dare not do

anything to make a connection with the John Wildcat they were trying to kill.

"I cry sometimes thinking of my woman, my children. I cry for them, and for my longing too, but . . .

"There is the one thing I didn't tell you . . . I already have been back there, trying to find that cave and . . . somehow I got turned around—I'm not sure, but the mountain wasn't there, the mountain I was on, I mean . . . The canyon, I couldn't find the canyon either . . . I know it's there, in the desert, somewhere. I know I will find it . . . and yet it's like a dream, the whole thing is like a dream in which I was dreaming other dreams."

Then he reached around with his hands and gently felt the scars on his own back, gently tracing the sides of his fingers on the marks up and down as far as he could go. A smile creased his face and he said quietly to himself alone: "No, it was real. The cave is there still. It is waiting for us Indians . . . and I will find it again, rest on its cool earth floor once more."

D ARRYL BABE WILSON is a poet and storyteller who shares the traditional tales of his native people (his father is A-Juma-We; his mother, Atsuge-We) who lived along the banks of the Pit River country of northeastern California. He has published poems and short stories in *Talking Leaves*, *Looking Glass*, and *News from Native California* and has edited a book on contemporary Native Americans living in California. Wilson has collected several hundred traditional stories of California's native people, which he will publish in a forthcoming book. He has also coedited a book entitled *Dear Christopher: Letters of Contemporary Native Americans to Christopher Columbus*, which was published by the Native American Studies Department at the University of California, Riverside, in 1992. Wilson is currently completing a graduate degree in literature at the University of Arizona.

AKUN, JIKI WALU: GRANDFATHER MAGICIAN

Darryl Babe Wilson

This was long ago when magic was a large part of the everyday life of the native people of "California"—the "Sacramento" and "San Joaquin" valleys were vast freshwater lakes, and the earth was young and still growing.

It had been dripping all day. One of those rainy days when the sky is gray-black and the drops are constant. Everything gets soggy. Inside the round house it was humid and smoky and in need of fresh air. There was a leak in the edge of the roof where the clay was not mixed properly with ashes and wild rye. The earth oozed to the touch where the water dripped down the support timber. The old chiefs argued when the day would be, but spring would arrive on time as it always did.

Everybody wanted to go outside, but it was dismal. As gloomy as it was boring inside—as dreary as their spirits. Earlier *Alliste* and *Tohe* had gathered wood for Grandmother's fire, and now they were just in the way. No matter where they turned, they either bumped somebody or knocked something over. They either stepped on the fingers of the baby playing on the dirt floor or mashed the tail of the little black dog. Or, worse, they stumbled over something precious that belonged to either *Amun* (Grandmother) or *Akun* (Grandfather). They were constantly scolded or so it seemed.

An idea!

They sloshed out of the round house through the rain-sloppy "crawl hole" and dashed into the forest, black dog right beside them. Their plan was to dig up one of the *mis-welo* (yew wood) shafts that *Akun* had readied. They had helped him char the ends of it and bury it two years ago. The *mis-welo* must be seasoned now. If so, they would now have something constructive and inventive to do, make a bow. They would not be in the way and *Akun* would be proud. Also, they would show the people that they were quickly growing into manhood as warriors!

The rain glistened off of their bodies and their soaked buckskin dangled here and there, annoying them both. Water trickled from their wet hair into their eyes and the salt of their sweat made its way into their mouths. They had their digging sticks and were trying to remember exactly where it was that they and *Akun* had buried the shaft. The old one taught them to heap the earth just a little and sprinkle it with leaves and debris so when it settled and the flowers and grasses of spring arrived, there would be no trace of the ceremony.

"When the sun was there, the tree was here," *Alliste*, the oldest by a whole year, said.

"But that was in the fall," *Tohe* answered. "The sun has moved to the south and your directions are not right."

"The tree hasn't moved, only the sun has," responded his brother. "Now sun has moved an arm's length to the south. So *mis-welo* must be . . . right . . . here!"

Tohe giggled a mischievous giggle. *Alliste* looked at him wondering with a smile playing in his eyes and at the corners of his mouth preparing for mirth. "I love *Akun*," *Tohe* said, "but sometimes he smells like old piss." This set them both laughing and rolling in the soaked leaves. Soon they stopped giggling and continued upon their mission.

The constant drizzle caused them to agree quickly and dig as fast as they could. Their dog joined in the excitement. "It is buried the length of the arm from the fingers to the elbow," *Tohe* remembered out loud. Soon the charred end of the *mis-welo* was uncovered. They both grabbed and tugged until they freed it slowly from the earth. It was like pulling on something with roots. Soon it was extracted. The pelting rain flicked much of the mud off of it, and they found it was still straight and solid. They gave a whoop of victory and their dog responded with excited barks. He danced in a circle looking at the boys over his shoulder. Stopped. Shook smelly water from his coat in every direction, then danced again.

As they hurried to their home, heads bowed to the lashing rain, *Alliste* said, "You know, *Akun* told us to prepare and bury wood for two bows each season. Let's burn one tomorrow and place it where we put this one. He promised that he would make a magic bow. Brother, if we think and sing like *Akun*, and do all of the things that he has taught us, we can make a bow too!"

Wet black dog beat them home and was being scolded and ran outside by their mother as they slid under the frame and back into the familiar odors of the round house.

As on every rainy day, evening came quickly. Darkness raced across the land like a summer cloud blotting the sun. *Akun* was at his favorite spot between the crawl hole and the fire. This was the seat of honor because he got both fresh air and warmth.

The old one knew what the boys were doing and he smiled a crooked crease across his face. It distorted like it was made of rubber. It stretched. Then it moved back to its original formation, slowly. Then he was the wrinkled old Grandfather again.

"Here is the *mis-welo*, *Akun*, let's make a magic bow!" cried *Alliste*, waking the baby from slumber and making it squall. Mother scolded the boys (in the same tone she had just scolded the black dog) and tried to quiet the infant. The boys excitedly positioned themselves beside *Akun* waiting for instructions of how to begin. They were careful to not get between him and the fire.

Akun held the seasoned staff softly in his hands. Carefully he examined it. He turned it slowly, studying it for defects. Then he looked "through" it at one end to learn how straight it was. He turned it to examine the other end in the same manner, searching for ripples in the wood that might show signs of weakness where the wood grew too quickly or too slowly.

The old one held one end of the shaft out over the soft fire for a little while, then changed ends with it. He sang a little song. He sang and sang. Each time he changed songs, he changed the end of the *mis-welo* to the fire. All was quiet. All around them their world throbbed like a great heartbeat.

Akun took the staff and struck the center post three times. Three times the earth vibrated. He knew that there was approaching a need for three events of magic. How he knew this always made the boys wonder.

With an old and gnarled curling of his lips, *Akun* blew upon the entire length of the *mis-welo*. He rolled it in his hands and continued singing. Then, using his talon-like fingers, he split the hard wood into two pieces. Although the boys watched every movement of *Akun*, listened intently to his song, and studied his every breath, they could not understand how it was that he could split seasoned yew wood with his old and worn fingernails, his fingers more like broken claws of an eagle.

They were astonished when he threw one half of the shaft into the fire. There was a defect in the wood that the young men could not see but that *Akun* "knew." The quiet of awe was broken when *Akun* began singing again. Once more he blew on the length of the split shaft. He sang again, and again he blew. Then he stood the split shaft beside the center post near the cradleboard and stuffed it between pelts of wolverine and coyote.

"*Lok-mi* (Leave it until first light)," he said softly with a throwing of his whiskered chin to the east. In his quiet the boys knew that they were dismissed and they knew that they could not touch the *mis-welo* until first light tomorrow. They wondered how long it would be before the old one worked the bow with them.

A coyote called across the mountain valley. An old and hoarse owl hooted from nearby shadows. The incessant rain slowed to a drop, drop. Then it ceased. Clouds parted. Stars danced, mosquitoes sang, and wind moved softly, wailing across the tops of the wet fields of grass and flowers. Fire whispered. Infants breathed. Softness dwelled within the rafters of the round house. Silently, in the warm darkness, little bugs and spiders moved throughout the home. Quiet reigned as the river sang and raced toward the distant ocean. *Tohe* said, in the velvet gloom, "That was a powerful song *Akun* sang." *Tohe* wrestled with sleep. *Alliste* rested.

Alliste dreamed of a powerful bow with arrows of the most beautiful balance, decorated with falcon feathers and the red-winged blackbird. He dreamed that he sang a song that instructed him how to chip a perfect arrowhead from a sliver of the distant glass mountain. As he moved slowly through his dream, he watched the willow sprout that was to be the shaft of the arrow. It grew straight up, powerfully, came from the earth. In his dream, Grandfather had made the bow and the arrow and as the old one tested the tautness of the string, *Alliste* learned the music coming from the bow. The rhythm made his spirit flutter. He moved through the stars softly like a salamander swimming cautiously to the surface of the water for a breath of air. He continued to dance, to move through the stars, and to dream in all of the colors of the world.

Tohe slept uneasily. He was worried. Since *Alliste* was the oldest by one whole year, he would get to be the first to test the bow. *Tohe* would not be allowed to touch either the bow or the arrows. When his uneasy sleep was over, he dreamed.

Tohe entered a rising sun, walking hesitantly as a fawn in a strange forest. Softly he felt the shining path with his bare feet. As he penetrated the sun's brightness he discovered a clean and fresh land beyond, just like after a rain when the sun is brighter than at any other time. It was peaceful, silent. The beauty rested upon his tongue like a butterfly. All around birds sang and a breeze whispered to the grass that lined the path. There was a buzzing of insects and perfume delight from the flowers. Oh, the color of the flowers! He studied the land of his dream. He breathed deeply of the wonder. He tasted the leaves of the trees and the petals of the flowers. Sweet, a rare sweetness.

Music came from an earth mound upon the path. *Tohe* peered down the smoke hole and saw a little fire in the darkness. There was *Akun* rubbing bear fat on an arrow shaft and talking with an invisible being. *Tohe* seemed to not be a part of the scene, just an observer. Suddenly their eyes met and *Tohe* was, magically, standing in front of *Akun* inside the sweat house. *Akun* spoke.

"Little one, you must not be troubled in your sleeping. Elder brother will not leave you out of *our* quest . . . Think always the good thoughts."

Tohe reached out and touched the earth. His dream had vanished. There was no sweat lodge with *Akun* inside singing. There was only his little pile of *teh-wali* (buckskin) to sleep on. He knew he dreamed but he remembered *Akun's* advice. He thought the good thoughts and slept to dream again.

The excitement of the day caused the boys to sleep beyond *loq-mi*. Sun was looking over the edge of the earth with a silver halo showering the universe and golden arrows spearing the darkness of the canyons. They looked out of the lodge. They stretched and turned back into the round house. *Akun* was not there. Fire smoldered. There were few sounds in the home. They wondered where *Akun* was.

"There! On the center post beside the cradleboard! Look!" *Alliste* shouted. As they both focused upon the objects in disbelief, they forgot to breathe—or think. With a soft glow emitting from them, the magic bow and the magic arrow hung there on a peg secured by a twine made from the threads of fern. Falcon feathers were bound to the arrow shaft with sinew and *Akun's* special glue made from pitch, salmon skin, and deer hooves melted together over a slow fire. The red feathers of the red-winged blackbird adorned the shaft. The scalp of a red-headed woodpecker was wrapped tightly just near the obsidian tip. It shimmered!

In their moments of disbelief there filtered a wonder. *Akun* said to wait for *loq-mi*. They had slept beyond first light and to the time when sun looked over the earth. *Akun* must have made the bow in the moments that they slept just before dawn—they slumbered through the one ceremony and accomplishment that they ached to know how to perform!

The bow was short and stout. On the back of it, the old one had fashioned the skin of a rattlesnake. The inside was painted in the diamond pattern—his special design. Rawhide was wrapped around the grip. On each end of the bow was a feather from the tail of the golden eagle. The string was made from the back strap sinew of a very old buck. It was strong and it too was wrapped with the *Akun*'s glue. It would never break and it would launch the arrow with rigid authority.

There was the bow and the arrow. Could they touch it? Where was *Akun*? Could they just take the bow and arrow outside and test them? What would *Akun* say? Sure, it's okay. Everybody is busy, they will never notice . . . Only if *Akun* returned would he know . . . One little touch would not hurt anything. Sure. One little test . . . Just one.

With excitement and hesitation meeting upon a huge battle-field within his being, *Alliste* took the glowing bow from the peg, softly touched the taut string, listened to the music and felt the vibrations all around him. It brought a beautiful hum to his world. He took the bow and arrow outside. *Akun* was not in sight. They thought that he must be down at the river washing.

Just at the entrance of the round house, *Alliste* positioned the arrow neck on the still-vibrating string—just for fun. He pulled on the arrow and the string simultaneously—just testing its strength. He aimed the arrow toward the huge, endless sky—just in case. He pulled the string with a constant pressure as Grandfather had taught him. The bow bent, obeying his command. It quivered a little as *Alliste*'s strength was at its peak.

His fingers slipped!

The arrow darted skyward!

It traveled at a constant, flashing speed. Ever upward. It was frightening. The boys watched the red streak that the bright feathers and the glistening shaft left in its wake. Ever upward. They waited for the arrow to peak. Ever upward. It had not slowed down at all. The arrow pierced the silver-blue of early morning sky and kept climbing!

The arrow disappeared. The boys quickly oriented the arrow with the earth. They used the curve in the saddle of the mountain and four tall trees as points of reference. Straight above the second tree from the left for the distance of an arrow shaft held at arm's length was where the arrow vanished. Again the boys marked the spot. Again they measured it. For now they must tell *Akun* what had happened. *Tohe* observed, "That is very near where the North Star lives."

In their being they knew they were very wrong in taking the bow and arrow without asking permission from *Akun*. They knew also that they should not have tested it without his instruction. And they knew that under no circumstances should they have released the arrow! Yes, the old one would be very angry with them!

Black dog barked as *Akun* hobbled from the direction of the river. He noticed the boys standing uneasily in front of the round house. He shuffled slowly. When he reached the boys he looked into their eyes and he reached a gnarled hand out. *Alliste* placed the still-glowing and vibrating bow into it. *Akun* turned and entered the round house without a word. The atmosphere was brittle and fragile—like floating sheets of thin ice on a lake in the early spring.

After a night of broken sleep and scattered dreams, the boys slowly awakened. Their disturbed night was because *Akun* had not spoken to them and they could not locate the arrow, no matter how hard or how long they searched. Also, their mother and father had scolded them for being irresponsible. They stepped out into the early light. Dawn had just begun to tickle the eastern sky. It was silver and there was a tinge of pink in it.

There was one small cloud brighter than the other pink and it was brightly smiling. The early air was damp and it smelled like the moments just after a fresh rain. Still, their spirits were down.

Their father was in the deep shadows rustling and shuffling the oak leaves. They could see a deer hanging there, an oak limb spreading its hind legs so their father could skin it with the precision that he was so proud of. Earlier, the entrails were taken out in the forest to feed nature. Only the heart, liver, kidneys, and scrotum were saved—the most tasty of all the parts of *qessa-wi* (buck). It was early spring. If it was winter, Father would have saved the contents of the stomach to use as a salad for supplying the family with vitamins.

As they approached, their father was removing the skin from the neck with short, artistic strokes of the freshly flaked obsidian. Around the neck as a protective device the skin is thick and tenaciously attached to the meat. It cannot be peeled from the carcass and must be carefully cut free. The skin was a pile of white mingled with blood and gray on the ground. Later they would find four holes in the hide showing where the animal was shot twice—one time near the heart and another in the neck. Father had pushed the arrows on through the animal in order not to damage the obsidian tips.

Silently they watched the precision with which their father labored, knowing that they were still being punished for violating the trust of *Akun*. Any comment from them now would be met with chilly silence. And they would hurt all the more.

Akun slowly climbed up the ladder and emerged from his earth dwelling through the smoke hole in the roof. He reached out and wiggled through the hole like an awkward crayfish. Once free and on top of the dwelling, he tried to stretch his old muscles and managed to pop some weary ligaments. Then, with old bones that seemed to rattle, he shuffled down the roof and toward the boys. They deliberately watched their father "work" the *qessa-wi* that he had taken just before first light down by the edge of the placid lake. They avoided all eye contact with everybody. They were nervous. Deep inside they were crying. If they received a good, hard talking to, they deserved it! And they were prepared. But they no longer deserved to be ignored.

After clearing his throat several times and spitting a glob of something yellow that, almost alive, curled slowly in the dust, *Akun* said, "Children, I know that you could not find the arrow. When I was sleeping, I saw it in my dreams. It is lodged somewhere in the North Star. It may stay there for all seasons.

"When I was young, it is said by my mother that I did many things. The people worried if I would grow up—if I was ever going to be responsible. Often those things that I did were less than a dog would do and sometimes I was proud of being bad. My grandmother said that it took me a long time to grow up. But she always encouraged me to try again. Sometimes I am not grown up yet. When I see a pretty girl, I wish that I was young again, and careless." *Akun* smiled that rubbery twisting of his face. The boys relaxed.

"Now you must hurry. You, *Alliste*, go to the grove of yellow pines and capture a red-headed woodpecker. *Tohe*, go to the marsh and catch a red-winged blackbird. I will go to the willows to find a shaft. *Tohe*, you will have a chance to shoot the bow also."

A grinding stone weight was cast from their spirits as the boys scurried to fulfill their assignments. "When you finish, go to your mother and eat, you will need food in you," *Akun* hollered after the fleeing boys.

Akun was no longer angry at them! He had located the arrow, and when they returned from the task, Mother would have fresh-cooked meat and bread for them. It was a most beautiful sunrise —the one across their hearts that shined into their spirits and smiled.

Alliste took two cone-shaped "cages" about a foot long. These he fastened over different nesting holes of the woodpecker. Father had shown him how to do this. Since the woodpecker cannot back up, when it is committed to exit its home, it must continue out—there was no turning back. In this way the bird catches itself in the small cage. It is then sacrificed for the red feathers on its crown. Before noon he had taken one bird. This he delivered to *Akun*. *Alliste* lazed around the camp and in a daydream a beautiful girl with a turquoise necklace danced across his private world.

The job for *Tohe* was much more difficult. He had to make a series of foot snares out of the fiber from strips of bear grass, making certain that the knot would "slip." He had to take the pine dugout canoe and carefully place the snares near the nests of the blackbirds among the tules in the marsh. This is a solitary job, but one that was most rewarding, for the red feathers of the blackbird are highly prized for decoration and "power." At times it was difficult maneuvering through the shallow waters and the thick water grass with his pine canoe.

It was dark when he returned, but *Tohe* had a single blackbird with vermilion feathers on its wings. His foot snares did not work as he had hoped so he shot the bird with a blunt arrow. It took fifteen shots and fifteen lost shafts, but he had accomplished the mission. *Akun* was at the little fire singing and holding a new and magical arrow shaft over the smoking fire in order to season it quickly and make it light. After eating, *Tohe* joined *Alliste*. They walked in the evening, studying the North Star. Yes! There it is, flickering red from the North Star—the feathers of the magic arrow!

They hurried back to the lodge. There was a higher than normal pitch in the feminine voice coming from their home. Peering in, they found *Ta-teece* scurrying around the fire helping their mother clean the cooking area and the cooking baskets. They were chatting about everything. *Ta-teece*, the young woman from the forks of the rivers! The daughter of Black Bull Elk. *Tohe* elbowed *Alliste*. *Alliste*, in the soft evening, blushed. He was the oldest and *Ta-teece* was older than *Tohe*, so that meant that she was not there just to help their mother, neither did she come to visit *Tohe* . . .

Silently they slipped into the shadows of darkness and hurried to the fire where *Akun* was at war with angry mosquitoes. The kind that you swat and they return instantly. They get into your eyes and up your nose. And every bite is a sting. When they get into your ears they scream. Yes, there was a battle going on. It was one of sheer survival. The boys ran and collected some green cedar boughs to make smoke to drive the pests away.

"Black Bull Elk's daughter is with your mother. Go. They may need wood or water. Don't spend time. They may be speaking about something important," *Akun* said after a few moments of rubbing ashes upon the arrow shaft, swinging at the lingering mosquitoes and not looking at them.

"I'll give you my obsidian knife if you will go and see by yourself—the red one with a streaking cloud in its heart," *Alliste* bargained with *Tohe*.

"No, I think *Akun* wants you to go to help them more than me," *Tohe* countered. "Besides, you wouldn't let me touch the bow or the arrow that was made for both of us. I already have a good knife."

They entered the lodge. After an awkward silence, *Alliste*, looking only at his mother, asked if she needed help. The daughter of Black Bull Elk was silent. She looked softly upon *Alliste*. Mother, with a quick look in their direction, waved them away with her hand. They quickly left the lodge but at the moment of their departure they heard the giggles of both *Ta-teece* and their mother. *Alliste* knew that both he and *Ta-teece* were growing up. Again he blushed as the evening star watched over the evening and looked into a vastness that has neither beginning nor ending.

Her skin was honey-red. Soft, no blemishes. No tattoos. Her ears were not pierced. The eyes were shiny black and flickered as the fire danced. Her teeth were small and like a softly curving string of pearls. Yes. She was a beautiful woman with long hair falling far below her shoulders. When she tossed the hair from her eyes, her action was one of pride, a pride filled with an unknown mystery. And, ho! that smile. *Ta-teece* was staying with his mother only for tonight. She wore a plain yet delicate doeskin dress, she was barefoot. Around her neck, a turquoise necklace. It was a long time before *Alliste* slept. Again and again he heard *Ta-*

teece giggle at the same moment he left the lodge with *Tohe*. She giggled again, just before a dream wrapped itself around his spirit.

The hard feeling that *Tohe* has had for *Alliste* because of the arrow incident quieted. He was again comfortable. *Akun* was making an arrow for him, and *Alliste* had already helped. Everything seemed to be working out just right. But what was he to do? Lose another arrow? He would ask his father in the morning. But Father would just say to ask *Akun*. So, he may as well just ask *Akun*. No, his father may have some special instructions. He would ask his father first. *Tohe* slept. He dreamed about the red arrow flickering in the night sky . . .

"Father, maybe today *Akun* will have an arrow made for me," *Tohe* softly said over the early morning fire. "Is there something that I should do? Is there something that you should tell me? Is there something that I should know about the magic bow and the magic arrow?"

His father looked at him for a lingering moment and said, "Yes, there are many things that you should know about magic. Also, you should seek the answers from the person who knows the answers to all of your questions. Sometimes the words of the mother and father are not strong enough, not proper. Sometimes the answers to your questions are deep within yourself. Sometimes you must search there, deep within yourself. *Akun* will answer all of your questions that you cannot find within yourself —even as he answered all of my questions long ago." *Tohe*'s father put his arms around his son and squeezed him like a big bear would a cub. Then, with a tear at the bottom of his powerful heart, he turned away and proceeded to wrap a crack in the long salmon spear handle with sinew and pitch from a bull pine. His little son was growing into a warrior.

Like a spotted deer entering the meadow in the bright light of a full moon, stepping softly and making not a sound, *Ta-teece* moved with the grace of a dream beside the rushing river. She was there in the silver of dawn to bathe. She had already helped with the morning fire and was dismissed for a short time by *Alliste*'s mother.

Alliste was also at the river refreshing himself from the drowsiness of sleep. He saw her moving in the early light and went, hesitantly, in her direction. He was hoping that he could meet her but make it look like an accident. His carelessness brought on by a wave of passionate pretending made him step on a dry branch that cracked in the early morning like two rocks striking each other! *Ta-teece*, startled, looked up into the eyes of *Alliste*.

Silently and for a fleeing moment they searched the spirit of each other. *Ta-teece* saw all that she dreamed was there. *Alliste* melted before her eyes. She heard no sound as he, in his moment of near embarrassment, departed. She smiled and proceeded to the quiet waters of the river. *Alliste* would need her soon.

Black dog danced in a circle in the dust. *Tohe* was in the lodge of *Akun*. Black dog wanted to run and play and hunt. *Tohe* wanted to know exactly when *Akun* had completed the arrow. He wanted to study the "ways" of *Akun* so that he could accomplish, some day, the same feat of magic. He noticed that *Akun* always sang a beautiful song while he was making those things that he instilled with magic. He hummed the song of *Akun* wondering what the words meant. Maybe there aren't any words, just meaning, he thought.

The old hands wrapped and glued, weighed and balanced, studied and straightened. *Akun* polished the shiny shaft. As he did all of these things, he continued his little song. Soon the arrow was completed but for the decorations.

Akun took the scalp of the woodpecker and wrapped it snugly behind the obsidian tip. He then glued three vermillion feathers to the middle of the shaft, and laced three more among the three eagle feathers that made the glide of the arrow a balanced and delicate creation. Arrow was ready!

"*Akun*, Father told me to talk with you. I wonder what to do before I shoot the magic bow. Father said for me to search within myself and when I had a question that I could find no answer for, to ask you—that you always have all of the answers. So, what do I do before I shoot the magic bow?"

With the slow movements of an aged porcupine, *Akun* turned

his head and, with cloudy eyes looking deep into a life experience that spanned nine of *Tohe's*, said, "It may be that you must find your answer in a dream."

Wandering, *Tohe* walked through the forest. He went to the placid places of the river and to the foaming ripples. He stopped at the bubbling spring and "talked" with the blue juniper growing there. He cast a "thought" to the four eagles circling in a mating dance high overhead. He cast a "thought" to the buzzard eating carrion in the golden field. In his state of wondering and searching within himself, *Tohe* decided, as had all of the warriors of his nation before him, to seek answers from the Great Power that can be contacted only after humbly climbing the highest mountain in the land, *Ako Yet*.

Amun (Grandmother) made him a little bundle of dried meat and smoked salmon. He took a beaver-skin water bag and long before sunrise set off to climb the mountain. He knew that he must stay there for one night, and might have to stay longer.

Breathing rapidly because of the thin air, *Tohe* reached the top of the mountain. He refreshed himself with some smoked salmon and a cool drink of spring water from the water bag. What a panorama. He could see in all directions for distances that he only dreamed of—like an eagle soaring high above the forest, he looked down upon all of the world—and knew all things. Resting, he dreamed.

When he awoke, the sun seemed to be just an arm's length away, and it appeared to be huge and almost menacing as it sat on the distant mountain range before it fell off of the earth and darkness was all around.

Tohe studied the universe. Sky was milk white, sparkling with red, blue, green, and lavender. There was the North Star, bold among all of the whiteness. Over there, the dancing one that glinted the colors of the rainbow, the magical power of Black Bull Elk's tribe. The "Milky Way" was barely discernible from all of the white of all of the millions of stars. Far below, a vastness of silence. The call of the coyote could not reach the mountaintop. It was pure. Solitude.

Tohe studied the stars entering their individual worlds. His body was only a place for his spirit to return to after its journey through a thousand eternities. He wondered. He slept. He dreamed dreams that never were dreamed before . . . and never dreamed again.

When the first silver arrows of sun shot up over the eastern horizon, *Tohe* bid peace to the spirits that dwell within the universe and turned homeward. He ascended the mountain and made his way through the pines and firs and down into the dusty oak and brush country again. There! A rapid fluttering. A bird. A hummingbird. He cast a "dream" to the blur of green, blue, silver, and lavender hovering among the flowers. Bird vibrated, then darted up and away—as if it were going to the North Star.

The North Star!

Tohe remembered his dream. Instantly his wondering was answered. If brother could make an arrow stick in the North Star, maybe he could knock it loose, then they both would have a magic arrow. *Akun* would be happy and his mother and father would be proud! *Alliste* could give his arrow to Black Bull Elk and for sure Black Bull Elk and his tribe would not deny that *Alliste* and *Ta-teece* should live together when they grow up. Somehow little brother knew that they would.

Akun was waiting for *Tohe* and he explained the turning of the earth and the spinning of the universe. He also explained the necessity of knowing magic and of being a brother to magic as much as a brother to *Alliste*.

The fire in the early evening had turned to glowing coals with only wisps of smoke occasionally emanating from it. *Akun* said that it was time for *Tohe* to move into his adventure. After a little, vibrating song, they moved through the black shadows and into a wide field. Evening sky was white with stars. Silently they viewed the North Star. "There it is, *Akun*," *Alliste* whispered. "On the left and almost at the bottom of the star, the dancing arrow."

As if it were a dream, *Tohe* took the magic bow in his little hands. He knocked the magic arrow to the singing strands of braided sinew. The forest, the river, the moon, and his nation watched. He bent the bow with all of his strength. His muscles were taut and quivering, and, with a sight on the North Star, he released the arrow.

A flash of red in the night. A streak, arrow darted skyward. They waited . . . And they waited . . . Some of the people gave up and returned to their dwellings and to their dreams. Many waited . . .

Then!

Streaking toward earth they saw a single flash. One arrow had returned. It landed to the west, near the great salty waters. (In those early times they did not know it but that arrow would be the father and mother of all the redwoods of the western hemisphere.)

That night he did not think about *Ta-teece*. Instead, *Alliste* wondered about the arrow and wondered if it was his or *Tohe*'s. *Tohe* dreamed. In the slow replay of his dreams, he saw his arrow approach the North Star. He saw it land ever so close to *Alliste*'s. He saw the "earth" give way around the shaft of *Alliste*'s arrow, and he saw it turn and fall back to earth. Yes, that was *Alliste*'s arrow that fell. *Tohe*'s arrow remained thrust into the North Star.

Yet *Alliste* wondered . . .

(*Alliste*'s *arrow has just returned to earth and he wants to go find it. Akun has given his permission to both boys to travel—to enter a new era. Ta-teece is there with the family when Alliste departs. The young warriors set out on the adventure at breaking light!*)

Their fingers just touched in the velvet of darkness and they both tingled.

The little fire was flickering and dancing in the soot black of first light. *Akun* was humming his little song. Black dog lay in the dust, head on the ground between his front legs, looking up at the people with sad eyes. From a distant cave's mouth, a mountain lion screamed; a single ear of black dog twitched. The scream rolled across the flat waters and into the distance. The canoe was filled with provisions. *Amun* was giving last-minute instructions. Father and Mother worried of this adventure. Bats dipped and spun across the light of the fire—then were gone. Mosquitoes hovered just beyond the smoke. Moon looked with a full face upon the gathering.

With "traveler in peace" stained with blackberry juice upon their faces and each with a bow and ten arrows and a long spear, the boys set out as the waters rushed in and rolled and crashed. They jumped into the rocking canoe, corrected it, waved with a single backward glance, and entered another adventure. *Akun* continued singing. Black dog yet lay on the earth. With their paddles flicking in the early light, the boys, whispering upon the water with a wake behind their muscle-powered vessel, moved away from their homeland in search of the magic arrow.

"Do they have enough water?" *Amun* nervously asked *Akun*.

"This water is the length of the land, it is said. And beyond the distant mountains there is another water that goes around the world," *Akun* answered. *Amun* was just nervous and forgot that the entire lake was fresh water.

"It is said that at the other end of the great salt waters another people live there—different from us. Where they came from, nobody seems to know," *Akun* offered, talkative this day when his grandsons departed for a "traveling"—and he was too old to lead with them.

In the moments of silent departure, a little tear appeared and moved down a honey-soft cheek. It reached the curve of the face and dropped to earth as a little puddle that seeped into the dust. A delicate hand reached up and nervously twitched a chunk of turquoise on the little necklace. The earth trembled.

Some of their people returned to the mountain dwellings. The sun moved across the sky two times before the young men touched land. On the second morning they saw islands (Sutter Buttes) far to the south. Pointing the canoe to the west, they continued on their journey. *Akun* had told them that they would have to walk for two suns in order to reach the great salt waters once they had touched land beyond the great lake. *Amun* had made them a bundle of dried meat that should last them for over a week. They could gather pine nuts and berries and catch fish and frogs in the streams. And there must be the root called *apas*.

They slid the canoe out of the water and dragged it into the bushes and covered it with brush and leaves, then, with a limb of a small pine tree, erased their tracks and the skid marks of the canoe bottom. They turned their faces to the west and continued their quest.

That night, in a land that was almost strange to them, they slept in shifts beside a little fire at the mouth of a cave that had a little stream running through its center. The water was good. The quiet was good. They found new aromas and different tastes. And they wondered where the arrow lay. In the silence, *Alliste* could hear a song from the distant mountains. It came across the wide lake and moved his other thoughts aside. It was a sweet song.

They approached a soft valley. There in the heart, a mound with smoke coming from it. An earth lodge! Cautiously they moved toward it, alert. From a distance they hollered to the lodge. "Ho! Hooo!" A worn hand, much like *Akun*'s, reached out of the smoke hole. A gray head followed. Presently there was an old person standing on the lodge. A ragged headband of beaver skin held his white hair in place. A single feather hung askew at the back. Around his buzzardlike neck hung a jet-black chunk of obsidian suspended by a worn piece of buckskin. He was slender and he had wrinkles everywhere—even on his knees. The breechcloth was made of a soft grass woven with the designs of many nations. His eyes were silver-white and clouded, although he could see very well. Barefoot and confident, he waved to the young men to come and enter his lodge.

This new grandfather had no tribe or nation; he claimed them all as his very own. He was a spiritual person and lived upon this land for as long as he could remember. He spoke. *Tohe* and *Alliste* listened intently. Fire danced as the winds whispered through the gigantic forest that lived behind the earth lodge and reached the sea and dwelled the length of the land.

"As I was talking with the power that dances within the North Star only a short while ago, and all of the mountains and hills were bare and there were but few trees and brush along the coast of the great salt waters, a red streak emerged from the night sky and dove to earth. I hurried out to see what the shiny thing was that came from beyond the darkness. It landed just beyond that hill." The old person pointed a crooked finger to the west of his dwelling.

With fascination the boys listened as this new grandfather continued the story. "Quickly I went to that place where it landed. I could not find it—whatever it was. But I found, instead, a new tree growing. As I watched, it grew greater and greater. It dropped some seeds, and it grew greater and greater. Its seeds sprouted and they grew, as I watched, into huge trees of red bark and massive limbs. The base of the First Tree grew to be larger than this round house and it was so tall that it touched the sky. There was a power in the growing. All around the earth was popping and rocks were being moved as the forest grew. There was a strength growing there that came from the North Star.

"It was only two days and the forest had grown, so I have heard, the length of the land. The trees are all beautiful and strong and they have an amazing spirit. Somehow the trees have been made responsible. Many birds live in the branches and many animals find shelter in their shade. They are magic trees, a magic forest. They came from the North Star as I sat outside by my little fire not long ago. It is said that they drink from the clouds and feed water to the little flowers at their bases. They are most wonderful."

Their eyes met in the darkness. The young warriors were silent about the arrow and the North Star. If need be, *Akun* could travel the lake and tell the story to this old person who knows many things also. They left a "diamond" found singing in the heart of the powerful mountain, Akoo-Yet (Mt. Shasta), with the ancient and wise person. Their mission accomplished, and after examining some of the massive trees of the gigantic forest, the young men departed while the sun was overhead. They said farewell to their new grandfather and turned to the east, to their canoe, to their homeland.

Whispering across the waters in the early evening, they spotted a little fire. They pointed the pine dugout canoe toward it. They found *Akun* sleeping by the little fire, swatting, unconsciously, at hovering mosquitoes. *Tohe* stirred the fire and the sparks flew skyward and disappeared. *Alliste* looked for fresh food. He found some pine nuts and a little damp basket filled with *apas*, the roots that taste like sweet earth, the earth of their people! *Akun* slept, they feasted. Fatigued, they slept also.

At the break of day, *Akun* shook them awake. "Hurry! We must leave this water soon. We shall be two days returning home. Wake up!"

Like puppies that have been nuzzled awake by their mother in order for them to eat, *Tohe* and *Alliste* stretched and yawned, stretched and yawned, then opened their eyes. They were near their homeland! They had a wonderful story to tell all of the people! Yes, they must hurry!

"Leave the canoe in the shade. Turn it over. Cover it with brush and leaves. Throw water on the leaves so it won't dry and crack. We may need it soon," *Akun* commanded. The boys ran to the lake, splashed water all over themselves and, shining in the early light, carried out the orders of *Akun*. With a final splashing in the clear lake water, they grabbed their packs and their weapons. Following *Akun*, they turned toward the snow-capped mountains to the east and the comforting warmth of *Amun*'s fire in the round house.

As they approached their homeland and dropped from the rugged mountain forest onto a little grass valley, they encountered a person standing there. Black Bull Elk!

Akun greeted him in the usual manner, hand signals. The four of them walked to the shade of a juniper tree. *Alliste* wanted to see *Ta-teece* first, to tell her the story of the magic arrow and the gigantic forest, but here, in the path, they met her father. *Akun* and Black Bull Elk smoked in the cool shadows of the juniper.

Looking directly at *Alliste*, Black Bull Elk said, "You have been searching for the magic arrow. Have you found it?"

Alliste nervously hesitated, then said, "Yes, we found it."

"Show it to me," Black Bull Elk said with a tone just a little short of a command.

"You may see it but you will have to travel many days," *Alliste* said. "It has turned into a giant forest that grows the length of the land near the salt waters. A person may travel for an entire moon and never step out of its shadows. The trees drink from the clouds and at the bases they are larger than a round house. There is much life among the branches and upon the forest floor."

Black Bull Elk knew that *Ta-teece* was at the dwelling of *Alliste* and *Tohe*'s mother. Now he knew why she wished to remain there waiting for the number of suns counted upon the fingers of both hands.

(Akun *puts the magic bow away. In this manner he knows that it will encourage the boys to work together and try to make their own bow and their own arrows—it is time for them to grow in another dimension.*)

"Here is the song that you must sing while making your magic bow," *Amun* said to the boys as they sat at the fire tearing at the fresh bread that she had just made. "And don't eat like a wolf. It is not good for you. When you are old you will remember my words."

Hay konni-kiti hay we hay
hay konni-kiti hay,
Hay konni-kiti we hay
hay konni-kiti hay . . .

"This means 'Great Wonder, Great Power, we know that we are nothing, nothing, we know we are just nothing.' You must sing this song."

As they did for the first magic bow, they went to their secret place and dug up another *mis-welo*. They thought long and hard about the wood knowing that they would have to work it with all of their spiritual strength in order to create a bow and an arrow. Spring quickly turned to summer. They had the bow worked almost into form and had the arrow shaft prepared for the feathers and the obsidian tip.

The bow and arrow were complete, except for the power that only *Akun* could instill through spirit to the bow and arrow. The boys asked him for his help. *Akun* quickly agreed and made the backing for the bow but insisted that the boys make their own designs on either side of the grip. He twisted the sinew into bowstring and sang a song as he placed the feathers in a balanced position along the arrow shaft. Soon all was prepared.

Again, with their people watching, the boys proceeded into the open field, silver under the vibrating moon. Together they nock the arrow. Together they bend the beautiful bow. Together they aim at the North Star. Together they release the arrow with a singing of the sinew string and watch it streak skyward. They waited . . . and waited . . . and waited.

Then, like two bolts of lightning, the red arrows fell back to earth. One landed in the north and the other nearby. In the darkness they hurried toward the arrow that landed nearby. They stumbled and fell and stumbled again. Almost drunk with panic to locate the arrow, they rushed through darkness, skirted the river, crossed it as a shallow ripple, darted across an open field in the silver of the moon. They burst through the thicket near the big river into an opening.

"Look! Over there at the base of the hill! My arrow growing into a glowing pine tree!" *Tohe* shouted.

"And there where your tip pierced the earth, a spring. It is a little spring with a pine tree protecting it," said *Alliste*.

When they had returned to the people and the excitement

and wonder of the arrow the spring and the tree had abated some, the boys asked *Amun* about the event.

"It is said by the old ones that magic waters dwell within the earth, that these waters are held in beautiful baskets made by magic grandmothers long ago. It may be that the arrow struck such a basket. I will look in the morning. It is said that the water coming from the basket gives long life to everything—that some things never die when drinking or touching this water. I will see in the morning. I must see it to know if it is as my grandmother said it was to be long ago . . ." The boys knew that *Amun* would say no more about it until she was able to see the tree and the spring for herself. That night they slept, wondering about the arrow that landed far to the north.

"It is one of the baskets," *Amun* said to the boys in the early light. She had made her way there and in the quiet of the morning discovered for herself that precious place. "We must be careful. Keep this place a secret. If not, many people will come and they might ruin it," *Amun* cautioned the boys. They obeyed the warning of *Amun* as if it were a command.

On the fourth day after the arrows fell from the North Star, a stranger approached from the north. He was welcome and, after being fed, he talked with the gathered people in *Akun*'s earth lodge. He had a small pouch, which he produced. From the pouch, very deliberately, he took three vermilion feathers—those from the red patch on the shoulders of the blackbirds.

"My people live in a great circle around the lake that has an island floating within it. It is north of the great white mountain, the traveling of two days and two nights. The old ones say that long ago a huge fire was where the lake now sparkles and that the fire of rocks lasted for all seasons until a long and harsh winter filled it with cold water. The waters extinguished the flames. In the center of the floating island there was a fire that burned longer than all of the rest because the water could not get in there. For many seasons now the island has been sleeping. There has been no fire.

"As my people gathered around the shores of the lake to

watch a falling fire streak toward our lake, we wondered. In fear we wondered. The streak of fire landed on the floating island. We made plans to go to the island in the morning, then slept.

"We were greatly surprised. In the morning there was a huge tree standing in the middle of the island where there was nothing before, and we noticed that the forest all around our land began to grow larger. It was frightening, but some of us ventured to the island, looking for something that would explain the existence of the huge tree. At its base we found three feathers. We recognized them as being from the red wings of the blackbirds that grow in your valleys here. That is why I have come—to return the magic feathers to you and to tell you this story." He had a small pouch, which he produced. From the pouch, very deliberately, he took three vermilion feathers—those from the red patch on the shoulders of the blackbirds.

"As are the instructions of my chiefs, I must return quickly to our land. Who shall receive these feathers? Who shall my people recognize as a great warrior?"

After a long silence, *Tohe* and *Alliste* stepped forward and claimed the feathers from the stranger. "The feathers belong to us both," *Alliste* said. "They were fastened to an arrow that we used to knock another arrow from the North Star. When you arrive in your homeland, say to your people that the feathers have been returned to the proper people, but that we are not great warriors."

The stranger listened intently. After *Alliste* concluded, he said, "I shall tell my people that there will soon be a day when the owners of the magic red feathers are great warriors. I will tell them that in five snows that you will have that honor. Until then, as soon as you can, you must come to my land and see the tree that grows there on the island in the lake. It is so tall that it pierces the clouds and its spirit glows in the night."

As the stranger melted into the night, *Akun* began, "You have seen how it is that these young men learned that in working together they could accomplish something that many of us would not dare to do. To the west there is a huge forest made by one of their falling arrows. Here in our land there is a spring with a magic basket of water that is nestled beneath its roots. The water comes from the heart of a basket. To the north there is a huge tree growing upon a barren island. Those three shall produce entire forests, for I have seen it in my dream.

"Within five snows, *Alliste* shall be the son-in-law of Black Bull Elk and he shall be a great warrior. *Tohe* shall learn the medicine way and he shall be a great healer and a great dreamer. I grow old. *Amun* grows old. Soon we shall enter the spirit world. It is good for my heart to know that our young ones are so strong. We shall not perish as long as we have dreamers and warriors, for as long as we unite as a quiver of arrows and stay strong, for as long as our women bear children that are just and have a purpose to fulfill."

a NITA ENDREZZE, a Yaqui Indian who received her master's degree in creative writing from Eastern Washington University, is a professional storyteller, teacher, and writer living in Spokane, Washington. She has published her poetry and short stories in several collections, including one in French published by Rougerie. Her works have been published in *Poetry Northwest*, *Words in Blood*, *Anthology of 20th Century Native American Poetry*, *Poesie Presents*, and *Zyzzyva*. Endrezze's work has recently appeared in Joy Harjo's *Reinventing the Enemy's Language*, and her new book, *at the helm of twilight*, won the Weyerhauser/Bumbershoot Award for the best volume of poetry produced by a small press in the Pacific Northwest.

MARLENE'S ADVENTURES

Anita Endrezze

The morning of Marlene's fiftieth birthday was clear and warm. As she drove in her sister's driveway, she could see the chickens pecking around the damp earth by the water trough. Two horses were waiting, their reins tangled around the fence posts, their tails swishing away flies. The big horse, Old Mary, was half asleep, her eyes closed, one hind hoof lifted lazily. She was so round that she made the barn look small. Marlene was going to ride her today, come hell or high water.

Standing by the other horse, a young mare named Frenzy, was Marlene's niece, Tina. Tina was brushing Frenzy's back with long sure strokes, sending up puffs of dust.

Tina raised her hand in greeting as Marlene got out of the car. She looked around for her sister, Darlene.

"Where's your mom?" she asked.

Tina grimaced. "She came down with the flu last night. She's really sick. She's been throwing up all morning."

Marlene almost smiled. "So, the horseback ride is off?"

Tina laughed. "No such luck, Aunt Marlene! I'm going with you."

Marlene's fear of horses was well known in the family. In fact, that's why she was here today. She was going to force herself to get over this ridiculous fear. Horses were just animals, after all. Big animals, to be sure. With hooves and teeth and wild eyes. Well, maybe not Old Mary.

In a way, it was all her husband's fault. Just last week, Marlene had been grumbling about her upcoming birthday.

She warned her husband, "Don't you dare get me any of those supposedly funny presents. You know the ones, they're always in black. And no surprise parties. It's bad enough turning fifty without having to be happy about it in front of a bunch of snickering friends."

Sonny had just smiled. "Honey, we're all in the same boat." She had sniffed.

He got up out of his favorite chair and came over to her. "You know, hon, I don't think you look a day over . . . well, thirty!"

"Liar." She sat down, depressed. "If only I was thirty again . . ."

He put his hands on her shoulders. "What if you *were* thirty? Would you change your life?"

She thought about it. "Yeah, I would." Quickly she added, "Well, not the big things, like you and the kids. I'm happy about that."

"Well, what then? What would you do?"

She sighed. What had been missing from her life? She'd done everything the way it was supposed to be done. Marriage, kids, a job at the beauty parlor. Her life was pretty normal. And that was the problem. No adventure. No surprises. No stretching her limits.

"Okay," she said. "For one thing, I wouldn't be so afraid of everything. I'd be more adventuresome!"

Sonny lifted her head until she was staring directly into his eyes. "Dear, you can start doing all that right now!"

She shook her head. "No, I can't."

"Why not?"

She didn't know why not. It just didn't seem right. To change her life now? But, really, why not?

Sonny went over to the desk and came back with paper and pencil. *That* was so predictable, she thought wryly. He was a great one for making lists. But, after all, he was the owner of Sullivan's Staple Supply Senter (she hated the way he spelled center, but he couldn't be talked out of it, and after nineteen years of the business, she'd gotten kind of used to it. At least she had managed to talk him out of his original idea: Sonny Sullivan's Staple Supply and Stationery Senter.)

So he had handed the paper to her and suggested she make a list of some adventurous things she really wanted to do.

Number three on the list was to ride a horse.

Old Mary, the safest horse you could ever wish for. Darlene had promised Marlene that riding Old Mary would be like sitting in a rocking chair.

It had been forty years since Marlene had vaulted up into a saddle. Now she looked doubtfully at Old Mary's saddle. It was straddling the corral railing. She'd rather ride the fence, she thought, but she had to prove to herself that she could do it.

"Need a hand?" asked Tina. She pushed back her long hair, flipping it behind her ears.

"No, no," replied Marlene. "I think I remember how to do it."

She hoisted the saddle off the railing. Wow, it was heavy. Puffing a bit, she turned toward Old Mary. Now what? Could she lift the saddle up and get it in the right position on that broad back?

"Hold it, Aunt Marlene! You forgot the blanket!" Tina quickly put the saddle blanket on Old Mary's back, then, grabbing part of the saddle, she helped Marlene.

Old Mary hadn't moved an inch. She seemed to be sleeping. Frenzy, on the other hand, was aptly named. She was rolling her eyes and flicking her ears. She shifted her weight from one leg to the other impatiently.

"Want more help, Aunt?"

Marlene shook her head. While Tina started saddling up Frenzy, she eyed the stirrups. She always had to shorten them, she remembered. Now how the heck did you do that? She fumbled with the straps and managed to pull up the stirrups a few inches. She walked around to the other side, making a wide foray around the hind quarters.

Okay, Marlene was ready to get up on the saddle. But Marlene's head just reached the top of Old Mary's shoulder. She could no longer jump like a grasshopper.

Tina must've been watching because she was offering to help Marlene. Tina had linked her fingers together, forming her cupped hands into a mounting position. "Here," she said.

Marlene grabbed the saddle horn and put one foot into Tina's hands. She heaved herself up, raising the other leg to swing on to the saddle.

Two things happened. First, the power of Marlene's thrust sent Tina backward. Second, the saddle had not been cinched around Old Mary's big belly. It slipped toward Marlene. Marlene had one leg hooked over Old Mary's back and the other was dangling in the air. But only for a brief second. Then gravity took hold and Marlene ended up under Old Mary's belly. She stared up at the massive weight above her and tried to breathe. Old Mary didn't move.

"Oh migod!" Tina quickly pulled Marlene out from under the horse. "Are you okay?"

Marlene nodded. She didn't know what happened.

"Gosh, I guess you forgot the cinch," Tina pointed out.

Marlene slowly got up. She dusted herself off. By the time she had finished, Tina had saddled Old Mary again. Marlene sighed.

Tina untied Old Mary, who barely opened her eyes. She ambled along. Tina took her over to the wood pile. There was a chopping block. Marlene got the idea. She stepped on to it and pulled herself up.

Wow! Things looked different from this high up, thought

Marlene. It was kind of like riding in a big semi. Old Mary seemed to be breathing; otherwise there was little sign of life. Marlene was deeply grateful.

There was something wrong though. Her legs were all bunched up, like a jockey's. The stirrups would have to be lengthened. Marlene realized that she had set them in the position that a ten-year-old would've needed. It made her feel kind of sad that the years had gone by so quickly and that the little girl she had been was no more.

She called over to Tina for some help. Her niece fixed the stirrups and then nimbly vaulted up on Frenzy. She clucked her tongue. Frenzy pranced sideways in her eagerness.

"Hey!"

Marlene heard her sister's voice. She looked up at the door in her sister's trailer home. It was a white single wide. Darlene was peeking around the screen door. She was wearing her old bathrobe. Her hair was all tangled and her face looked pale. She waved and called out, "Have a nice ride!"

Marlene waved back. "We'll talk when we get back, if you feel up to it. So long!"

Marlene dug her heels in Old Mary's side and flicked the reins. "Giddyup!"

Nothing happened.

She clicked her tongue the way Tina had. Nothing happened. She rocked forward in her saddle. "C'mon, Old Mary. Get your rear in gear."

Old Mary's ears twitched. She heaved a great sigh. But she didn't budge.

"Tina! Tina! Where do I put the quarter?" joked Marlene. Tina turned around and rode back to Marlene. She reached down and pulled on Old Mary's reins. Old Mary pulled her head back, chewing on the bit, and then gave in. She plodded on, following Frenzy.

It was a lovely morning, thought Marlene. And riding a horse wasn't so bad. She was glad she had decided to do it. After all, who ever heard of an Indian who was afraid of a horse? Old Mary wasn't like her previous experiences with horses. Marlene remembered the little horse she had had when she was ten. One day it had chased her around the corral, teeth snapping, hind hooves flailing away as it bucked and twisted, its eyes showing more white than brown. Luckily, there was a big rock in the corral and Marlene had scrambled up. She had waited for an hour until her brother came to rescue her. Every time she had tried to get down, the horse would try to climb up the rock. It was a wild thing, a wiry mustang full of hate. She'd found out later that its previous owner had abused the mare. After one scary ride, when the horse had tried to run Marlene into barbwire fence, Marlene never rode her again. Or any other horse for that matter. Not even the plastic horses on the carousel.

Tina and Marlene chatted as they rode down a dusty road. The road was lined with pine and cottonwood. Sometimes, like now, Marlene realized how much she missed living in the country. Darlene had never moved off the reservation, which was strange in a way, since she was the "wild" one. She liked to party; in fact, Marlene was wondering if the flu was really a hangover. Marlene, on the other hand, was the quiet type. But she liked living in the city and, really, it was only a forty-five-minute drive to the res.

The wild roses had finished flowering. The rosehips were swollen and green. She liked them after the first frost, when they became sweeter and turned bright red. She had eaten handfuls of them as a child.

Old Mary rolled along, like a big ship at sea, thought Marlene. Tina turned her attention toward a small trail off the road. They followed it into a meadow and rode silently for a while.

Marlene thought about her husband. The reason they lived in town was because that's where the work was. Sonny's business had done well enough, even though Sonny griped about spending his whole life selling staples. He'd get in one of his moods.

"Marlene," he'd say gloomily, "my grandfather was a leader of the people. He outwitted soldiers and gold rushers. He fought to save my grandma when that farmer chased her off the tribe's old berry patch." Sonny would pause and sigh. "And look at me, I'm spending my life selling staples."

Or else he would mutter, "Hon, my mother almost died giving birth to me. She was in the hospital for two weeks. You'd think for all her trouble, she'd have a son that'd amount to more than a staple seller."

Or he would grumble, "My dad almost died in the war. Got a bullet that chipped his rib. Another inch and he would've died. But what have I done in my life? Sell staples."

Marlene, in an attempt to bolster his spirits, would add, "Well, Sonny, it's not just staples, you know. You are the main supplier of office supplies in the city."

But, if Sonny was in that mood, it wouldn't make a difference if he sold gold-plated staples. He just had to work his way out of his depression.

Marlene thought of him fondly. He really was a dear, she mused. She looked up at the sky. It was a perfect blue. Too bad he wasn't on the ride with her.

Suddenly Old Mary stopped. Marlene flicked the end of the reins on the horse's shoulder. Old Mary just reached down and yanked a mouthful of grass. Lunchtime and Old Mary wasn't going anywhere.

Tina turned back to see what was keeping Marlene. Sizing up the situation, she shrugged her shoulders and rode back toward her aunt.

"Time to go home," she said. "When Old Mary stops to eat, she won't go any farther. But if we head for home, you'd think she was a two-year-old again. She can really move."

Tina grabbed the reins and jerked Old Mary's head around. Now she was facing home and she knew it. She picked her head and almost trotted down the trail. Marlene bounced and bounced in the saddle. She was feeling a little sore. The saddle was hard, even if Marlene had a little too much padding of her own. She'd put on a bit of weight in the last few years.

With each jolt, Old Mary grunted. Her ears were pointed determinedly ahead. She walked clumsily, her nose quivering with the smell of home. She didn't pay much attention to the topography of the trail. Marlene felt bruises forming in embarrassing places.

"Whoa!" she urged, but the horse ignored her. Tina trotted past Marlene and placed Frenzy in front of Old Mary. Now the old horse was forced at a slower pace. Marlene called her thanks to Tina.

Tina was a confident, healthy young woman. At sixteen, she was more worldly than Marlene had been at twenty-six. Well, Marlene thought, kids grow up faster and faster with every new generation, it seemed. Tina had thick, shiny hair and a smooth golden complexion: gifts from her mother. She also had green eyes and freckles. Her father was the son of Norwegian immigrants. Tina rarely saw her father. After the divorce, he signed on fishing ships off the coast of Alaska. Darlene did her best to keep him there. So with an absent father, a broken family, a mother with "high spirits," you'd think Tina would've been a needy child. Or maybe one that turned to drugs or drinking. But Marlene considered Tina to be one of the most capable people she knew.

"How's your summer vacation going?" she asked Tina.

Tina turned around in her saddle and spoke over her shoulder, "Borrring!"

"Why?" asked Marlene, although she could figure out pretty well why a teenager would like more action than feeding the chickens.

"I never go anywhere. Maybe I could come and stay with you for a while?"

"Sure. That'd be great."

Marlene knew that life could be boring in the city too. But it was the change of scenery that made the difference, she decided. She leaned over and scratched Old Mary's neck. It must get boring for Old Mary fenced in the pasture all the time. Marlene contemplated her own life. She felt fenced in also. Old Mary: Old Marlene. Both plodding along life's roads.

Tina pulled up on the reins as they left the meadow trail and turned down the road toward home. Old Mary kept her head down, watching the dust puff up from her hooves. She seemed to have lost her excitement about going home.

Tina rode next to her aunt. "Mom told me about a list you made. Of adventures? And that riding a horse was one of them."

"Well, yeah." Marlene laughed. "I guess this isn't much of an adventure to you!"

"Well . . ." Tina laughed too.

"Now that I've done it," confessed Marlene, "it doesn't seem so wild after all to me either."

"So, what other adventures are on your list?"

"Oh." Marlene hesitated, she felt a little embarrassed. "I, um, well . . ."

"C'mon, what is it?"

"Okay. Number two on my list is to ask a man to dance. Since it's my birthday today, I'm going out dancing tonight."

Tina looked puzzled. "What's so wild about that?"

Marlene sighed. "When I was your age, girls just didn't ask a guy to dance! Never!"

"That's so weird." Tina thought for a second. "But what's Uncle Sonny going to think about your asking a man to dance?"

"Who do you think I'm asking to dance?" Marlene roared with laughter. Actually, it was a bit frustrating trying to be wild and crazy. She was beginning to feel like a fool.

Tina shook her head. "Well, if you ask me, your adventures are really tame. No offense intended."

"I think you're right." Marlene had to agree.

"What's number one on your list?"

"I don't think I should tell you!"

Tina grinned. "What is it? Something crazy like watching M*A*S*H instead of *Wheel of Fortune?* Or drinking lite beer instead of the regular stuff?"

"Go ahead and laugh." Marlene was feeling more and more desperate. She was just boring, she ought to face it. She couldn't be adventurous; it just wasn't in her. On the top of her list was a risqué adventure, she had thought. But now it seemed tame too.

Tina was laughing at her. Well, thought Marlene, I deserve it. But there was no way that Tina would provoke her into telling her last adventure. She kept her mouth shut until Tina gave up and they rode on, nearing the farm.

The number-one adventure was to make love in a strange place.

When Marlene had told her sister all about the list on the phone last week, there had been a puzzled silence. Then she had giggled. "What? Is there some part of the body you can do it with that I don't know about? Tell me!"

Marlene had been mortified and shocked. "Oh, no! I mean like making love in the kitchen or something like that."

Darlene had laughed at her too. "The kitchen! Is that as far as your imagination can go? Wait until you hear where I've done it!"

Marlene refused to listen. Now she wished she had. She had no idea how she could fulfill her last adventure so that it would be more exciting than this trail ride.

Tina and Marlene rode up the driveway. When they got to the barn, Tina swung down and offered to help her aunt dismount.

Marlene, still stung by the memory of Darlene's laughter, waved away Tina's help. She could get down by herself!

And she did. But when she tried to straighten her legs out, she found they were permanently bowed and her back was bent over. She groaned. The saddle had rubbed her in such a way that she didn't think she could do number one on the list. She walked like a bow-legged crab over to the fence and tied up the reins.

She looked Old Mary in the eye. "Thanks," she said, "for nothing."

Old Mary didn't even blink. She was still chewing the grass from the meadow. Her lips were smeared with a frothy green foam. Her muzzle was white-haired. She didn't give a damn about Marlene and her aches and pains.

As Marlene tried to stand up straighter, the door to the trailer burst open. It was Darlene and she looked alarmed.

"Oh, thank God you're back! Marlene! Sonny's been taken to the hospital! He had a heart attack!"

Marlene's own heart seemed to stop beating. Sonny! She stumbled toward her car.

"Can you drive all right?" called her sister. She eased over the porch handrail and vomited. Tina ran to help her mother.

Marlene turned the car around and began the drive back to the city. Afterward, she never remembered the drive. She could remember turning the key in the ignition at her sister's farm. Then she was suddenly turning the car off and parking in the hospital parking lot. Everything in between was a blank.

The nurses directed her toward the emergency room. There she was advised to sit and wait for the doctor.

They gave her a cup of coffee. She drank it but never tasted it. She sat and waited, her hands cold and with tears in her eyes. She should call the kids. No, better wait until she knew more. No sense that they worry too.

She tore the coffee cup into little pieces. Her life was falling apart. Without Sonny, there was no life. He had been her adventure for twenty-eight years.

A woman in a white coat entered the waiting room.

"Mrs. Sullivan? I'm Dr. Valencia."

They shook hands. Numb with dread, Marlene listened to the doctor. Sonny had collapsed at work. A customer had called 911 and, while waiting for the ambulance, had noticed that Sonny was clutching his chest and stomach. When they got Sonny in the ambulance, they began treating him for his heart after noticing rapid heartbeats and some missing beats as well. But when they got to the hospital, they had examined him and felt a mass in his upper stomach and intestinal area. Something was there. X rays had been ordered and were now being processed. They think that the mass was pushing against his lungs and, possibly, his heart. They would have to operate. It could be cancer.

Cancer.

Marlene heard the word.

Or it could be benign, the doctor pointed out.

Cancer.

Marlene started to shake.

The doctor called for a nurse to help. She had to see about the X rays. Mr. Sullivan was being prepped for surgery now. There were papers to fill out. And hours to wait.

And so Marlene waited. She prayed for Sonny. She wanted their life to be together. A long life. They had plans for retirement. Travel. Lazy days. Grandchildren. Powwows. Movies. She wanted everything to be normal. It was all her fault, wanting more from life than was good for her. She cried and paced the room.

She knew it wasn't really her fault, but she had to blame someone or something. She alternated between begging God to heal Sonny and wondering if it was God's fault. Or if there was a God. Her life hung on a series of meaningless ifs.

Finally, out of weariness more than sense, she began to calm down. The only "if" that mattered was that if Sonny got well, then living their lives as lovingly as possible would have to be the answer.

She felt a certain amount of peace with this, but it was also with a sense of resignation. It was all out of her hands. She couldn't influence the chain of events. She got up and began to call her kids.

Just as she had spoken with the last one (he was at college on the coast), the doctor came back.

"Mrs. Sullivan." The doctor was smiling tiredly. That was a good sign. Marlene breathed slowly.

"Mrs. Sullivan, your husband is going to be all right. There was a mass in there, but it was benign. We removed it and part of his stomach and intestine. We stapled the healthy parts together. We have to watch him for a few days in the hospital, but he should be able to go home at the end of the week. We're very happy that everything turned out so well. He'll need to have periodic checkups. We want to make sure that we rule out cancer in the future, but he really should be fine."

Marlene's legs buckled under her and she sat down heavily on the chair.

She thanked the doctor and then thought over everything the doctor had told her.

Staples!

Sonny had been stapled together!

Marlene didn't know whether to laugh or cry.

She did both.

S HERMAN ALEXIE is a Spokane and Coeur d'Alene Indian who grew up in his native Pacific Northwest. He lives on the Spokane Indian Reservation in northeastern Washington, where he writes poetry and fiction. He has published in several journals and magazines. His recent work, *The Business of Fancydancing*, "paints painfully honest visions over our beautiful and brutal lives," according to Paiute Indian writer Adrian Louis.

THE APPROXIMATE SIZE
OF MY FAVORITE TUMOR

Sherman Alexie

After the argument that I had lost but pretended to win, I stormed out of the HUD house, jumped into the car, and prepared to drive off in victory, which was also known as defeat. But I realized that I hadn't grabbed my keys. At that kind of moment, a person begins to realize how he can be fooled by his own games. And, at that kind of moment, a person begins to formulate a new game to compensate for the failure of the first.

"Honey, I'm home," I yelled as I walked back into the house.

My wife ignored me, gave me a momentary, stoic look that impressed me with its resemblance to generations of television Indians.

"Oh, what is that?" I asked. "Your Tonto face?"

She flipped me off, shook her head, and disappeared into the bedroom.

"Honey," I called after her. "Didn't you miss me? I've been gone so long and it's good to be back home. Where I belong."

I could hear dresser drawers open and close.

"And look at the kids," I said as I patted the heads of imagined children. "They've grown so much. And they have your eyes."

She walked out of the bedroom in her favorite ribbon shirt, hair wrapped in her best ties, and wearing a pair of come-here boots. You know the kind with the curled toe that looks like a finger gesturing *Come here, cowboy, come on over here.* But those boots weren't meant for me: I'm an Indian.

"Honey," I asked, "I just get back from the war and you're leaving already? No kiss for the returning hero?"

She pretended to ignore me, which I enjoyed. But then she pulled out her car keys, checked herself in the mirror, and headed for the door. I jumped in front of her, knowing she meant to begin her own war. That scared the shit out of me.

"Hey," I said, "I was just kidding, honey. I'm sorry. I didn't mean anything. I'll do whatever you want me to."

She pushed me aside, adjusted her dreams, pulled on her braids for a jumpstart, and walked out the door. I followed her and stood on the porch as she jumped into the car and started it up.

"I'm going dancing," she said, and drove off into the sunset, or at least she drove down the tribal highway toward the Powwow Tavern.

"But what am I going to feed the kids?" I asked, and walked back into the house to feed myself and my illusions.

After a dinner of macaroni and commodity cheese, I put on my best shirt, a new pair of blue jeans, and set out to hitchhike down the tribal highway. The sun had gone down already so I decided that I was riding off toward the great unknown, which was actually the same Powwow Tavern where my love had escaped to an hour earlier.

As I stood on the highway, with my big, brown, and beautiful thumb showing me the way, Simon pulled up in his pickup, stopped, opened the passenger door, and whooped.

"Shit," he yelled. "If it ain't little Jimmy One-Horse! Where you going, cousin, and how fast do you need to get there?"

I hesitated at the offer of a ride. Simon was world famous, at least famous on the Spokane Indian Reservation, for driving backward. He always obeyed posted speed limits, traffic signals and signs, even minute suggestions. But he drove in reverse, using the rearview mirror as his guide. But what could I do? I trusted the man and when you trust a man, you also have to trust his horse.

"I'm headed for the Powwow Tavern," I said, and climbed into Simon's rig. "And I need to be there before my wife finds herself a dance partner."

"Shit," Simon said. "Why didn't you say something sooner? We'll be there before she hears the first note of the first god-damned song."

Simon jammed the car into his only gear, reverse, and roared down the highway. I wanted to hang my head out the window like a dog, let my braids flap like a tongue in the wind, but good manners prevented me from taking the liberty. Still, it was so tempting. Always was.

"So, little Jimmy Sixteen and One-Half Horses," Simon asked me after a bit, "what did you do to make your wife take off this time?"

"Well," I said. "I told her the truth, Simon. I told her I got cancer everywhere inside me."

Simon slammed on the brakes and brought the pickup sliding to a quick but decidedly cinematic stop.

"That ain't nothing to joke about," he yelled.

"Ain't joking about the cancer," I said. "But I started joking about dying and that pissed her off."

"What'd you say?"

"Well, I told her the doctor showed me my X rays and my favorite tumor was just about the size of a baseball, shaped like one too. Even had stitch marks."

"You're full of shit."

"No, really. I told her to call me Babe Ruth. Or Roger Maris.

Maybe even Hank Aaron 'cause there must have been about 755 damn tumors inside me. Then I told her I was going to Coopertown and sit right down at the lobby of the Hall of Fame. Make myself a new exhibit, you know? Pin my X rays to my chest and point out the tumors. What a dedicated baseball fan! What a sacrifice for the national pastime!"

"You're an asshole, little Jimmy Zero-Horses."

"I know, I know," I said as Simon got the pickup rolling again, down the highway toward an uncertain future, which was, as usual, simply called the Powwow Tavern.

We rode the rest of way in silence. That is to say that neither of us had anything at all to say. But I could hear Simon breathing and I'm sure he could hear me too. And once he coughed.

"There you go, cousin," he said finally as he stopped his pickup in front of the Powwow Tavern. "I hope it all works out, you know?"

I shook his hand, offered him a few exaggerated gifts, made a couple of promises that he knew were just promises, and waved wildly as he drove off, backward, and away from the rest of my life. Then I walked into the tavern, shook my body like a dog shaking off water. I've always wanted to walk into a bar that way.

"Where the hell is Suzy Boyd?" I asked.

"Right here, asshole," Suzy answered quickly and succinctly.

"Okay, Suzy," I asked. "Where the hell is my wife?"

"Right here, asshole," my wife answered quickly and succinctly. Then she paused a second before she added, "And quit calling me *your wife*. It makes me sound like I'm a fucking bowling ball or something."

"Okay, okay, Norma," I said, and sat down beside her. I ordered a Diet Pepsi for me and a pitcher of beer for the next table. There was no one sitting at the next table. It was just something I always did. Someone would come along and drink it.

"Norma," I said. "I'm sorry I have cancer and I'm sorry I'm dying."

She took a long drink of her Diet Pepsi, stared at me for a long time. Stared hard.

"Are you going to make any more jokes about it?" she asked.

"Just one or two more, maybe," I said, and smiled. It was exactly the wrong thing to say. Norma slapped me in anger, had a look of concern for a moment as she wondered what a slap could do to a person with terminal cancer, and then looked angry again.

"If you say anything funny ever again, I'm going to leave you," Norma said. "And I'm fucking serious about that."

I lost my smile briefly, reached across the table to hold her hand, and said something incredibly funny. It was maybe the best one-liner I had ever uttered. Maybe the moment that would have made me a star anywhere else. But in the Powwow Tavern, which was just a front for reality, Norma heard what I had to say, stood up, and left me.

Because Norma left me, it's even more important to know how she arrived in my life.

I was sitting in the Powwow Tavern on a Saturday night, with my Diet Pepsi and my second favorite cousin, Raymond.

"Look it, look it," he said as Norma walked into the tavern. Norma was over six feet tall. Well, maybe not six feet tall but she was taller than me, taller than everyone in the bar except the basketball players.

"What tribe you think she is?" Raymond asked me.

"Amazon," I said.

"Their reservation down by Santa Fe, enit?" Raymond asked, and I laughed so hard that Norma came over to find out about the commotion.

"Hello, little brothers," she said. "Somebody want to buy me a drink?"

"What you having?" I asked.

"Diet Pepsi," she said, and I knew we would fall in love.

"Listen," I told her. "If I stole 1,000 horses, I'd give you 501 of them."

"And what other women would get the other 499?" she asked.

And we laughed. Then we laughed harder when Raymond leaned in closer to the table and said, "I don't get it."

Later, after the tavern closed, Norma and I sat outside on my car and shared a cigarette. I should say that we pretended to share a cigarette since neither of us smoked. But we both thought the other did and wanted to have all that much more in common.

After an hour or two of coughing, talking stories, and laughter, we ended up at my HUD house, watching late-night television. Raymond was passed out in the backseat of my car.

"Hey," she said. "That cousin of yours ain't too smart."

"Yeah," I said. "But he's cool, you know?"

"Must be. Because you're so good to him."

"He's my cousin, you know? That's how it is."

She kissed me then. Soft at first. Then harder. Our teeth clicked together like it was a junior high kiss. Still, we sat on the couch and kissed until the television signed off and broke into white noise. It was the end of another broadcast day.

"Listen," I said then. "I should take you home."

"Home?" she asked. "I thought I was at home."

"Well, my tipi is your tipi," I said, and she lived there until the day I told her I had terminal cancer.

I have to mention the wedding, though. It was at the Spokane Tribal Longhouse and all my cousins and her cousins were there. Nearly two hundred people. Everything went smoothly until my second favorite cousin, Raymond, drunk as a skunk, stood up in the middle of the ceremony, obviously confused.

"I remember Jimmy real good," Raymond said, and started into his eulogy for me, as I stood not two feet from him. "Jimmy was always quick with a joke. Make you laugh all the damn time. I remember once at my grandmother's wake, he was standing by the coffin. Now, you got to remember he was only seven or eight years old. Anyway, he starts jumping up and down, yelling *She moved, she moved.*"

Everyone at the wedding laughed, because it was pretty much

the same crowd that was at the funeral. Raymond smiled at his newly discovered public speaking ability and continued.

"Jimmy was always the one to make people feel better too," he said. "I remember once when he and I were drinking at the Powwow Tavern, when all of a sudden, Lester FallsApart comes running in and says that ten Indians just got killed in a car wreck on Ford Canyon Road. *Ten Skins?* I asked Lester, and he said, *Yeah, ten.* And then, Jimmy starts up singing, *One little, two little, three little Indians, four little, five little, six little Indians, seven little, eight little, nine little Indians, ten little Indian boys.*"

Everyone in the wedding laughed some more, but also looked a little tense after that story, so I grabbed Raymond and led him back to his seat. He stared in disbelief at me, tried to reconcile his recent elegy with my sudden appearance. He just sat there until the preacher asked that most rhetorical of questions.

"And if there is anyone here who has objections to this union, speak now, or forever hold you peace."

Raymond staggered and stumbled to his feet, then staggered and stumbled to the preacher.

"Reverend," Raymond said. "I hate to interrupt but my cousin is dead, you know? I think that might be a problem."

Raymond passed out at that moment and Norma and I were married with his body draped unceremoniously over our feet.

Three months after Norma left me, I lay in my hospital bed in Spokane, just back from another stupid and useless radiation treatment.

"Jesus," I said to my attending physician. "A few more zaps and I'll be Superman."

"Really?" the doctor said. "I never realized that Clark Kent was a Spokane Indian."

And we laughed, you know, because sometimes that's all two people have in common.

"So," I asked her. "What's my latest prognosis?"

"Well," she said. "It comes down to this. You're dying."

"Not again," I said.

"Yup, Jimmy, you're still dying."

And we laughed, you know, because sometimes you'd rather cry.

"Well," the doctor said. "I've got other patients to see."

As she walked out, I wanted to call her back and make an urgent confession, to ask forgiveness, to offer truth in return for salvation. But she was only a doctor. A good doctor, but still just a doctor.

"Hey, Dr. Adams," I said.

"What?"

"Nothing," I said. "Just wanted to hear your name. It sounds like drums to these heavily medicated and heavily Indian ears of mine."

And she laughed and I laughed too. That's what happened.

Norma was the World Champion Fry Bread Maker. Her fry bread was perfect, like one of those dreams you wake up from and say, *I didn't want to wake up*.

"I think this is your best fry bread ever," I told Norma one day. In fact, it was January 22, 1978.

"Thank you," she said. "Now you get to wash the dishes."

So, I was washing the dishes when the phone rang. Norma answered it and I could hear her half of the conversation.

"Hello."

"Yes, this is Norma Many Horses.

"No.

"No!

"NO!" Norma yelled as she threw the phone down and ran outside. I picked the receiver up carefully, afraid of what it might say to me.

"Hello," I said.

"Who am I speaking to?" the voice on the other end asked.

"Jimmy Many Horses. I'm Norma's husband."

"Oh, Mr. Many Horses. I hate to be the bearer of bad news,

but, uh, as I just told your wife, your mother-in-law, uh, passed away this morning."

"Thank you," I said, hung up the phone, and saw that Norma had returned.

"Oh, Jimmy," she said, talking through tears.

"I can't believe I just said *thank you* to that guy," I said. "What does that mean? Thank you that my mother-in-law is dead? Thank you that you told that my mother-in-law is dead? Thank you that you told me that my mother-in-law is dead and made my wife cry?"

"Jimmy," Norma said. "Stop. It's not funny."

But I didn't stop. Then or now.

Still, you have to realize that laughter saved Norma and me from pain too. Humor was an antiseptic that cleaned the deepest of personal wounds.

Once a Washington State patrolman stopped Norma and me as we drove to Spokane to see a movie, get some dinner, a Big Gulp at 7-Eleven.

"Excuse me, Officer," I asked. "What did I do wrong?"

"You failed to make proper signal for a turn a few blocks back," he said.

That was interesting because I had been driving down a straight highway for over five miles. The only turns possible were down dirt roads toward houses where no one I ever knew had lived. But I knew to play along with his game. All you can hope for in these little wars is to minimize the amount of damage.

"I'm sorry about that, Officer," I said. "But you know how it is. I was listening to the radio, tapping my foot. It's those drums, you know."

"Whatever," the trooper said. "Now, I need your driver's license, registration, and proof of insurance."

I handed him the stuff and he barely looked at it. He leaned down into the window of the car.

"Hey, Chief," he asked. "Have you been drinking?"

"I don't drink," I said.

"How about your woman there?"

"Ask her yourself."

The trooper looked at me, blinked a few seconds, paused for dramatic effect, and said, "Don't you even think about telling me what I should do."

"I don't drink either," Norma said quickly, hoping to avoid any further confrontation. "And I wasn't driving anyway."

"That don't make any difference," the trooper said. "Washington State has a new law against riding as a passenger in an Indian car."

"Officer," I said. "That ain't new. We've known about that one for a couple hundred years."

The trooper smiled a little, but it was a hard smile. You know the kind.

"However," he said. "I think we can make some kind of arrangement so none of this has to go on your record."

"How much is it going to cost me?" I asked.

"How much do you have?"

"About a hundred bucks."

"Well," the trooper said. "I don't want to leave you with nothing. Let's say the fine is ninety-nine dollars."

I gave him all the money, though, four twenties, a ten, eight dollar bills, and two hundred pennies in a sandwich bag.

"Hey," I said. "Take it all. That extra dollar is a tip, you know? Your service has been excellent."

Norma wanted to laugh then. She covered her mouth and pretended to cough. His face turned red. I mean redder than it already was.

"In fact," I said as I looked at the trooper's badge, "I might just send a letter to your commanding officer. I'll just write that Washington State Patrolman D. Nolan, badge number 13746, was polite, courteous, and, above all, legal as an eagle."

"Listen," the trooper said. "I can just take you both in right now. For reckless driving, resisting arrest, threatening an officer with physical violence."

"If you do," Norma said, and jumped into the fun, "I'll just tell everyone how respectful you were of our Native traditions, how much you understood about the social conditions that lead to the criminal acts of so many Indians. I'll say you were sympathetic, concerned, and intelligent."

"Fucking Indians," the trooper said as he threw the sandwich bag of pennies back into our car, sending them flying all over the interior. "And keep your damn change."

We watched him walk back to his cruiser, climb in, and drive off, breaking four or five laws as he flipped a U-turn, left rubber, crossed the center line, broke the speed limit, and ran through a stop sign without lights and siren.

We laughed as we picked up the scattered pennies from the floor of the car. It was a good thing the trooper threw the change back at us because we found just enough gas money to get us home.

After Norma left me, I'd occasionally get postcards from pow-wows all over the country. She missed me in Washington, Oregon, Idaho, Montana, Nevada, Utah, New Mexico, and California. I just stayed on the Spokane Indian Reservation and missed her from the doorway of my HUD house, from the living-room window, waiting for the day that she would come back.

But that's how Norma operated. She told me once that she would leave me whenever the love started to go bad.

"I ain't going to watch the whole thing collapse," she said. "I'll get out when the getting is good."

"You wouldn't even try to save us?" I asked.

"It wouldn't be worth saving at that point."

"That's pretty cold."

"That's not cold," she said. "It's practical."

But don't get me wrong either. Norma was a warrior in every sense of the word. She would drive a hundred miles round trip to visit tribal elders in the nursing homes in Spokane. When one of those elders died, Norma would weep violently, throw books and furniture.

"Every one of our elders that dies takes a piece of our past away," she said. "And that hurts more because I don't know how much of a future we have."

And once, when we drove up on a really horrible car wreck, she held a dying man's head in her lap and sang to him until he passed away. He was a white guy too. Remember that. She kept that memory so close to her that she had nightmares for a year.

"I always dream that it's you who's dying," she told me, and didn't let me drive the car for almost a year.

Norma, she was always afraid; she wasn't afraid.

One thing that I noticed in the hospital as I coughed myself up and down the bed: A clock, at least one of those old-style clocks with hands and a face, looks just like somebody laughing if you stare at it long enough.

The hospital released me because they decided that I would be much more comfortable at home. And there I was, at home, writing letters to my loved ones on special reservation stationery that read: FROM THE DEATH BED OF JAMES MANY HORSES, III.

But in reality, I sat at my kitchen table to write and DEATH TABLE just doesn't have the necessary music. I'm also the only James Many Horses but there is a certain dignity to any kind of forced tradition.

Anyway, I sat there at the death table, writing letters from my death bed, when there was a knock on the door.

"Come in," I yelled, knowing the door was locked, and smiled when it rattled against the frame.

"It's locked," a female voice said and it was a female voice I recognized.

"Norma?" I asked as I unlocked and opened the door.

She was beautiful. She had either gained or lost twenty pounds, one braid hung down a little longer than the other, and she had ironed her shirt until the creases were sharp.

"Honey," she said. "I'm home."

I was silent. That was a rare event.

"Honey," she said. "I've been gone so long and I missed you so much. But now I'm back. Where I belong."

I had to smile.

"Where are the kids?" she asked.

"They're asleep," I said, recovered just in time to continue the joke. "Poor little guys tried to stay awake, you know? They wanted to be up when you got home. But, one by one, they dropped off, fell asleep, and I had to carry them off into their little beds."

"Well," Norma said. "I'll just go in and kiss them quietly. Tell them how much I love them. Fix the sheets and blankets so they'll be warm all night."

She smiled.

"Jimmy," she said. "You look like shit."

"Yeah, I know."

"I'm sorry I left."

"Where've you been?" I asked, though I didn't really want to know.

"In Arlee. Lived with a Flathead cousin of mine."

"Cousin as in cousin? Or cousin as in I-was-fucking-him-but-don't-want-to-tell-you-because-you're-dying?"

She smiled even though she didn't want to.

"Well," she said. "I guess you'd call him more of that second kind of cousin."

Believe me: Nothing can ever hurt more. Not even my tumors, which are the approximate size of baseballs.

"Why'd you come back?" I asked her.

She looked at me, tried to suppress a giggle, then broke out into full-fledged laughter. I joined her.

"Well," I asked her again after a while. "Why'd you come back?"

She turned stoic, gave me that beautiful Tonto face, and said, "Because he was so fucking serious about everything."

We laughed a little more and then I asked her one more time, "Really, why'd you come back?"

"Because someone needs to help you die the right way," she

said. "And we both know that dying ain't something you ever done before."

I had to agree with that.

"And maybe," she said, "because making fry bread and helping people die are the last two things Indians are good at."

"Well," I said. "At least you're good at one of them."

And we laughed. Yes, we laughed, because most of the time that's all that really matters.

CAIT FEATHERSTONE, who is of Arapaho and mixed European ancestry, has had poetry and fiction published in journals and anthologies, including *Tidepools, Lemming, Southern California Literary Scene, The Shore Poetry Anthology, The Little Valley Collective*, and the international collection *Angels of Power*. She lives in Vista, California, with her husband and two sons.

SHADOWS AND SLEEPWALKERS

Cait Featherstone

He'd been in the area a long time, long enough to become background. When he first emerged, a tall thin dark and silent presence on the local scene, everyone talked about him, asking one another variations on the same question: Who is he? He never spoke and, without any answers, like children chasing their own shadows, people soon began to make up stories about him. Maybe he'd been a Vietnam vet, some would venture. Others suggested that this seeming monastic stranger had come from some ashram in Tibet. Or perhaps he was a Somalian refugee, his African black skin seemed so thin as to barely stretch around his bones. Eventually, the qualifying "maybes" and "perhapses" were dropped, and fiction was passed as fact.

Soundlessly he looked straight through things, his eyes telling of unspeakable things. And I wondered. Had he run barefoot, like a crane skimming the surface of a lake, through the rice paddies of Vietnam? Had he seen a fatal flash? Were his saints beheaded? Did a torch emblazon on his breast the mark, the scar of war? Had the earth become a molten sea, a hardened moonscape surface? Was there an immutable point at which he thought—he knew—that every living thing had ended? And so he had stopped breathing, had become shadow? Did he know what we would all come to know?

Too often to be mere coincidence, our paths crossed and converged daily. It seemed as if he was everywhere I went, like a parallel life or a shadow I'd owned in another lifetime. Often he'd be in the crosswalk when I was in my car at a stoplight. Before work in the morning, I usually stopped at a local diner for coffee and he would walk past the window, past the table where I sat, separated by only a pane of glass. As an assistant manager of a local bookstore, I usually opened the place early in the morning. He would show up before any of the other employees did, gazing at the books on display in the front window, yet never looking directly at me.

I began to change my routine slightly. Sometimes I would go down to the beach to take an early walk before going into work. He would be walking at the edge of the shore, the sea a blue backdrop to this moving shadow, this tree with legs. I began to take my walks at sunset instead, and there he'd be, at the edge of a cliff above the sea, at the edge of the world. He'd stand like a tall dark crane balanced on one leg. Then poised and positioned on both legs, he'd begin a series of undulating, flowing movements. In Ina Coolbirth Park in San Francisco, I'd often seen Chinese people exploring the air with fluid movements, their bodies and the air in harmony. Though this was not Tai Chi, it seemed clearly ceremonial, religious, holy. His silhouette formed the character of a word in Japanese script; his movements shaped haiku. What had seemed the figure of a black crow, a disquieting deathly form, through movement became a dark light, a black sun.

Then one day I stopped at the diner for a morning cup of coffee. I walked down the aisle toward my usual booth and noticed that the shadow man was sitting there. He was taking what looked like tea leaves from a small leather medicine bag that hung around his neck and placing them in a cup of hot water. As I came nearer, he looked up, and for the first time he was seeing me, not seeing through me. His look was clear, not shrouded with darkness nor veiled with otherness as I had come to expect. He had seemed to journey momentarily out of that dark place. I returned his look, nodded my head. And for the first time since I'd seen him, he smiled at me. He opened his mouth, to speak, to speak to me. And I, in awe, awaited the sound of his voice, the words sure to shape around some thought sprung from the well of silence he occupied. A sound emerged, high and light as air, full of jive and jazz, as he said, "What's happenin', mama?"

Michael came back in 1969, and he never spoke a word about what happened to him over there, until two months ago when I told him I couldn't do it anymore, couldn't live with only the memory of who he'd been, couldn't be a wife to a man who was just sleepwalking through this marriage. That had been the first time that he spoke about Vietnam, eleven years after he'd come home.

But he hadn't really come home, I learned, as he told me about a night in Da Nang (rocket city, they called it), when they were under a mortar attack and one landed about six inches from his head and when he saw it he knew, he knew in his bones, that he was dead. Only thing was, the rocket didn't go off. It was a dud.

But it killed him anyway.

So we began to come here, to the Vietnam Vet Outreach Center, to see if he could get some help to find a way back, so he could really come home. Ben, our therapist, was a medic in Vietnam for two tours. When he came home he used his GI benefits to pay for a degree in psychology. Then two years ago he left his lucrative private practice to work for next to no pay at the Outreach Center. The cops often call him when they're dealing with a vet on the streets or a vet in a hostage situation. Usually the hostages are family members, a wife, children. Ben tells me that Michael is a textbook case.

Michael and I used to meet with Ben as a couple, until things began to break down, until we couldn't even be in the therapist's office together without all the rules being broken. Once, as I was telling Ben how afraid I'd become, Michael sprang out of his chair and lunged at me, shouting "Why? How can you be afraid of me?" I responded to his sudden movement reflexively, leaning back in my chair with my hands and arms up around my head and face. But before contact could be made, Ben stepped in between Michael and me, calmly yet urgently saying "Look at yourself, Michael." That was the last time we met with Ben together.

So here I sit on the olive-green Naugahyde couch in the waiting room while Michael meets with Ben. Afterward I will meet with him.

Things haven't been going as I expected. The more our therapist has helped me, the worse Michael has become. He began taking the keys to my car everyday when he went to work so that I couldn't go anywhere. He unplugged the phone. He has suspected me of every betrayal he could think of, mostly, I think, because if he could blame our problems on another man, he wouldn't have to make that long journey back from the jungle.

And he has become more and more physical, violent. Sometimes even in the middle of the night, in the dead of my sleep, I wake up to find him standing over me. "I'll never let you go," he says.

So I sit here, waiting. A vet who's been watching me for some time crosses the room and sits down beside me.

"You weren't in Nam, were you?" he asks.

"No," I answer, "but it was my war too."

"Your old man?" he asks.

"Yes."

He has that look, clouded and vacant, that many vets I've met have. He holds out a weathered black address book to me. "I've kept them all in here," he tells me in a hushed tone, leaning closer, as if sharing a secret. "The names of the dead. Their addresses, birth dates, and the day they died. Sometimes I go to visit their hometowns for them, check in on things, talk to their families."

I take the book and slowly open it to page after page of name after name. I look into his eyes, familiar and hollow and dead. "May I?" I ask, and taking a pen out of my purse, I turn to the appropriate place in the book and write my husband's name.

DUANE NIATUM is a Klallum Indian from his native Pacific Northwest. He is a specialist on Northwest Coastal Indian art, but he is best known for his poetry and short fiction. His stories have appeared in many journals, and they have been translated into twelve languages. He has edited and authored several works, including *Songs for the Harvest of Dreams*, *Digging Out the Roots*, *Ascending Red Cedar Moon*, *Carriers of the Dream Wheel*, and *Harper's Book of Twentieth-Century Native American Poetry*. His poems and stories have been widely anthologized. His most recent work is *Drawings for the Song Animals*.

FOR HER WITH NO REGRETS

Duane Niatum

Did I hear a key make music out of glass: tap, tap, tap? The clock glared six or seven. Was I dreaming or what? Then the cadence of those unforgettable words that followed told me this was no dream. "Wake up, wake up! Ernie says it's time to let me in your life. It's time to play—wake up, wake up! I'm bringing you the morning, and everything's the color of oranges." As I rubbed confusion from my eyes to let her in, Suzanne pointed to her watch's face, and sure enough, Ernie's smile and the two oranges she put up to my nose lit the room with seven o'clock. I made an effort to act amused and delighted that she and Ernie had decided to bring me a taste of the dawn. It isn't easy, however, for this nighthawk to dance the *Sesame Street* rag so bloody early in the morning. But I gave it a whirl, and when my sweet Suzanne began undressing, the world quickly seemed as it should be, and my eyes did cartwheels of anticipation. Sex may not be the complete cure for our century's decline, as well as our own, but it helps.

I think it was the next day that convinced me the mind is the joker. I was sitting in a Laundromat, waiting out the machine, when this subliminal image of a wild redskin jumped out of the magazine I was attempting to read, carrying a shield with words clearly carved in red: "Laugh, goddamnit. She's Jewish and that tribe is as crazy as ours. Don't give her up without a chase!" What can I tell my spirit helper? I took its advice. I stood and did a little round dance from one end of the Laundromat to the other in Suzanne's name. Pain'll do it, I tried assuring those staring at me with disapproving eyes. I said to them that this was the only way to stop it from playing to the ends of our nerves, the first move in pulling yourself out of the black hole. With luck this could pad the next fall; make the ground a little less concrete. You then manage to keep one skip and a zag ahead of the demon's claw club, its spikes, working hard to flip you off like a light bulb. The Laundromat gang pointed toward the door so I did not look back.

As my frustration became more acute, a friend was most helpful when she suggested my walk down the boardwalk of adultery would improve if I saw my little siren with a sense of humor, not to mention my place in the drama. As she reminded me, the story was already rumored that I would be the one left holding a blank page. Watch out, she warned, or it could be doom, doom, doom, all year long! My friend says humor is how to survive when you choose to set fire to your shoes while on the run. As she so candidly remarked, she might be forced into waving to me from the periphery of the city waste factory, as I go under the last time, hugging my love's Mediterranean doll of hysteria, hysterically to my chest. As my comrade of wrong roads later said upon leaving me the dark, "It rubs off—hysteria."

Granted, my coy mistress was passion-picking blueberries until the sun sets. She looked as sensual as her name, and a more playful woman I have never known. She had brain cells in abundance, but decided not to ask too much of them. When ambition steals the soul, trickster litters the road, and talent is the sacrifice.

How we leaped through the endless rings of the chaotic maze we had rapidly created for ourselves to make the hours a ritual of surprise. We did not have many, owing to the husband, but we frequently bowed to the illusion that even the smallest gift would bring us that much closer to the August field of the spirits. In the privacy of our nakedness, we applauded the band that played our secret nature. We were near the end of the song when she whispered: "It doesn't matter, Young. We'll find a way. I believe in you. I believe in me. I believe in us. Honest, Ernie." And for weeks I believed it too. Our beat seemed inexhaustible and without measure. Ah, for the pure blindness of the body! It even helped us face anxiety whenever that scarface changed the scene to fit the fear. I began shaking my nervous rattle around our heads the day she first admitted: "Look, I know I promised to get my own apartment. Why won't you believe I'm trying? Leaving him isn't easy. Ten years we've been married. Habit alone makes it scary to leave the roost."

"Suzanne, Suzanne, you don't want an answer. So I wonder how hard you looked. Yet I'll do us a favor and declare this subject a foreign issue. Someday you can let me in on the good news. Now let's smoke the pipe in peace."

But after her departure, you could have seen me asking the empty rooms why in the hell we got together in the first place. With my two or three mistakes in this area, dying to rise up in righteousness, rarely have I bounced so hard for another man's wife. In the beginning, the middle, and the end; it worried me. I chewed on the cuffs of my heart on several occasions. She thinks it was because we feel Woody Allen and Raven are the comic geniuses of the Void. She said it was really because I would gladly live in the Metropolitan Museum in New York City for the rest of my life, if the crummy guards could in any way be averted, along with their snapping-jaw dogs. She once teased that she liked the child and old man in me, not necessarily in that order. I had many reasons for dreaming of her, and these played a special part: Who do you know out there in the thick of our frantic footage, who might stomp on your heart with her verbal slammer for the fifty-minute tirade and then make love to you in such a manner, you would be quite willing to wear your masochist suit for the rest of the month? And I swear before Raven's feastbowl and the Wailing Wall, she was the greatest cook to beat her eggs in the Northwest. Gourmet and French down to the crêpe's edge. From the first meal my tongue wanted to do nothing but lay prostrate before her table. It never would admit to the idea of begging for more, but the thought had occurred. But this one is my favorite. Any woman who can read *Ulysses* straight through, book flaps and all—purely for the pleasure of hearing the pun bursts roll wildly down the page—can carry my little cache of faith in her bookbag any day she wants.

There were other reasons she had me whistling for weekends that went on into the middle of the next month. The ones that turned us into renegades, soulmates. We were drawn together as much from the blood's pull as the genitalia. Our ancestors, you see, taught us well how to make soup out of stones, a life out of nightmares. The grandfathers and grandmothers who speak in flames sang endlessly to us of how scars bind two together as much as tenderness. That they could just as quickly destroy what they brought together we had to learn on our own. We did. Although we started seeing the fragments of our childhood surface in each other's eyes, when anger and pain possessed us, we would always be grateful for the experience of the dance. We had found in the dark that we owed at least this much to the chanters calling us to sit before the fire of the old ones; listen to their story of the way love paralyzes your body with joy and pain each moment you hear your escaped cry.

It's funny how these things happen. I did know from the first time she smiled at me that she would not easily be forgotten . . . a tall, slim, angular woman, with gypsy hair, and the kind only the wind knows how to form. With eyes that hold you like the blue of a waterfall—dangerous water nymphs. The fantasy figures that choreograph your sleep. It just so happens I met her on a bus. As our circles merged, we swore we had touched the center of each other before. Maybe in New York. Maybe in San Francisco. Where, we never found out. We didn't let this bother us. We discovered by trial and error it wasn't a story we made up to keep us out of the boredom cage. The world was green opening everywhere we ran to hide. The sun spoke the entire palette of Monet. As usual, I was reading a book and only physically getting on the bus. Though it will appear slightly off point, as our brief little snapshot happenings are prone to do, she began to look up from her paper as my eyes found her and the source of the warmth. From that moment, when I returned from swimming in the eternal wheel of her eyes, I felt I was hers. What I hoped for, and believed did happen, was that she, for that interlude, and what went on into two more seasons, was also gladly mine. Body and soul. (It has never concerned me that all there is to be found of our trap of temptation is a vanishing spirit, another loss to welcome home, and no chance to do anything to change it.)

It was a leap in tall grass all that spring and summer. We can look back and feel good about the ruins. Once we called the bed our El Dorado, we reasoned that it was the perfect field to untangle our existential crises. The shadow offers nothing, but the body, oh the body is first teacher, and we attended every class we could. We became notorious hour-thieves. Day or night, we chimed in success. Now we reach the barbed-wire truth. When one of you is married, this can get you into more corners than a chess game. Still, we refused to throw in the sheet, and for more times than either of us thought possible, we played in top form against the counterrhythms of our bones. Yet the future continued to appear tenuous at best, since the husband was turning our world into a merry-go-round. So it was inevitable that I eventually heard her say "I can't make up my mind, Young. Damn it, I want you both!" Of course, this was after several flights she had made between her house and my apartment. When she disappeared in the night again, I nicknamed her "La Femme de Vacillation."

The heat was on. In Seattle that is a very special event. During summer the whole city skips for the open road. So I never thought the day would arrive when I would complain about the heat being too much with us. This summer I did. You couldn't cool down. I fried like a snake in the Gobi desert. Fortunately, it was late in the evening when she said, rather laconically, in her best Brooklyn College panache: "Young, why do I feel as if I'm skating into a wall? Can you please show me why I'm going on with this? You said I might soon be visiting you at the Thunderbird funny farm. What would you say if I said I think I'm already there?"

Trying to sound unthreatened, I said, "Come back, woman. All we need's to get used to thin ice. We've been doing it for months. We can't quit now." She looked as if she could feel the ground getting firmer, as I watched her go into a kindly acceptance nod. Oh, Sesame, the air was a bit smoky and our eyes were little Coney Islands and the thrill kept us humming in the corners.

Not long after I had a phone installed, Suzanne called: "Hello, hello. Young? Can you meet me downtown at the Squire's Tuck, seven P.M. sharp? I've got you something. Can't talk anymore. Terribly rushed here at work." *Click*. I went. She was at the door, all smiles and elation. I was curious. Special gifts people have given me have always made me uncomfortable, although never ungrateful. Awkwardness is clearly the first sensation.

Well, it turned out, she had chosen for me an incredible French sport coat. She said, "I want you to have this to remember me by, because I don't think we can go on. I can't stop thinking about my husband when I'm with you. Resentment's waving its ugly club. I don't know whether to hit him or you."

The month trekked on to its feeble end. I brought out all my old baskets and began to weave myself into another pattern. Shrinks were crossed off the option list; they seemed too much like stock brokers, building gibberish sticks and toy boats out of hundred-dollar bills. Better weave a basket; chant in tongues.

What to do? What to do? The weather was the same, warm as sea grapes, but my mind was an unhappy sailor with no passport. I attempted taking other women to movies and galleries and bars. Though this was her suggestion, it was hopeless. I tried singing for wrong numbers. Nothing worked. Suzanne was everywhere. On every street, in every shop, directing every dream, and alas, in other women's eyes. Ouch, I said, and returned to feeding time, the four walls. Then someone suggested I escape to the mountains of the coast. Let Nature do the healing. It was the perfect suggestion. I fled to the coast for a week. And before I could say *I will learn how to fall without a word*, I was drinking a glass of wine on a wind-carved beach, watching sand fleas climb their steep creations, fall back, and climb again. You can imagine how much I paid my respects to those fleas as the waves began to numb my history.

Back on the job and doing the cross-town routine, the heart gradually learned to take the ups and downs in stride. Days slipped off into weeks, weeks into old newspapers, and no smoke signal from Suzanne. Soon September dropped to its leaves and the crows reluctantly accepted the ice crystals of clarity. The first sign of frost had everyone looking. Then one night when the bars had failed to make me feel Halloween was so damn great, I came home to find her sitting on my stoop. I practically stumbled on her. She sang: "Hi, I changed my mind. I can't live without you! Can we have a drink upstairs? Face the witches and Frankensteins together? I'll be your cozy pumpkin!" She had become more clever each day. I was so happy to see her that all my reservations evaporated. We ran up the steps in a single lust. I whispered I loved her more than ten thousand choke cherries and she swore valleys of appley orchards.

Just as we had tossed ourselves into exhaustion, she leaped from the bed to announce: "I can't do this! I just can't! My husband needs me!" And away she went, following the demon calling from the night. I shrugged. My fairy princess is merely appeasing the inner creatures. I rolled over to face the wall; let the disconsolate selves posing as comics put out the dark; fighting the old question streaming just beneath my eyelids: Would she be back or what?

I awoke one dawn, from a week with no sleep, and pushed my panic buttons. (I'll do a lot for love since, I'd be the first to admit, it does a lot for you. Yet everybody could see this was getting ridiculous.) Dumped into the pits of insomnia for seven nights had left me pounds lighter and midnight's stutter-star. You could ask me to spell knots, and all that would fall from my lips would be babbling x's and m's. Was this the sign of imminent catastrophe? Hadn't she realized I had already opted for safer ground— the home sweet home of my own laughing walls—alone, alone?

It didn't take long after this for the worry bugs to make a harvest of our lives, gleefully chewing up the remains of our momentary trip to paradise. I watched the visible grow obtuse, as even the rats began to move on from our nest. She did pin one last note to my door:

> My dear Young,
>
> Even though we cannot be together, the past and our dreams remain. I must confess to you that I was afraid of taking the chance. I feared it wouldn't work, but refused to face my doubt until now. Can we ever be friends someday?
>
> Good-bye,
> S.

I am not ashamed to tell you I feel mortality is a good thing. From any perspective on the streets we call our running ground, the idea of immortality would most likely tip the scales of a balanced mind. The eternity that has always interested me is what my heart tells me feels good in parentheses. I live by the season. I am a loyal keeper of the cold's stone bell. The rest is better left to fleas and the gods who are more homeless and torn by grief than us.

Here is the last piece of the puzzle I cannot put into place.

Time, the medicine man in charge of us all—how can it be expected to heal such loss? Nothing out there or nothing inside has shown me the rite to grieve. Not even the grass in the field outside my window, with the wind that is neither of the earth nor the sky. Yet I bet you three strips of smoked salmon in a bagel jar, if chance called me to reach for her hand on this edge, I would do it. She said as much one good-bye. So I clap three times for our grand encounter. Toast the pieces that give us wholeness for a night. May her cup be full when this memory raises her sweet bird of a hand to the stars and the moon we followed so many nights, to catch one last glimpse of those exiles with no future whom only darkness will remember or name.

a NDREW CONNORS is a Bad River Ojibwe. Born in Ashland, Wisconsin, Connors earned a bachelor's degree in English at the University of Wisconsin—Milwaukee. A self-taught journalist focusing primarily on American Indian urban issues, he is editor of *News from Indian Country*. Connors has recently completed a chapbook for the American Native Archive Press and is at work on his first novel. He lives in South Milwaukee and has two children, Eric and Anna.

AVIAN MESSIAH
AND MISTRESS MEDIA

Andrew Connors

J anice Sebline scribbled lazy notes in a minute notebook while Reginald Throckmorton, rising young executive, rambled on about the company's success, his success, and the grand illusions of their future combined successes.

"Yes"—he beamed—"our projected urban development projects will not only be an economic boon for the city, state, and a national American blueprint for better tomorrows, but we at the Laurel Robins Corporation tower above our competitors. Our Human Services Division, for example, greatly benefits every man, woman, and child, regardless of their racial, ethnic, political, and religious background, here in this great country of ours."

Which made little sense to Janice, who popped chewing gum, reread her notes, noted Throckmorton's politically correct behavior—contrary to the Laurel Robins's record—and responded with "In other words you stand to make some money."

"I can't complain," Throckmorton tacitly acknowledged,

leaning back in his leather chair. "But of course that's off the record."

Janice nodded. "Yeah, yeah," she said. "We're going to need stills, Mr. Throckmorton."

"Just call me Reggie," Reggie said.

She ignored his overture, looked past him and out the window. "Maybe we can get a picture of you and this view?"

Reggie imperiously smiled. "Oh yes, you can see the whole city. We call it our regal view. I can see the marina from here. In fact, I can see my boat. Have you ever been on a sailboat before, Miss Sebline? Thirty footer?"

She walked to the window and looked down. The view from thirty stories up in the First National Wisconsin Building was breathtaking. Particularly when one had a fear of heights. She stepped back. "I've been in a sailboat, Mr. Throckmorton . . ."

"Reggie . . ."

". . . and I'd prefer things with motors. Sailboats bore me, take too long. We'll film your interview tomorrow morning."

"Sure, whatever you say," Reggie agreed. "This is just a public interest piece, right?"

"A dirty job, but somebody's got to do it," Janice replied, not too thrilled about this assignment. But that was the card she drew. Being cub reporter on an Old Boy station, she took whatever assignments they gave her.

"Perhaps lunch," Reggie offered, his choppers gleaming, brown eyes beading.

"Maybe another time," Janice smoothly rebuffed. She flipped the notebook into a backpack, a collegiate holdover, and headed toward the door.

"Maybe dinner," Reginald Throckmorton, young exec on the go, quickly suggested.

She rolled her eyes, cursed Fate, and turned stonily around. "Maybe not," she said malignantly.

Just then she spotted something from the corner of her eye and heard a dull *thump* bump against the window. She jumped somewhat, exclaiming "What was that?"

Throckmorton didn't notice. "What was what?"

"Something hit the window."

"Oh, that." He glanced outside. "Who knows, could be anything. Maybe the window cleaner dropped a rag? Maybe a bird hit the window? Up here, could be anything. Why, I remember that big hailstorm awhile back. The hail was slamming off the windows something fierce. Thought for sure we'd lose a window. Did I mention I own a Jaguar XKE?"

"Whatever," she remarked over an exiting shoulder. "We'll be here ten-thirty tomorrow morning to finish your interview segment."

"The public relations one, right?"

"Of course, public relations," Janice answered, slipping out the door. She sallied past his secretary, thinking perhaps the window cleaner would make a better interview. Probably had many interesting stories dangling forty stories up, overlooking beautiful downtown Milwaukee. She also knew Reginald Throckmorton, thwarted young VIP, had but one thing on his mind. And there'd be none of that, no sir and thank you.

Janice Sebline had a fledgling career to think of, one she worked hard for. Now it was all for one and that one is me. She shared once too often. Yet she had this effect on men, men in high places getting higher. Ah, a sigh, an unfulfilled moan, adieu; but love could come later, much later—considering what *he* did to her.

She waited for the elevator wondering if that big breaking assignment would ever come her way.

Meanwhile . . .

He didn't mean to say what he said; oh hell, he meant exactly what he said. Let's face it, he had enough of their bull—my food is undercooked, overcooked, and how do you cook this; and concluded food service was no longer what he wanted to do. Been doing food service for almost fifteen years. Much too long for any sane person.

So he went off on a customer: I'd like to speak to the manager; yeah, what do you want; you should do something about that rude employee over the phone; you want me to call a rude employee over the phone; no, the one that answered the phone was rude; did he do it with tact, though: What? Look, I'd like to register a complaint; will that be one room or two; what?

And that's what he said, going on and on with a customer, toying with his complaint, belittling his reasons, mocking hyperboles. He shouldn't of . . . but that's the restaurant biz. Sometimes a customer will go so far. Those of you who've worked in restaurants would know what I'm talking about. The rest of you are the cause of the restaurant worker's misery. Which is neither here nor there, unless you're Cloud, former pizza restaurant manager and bellicose busboy.

So Cloud walked away from his job feeling he'd had enough. Never occurred to him that he didn't have money socked away. Such was the whimsical price of split decisions.

Whenever Cloud needed a life major decision—like now, for example—he rode public transportation round and round the city. This put things in tactile perspective; particularly his lot, which at that moment was in low-wattage overload. This bothered him sometimes, like I suppose it'd bother most of us, yet he often used this as a brain cleaning: get the brains in order, move off and get on with life. Cloud, unlike most of us, gets away with irrational moves because he has no one to answer to. Which may or may not be why he's riding this particular bus on this particular day.

Maybe he likes bus people? Bus People gave him different life perspectives.

Bus People rode the bus because they had to. That was it, just it, and all it would ever be. Bus People had ends to meet, bills to pay, mouths to feed, and people depending on them for clothes, roofs, scraped knees, missed meals, and pure survival: survival without guilt. Bus People dealt with tight schedules, indifferent drivers, inclement weather, loud-mouthed children with blaring boom boxes blasting in confined spaces, standing room only, and missed stops, not because they wanted to. Egad no, no one in their right mind rode the bus when they didn't have to. Bus

People rode the bus because they had to, there was no other way. Real people.

While Cloud, rarely in a right mind, used bus riding to mellow mesmerizing life panoramas.

He took the 30 from Hampton to Sherman, Sherman to 43rd, 43rd around the bend to 35th, 35th to Wisconsin, and down the avenue. Which was about the farthest he'd normally travel to get his fill of real people. Route 30 took him through Milwaukee's heart, where all the real people lived. And once through the heart, you were on the East Side, where no one had any idea what was going on. A good place to raise money for any given cause. But not very conducive to real-world values, survival without guilt.

Cloud watched a toothless woman haul cart and all on the bus. She took her sweet time, and no one complained. That was bus riding in Milwaukee. Some kids cracked jokes about the woman, while other riders averted meandering attentions into space. Urban indifference, the bus rider's code. The toothless woman gummed verbal exchanges with silent wraiths, while spying everyone and thing around her, looking for the high ground. She pushed her stolid presence solidly into a side seat, shopping cart blocking the narrow aisle, and the driver rolls his eyes, closes the door, and moves on.

Yes, Cloud thought, she represents real-world values, survival without guilt. So I had a bad night with some bozo customers. Is that as bad as this woman's life?

The toothless woman spied him spying her and flipped him the middle-fingered salute, the silent bird of serious business. Truly, survival without guilt. That woman definitely came to terms with life. No problems.

She also showed him. Imagine, transferring our problem on another, hoping their problem is worse than yours. For what purpose? What is your means? She showed you with her salute, didn't she? Now Cloud's problem was twofold, a reluctant survivor struggling with guilt. He sat smirking, enjoying the joke played on him.

He told a customer off, so what, big deal. This woman told him. And so it goes. He stared out the window and realized he passed his usual stop. What the hell? Today he'd take a different stop.

Today is a good day to walk.

He got off at the next stop, 16th and Wisconsin, and strolled down the avenue, people watching. Some watched back from recessed doorways and porno shops, while others, Marquette students and total world survivors, watched themselves watching traffic. Traffic watched no one and proceeded willy nilly to and fro, prepositional wanderers along the straight and narrow byways of urban sentences.

Before long Cloud found himself standing before the First National Wisconsin Building. From 16th and Wisconsin to Jackson and Wisconsin. Where did the time go? Human patterns swirled around him. He didn't notice. Cloud was drawn to the building and its height. The next best thing to flying, way up there. Up there he could look out over the sprawling metropolis, see the world's problems in all their grimy splendor, and weight them against his own.

He rooted to that spot, lost in thought, staring at the forty-story icon. Two policemen across the street, however, took keen interest in Cloud.

"Whadda ya think?" Officer Krantz queried his partner.

His partner, Officer Matthews, munched doughnuts and slurped coffee. "I think we should form our own response to the League of Cultural Sensitivity," he said between bites.

Krantz whirled his eyes and sighed. "No, I'm talking about that guy standing across the street."

Matthews followed Krantz's directions. There was indeed a man standing across the street. But he didn't seem to be bothering anyone. He looked average, blue jeans, blue jeans jacket, red T-shirt, dirty tennis shoes, long black hair tied in a lazy ponytail, glasses, just an average-looking guy looking at a tall building. Matthews looked up at tall buildings from time to time. Nothing odd about that.

"Looks like an average guy to me," Matthews said.

Krantz studied the man across the street. "Hmm, I don't know . . . looks suspicious to me."

"You'd know," Matthews agreed.

"Damn right, I'd know, rookie." Krantz was pleased with himself and his nineteen years of experience. He'd get his rookie on the straight and narrow. "Ah-ha," he exclaimed knowingly. "Look at that, the security guard's going over to him. Observe, Officer Matthews."

"Whatever you say, George," Matthews acknowledged. "You're the boss."

Cloud felt the presence next to him. He continued studying the gleaming glass obelisk stretching above him. What was this building's purpose? Then he noticed little bodies littering the sidewalk alongside the building.

"Say, buddy, what do you think you're doing here?"

Cloud turned and faced a stocky man in pseudopoliceman blue nervously caressing his holster. The man's face was an acne-scarred paradise marooned on a flat head bobbing on a thick neck. Cloud couldn't help it. He smirked. The guard misinterpreted.

"I asked you what do you think you're doing here," the man repeated forcibly.

"Just standing, looking at this magnificent monument to man's technocratic achievements," Cloud replied pleasantly.

Immediately creating dubious notions in our friendly security guard. A troublemaker. "Well, I'm afraid you're going to have to move on," he returned, firmly pleasant.

"Why?" Cloud asked, turning back to the small bodies littering the sidewalk. They were minute avian ghosts attesting to mankind's preoccupation with itself. He looked for problems greater than his and found them lifeless on a sidewalk.

Meanwhile the guard quickly thought of a reason why Cloud should vacate this spot. "People are complaining. Move on."

Cloud surveyed the perimeter for complaining people. He saw people around a hot dog stand, probably complaining about

ketchup and onions; more things restaurant people had to contend with. He empathized with the hot dog vendor. Others
walked to and fro, watching themselves watching traffic—the
same old line in a new setting. No one gathered around the
security portal to watch him.

"What people?"

The guard searched for support. He was dealing with a live
one: *Now how did that manual say?* "Look, pal, you've been standing here for quite a while. Now maybe you're not up to nothing
in particular, but you just can't stand here all day."

"Why?"

"Look," the flustered guard pleaded, "if you don't get moving I
may have to run you in for vagrancy."

Cloud chuckled. "So that's it. Run me in for vagrancy? Is it
because I have a ponytail?" The guard stood motionless. "Is it
because I'm wearing blue jeans and dirty sneakers? You'd better
watch out, you'll never know who snuck up on you."

"What seems to be the problem?" Officer Krantz asked officially, magically appearing beside his comrade in security.

"This man refused to leave the premises after I've asked him to
leave," the guard replied, breathing easier now that official help
was on the scene.

Cloud beamed at the policemen.

Janice Sebline strolled out the front door steaming about this
assignment. Interview Laurel Robins Corporate officials about
their upcoming real estate developments in the Milwaukee area.
How interesting. How thought-provoking. Such human interest.
So far she laid out the groundwork with three high Laurel Robins
VIPs. They all said the same things, and they all tried to pick her
up—including a female. Yuck. Surely Janice Sebline was meant
for better things than this.

She walked straight through the crowd toward Jackson and
Wisconsin, hoping a parking ticket wasn't mocking her troubles.
A modest knot of people standing off to the side attracted her
attention, cueing the reporter's instinct screaming to erupt. She
moved through the throng toward the rapidly expanding crowd.

She noticed two police officers and a security guard questioning an average-looking man wearing blue jeans and a ponytail. Great, something humanly interesting going on here.

"I don't understand what all the fuss is about," Cloud said, somewhat amused. "I'm not bothering anyone."

"You're refusing an official order to remove yourself from a public premise," Officer Krantz explained.

Cloud looked puzzled. "I don't understand, I've only been standing here for ten minutes. Could I help it that I was attracted to this building? Do you realize this place is obscene from all over the city?"

"Do you have any identification?" Officer Krantz asked.

Cloud nodded. "Of course I do. Who in their right mind would walk around this place without proper identification?" He reached into a back pocket. "What if a person got hit by a bus or something?" His hand came away empty. "You know, sometimes a person leaves home with many things on his mind, and he forgets things."

Officer Krantz looked knowingly at his partner. "You mean you don't have any identification?"

Cloud looked knowingly at Krantz's partner. "Well, at least I know who I am."

"And just who is that?" Krantz asked.

"I am Aanakwad," Cloud proudly announced. "In your language that would mean Cloud."

"Cloud? That's it?" Officer Matthews asked.

Cloud nodded. "It's an old family tribal name, passed on to me from my granduncle Clyde Cloud, who got the name from Clinton Cloud. Seven generation that name travels. That name's worn many shoes. You see, my father, Cliff Cloud, couldn't come up with any more 'cl' beginnings, so he opted for just Cloud. Or that's the way I heard it."

Sebline latched on to the tribalness of the name: Aanakwad, Cloud. Now here is a human interest tale, one she'd been seeking since the degree arrived in the mail, five years too late. Her storytime instincts noticed the security guard slipping away.

Something more was afoot than the mere hassling of "a person of color," a true tribal man. Funny, though, his skin didn't look tribal. She edged closer to the trio. The crowd surged around them.

Krantz thought troublemaker. "Roy, run a make on that name, see if there's anything on Mr. Cloud."

"I've had that name made once before," Cloud rambled on, dismissing the officers. He had nothing to be guilty about, therefore nothing to worry about. He thought about an Abbott and Costello movie: *I fear nothing when I am in the right; whoever pushes me around will find me full of fight.* Odd how these things crop up at the strangest times.

He thought about the birds flying free and then smacking into this eclipsing monolith to progressive patterns and induced dreams. Now that was indeed a problem, a problem far greater than any problem Cloud-Without-a-Job had. Not even the toothless woman on the bus came close to this problem. The security guard returned and whispered something to the policeman. Officer Krantz nodded, staring victoriously at Cloud. Janice Sebline stepped between the foursome and into the spotlight.

"What seems to be the problem, Officers?" she inquired affably.

"I was just standing here mourning lost avian dreams," Cloud offered in an offhand manner.

"Just who in the hell are you?" Officer Krantz inquired in return.

Janice snapped open her wallet. "Janice Sebline, WMTJ News."

"Christ, a reporter," Krantz mumbled.

"Oh, yeah, where's your camera?" Officer Matthews added, for no apparent reason.

Cloud smiled while wild-eyed dreams danced within his mind. Real-world survival didn't exist on this dead square. Survival lay sprawled on a city sidewalk, and a lone man in khaki workclothes strolled nonchalantly among tiny corpses, quietly spearing and hiding them in a canvas bag.

"Our cameras are our eyes," Cloud announced, facing the crowd swelling around them.

Krantz moved to block Cloud, but Janice slipped between, asking "And what exactly did you do, sir?"

"I wondered how I could save myself from this," Cloud began, his hands animated motions of purpose and design. "But they drove me here." His eyes fell on the dead birds disappearing in a workman's bag. "Oh yes, what good is flight when demands keep pulling you back? Like take your extra cheese and feed it to the birds. That's all it's good for."

"What the hell." Krantz moaned. He saw Matthews dodging traffic, heading back.

Janice believed she was on to something big. "Exactly what do you mean, they drove you here?" she asked. "Who drove you here? The birds?"

"Will you please get out of here?" Krantz asked Janice through politely clenched teeth.

"I'm only doing my job," she said. The crowd began stirring. A few clapped and whistled.

Cloud stared at the sky. "I remember a Hitchcock movie. Oh, could their revenge be so sweet. And we think we've got it bad."

Neither Janice nor anyone else quite knew what to make of this. So Janice interpreted it according to her knowledge and dreams. "Are you saying that one day nature will rise up against humankind and put us back in our place?"

Cloud paid no mind to the gathering crowd, Janice's questions, or the policemen. He was thinking about next month's rent. Shouldn't have quit the job, he scolded himself. He shook his head: rash move, always with the rash moves. But those customers. He hated dealing with those customers. I want this, I didn't get that; Christ help me, those customers are getting to me. And then the cooler going out—rising dough everywhere.

"We've got to get them out of this place before they rise completely," Cloud said absentmindedly. "Or else everything we've worked for will be destroyed."

Krantz's orbs rolled with disgust just as Matthews joined the crowd, which by now had swelled to some fifty people. Many were dressed in business uniforms, while many were street people doing such things as street people do. The Streets had Security twitching.

"What kept you so long? Why didn't you call from here?" Krantz stared coolly at his partner, who stuffed a doughnut crumb into his mouth. "Well, did you get anything on this Cloud?"

"You won't believe this, but there is a Cloud," Matthews said. "I mean, just like that, Cloud. No first name."

"Did you cross-check?"

"Of course I cross-checked," Matthews said. "I found a lot of Clouds, but only one Cloud with no first name."

"An address?"

"Yup." Matthews wiped his mouth and studied the situation. "What's going on?"

"Nothing I can't handle," Krantz replied. "Did you find anything else on our Mr. Cloud? Parking tickets?"

To which Cloud responded, to no one in particular, "For thirty-five years, yea and verily, I have wrestled with the problem. Like sovereign birds blowing free, riding currents and waves, avian dreamers in urban lands. And then this . . . this eclipsing monolith of progressive patterns and induced dreams steals those dreams. Buries them away in canvas sacks, poof, gone." Cloud shook his head sadly.

A tear rolled down Janice's face. "O God, that was beautiful," she said. Some in the crowd sighed along with her, others engaged in conservative laughter.

Krantz motioned for his partner to stand ready. "Are you on some kind of drugs?"

Cloud shook his head. "Always demanding, give me this, give me that—how much, how much, how much? Can't they read?" Everything they need to see is right there in front of them. Oh, how they tie up phone lines with questions and petty complaints."

Janice furiously jotted all this down, wishing they had sent a television crew along with her. Oh, well, she'd write an article for the *Journal,* and for further developments she'd get a television crew.

Krantz noticed that the crowd was half Suits and half Streets. It wouldn't be long before the Streets outnumbered the Suits. There was bound to be an occurrence. Especially with this lunatic babbling nonsense; not to mention the guy spouting off about dead birds and unruly customers. Krantz decided to diffuse the situation before it became an incident.

"All right, Cloud, if that's your name," Krantz said officially. "I think you'd better come down to the station with us."

"But why?" Janice asked indignantly.

Cloud watched as the last bird was stuffed into the workman's bag. He scanned the forty floors searching for other tiny birds. "You know, those birds wouldn't have to suffer so much if we'd only take the time to really notice them. But who notices anything anymore? The only thing people notice nowadays is if they get sausage and wanted pepperoni. Oh, boy, they notice that, all right."

Krantz nodded to his partner. Matthews grabbed Cloud's arm. "C'mon, buddy," he said. "We're just going to take you downtown for questioning."

Cloud said nothing. He smiled, looked up, looked around, shrugged his shoulders, and said, "Sure, why not," because he had nothing better to do.

Janice turned on Krantz. "Exactly what has this man done, Officer?"

"Look, lady," Krantz said, prepared to politely squash this so-called reporter before things went any further. "It's just routine. Our friend here has no identification."

"But according to Cloud . . ."

"That's Mr. Cloud," Mr. Cloud added.

She continued without skipping a beat. ". . . Mr. Cloud was just standing here ten minutes," Janice persisted. "Now, I've been here for nearly six minutes, and from what I've heard, and I'm sure these people have also, he hasn't really said anything that warrants this type of action." The kid was on a roll.

"This isn't really any of your business," Officer Krantz said. Another squad car pulled alongside the curb. Krantz gave them the sign.

"Did it occur to you that maybe he was waiting for the bus?" Janice asked pointedly.

"I just got off the bus," Cloud offered. "Buses are little worlds unto themselves. They roll through this aimless urban universe like meandering starships through birdseed intersections climbing the walls."

Janice halted and asked him to repeat that. Cloud shrugged and smiled. "It's that extra cheese that really gets me," Cloud offered in explanation. "It's hardening their arteries like this building obstructs avian dreams. One day a dream bird will fly into their hearts, but that cheese, like this building, will stop that dream, dead, plop, into the workman's bag."

"Amen," some people in the crowd shouted.

"Jesus H.," Krantz swore. Now he had to get this nut case off the streets before some unsavory character took advantage of him. "All right, let's break it up. C'mon now, let's get a move on." Krantz and the squad officers began dispersing the crowd.

Matthews led Cloud across the street. "Having a bad day?" Matthews casually asked.

"Bad month," Cloud answered. "Sometimes it's like that. Tomorrow it'll be better. Come to think of it, I don't have any money to get home."

"In the wallet, huh?" Matthews opened the door for Cloud.

"Maybe the transfer's still good?" Cloud checked his pockets. "This will probably take awhile, right?"

Matthews nodded, patting Cloud down and ushering him into the backseat. "We have to verify your identity. You know, routine."

"Yeah," Cloud agreed. "Didn't have anything better to do today."

"Officer," Janice demanded, standing defiantly before Krantz. Now she knew what her mother was talking about. Dear old mom, a protest marcher from the sixties. "You just can't take a man in for questioning simply because he has no identification. What is this, the Soviet Union?"

"Yeah," people in the crowd chanted. "What is this, the Soviet Union?"

"Lady . . ."

"That's Miss Sebline," Janice corrected.

Krantz rolled his eyes heavenward, trying to keep his temper under control. Nineteen years of service, still the same old thing. "Look, Miss Sebline," he said, "this Cloud was asked to leave. He refused, and he also doesn't have any identification. We have to take him in—it's for his own good. You heard him . . . did any of that make any sense to you? And besides that, there isn't a Soviet Union anymore. What kind of reporter are you, anyway?"

Janice, though miffed at the last sentence, thought hard on the previous one. What exactly did Cloud say? "From what I understand, he only stopped here to say a prayer for the birds that were killed in front of this building," Janice offered.

"Bird killers," someone in the crowd shouted.

"They kill the birds, they kill us," someone else added.

At that moment, strange as it may seem, a WMTJ television van happened to drive by. "Hey, Joe, isn't that that new reporter?"

Joe looked out the window. "Yeah, that Sebline kid. Say, she ain't bad."

"I wonder what's going on? Cops here and everything." So the van stopped, which in turn stopped traffic on Wisconsin Avenue.

Two more squad cars appeared on the scene. Cloud greeted the officers with a smile when they stepped over to question Matthews.

Krantz rested his hands on his hips, taking a firm stance. "All right, all right, that's enough of this. C'mon, let's break this up. There's nothing happening here." Krantz and the officers moved through the crowd. The crowd decided it was time to party. You know how crowds get.

Joe and Fred, the WMTJ camera crew, walked up to Janice and Officer Krantz, camera shooting, and asked, "Say, what's going on here?" Which wouldn't have been all that bad, except at that moment a crosstown rival, WJTM TV, happened to be driving by. The same conversation as before ensued, and soon their cameras were in on the fray.

Camera lights flashed on the crowd. The crowd responded with a hearty "Bird killers, bird killers!" and put on a scene. The Streets loved it, while the Suits began backing out of the picture. Wasn't good for the image. Of course, a few liberal Suits stayed behind to watch. And many then discovered that their watches, among other things, were missing. One Suit turned just as a Street sneaked away. "Hey," he shouted, "that man stole my wallet!" The Suit chased the Street, two policemen joined the pursuit, and all collided with a little old lady on her way to pay her home mortgage under threat of eviction.

Meanwhile, another Suit broke away from the crowd, dropping a crisp new empty leather wallet in a black kid's hands.

The cameras caught it all.

Later that evening . . .

Cloud sat across from Officers Krantz and Matthews wondering if it would be raining when he left. He didn't mind the rain, it was walking west along Wisconsin Avenue that bothered him. Riding the bus and watching *real* people was one thing. But traveling among them, late at night . . . no sir, he'd have to find a way home.

Krantz glowered at Cloud, standing over him like a red bear in blue. "We should arrest you for inciting a riot," he growled.

Cloud looked at Matthews. "Do you think you could lend me a quarter to make a phone call? Someone I know must be home."

Krantz snarled. "That's what you said an hour ago. It seems nobody you know is at home. What, did they all know you were calling?"

"I'll pay you back," Cloud said. "If not, maybe I can use your phone. Have the city send me a bill."

The station sergeant, Murphy, strolled over to the desk. "Well, Krantz, we really have nothing to hold him on."

"What about that incident at the First National Wisconsin?"

"He was in the car when all that happened," Murphy said. "We don't have anything to hold him on. Why don't you let him go?"

Krantz couldn't let him go. Krantz had to have him because Cloud was responsible for that melee with the crowd. Splattered all over the local news, and Krantz with a torn pocket, gotten while avoiding the little old lady who belted him for running her over. In glorious living color on the Six O'Clock News.

At that moment a harried young lieutenant rushed into the office. "Good Lord, it's that reporter again. She's got an ACLU lawyer with her and they're clamoring for his release."

Krantz chuckled. "Where did you get a word like clamoring, Chris?"

"I read, I read," the lieutenant shot back. "Look, Krantz, we have nothing to hold him on. We're letting him go."

"Don't bother me," Matthews agreed.

"I suppose," Krantz relented. "But I'm going to be watching you, Mr. Cloud. No identification, no job . . . Christ, just what in the hell kind of city are we running anymore?"

"Does anyone know if it's raining?" Cloud asked.

"Not yet," Matthews said. Krantz slapped his shoulder.

"I suppose a walk would be okay. I'll take the long way around. No, that wouldn't be good, that's a long way." And Cloud rambled on as Officer Matthews led him into the lobby.

"You know, I get off in a half hour," Matthews said. "I'm heading toward the Northside, maybe I can give you a lift?"

"That would be cool," Cloud readily agreed.

"Besides, I'd like to hear more about that powwow you were talkin' about."

"You wouldn't believe the energy," Cloud said, pushing through a door. "Very high positive energies. I like them."

"Sounds like it'd be a good time," Matthews said.

The high-wattage television lights blinded Cloud, Officer Matthews, and anyone else unfortunate enough to be standing behind door number one. Fortunately for Cloud, his right hand managed to shield the glare and save his front teeth as Janice

Sebline, WMTJ TV's newly created Video Crusader, thrust a microphone in his face.

"How have they treated you, Mr. Cloud? How were your conditions? We've been talking with some of your supporters and they're behind you one hundred percent." Janice Sebline didn't pause for breath.

"Supporters?" Cloud and Matthews asked.

At that moment, large hand-painted signs filled the lobby. A MAN HAS A RIGHT TO PRAY. HONOR THE WORLD, SAVE THE AVIAN DREAMERS.

Twelve more microphones snaked around Miss Sebline, and she presented her best profile.

Cloud stepped back when he discovered that his supporters consisted of the Sorority Sisters of Misguided Multiculturalism; various American Indian college student organizations bearing names like the Native American Student Movement, the American Indian Student Association, and the American Indian Native Student Coalition; local conservation groups—college and radical fringe; a multitude of bird-watching societies; the curious with nothing better to do; and people milling around in the police lobby waiting to pay fines and other police-related events.

"Supporters?" Cloud asked once again.

"Oh yes, Mr. Cloud . . ."

"Cloud would be fine," Cloud said.

"These people have heard your message," Janice rapidly continued. "It's the message your people have been trying to tell us for so long."

The crowd cheered.

"Tell me, Mr. Cloud," a reporter began before Janice could, "what was it that drew you to the First National Wisconsin?"

Cloud gazed at the man, trying to figure out what was going on. He barely remembered what he had said. That was hours ago. Cloud recalled going there because he had nothing better to do. Which is why he easily agreed to coming down to the station. All he wanted to do was go home and think about asking for his job back. After seeing the birds sprawled along the sidewalk, he knew he could deal with extra cheese no pepperoni for a while longer.

"Did the First National Wisconsin have you arrested because of some alleged involvement in the Indian bingo fiasco?" the same reporter asked.

"Well," Cloud began, figuring out a way to get these people off his back. "I no longer had a job and I wanted my job back . . ."

"So," another reporter interjected, "then you were one of the displaced tribal workers."

"I displaced myself," Cloud answered.

His answer was drowned out by a host of shouted questions that, somehow or another, were answered before a word slipped from Cloud's mouth. Questions like did he approve or disapprove of the Columbus Highway? Or some large corporation's involvement in Indian gambling interests? Or humankind's disrespectful treatment of the natural world, as evidenced by the monolithic First National Wisconsin building? Even one on personal karma was asked and answered. Each question built on the other, and the reporters and supporters were confusing themselves more than Cloud confused himself.

What to do, what to do?

Cloud wanted to go home. The police officers wanted Cloud to go home so things could resume their normal chaos. But no one else seemed to want to go home. Maybe they didn't have any homes? Who knows? It was clear, however, that one thing was getting accomplished, and that was a protest rally against the Avian Dream–stealing (as it was now called) First National Wisconsin building and all that it represented. And Cloud would be the spokesman.

Lights, camera, action.

Cloud tossed a few Grouchoisms at the reporters and managed to slip away. The reporters noted every word and slipped off to make their copy. The show must go on. The college students and various social organizations slipped off to plan tomorrow's rally. The station captains slipped off to try to figure out where in the budget was the money to police this rally.

Unnoticed to everyone, one lone old man sat in the lobby corner, watching everything. His face was masked by a wide-brimmed hat. He was furniture quietly surveying the madness around him.

That night, Cloud's face was flashed across the local media and into everyone's home. Raymond Felician, his wife and daughters were sitting lazily before the television, not paying much attention. Ray's wife looked up and tapped his shoulder. "Say, isn't that Cloud?"

Ray shifted his glasses, marked his place in a book and looked up. "Well, I'll be damned, what has the boy gone and done now?"

His daughter listened closely. "I think he said he was thinking about asking for his job back."

Ray chuckled. "Had to go on television to do that? Of course he can have his job back."

In another living room another couple watched the evening news. "Say," Man said, "that's the jerk that told me to take my extra cheese and stuff it."

Woman glanced at the television. "Sounds like he was preoccupied with something else when he yelled at you."

Man listened to Cloud's interview. "You know, honey, he has a point there."

Honey snuggled next to Man. "Maybe we should go to that rally tomorrow?"

Man caressed Honey. "I think we should do something about those birds. Imagine, flying all that way only to smash against that building."

Cloud walked into his apartment and flopped into a chair. "I don't need another day like this," he told a large Groucho Marx poster.

The phone rang. It was Sebline. "Hello, Cloud," she began cheerily. "I just wanted to tell you that we're all behind you. You did disappear rather quickly. Did you watch the news tonight? You looked great. I just got word that CNN is sending a crew up here to cover tomorrow's rally. That's at two o'clock, just in time for the Six O'Clock News. You will be there, you're the main speaker. We're all behind you one hundred percent. If you'd like, I'll come by and pick you up?"

"Er," Cloud said.

"Fine, I'll see you tomorrow at one-thirty. Have a good night, Mr. Cloud. We won't let you down." *Click.*

Cloud shrugged, replaced the phone, popped *Duck Soup* into the VCR, and fell asleep happily.

The next day Cloud was on the phone talking to Raymond about a possible vacation when there came a resolute ringing of his apartment doorbell. Cloud excused himself and answered the door.

"Good afternoon, Cloud," Janice greeted cheerily. She looked stunning, and quite overdressed.

Cloud wore blue jeans, one sock, and nothing else—he too was dressed for the occasion. "What do you want?"

"Surely you haven't forgotten," Janice answered, barging into the apartment. "You're not even ready. Cloud, it's almost one-thirty."

Cloud looked for a working clock. The VCR flashed 12:00, 12:00, 12:00. "What's going on at one-thirty?"

"You mean you've forgotten the rally?"

"You must be looking for my brother," Cloud said, hanging up the phone.

"I'm sorry? Were you talking on the phone?"

Shit, I hung up on Raymond, Cloud thought. Oh, well. "Yeah, I forgot about the rally," Cloud answered. "I thought I was just dreaming yesterday."

"No, sir," Janice said. "*CNN, ABC, NBC, WMTJ, WJMT, WITV,* and *92 'LIP* will be covering the rally."

"All them, huh?" Cloud found a shoe. "I have just one question." Cloud found yesterday's T-shirt. He put on what he found so far. "What exactly is this rally all about?"

Janice hesitated, then smiled broadly exposing gleaming white teeth. "You are such a kidder." She tapped him on the shoulder. Cloud smiled. "Do you know you don't have a sock on that foot?" She pointed to his foot wearing a shoe and no sock.

"I'm making a fashion statement," Cloud said. "And you're going to drive me there?" He found his other shoe.

"Are you going dressed like that?"

Cloud looked himself over in the mirror. "I suppose I should throw on a jacket. It might rain, you know."

The drive to the First National Wisconsin building was uneventful. Janice chirped all the way. Cloud watched the people. They didn't appear concerned about the great rally, if they even knew about it. They went about their business and Cloud wanted to join them.

It would be good to get back to work.

The west wall of the First National Wisconsin was jammed with people. Surrounding the people were police officers, and surrounding the police officers were news cameras. Banners proclaiming avian dream rights and denouncing Laurel Robins's alleged misdeeds flowed on the left. Banners decrying the liberal banners and sprouting *Pro-American* locations and promoting progressive anti-everything causes flapped on the right. The media were having a field day as slogans were belted back and forth like a rampaging porcupine in a nudist colony. The crowd cheered and jeered when Janice Sebline, the Video Crusader, and Cloud stepped from the car.

"Save the birds, down with Laurel Robins," one side shouted.

"USA, USA, USA," the other side screamed, for lack of anything better to say.

Petty arguments erupted around the fringe, neither side making much sense, and the newscams gleefully recorded it all for posterity and a possible jump in the ratings. Reporters stood on the perimeters babbling incoherent nonsense and hot dog vendors closed their stands, having sold their supply in less than one hour.

A police escort guided Janice and Cloud through the crowd. Janice loved it all. She smiled and waved, shook hands and showed her best profile. Cloud wondered where his other sock was.

A pole of a man with red hair, a large nose, oversized glasses, and casually dressed in a tweed sport coat and gray corduroys stepped up to the podium when Cloud reached the makeshift stage. "As mayor of the City of Milwaukee, I would like to acknowledge your cause, Mr. Cloud," he saluted (if there is such a word?). The crowd roared. The mayor stretched out his arms looking like a windswept clothesline pole and continued. "As our fair city suffers through these trying times, times of racial discord and mutual suspicions, of economic crisis and environmental distress, of the homeless and the downtrodden, of the . . ."

"Enough already," someone shouted.

". . . inclement weather and depressing headlines," the mayor, who wasn't doing well in the opinion polls, rolled on. "You, Mr. Cloud, have presented our city with a simple message, one that we, as citizens, have been seeking for a long time."

"Save the birds, save ourselves," the avian dreamers sang.

"USA, USA, USA," the Pro-American progressive conservatives hooted.

Cloud studied the dias. He recognized various "people of color" leaders who stood by politely clapping. He glanced out at the faces, a lively sea of clashing hues, waiting expectantly for him to say something wise and enlightening, or vicious and slandering, depending on your political stance. The college students looked adoringly at him and flashed their banners. Cloud stepped up to the mayor, shook his hand, and stood before microphones, video cameras, scribbling reporters, and what looked like a million eyes, friendly and otherwise. He cleared his throat.

"Tell it to the world," the Reverend Curtis R. Porter, of the Northside League of Urban Justice, belted out.

Cloud smiled at the man wondering what he was talking about. The mayor hesitated, then said, "We know how overwhelming this must be, Mr. Cloud." Once again he thrust out his long arms, looking as before. "The fine citizens of Milwaukee are waiting for your words. We support your cause."

"Words," Cloud said, puzzled.

"Save the birds, save the birds."

"USA, USA, USA."

An austere-looking woman leaned over the podium and said, "We are with the avian dreamers. For too long we have asked how much, how much, how much? Do we really need the extra cheese?"

"You sure don't," someone called out. The crowd laughed.

"And we've forgotten our purpose," the woman continued, unruffled. "We have forgotten about the simple things. Must the birds pay for our arrogance?" She was on a roll. "What you said was true, Mr. Cloud, we are all tribal sisters and brothers, despite our differences in color."

The crowd was silent, trying to decipher what Lady Gregory Denise Hill-Quickdraw was saying this time.

The reporters chuckled. "Thank you, Alderperson Hill-Quickdraw," the mayor said.

"Tribal brothers and sisters?" Cloud asked the mayor.

The crowd erupted in a cacophony of cheers and jeers. One rather large man wearing a pronounced American flag pin and girlie tattoos bulled through the crowd. "Der ain't nothing tribal about me," he shouted, shaking a hamfist at Cloud. "Why don't youse go back wre you came from and leave the bingo to da churches?"

"Bingo?" Cloud inquired. Bits and pieces of yesterday's folly were beginning to filter back to him. He remembered some things he said, but this?

"Oh, why don't you chucks go back home and let the man speak?" a small, wiry African-American man shouted back.

"You can't stop us from talking anymore," a burly Latina woman added.

"Why don't you people get jobs and quit bitchin'?" a handsomely chiseled Adonis in a Khan's three-piece said.

"Dream stealers, dream stealers," one side of the crowd erupted.

"USA, USA, USA," you know who added.

The cameras whirled merrily along.

A wordball formed in Cloud's throat. If he could only remember what he said. Yesterday he had nothing to do and was in a very snide mood. A mood brought on by self-pity and rash decisions. A guilty mood, actually.

Guilt. There was an answer. He scanned the crowd. The crowd looked for a cause, any cause, because they had nothing better to do. Their world was guilt, thriving and dying with it. He remembered the bus ride. He looked up suddenly.

There, standing ten feet in front and protecting a shopping cart loaded with refuse, was the toothless woman. She spied him spying her and flipped him the bird.

Cloud erupted in laughter. The crowd paused.

"Guilt, that's what's been bothering me," Cloud said, his words echoing between buildings. The crowd waited expectantly, waiting to pounce in either direction.

"How do we survive without guilt?" Cloud asked.

"Learn from the birds," Alderperson Hill-Quickdraw shouted.

"Go back to the Southside," someone shouted.

"Tell the world about the sins committed against us tribal people of color," Reverend Porter wailed.

"Reverend, could you tell us about the alleged mishandling of League funds?" a reporter loudly asked.

The reverend shook his head. "There it is," he hollered, standing up and looking defenseless. "They always attack us with lies and heresy. They don't want us coming together. They're suppressing us and denying my rights."

Cloud shook his head, saying to himself "And what have I done?"

"You have given us a voice," a man shouted.

Cloud continued talking to himself. "I suppose I can deal with the extra cheese—that's the way it is. But they always want so much."

"How much?" a heckler queried.

"Why don't you let the man speak?" a woman retorted briskly. "He has come from the Indian lands, ready to tell us what the Indians have to say about this."

"Wait a minute," Cloud began, realizing his voice was carrying.

"Tell us what the Indians know," the crowd chorused. One side anyway.

"Indians?" Cloud stared at the crowd. "I just don't know," he said softly.

"That's an Indian for you," someone screamed. The crowd hissed and cheered the man.

The mayor smiled, waving for cooler heads to prevail. The police readied themselves. The newscams whirred and clicked. Cloud stepped back and looked up at the First National Wisconsin building. He looked back at the crowd.

A tall old man wearing a floppy-brimmed hat stood across the street, watching everything around him and, yet, looking directly at Cloud. Cloud heard a small thump-bump against something far away. He faced the sound just as a tiny body hit the sidewalk behind him.

The crowd had long ago decided to carry out its own agenda. Both sides stood toe to toe, accusing each other of every social and environmental ill in history. Some pushed, some shoved, and a long line of blue wearing white helmets and dark visors moved through the crowd. The cameras whirled. Janice Sebline twitched excitedly, speaking to a camera. "This is Janice Sebline, the Video Crusader, reporting on the spot for WMTJ News. As you can clearly see, the city is divided over the issue of saving the poor birds that have no place to call home . . ."

Barry Martin, WJTM reporter, talked with a Laurel Robins corporate official. "I don't know what all the fuss is about," the official officially said. "After all, we here at the Laurel Robins Corporation helped support the peregrine nestings on the top floors of the First National Wisconsin building. We at Laurel Robins support any and all causes that benefit mankind."

Barry Martin smirked knowingly. "Yes, Mr. Talltale, but isn't it true the peregrine is a bird of prey, and isn't it true that the Laurel Robins Corporation is preying on the socioeconomic depressive state of the near Northside?"

The Laurel Robins official officially excused himself.

Cloud stood over the sparrow watching it twitch. He stooped

down and studied the bird. Its eyes moved slowly back and forth, its beak hung open, its little bird tongue lolled listlessly, and it flopped weakly about, struggling to maintain a hold on life. Cloud picked the bird up gently. He cupped it in his hands and faced the crowd.

"All you want to do is survive without guilt," he said softly. "This isn't your fault."

He looked out over the crowd, which had begun a shouting match that drowned out a low-flying jet passing overhead. No one was paying any attention to the dias. The mayor slipped away. The reverend got into a shoving match with the nosy reporter. Alderperson Hill-Quickdraw and her women's rights supporters got into a free-for-all with antitreaty rights protestors —who showed up anywhere the word Indian was mentioned. News crews got into fistfights with other news crews for the best angles. Officer Krantz got into a procedural argument with a liberal station captain.

And the lone man standing across the street stared at Cloud, nodding his head.

Cloud floated through the crowd like a passing cloud, gently carrying the bird to the lone man. No one noted his passing. The lone man was a vision, a face Cloud had seen in his past. He stood before the man, holding the bird out.

"Can we save it?"

The lone man smiled and led Cloud away.

And the cameras whirred and clicked, flashed and popped, catching nothing and missing it all.

"This is Janice Sebline, reporting from the scene."

g R E G   S A R R I S is a California Indian of mixed-blood ancestry, Coast Miwok and Kashaya Pomo and Filipino on his father's side, and Jewish, German, and Irish on his mother's. His forthcoming books include *Keeping Slug Woman Alive* (University of California Press), *Prayer Basket: Hearing the Life Stories of Mabel McKay* (University of California Press), and *Grand Avenue*, a collection of short stories that includes "How I Got to Be Queen," which has been optioned by American Playhouse. Sarris is currently an assistant professor of English at the University of California, Berkeley.

SLAUGHTERHOUSE

Greg Sarris

I was fourteen. Thirteen maybe. I was worried I couldn't shoot. I mean take care of business once I got there. That's all us guys talked about. And I had a girl who would've let me. Her name was Caroline. An Indian just come to town and winds up in the Hole. Eyes pretty as nighttime sky in the country. Believe me, fine. And she's looking at me like I'm something, even I'm a Indian, but a half-breed. But I'm scared about this taking-care-of-business stuff. Then luck gives out on me and I win a trip inside that slaughterhouse barn and know I'm a man no matter what.

The slaughterhouse barn was down Santa Rosa Avenue, where folks had animals and stuff. Chickens in the yard, cows. But the houses didn't look like anything, no better than ours. Small and needing paint. Stuff like refrigerators and washing machines here and there where you could see them if you looked. Around the sides of houses, on back porches and in garages, like folks didn't think stuff that didn't work wouldn't stand out. Either that or they wanted you to see the stuff, like it was something, which everyone knowed was nothing. Falling ragged barbed wire fences surrounded the places, except for the slaughterhouse where there was thick plank boards. Along the street plyboard was nailed to the planks so you couldn't see the horses. On the plyboard you could see advertisements for things in town. Coca-Cola. Cherri's Chinese Kitchen. Hamburger Dee-Lux. The freeway wasn't finished yet so folks coming north drove through town, up Santa Rosa Avenue.

It was two barns at the slaughterhouse. One was in the middle of the corral. Its roofline sagged like the swayed back of one of them horses. It's where the hay was, where the horses fed. From there we watched the goings-on in the other barn that was across the way. It was three stories high and painted. I say watched the goings-on, but we couldn't see nothing. Just trucks carrying in horses and carrying out pet food. But it was no secret what happened in that place at night. Smoke and Indian Princess Sally Did sold girls.

Smoke had eyes the yellow color of his straw hat. The eyes looked out from his black face just like they was set in a dark wall. Folks said they was goat eyes, square in the iris. I wondered if the white people who came about the horses seen his eyes that way. Smoke looked like the devil. Indian Princess Sally Did was worse. She was the one who went around talking to folks. She had balled-up black hair with a white stripe down the middle. She never took off her sunglasses and she dressed in a purple get-up and high heels. Thing is she thought she looked like she was society. I remember seeing her in the market on Grand Avenue. I thought she couldn't see I was looking because she didn't pay attention to anything that wasn't of use to her. She was reaching for a can of coffee when I seen it on her leg, just above her knee —a tattoo that said 1946. Whatever that year was to her. "What you looking at, smelly Indian scoundrel?" she snapped, scaring me half to death. Made you feel she had something personal against you.

Anyway, it was out of Sally's Cadillac we stole the girlie magazine, one showing everything on a body. Me. Buster Copaz, who was the oldest and the leader of our gang. Micky Toms, another Indian, like me and Buster. Victor James, who was black. And the angel-face Navarro twins, Jesus and Ignacio, who we called Nate. I seen the car parked in our neighborhood, and it was Buster who spotted the magazine and told Micky to reach in the open window and take it. There was paper and stuff like phone numbers that flew out the magazine as we tore down the street and made our way to the barn. "Good thing," Buster said, "because if we get caught with this there's no proving our connection to it. Like it could be anybody's." It was summer and we was too young for the cannery and too old for our mothers. We was fourteen or so, like I said. So we messed up like this.

Up in the hay, Buster started looking at the pictures. From where I was I seen the curves of naked women, softlike and the pale color of a half-cooked hotcake. Micky, who don't have much of a neck to stretch, sat next to Buster. The rest of us looked from where we sat, even if what we seen was upside down.

"Turn it so we can see," Victor said to Buster, who hogged the pictures on his lap. But I knowed what was next.

"Just picture it like it's real," Buster said.

See, Buster couldn't control himself. He made it like if we didn't follow we wasn't cool. We had ourselves a hideaway in that barn, a fort made by moving hay around so we couldn't get seen. Just then it looked like Buster was going to share the pictures because he put the magazine in the middle of our circle. But it was only so he could get his drawers down and have us look at the pictures and do the same. So he wouldn't be alone not controlling himself.

"Close your eyes," Buster said.

By this time we was exposed too. Or partway. The closing eyes part I went along with. You know how guys check each other out, and no one compared to Buster then. Least of all me and the Navarro twins. Which caused the shooting worries. But I seen Buster's eyes closed but not closed, all glassy, like hard murky marbles over them pictures. He was gone already. Then I closed my eyes completely. I tried to keep seeing the picture that showed a woman in black stockings. Never mind the hay poking my ass and the back of my legs, I was starting to feel pretty good, like things was working, when what I seen was Caroline. It was her come to my mind, and I kept on.

I thought first it was them stray cats, which had a way of coming out of nowhere in that barn and scaring the hell out of us. Things got still and at the same time voices. I heard Buster jump, then the others. I opened my eyes. Buster and them wasn't there, but moved, over the side of the hay looking down on the mangers. I blinked a few times to catch what just happened. Then I pulled up my pants and joined the others. Buster turned and put his finger to his lips for us to shut up. I moved between Micky and Victor and seen what Buster was looking at. It was Smoke and some black girl talking.

"You just shut up and never mind," Smoke was saying. He chewed her out like nobody's business.

"Well, I—" she started to say with her hand on her hip.

"Well, you nothing," he said. "You jealous 'cause you old whore. Let me and Sally run things. And tonight we done a run and it ain't just you."

It was like he said something all of a sudden took the air out of her. Her hand fell from her hip, like she wilted. She stood there looking foolish even to me just then. Standing in that short black shirt two shades darker than her skin. Standing in high heels sunk flat in the dusty horseshit. I could see the black where her orange hair growed out.

"Now you just get," Smoke said. "And you go through the fence there. Go up the railroad tracks and don't be coming around here in broad daylight. You look worse than you is."

The black girl disappeared. Smoke lifted his straw hat like to cool his head. He was dressed in overalls, like someone who just works with horses. After a minute, he left too. Only he went through the gate to the other barn.

"We're going in there tonight," Buster said like he'd been thinking it over the past two days. We sat back in our spots and Buster closed the magazine and stuffed it between two bales of hay.

It was Smoke saying tonight that hung in our ears and then grew inside our brains. Like tonight was a star just now so close we might touch it.

"We can't all go in," Victor said, "because there's a big pit in there full of dead horses and we could all fall in."

Pit or no pit, that wasn't the point. Nobody knowed for sure what was in that other building. Sure they killed horses in there and folks talked about a hole where they ground up the meat. But Victor was just talking to cover what we was feeling. It was dark, scary. The only way to get in that place besides the front was to sneak up the chute in back where they took the horses to kill them. No one wanted to go through that to see what tonight was all about. No one had the guts.

Buster acted a smartass. "We all die," he said. But he had things figured out. He played on what Victor was saying. "If we're dead then there's no way anybody knows what's going on in there. So one of us is going to stand near that chute and the rest is going to watch outside the fence—" He stopped for a second, breaking up his line of words like he was in a movie. A cool guy. "Oh, and in case you all forgot, *one* of us *is* going inside."

He grabbed six pieces of straw and started arranging them in his hand, like he couldn't see what he was doing. "There's one short one," he said.

Victor's eyes popped out of his head. He must've been picturing himself drowning in a hundred feet of molding horse intestines. He had a sister who rode off with Smoke one night, at least somebody said that, and when one of us, I forgot who, asked him about it, his eyes got big like now and he looked over his shoulder like his mother or somebody was listening. He was quiet as cat walking, and just turning his head to see behind him.

"Think of the girls," Buster said. "Girls."

I must've looked scared as Victor. Thinking of girls in that barn didn't help none. Thinking just then couldn't have changed what happened. I picked the short straw.

"Micky, you stand by the chute. Me and everybody else stand guard." Now Buster was a commander of the troops making his strategy, all business. He looked at each of us. Then stopped on me. "Frankie, if you don't show up . . ." He stopped and spit and looked at me again. "Get some points, Frankie."

The plan was to meet at nine o'clock, when it was dark. I was standing outside the market on Grand, just about home, and I seen on the store clock it was only three. Six hours, I thought, and I'm superstitious. Six ain't a good number. Buster and them split, went home. I couldn't just sit. I went back to the slaughter-house, probably just to see where I was going.

Nothing seemed the same in that haybarn. I thumbed through the magazine, but without the guys there I felt like pervert or something. I seen the cobwebs on the old roofboards and the way the main beam swayed under the weight of the roof. Like them endless spiders had eyes and was seeing me in my secrets. The beam would snap, coming down, keeping me forever with the whole world to see with them pictures in my hand. I thought of Mom or Sis finding me like that. And Dad. "Can't you get the real thing, boy? That's okay to study, but don't be no fool. Re-member what I tell you." I heard that drunk talk of his with me and my friends about what you're supposed to do with a woman to make her happy.

I put the pictures back between the hay bales and crawled to where I could look to the other barn. It was quiet over there and I seen Sally's gold Cadillac like it was resting. It looked small, miniature-sized against that large white barn growing up all around it. In the corral just below me them horses stood swatting flies like they had a million tomorrows. I couldn't sit still.

I went out, behind the barn, and made my way along the railroad tracks. Lots of times us guys followed the tracks, which cut right through town, from the slaughterhouse north to the station on lower Fourth, where there's bars and poolhalls. The tracks pass back of that white place. Which is where you can see the chute they take the horses up to meet the gun, which is where I was supposed to go in a matter of hours. I came to the fence and saw the burlap hanging from the top of the chute, covering half the gaping black hole that led inside. All at once an old white cat appeared. Scared me on account I was just starting to picture myself up the chute. It stopped and looked at me then came down the ramp like I was nothing. In the sunlight it was old and matted, white hair gray and dusty looking. It moved slow, stiff-legged. What that cat must know, I thought, watching it cross the corral to the other barn.

It was then I decided I needed luck.

Do a good thing, Grandma says. I thought of her cousin, Old Julia. They didn't talk much, even though Julia just lived around the corner. Something about something Julia did a long time ago, which had Indians mad at her. Something about who she married, some white man. I don't know. Folks don't talk. Point is she had no friends and lived alone. When I got to Old Julia's, I seen her front door was open and I walked up and tried seeing through the screen.

"Auntie Julia," I called.

She came through the kitchen into the front room and I seen her face all pushed up, set hard. Like she was going to talk back to someone, madlike. Or not talk at all, refuse to answer up to all the things folks accused her of. Then she let down, and her eyes came out big and watery. "Frankie," she said, pushing open the screen.

"Auntie," I said, "them weeds out back of your house, they going to catch fire and burn you down."

She giggled and covered her mouth with her hand, like a young girl. "Oh, gee," she said, and you'd think I told her her slip was showing. I seen lots of old Indian ladies do this. Grandma does it and it's her way of covering how she's thinking in the situation. And Old Julia, I should've figured the range of her thinking after I'd just found her face hard as the porch I was standing on.

"Now come in," she said, shaking the screen door she held open.

Inside Old Julia's place you'd think time stopped. The world hadn't touched her. Not a speck of dust. Not a scratch. Not a dent or sign anyone sat on the puffy couch or rested their elbows on the pressed white doilies over the arm rests. The purple and pinkish blooms of her African violets in the windows looked fake, clothlike. It looked like she'd just put the pictures of her one daughter and grandson in new frames and placed them perfect on the walls that morning.

In the bright yellow kitchen her redbud and sedge roots for basketmaking sat on the table in neat coils wrapped and tied with strips of yellow cloth. Like my grandma, Old Julia was what they call a famous Pomo basketmaker. But there were no signs except her roots, no peelings on the floor or wet hairy sedges drying on newspapers. No signs of her weaving. She poured me a glass of milk, placed it in front of me on a napkin, then stood by the counter, like she was waiting for what I wanted next. I sat down. I felt like she'd been waiting and hoping all day for me to come. Like she had that milk just for me and the house perfect the way she thought I liked it.

"I don't have much to do today, Auntie, so I thought I'd take care of your weeds out back and side of the house." It felt good telling her this, seeing how she was. I sipped my milk.

She shifted on one foot. "Oh, dig them out? That's too much work." Her voice was steady but tiredlike.

"Someone could throw a match, Auntie, and that's it."

"True," she said, shifting again. She looked old. She wore a red scarf and wisps of white hair stuck out bright against her sagged brown face. Her slip showed below her faded print housedress. It was like she didn't belong in that house. Her eyes was still big and watery. "That would be nice," she said finally.

She offered me a plate of cookies, but I wanted to start on the weeds. I couldn't sit still. I went out the front door and started pulling the tall oat grass that lined the sides of her house and filled her garden. I seen a couple of her window screens was rusted out. Really, her place was like anybody else's, only she had no junk, refrigerators and stuff, sitting around. In-town-reservation-living we called it. I was at the oat grass half a minute when I realized I couldn't pull it out. It was summer, like I said, too far in summer, and the tops of them dried oat stalks just busted in my hands. I should dig them, I thought, turn over the soil. But that would take too long, too hard. The earth was dry clay packed tight as stone. A small plot was all I could do.

I thought on this.

Then I seen the scythe. It was leaning upright against the fence. Its wooden handle growed out of the grass like something looking at me just then. I walked over and seen the blade was rusty, but it cut. Not good, but it cut. I'd do the whole place, surprise Old Julia. I swung that scythe like crazy, and in a hour or so I'd hit everywhere, alongside the house, in front by the rose hedge, the whole back.

I was standing catching my breath and admiring the territory I covered when Julia stepped out on the back porch. I started to gesture with my free hand, as if to say look, when I seen she was chuckling to herself.

"Oh, gee," she said. She was looking down where I butchered her small roses by the porch, not just those but the ones beneath the back window.

I seen the chipped paint now and the rusted-out screens and I seen Old Julia's hanging slip. But there was nothing sorry about her. Her whole body started shaking, the slip and housedress jumping up and down, and she done nothing now to cover that laugh sounding like a crow calling and shrinking me to the size of a pea. I looked away and seen the yard like a blond kid with a bad haircut. I wanted to apologize about the roses, but she was laughing so loud and hard I couldn't get her attention to say a thing. She stopped a split second and her face changed hard. She looked at the chopped oat grass then at me, and before she busted up worse than ever, I see what her squinting birds' eyes said: Throw a match and that's it.

I went home and sat in the shed back of our house. Just

plopped myself on a prune crate in the dark. I seen my luck like it was a movie in a theater. The short straw. Old Julia's cursing laugh. She'd seen what would happen the minute she found me on her porch, and she let me fall in. She tricked me. Tricked me into entering that strange cleanlike house where nobody lived because Old Julia wasn't a person. Tricked me with them watery eyes like she done that first time at the grocery store so I would carry her groceries. Hooey about some white man, whoever she married. The old folks knowed. Old Julia was a witch, a poisoner. Why else would Grandma and them keep away from her? Not because of a white man. Indians around here got secrets. Don't want people knowing certain things. Make us forget, not think of stuff. But they wasn't hiding nothing from me. Old Julia seen where that straw torn me wide open. She seen the hole and hooked herself there, and then like she had that straw in her hand, she tickled me with it for no reason except to laugh at me and feed her evilness.

I had to turn things around.

I went to Caroline.

That movie was still going in my mind. I wanted a different picture, and it was Caroline I thought of because no matter how low I was I felt high as the tallest tree around her. And none of the guys was around to make fun of me and her. I'm not lying, she was fine. But she was different.

"She's weird," Buster said. "Stinky virgin."

That was on the first day I really noticed her. Buster and me and Micky was sitting on the bike racks in front of the market and she comes walking up the street. Looked like a schoolgirl, white bobby socks and tennis shoes, pants rolled up at the cuff, plain white blouse. She tossed her silky black hair around to keep it out of her face, and the way she walked she could've been anywhere, going down the hall at school, at the fair. Like she wasn't paying attention to nothing. Maybe that's what caught my eye, because to me just then there was something woman about her, no schoolgirl.

"Hah! She's your cousin," Micky said, laying one into Buster.

"Shit, I don't know them drunks from Graton. Stinky Indi-ans," Buster said.

I knowed she was Buster's cousin first day in history when the teacher called her name—Caroline Copaz. That and she was some relation to that lady Grandma knowed in Graton with the same name. But it wasn't till just then on the street I see her potential, like I said.

Anyway, that same afternoon I went to the Hole, where she lived, and played like I was visiting old man Toms, Micky's grandpa. The Hole is in our corner of town that is called South Park. Only it's in the worst part of South Park, south end of Grand Avenue. It's two lines of brown army barracks separated by a potted dirt road. All kinds of Indians end up there. Blacks too. Micky's grandpa lived in a place at the end, just across from Caroline. I found him sitting on his ripped-apart piss-stained–looking couch halfway in the middle of the road. Like him and that couch was a roadblock at the end. He sat all day like that, watching folks and sucking his empty pipe. I greeted him and sat on the wobbly armrest. He asked how Grandma and Old Uncle was and then laughed showing a long yellow tooth, his big belly with his pants pulled up quaking up and down causing his half-undone zipper to come open more and more.

"Mata," he said, which means woman, and I seen Caroline come out her door.

I seen the old man's Stetson hat on the couch and I picked it up and make like I just took it off my head for Caroline. Like a dude of high class. "Good day, lady," I said.

I stopped her short. She studied me like. Her eyes focused and then I seen her face changed like she knowed me half her life and just then remembered. "Good day, sir," she said in the same kind of voice I used.

That's how I got to know Caroline. And how I knowed she was different.

I struck a lucky note. Caroline loved games. We played we was different people. Used accents and that stuff. Sometimes we'd be married and discuss our children. Oh, Peter has such a problem with his homework. And what is it, my dear husband, that keeps our Allison brooding? Mostly Caroline. She'd start like out of nowhere. We're just walking along or sitting back of the fairgrounds and she'd start into something. I couldn't keep up with her, all that different kind of language. She lost me. I felt funny or something.

"You read too many books," I told her.

It was me started the Romeo thing one day. Except she thought it was a damsel in distress story. Point is Juliet wanted same as Romeo, which Caroline hadn't figured out. We was in our spot under the cypress trees back of the fairgrounds. I help her down where she could sit.

"Thank you, kind sir," she said. "I narrowly escaped."

I kissed her, started pressing on her too. I moved up her skin, under her blouse. She pushed up and hunched over kind of. She was that girl again, the one I didn't look at in history class. Only I seen her now, and when she turned to look at me I was something cool, the toughest guy on earth.

She looked away and let out a sigh like she was tired. But she was already somewheres else. "Peter got another note," she said, disgusted like.

It was almost six when I knocked on her door. It was bright outside still. Old man Toms was watching from under the Stetson hat that shaded his face and his big belly started heaving again but I turned away. I was about to leave when the door pulled open then closed just as fast. Like a window shade popping up then down. Now you see, now you don't. Then the door opened a couple inches, then slowly a couple inches more until Caroline's mother was there. Only her face and fingers on the door. The face just appeared, come into the light and wasn't attached to nothing. It was a mask, painted orange lips the same color as the nails on the door, pencil brows and false eyelashes, one of the lashes drooping over eye like on a busted doll. She moved so slow and strange and stared with that drooping eye like she was looking at something beyond me.

"Carol, your nigger boy's here," she said without putting expression in that puppet face.

Her voice swerved and bumped, like a car out of control. It told everything you couldn't see past the mask. She was drunk, as usual. The booze smell coming from that brown painted-up head enough to knock old man Toms off his couch. I knowed what she meant saying nigger boy. My father and uncle them's all Portuguese. Part black, folks say. But this woman's thing was something with my dad. I don't know. It didn't bother me none. I didn't say nothing, not then, or even before when she first showed her face. I just waited. She said something again about me being a nigger, then Caroline came out and the door closed behind her.

She was bright-looking, clean with her white blouse and tennis shoes and socks, her pants rolled up just so. Only thing, she didn't give them eyes. No princess look. Not the wife either. Nothing. Like she didn't even look at me. She brushed past me. "Come on," she said. Old man Toms was laughing so loud I wanted to kick him one in that fat unzipped gut.

I figured Caroline was mad on account I hadn't come by for a while. She was stepping fast and big, like she knowed where she was going. I trailed behind her and kept asking over her shoulder what was the matter. I thought it might be her mom being drunk and all that. After all, it was just Caroline and her mom in that place. Living with the foul-smelling puppet head was no pleasure. But it wasn't her mom. It was me, what I first suspected.

She led me to the cypress trees and then sat down. I caught her eyes once but she looked away.

"You're just a dumb boy," she said.

Her voice was different. Nothing I recognized. None of the voices I knowed from her. Caught me off guard, but it went along with her being pissed like. She had her face in her hands, the long fingers up her cheeks, and she was looking back down the street, toward Grand. The sun showed her eyes, but I couldn't see her straight on.

"I been looking for a job," I said.

"You lie, Frankie. You can't get no job." She wasn't moving.

"I want to do something. Not just sit around here all day like a nobody bum."

"You're a nobody."

Her voice was ten miles away same time it was right there. I wasn't stupid. She was mad on account I kept reaching for more than she wanted to give and then stopped showing up to see her. Which was the truth. She pushed me to it.

Then I put my arm around her. I felt good. But she was hard as a rock, unmoving yet.

"I never went to the park with Buster to see them other girls."

The soft sell. I figured I'd play it from her point of view. I was telling the truth, even if the truth was them girls around the park moved too fast. But nothing seemed to matter to Caroline. I had to approach it different.

"Me and Buster's going to do something tonight. I'm . . ."

"Probably you are," she said, "because you're a nobody."

It was like she talked all of a sudden. Cut me off without thinking about it. Like her voice come out of the sky and then was gone so you didn't know if you heard it or not. It was strange. Sounded something like a disgusted mother, but it went too fast for me to say for sure. She went with her voice, farther away. It wasn't what I wanted. I heard my own words about tonight, me and Buster, and I remembered why I was sitting there just then. Where I'd started to feel good with Caroline, now I was sinking. The stakes was high. I had to win. Even if she just looked at me in that certain way said I was something cool. I held on to her like she was a card I could will into an ace. Time was all I had. I knowed if I just held, and I would've held till dark, she'd give in. And I was right.

The sun dropped two fingers' worth in the sky. That's how I was measuring time, with my free fingers against the sun. I first seen her kicking at the dirt, just a little with one foot, then she adjusted her shoulders. I started moving too, but not where she could see. The tide turned, the ace came up and got me moving. I leaned over and kissed her. Her eyes were open and holding that sun in little dots of light, and if I hadn't closed my eyes just then and kept looking I would've seen the mountain range, everything in her eyes clear to the ocean and back. She put her arms around me like never before. I felt her hands back of my shoulder holding on. I leaned her against the tree. Then, all at once, she twisted and bolted upright, and when she pulled away my hand was caught in her blouse which pulled her toward me and made her pull back again so we was caught together and when she jerked free she flew against the tree and hit with a thud.

I jumped to her then coiled back. Her eyes shot through that tangled mess of hair at me like I was the devil himself. She pushed herself upright with her elbows, still glaring at me, then faced the sun and started clearing the hair out of her face.

"It's no use," she said. "You're just like all the rest. It's all the same. Mama's right."

I didn't follow her. Everything changed so fast. She arched her back, stiff. The wife, I thought. I worked my throat so my voice would be the husband. Caroline's lips started, but nothing came out, no words. Then she wilted, folded up into her lap, and I could tell what she said before she said it.

"It's no use," she said into her hands.

She crossed the line. She was on the other side, gone. I felt we wouldn't be friends after that. I cramped up, felt sorry, because just then I also knowed I liked her special. I found out too late. I cramped up, felt sorry and mad at the same time.

She braced herself, hands on knees, like she propped herself up, then she was on her feet. I seen the sun glistening down one side of her face. Then she was running. She'd gone halfway down the block before I could move. I chased her far as Grand then quit.

I was just plain mad. Mad at her, Buster, everybody. Mad at myself. Damn this sex business anyway. Damned if I did, damned if I didn't.

I went home.

The house was noisy and stuffy-smelling. Kids everywhere.

The TV. Mom cooking. Dad and his brother, Uncle Angelo, and their six-packs of beer at the kitchen table. Mom over the stove with the pink plastic curlers in her hair from morning. Grandma and Old Uncle in their spots next to the stove, two old Indians, sitting like they was in the park or on the front porch, just watching.

"Frankie, you want some beans, here?" Mom asked without turning to look at me standing behind her. She's like that. Got a sixth sense where she knows each of her eight kids without look-ing.

She dished a bowl of chili from the big pot she was stirring. "Get yourself a spoon," she said, and then dropped a spoon in the bowl she handed me. I looked for a place to sit. The chairs and couch was filled in the front room so I sat at the table across from Dad and Uncle Angelo. Which I didn't want to do on account of their getting drunk and loud. Mom handed me a warm tort in a paper towel. "Where you been?" she asked, turning back to the stove.

Just then Uncle Angelo's fists hit the table causing my plate of beans to jump half an inch. "Son of a bitch, the bastard was in his car already," Uncle Angelo said.

It was something about somebody Uncle Angelo wanted to beat up at work. Him and Dad always talked like that when they was drinking. Fighting and women. They was more drunk than I first figured. Both of them cussed up a storm. They looked the same, curly black hair, lightish skin, tight faces that opened and cracked in lines when they laughed. And when they was drink-ing, their eyes got small, black beads like rats' eyes, so you couldn't tell what they was thinking and what was coming next. I looked to Grandma in the room with all that talk. She seen me and she giggled, lifting her hand to her mouth. Mom lifted the pot of beans to the sink. At least I got interrupted and didn't have to think of an answer for her about where I'd been. I could thank Uncle Angelo's fists for that.

Most of the time I wanted Dad and Uncle Angelo to leave, get on with their routine, which was drinking then out on the town to the bars and pool halls on lower Fourth. They picked on everybody. Old Uncle about never being married. Me if I got a piece of ass yet. But just then, watching for what was coming next out of them, I didn't have to dwell on the fact I was sunk worse than a brick in a fish pond. I did start thinking about the scene, though, Sally Did and Smoke. I thought of asking Uncle Angelo about Sally on account his wife was related to Sally, sister or something, which is how we knowed Sally was just another Indian from around here and not a princess from some faraway tribe like she was claiming. See, I was thinking if I could find out something about Sally and the goings-on in that slaughterhouse I wouldn't have to go all the way inside. Just fake it, go in a little, then tell the guys a story.

But I wouldn't get a chance to ask Uncle Angelo nothing.

Everything got quiet. Just the TV and Mom taking plates from the cupboard. I kept my eyes on my food. I kept eating. I felt Dad and Uncle Angelo move past me, behind me. They were going to tweak my ear, pinch my chest. I could hear even what they was going to say. "You get your whistle wet, boy?" All that stuff. I just kept my head down, chewing my beans, and because the longest time went by, I figured the worst possible thing would happen. Like they'd hit me a good one upside the head and then I'd have to sit there watching them laugh at me. Like I was supposed to be quicker and outsmart them. What could I do? Then from the corner of my eye I seen Mom picking up the empty beer cans. And I seen Dad and Uncle Angelo was gone, not anywhere. I turned clear around until I seen the open front door.

Mom put plates of beans on the table for Grandma and Old Uncle. The two of them sat down with me. But I didn't look at them any more than I looked at Dad and Uncle Angelo. I seen only the open front door and the streetlight shining beyond. It was my time to go too.

I started seeing my live movie again. Not like I turned it on, but like it turned itself on, the whole day's events running past my eyes. And this time Caroline added in. I had nothing to take out that door with me. No luck, only an empty barrel. I looked at my sisters and brothers in the front room and then at Grandma and Old Uncle. I was alone all of a sudden. I started to shake like. I thought of Buster and them out back of that slaughterhouse. They'd be waiting for me. Points. Points. Points. I have no points. I was washed up, broke. Sunk. Then something come to me, not in my head, but in my shaking. Like something just give up in me and let me go. I seen my movie still going and it wasn't just Buster and them. It was the whole thing. And me. Me. What was I holding onto anyway? Nothing. What did I have to lose? What I had was one more chance not to lose, to turn the whole picture around. The short straw, Old Julia, Caroline. Everything. I was my only chance. So I got up and left.

It was cool, clear. The night opened itself for me. I slipped down Grand and up Santa Rosa Avenue like a eel in water. Nothing stopped me until the slaughterhouse fence. Turns out I was the only one there. Seemed like forever but Victor and Micky finally showed. Buster didn't turn up for another half hour it seemed. The Navarro twins didn't show at all.

"Okay," Buster said, "it's just us." He looked at me and then started explaining how I just walk up the chute. He talked like it was some technical maneuver, as if I couldn't figure out how to walk up a ramp and hadn't thought way beyond that the whole time I was waiting for him. But he was going through the motions, saying stuff so he could still play Buster. He didn't know what to do after going up the chute. He couldn't say if he had to and he knowed it. Nobody could. It was a big deal. "All clear," Buster said, but I was already through the fence.

The chute had cross boards like steps so the horses wouldn't slip or fall. That struck me funny. Like to make sure the horses would go in and not hurt themselves and miss out on dying. But soon as I was under that burlap and in the dark I had to pay attention. I couldn't see a damn thing. And the horse gut pit and all that come to mind. But funny thing, it never crossed my mind to lie just then, like I planned at home. I never thought of stopping and hiding in the dark. I already done more than Buster or any of them.

I followed a fence railing. I walked sideways, like a crab, never letting go of that railing. I was thinking. Like I said, that hole of horse guts was on my mind, and I took little steps, holding on to the railing and testing with each step to make sure I had solid ground. I looked back to the light from the chute hole every once in a while. Then something happened. I couldn't see anything. Frontward or backward. My way out was gone. I couldn't see the chute hole. I must've rounded a corner. Things shifted. The railing stopped and I was clinging to a flat wall. I froze up, spread-eagle on the wall. I was completely lost.

I thought of tearing out of there, making a mad dash for the chute hole. The place had no windows, so I couldn't think of that. There was no way out but the chute and the front door, and I was a far ways from the front door. I was on the second floor somewheres and the front door was on the first. I almost panicked. But I had enough reason left to tell me that tearing off in that darkness was likely to land me in the horse pit or something worse. I stood there awhile, my palms flat against the wall. I was spread-eagle, like I said, facing the wall like I was caught and waiting for cops to frisk me. Then I started moving real slow, going sideways with the toes of my tennis shoes and my palms holding on to the wall. I'd gone about five feet when I heard it. Actually, I felt it, a vibrating sound in the wall, like a bass pounding through the wood. I stopped, then moved a little backward then forward. Forward it was stronger. I followed and it got stronger, louder so that it was music I was hearing. A clear beat, a drum beat for some rock and roll song or something. Still I took small steps, testing that I had solid ground beneath me. I kept moving sideways. And for reason. I started smelling something like meat, a thick copperlike smell that was warm and damp. It choked me. I felt like I was moving between flesh. Like it was hanging on either side of me, all around. But I kept going, a little forward then stopping then on again. Like that I kept moving. I was following the music, and then just as fast as that meat smell come, it disappeared and I was standing on a landing looking down a flight of stairs to light below.

It was the Supremes singing "Got Him Back in My Arms Again." The way was clear, just down the steps. But I was more scared than ever. Like down those steps I would see the goings-on firsthand. I could hear people moving and talking. What if it was nothing, just some folks partying? What if it was something and I got caught? Like I seen something illegal and they killed me so I wouldn't tell. It was this last thing pushed me on. Fear, it was what I knowed best. Not Buster and them. They was so far behind me now. I was alone and scared to death and if I stopped I might've lost my fear. I went down one step at a time. The boards creaked but by now the music was so loud nobody below could hear. Two steps from the bottom I stopped, and when I peeked around the corner, bracing myself against the wall, it all come into plain view, the room with Smoke, Sally, and the girls.

I moved down one step and situated myself so I could watch. It wasn't really a room but a clearing of cardboard boxes stacked nearly high as the ceiling. That was three walls, and Sally's gold Cadillac made the fourth. Like it was a movable wall and it was in place now. A big transistor radio sat on the hood of the car and a black girl in a short dress that looked like a pink-flowered towel around her body played with the dials trying to find another song. The rest of them was in the middle of the room. But they hadn't stopped. They was still moving like the music was still playing. They wasn't dancing really, but walking in a pack slowly around the room, going in a circle. Like in some ceremony. Smoke out in front a little with a wine jug in a brown paper sack, his straw hat on and overalls. Sally was in the middle, her skunk-striped hair showing in the small crowd. They turned so that they had their backs to me, and when they turned again, coming in my direction, I see a smaller girl in the middle, between Sally and the orange-haired black girl, and Sally and the orange hair was holding on to her arm in arm, walking her along. Sally yelled for the pink dress one by her car to hurry and find some music. The girl Sally was holding on to wore a dark shawl, and when a song came on booming into the room, I seen the fringes of the shawl started shaking, dangling. I must've had my eyes fixed on that shawl because I didn't see if any of them started moving faster or not. I didn't see that the girl had stepped out of the crowd, not until the shawl dropped on the floor, and when I looked up I seen the girl was Caroline. She was still moving, taking little steps, one at a time by herself, wobbling some, like she was just learning how to walk or had too much of Smoke's wine. Caroline with lipstick and done up hair, and even in that tight red dress that would never let me see the color red again in peace, she looked to me like a butterfly just out of its cocoon. Nothing I had known before. And she was looking right at me, her eyes in mine and mine in hers, and not knowing it. Then she looked up, like she was looking to heaven, and she couldn't have seen any more than I did, which was that blasted naked light bulb over everything. "Over here," Smoke said, and I seen he was next to the Cadillac, holding the door wide open.

I pushed myself back up the stairs to the landing. Somehow I had sense enough to know if I stood there any longer I'd likely fall forward out of the stairwell in front of all those people. Somehow, even when you're dead inside, you think how to live. Something takes over. I should've just collapsed there, letting Caroline and everyone else see how small and dumb I was. But, like I said, something takes over. A million things raced through my mind. I thought of rescuing Caroline. I pictured myself charging down the stairs and whisking her out the front door and us running along Santa Rosa Avenue to safety. I must've been standing there awhile like that because I heard Sally's car start. I thought of Caroline. But it was no use. Things was bigger than me.

I groped in the dark and found the railing. Going out was easier. I came under the burlap and stood on top of the chute. You'd think I was a king or something by the looks on the guys' faces. I had a long view of the empty railroad tracks leading into town. I didn't want to move, but I was already going down the chute.

"What'd you see in there?" Micky asked.

"Nothing," I said, crawling through the fence.

Victor stood with his eyes popped out of his head. I looked to Buster who was quiet. He knowed like the rest I'd seen something. Must've been on my face.

"Just some people dancing around. That black whore with orange hair. There's no horse gut hole or nothing," I said, and spit. My voice scared me. Like it was telling what I just won was nothing to wear a crown about.

"Man, you *did it*," Micky said.

"Shit," Buster said. "It ain't no big deal." He spit like to outdo me. But he didn't believe himself and nobody else did either.

I looked back at the burlap hanging over the top of the black hole.

"Shit, let's go to the park and get us some chicks." Buster was still at it. He turned up his T-shirt sleeves to show his muscles.

We started making our way back to Santa Rosa Avenue.

"Frankie, you smell like meat or something," Victor said, first time opening his mouth. "You better go change your clothes."

"Yeah," I said, and looked up, and there was nothing in the sky.

*i*NEZ PETERSEN was born before the Indian Child Welfare Act could protect her family rights. As a child, she was removed not only from her mother, but also from her extended family of the Quinault Tribe of Washington. She survived the foster-care system, lived some years apart from any awareness of belonging. Years later, at the University of Oregon, her writing elicited a strong emotional response when read in an advanced fiction writing course. She learned of those marginalized and silenced. "I recognized how close I came to being one of those silenced by birth, gender, race, social standing, and education." Circumstances changed. Now she is blessed with the fortunate combination of opportunity, community, belief, and desire to speak. Petersen is completing a graduate degree in English at the University of Oregon in Eugene.

JOSEPH'S RAINBOW

Inez Petersen

The road that winds out of Aberdeen, one of the last big towns before reaching the village of Taholah, passes by an empty lot. Now it holds tall grasses whose movement reveals only the passing of small hunters searching out smaller prey. All traces of the weathered gray shacks that once stood roadside are hidden under the rippling tangle of weeds.

Both the inhabitants and the structures had in common a shabbiness and determination remarkable only in their constancy. Shushing sounds of tires on wet pavement as cars passed by served to remind us shack dwellers to keep our secrets.

A small clan of Indian kids gathered around Joseph in the dirt drive outside his grandfather's home. Intermarriage to nontribal members had noticeably diluted bloodlines. Skin color merged in shades from mahogany to deep amber, to pale olive; while hair colors crossed the spectrum between char black, brown-black, and light brown.

Even within one family colors contrasted sharply: Joseph in-
herited the darkness recognizable as Indian, although his almond
eyes suggested further blood mixture. His younger brother and
sisters, Bobby, Chloey, and Teena, were lighter in complexion
and their hair colors varied. Chloey's green eyes were exceptional
even within the broad range accepted as normal in the Quinault
Nation.

Cousins, siblings, and neighborhood kids listened to Joseph as
he explained his latest plan. He began:

"We'll make a rainbow in the woods."

"Really? How?"

"You can't do that! Hey, quit elbowing me, you runt."

Ignoring the commotion, Joseph continued. "First off comes
Plan A. We hijack yarn from Granny Rose's stash."

"That's flat-out stealing," said Arthur. He was the son of
Victor Labush, Taholah's only preacher.

"It's not stealing, we are only relocating necessary material to
a strategic location. Besides, Granny Rose can't knit a rainbow
and she always wants us to use our talents, right? What does she
always tell you when you try to get out of dancing at the giveaways, Arthur?"

His mumbled response came out. "Ifyoucanwalk, you-
candance, ifyoucantalk, youcansing."

"Right. Now, listen up. Granny Rose cleans her teeth and
then glues them in at nine A.M. every morning. Earlier in the day,
she likes naked gums."

Joseph mugged, as if smacking together naked gums. The children nudged one another and giggled. He continued. "The first
thing she does is turn off her hearing aid."

Puzzled expressions questioned this information. He explained
further, "It's like church prayers—she does it religiously and it
takes forever."

The older children perked up, realizing the importance of
Granny Rose's deafness in her morning ritual. The younger ones
pretended to know and nodded wisely.

It worked too. The very next morning, seven untried warriors passed by Granny Rose's rocking chair with a studied nonchalance. On the shelves behind her chair, brightly colored skeins of yarn vied for space alongside Granny's books. Their eager hands scooped up loads of yellow, purple, red, and blue. Even four-year-old Chloey managed to escape with three balls of yarn held aloft in triumph.

The screen door banged shut behind them. Several stealthy bodies froze midstride. Their fearless leader reminded them "Plan B! Run like hell!" They scattered like shot from a twelve-gauge, each clutching trophies.

A few hundred yards past the end of the dirt and gravel drive, bracken ferns and huckleberry bushes closed over human signs. Hidden from view, a water spigot dripped into the remains of an MJB coffee tin, riddled by practice shots. Rivulets of moisture condensed and fell through the many holes. The rendezvous point was just after a bend in a rutted track known as Tale's End Road, a longtime trysting place. The legend of Tale's End Road centered around questions concerning the unfortunate ending of Dixie and Walter's love affair.

It happened, or it could have happened, that Big Pete was setting snares one day. He might have come across his wife, Dixie, and Walter all tangled together in Walter's cousin's pickup truck near Tale's End. Maybe Big Pete let the air out of the two back tires. Maybe he helped himself to the crowbar in the back. One thing is for sure: Big Pete took care of business.

Sometimes that meant Dixie'd wear bright-colored scarves around her neck. Eventually, purple and green discoloration would tentacle out from behind the knotted bandanna. No cheerful scarf could hide from view the choke marks left by Big Pete. The bruises spoke the truth while Dixie herself insisted in a hoarse voice, "Must be having asthmatics again. Runs in the family, you know?" We knew.

So, when Dixie got all womanish when Walter came around, no one was about to notice. Dixie looked good in dimples.

No tribal cop ever poked around, looking for Dixie and Walter. No one questioned Big Pete concerning his new collection of tools. Walter's cousin didn't even claim his old truck.

Instead, the Pacific Northwest rain forest rusted out that one-eyed Ford. Rotting seat covers reupholstered themselves in velvety moss. Maidenhair ferns nodded, delicately covering what could have been bloodstains. Held in a damp embrace, death nurtured life.

The pickup truck became a beacon of warning and welcome: warning to any unsure of their love and welcome to any willing to die for their desire.

En route to the trysting site, Bobby stood guard. His duty was to decoy passersby. Down the road, Joseph lined up the other renegades according to height. He handed a ball of yarn to each one.

"First, tie one end around that sapling." He motioned with his chin, a quick jutting indicating which one he meant. "Victor, you help the little kids."

They followed his instructions.

"Now. Walk across the path, go around that tree, and come back. Good."

"What happens when this here yarn runs out, huh?" questioned one of the girls in the middle of the line-up.

Joseph answered, "Tie a knot and add another one to it, whatever color you want."

Plan C took longer than Joseph had anticipated, but the finished webbing worked. Strand by strand, shades of color stretched between two saplings that stood across the road from each other. Their limbs became the frame of a weaver's creation. Around and around, until there appeared a solidified section of rainbow; a wondrous trap.

"Spider Woman would be proud of her daughter's children," said Joseph. "Now, we wait." Like wood spirits the children seemed to dissolve into nearby foliage, prepared to wait for unsuspecting prey.

Sure enough, an old two-door sedan came crawling into view.

The broken windshield cracked into separate but spiraling mosa-ics. Shafts of sunlight reached through the overhead canopy of branches and hid the driver from view. Everyone knew it was William Kitsap. Who else could keep this heap plugging along on four or five cylinders?

Faces peered out from hiding places, all eager to learn the punchline in their elaborate joke.

Startled green eyes peered into darkness; Chloey awakened to the sound of angry voices in the next room. Troubled, she slipped wraithlike, unseen and unheard, into Mama's bedroom. She stopped at the corner of the cedar stand-up closet, then stepped inside. The scent of must wafted up as she sank onto piled sweat-ers. Chloey pulled a comforter up over her head then pushed it down so she could hear better.

"Why are you looking at me?" Mama's warm honey voice sounded warped and speeded up. "Her crying drives me crazy."

"But, Mama, not baby Teena. You can't do that," Joseph pleaded.

"Don't you understand? Why do you think I go out all the time? That constant crying! I want to protect you," Delores said.

"Not our sweet baboo." Joseph's voice faltered.

"You shut up! I didn't mean to hurt her."

Chloey heard the resounding snap of flesh against flesh but did not see Joseph touch his cheek where a handprint remained. She heard footsteps pounding past her hiding place and out the front door. In the silence that followed, she heard the ragged breathing of a monster.

Fear clamped tight her vocal cords. She practiced the pretend sleep Joseph had shown her. Sometimes monsters came up and snuffled with fumy breaths when she lay in bed at night. Some even wore Mama's perfume to fool her, but nothing bad would happen if she played possum.

Drifting off, Chloey decided she'd better teach Teena the pos-sum trick soon. Sounds haunted her dreams that night. Again and again she heard a baby wailing, then a sickening thump.

Heavy silence, then footsteps pounded by, leaving Chloey alone. As she opened her dream eyes, Chloey could see the tiny form crumpled on the floor. She begged her baby sister's forgiveness.

On a cloudless day, Joseph and Cousin Rosie plotted together sitting huddled on the back porch at Uncle Ronnie's.

Joseph suggested, "We could dump nails into Old Man Hall's driveway. He's so mean it'd serve him right to get a flat."

"Or two," Rosie answered. She smiled then shook her head. "We should wait until he evicts someone again. Remember when Jamie had to bail Pauline out of jail? He kicked them out for being just two days late on rent."

Joseph nodded. "Old Man Hall's gonna get it someday. Okay, then how about . . ."

Just then Uncle Ronnie lumbered out the door and passed them while warning under his breath, "Here she comes."

Too late, for on the very heels of their uncle's departure, Auntie Vi appeared. She held out two vegetable peelers, and out of nowhere produced what seemed like a whole gunny sack of No. 2 potatoes.

"Peel these." Auntie Vi didn't mince words: You always knew where you stood with her.

From where he sat on the porch, Joseph could see his little sister practicing "the bird." He groaned, imagining the worst if Auntie Vi caught sight of her.

"Look! I can do it! I can do it, huh, Joseph?" Chloey displayed her handiwork.

"Don't show that right now!" hissed Rosie.

"Wait until we play Fuck Off," hissed Joseph.

Just then a dusty station wagon pulled to a stop by the wood-pile. Their relief turned to dread as each recognized the bulk of the current CSD worker behind the steering wheel.

"Joseph, lookit! Miss Bunton is coming," a younger cousin joined them.

"She's coming to take you away, ha-ha."

"Not funny, Rosie." Auntie's terseness silenced the children. Miss Bunton pulled herself out of the car, rumpled as usual. Her gentle voice frightened them. "Violet Boyer? I am here by court order to collect the children of Delores Marie DuBois: Joseph Lee, Chloey Ann, and Teena Michelle. They are now wards of the court of the county of Gray's Harbor and will be taken immediately into custody." She held out a pen and an official-looking document. "Please sign this form."

I remembered that decree today when we headed north. She had handed it over to my aunt, it was legal all right. I remembered that Auntie's hand trembled as she wrote her name. Today as we traveled, I looked over at Chloey riding shotgun. Sound asleep, as usual on our roadtrips. I don't know how she does it; she can sleep through anything. Chloey held a tattered letter. The pages had started out fresh and new at the beginning of our trip just yesterday morning. Since then she'd worried the edges soft. Maybe it was the continuous handling, or maybe the message itself blistered and withered. I knew she intended to place that letter in the casket once we got to Taholah. I kept telling myself that someone should know what she wants to tell Mama. So I read it:

> So many things I don't know. Is it okay if I ask now? I always thought I would hurt you if I asked, but Mama I want to know: Where were you that day? What did they tell you? What did you do? Tell me what happened. I don't blame you for our past, I just want to hear your part of the story. How did you feel when you found out all of your children had been taken away?
>
> Placed in foster homes is what the record says, but to me it felt like being torn up and thrown away. Mama, so many things I don't know or don't remember. Now that the questions have started, I have more: Were you happy to give birth to a baby girl for

the first time? Tell me about that day. Did you and my father want me? Who was my father? Who was Joseph's father?

I know there was another brother. What was his name? Who was his father? This isn't meant to shame you or be disrespectful; I just want so much to have some history. Tell me please about that brother. I don't remember him at all. Someone told me he left when I was four. What happened?

I can't imagine how you managed to survive as long as you did. Your pain must have been endless. First, I need to embrace you, embrace our past; then I need to let you go. You were an incredibly beautiful woman; I know because I remember. Rest in peace, Mama. No matter what happened.

With care, I tucked Chloey's questions back into the envelope. I replaced it exactly as found, into her upturned palm. The monotony of I-5 no longer hypnotized me. My thoughts disrupted only by the irregular rhythms of memory.

Distance. Once upon a time we had distance to protect ourselves from knowing our history. As we approached Aberdeen, my palms began to sweat. Familiar landmarks glided by. Thinkamee Hill was the first. Distance no longer comforted me.

"Chloey, wake up. I want to tell you something. See that lot over there, where the grass is waist high? We used to live there in a tumbledown shack. We lived there with our brother, Bobby."

"No. I am Batman and you are the Joker this time, Joseph." Bobby's face spoke more eloquently than did his words.

Convinced, Joseph agreed. "Okay; meet me at the Bat Cave in ten minutes. I gotta check on Mama and the girls." He never let Bobby forget who was the boss, who was twelve, and who was man of the family.

Running home, Joseph didn't notice that more driftwood and debris had been tossed onto the rocky beach from the previous night's storm. He didn't hear the sudden growling of three all-terrain vehicles, as one by one they began clawing through the dunes a half mile up. He passed by gulls fighting over scraps of rotting fish, their scraw and scree noises bright notes over his thoughts.

Joseph pondered his self-imposed duties: Keep Mama from drinking and from men; keep Miss Bunton away from Mama; keep an eye on Chloey and diapers on Teena. A line from Victor Labush's sermon popped into his thoughts. *Am I my brother's keeper too? Nah, Bobby did good on his own.*

"Batman wins round one!" Bobby crowed, delighted in his easy victory. He scrambled over boulders, slippery and barnacled.

These rocks were piled at the base of a 250-foot embankment that overlooked the ocean. Fifteen feet from the top of the cliff, erosion had begun the makings of a fine cave. The boys digging had completed the job. They created a pirate's den. Sometimes it turned into a hide-out or fortress. Other times, like today, it was the Bat Cave.

Entering the dimly lit space, Bobby whistled and gradually transformed into Batman, Prince of Darkness. He began by emptying his pockets. They bulged with a careful selection of rocks and pebbles.

"Ammo! Just for you, Joker!" he shouted his challenge, gaining courage. Bobby-into-Batman furrowed his brow, thinking. *Better stash these in the back of the cave where it's harder to see.*

In her darkened bedroom, Delores resurfaced to consciousness. She groped for the tasseled pull-chain of the overhead light bulb, then decided against glare. Somewhere, a kimono-style robe disguised itself amid the tangle of sateen bedding and eluded her searching fingers.

Not finding the robe, Delores wrapped herself in sheets, took a deep breath, and wondered what the day would bring.

Her bedroom "door" consisted of colorful strands of faux beads. Sapphires, emeralds, and rubies clicked and mixed with equally faux pearls.

The sound of their rippled clatter beckoned to Chloey. She raced from another room where the antics of J.P. Patches, the clown, continued on Channel Nine. In the hallway she watched wide-eyed as another vision appeared: yards of royal blue shimmering around her mother.

"Good morning, Queen-mama."

Grateful for direction, Delores adjusted to fit this royal image. She realigned her posture. Straightening her shoulders and lifting her chin, she answered, "Good morning, Princess."

"Where is your crown?" Chloey asked. "And mine?"

"Robber birds stole them in our dreams. We will find their nests and get our crowns back right after breakfast," declared the queen. Improvisation came easily for Delores once she had a script.

Satisfied, Chloey brightened and nodded. The sound of J.P. Patches honking his bicycle horn caught her attention. Princess Chloey skipped back toward the sound.

Bobby felt more than heard the growling and ripping of dune buggies that sent tremors through the sandy embankment. The ceiling held up mainly by the root systems of dune grasses.

He focused on finding the bundle, previously stashed for today's adventure. As he groped in the recesses of the back wall, his fingers recognized the slippery feel of the material.

"Everything is working, just as I planned." Bobby shook out "the Bat Cape." Delores's kimono shimmered dimly in the half-light. Bobby tied the arms of the robe around his neck. Ta-dah! The Prince of Darkness practiced swooping about, but kept getting his feet tangled in the cape.

A fine sifting of sand dusted him. Bobby looked up.

"Holy batshit, I gotta get out of here!" His arms and legs churned through sandy clumps of earth. He tripped again in the folds of his cape. "I'm sorry for taking your robe." Bobby begged forgiveness of the only goddess he knew. His gold-flecked eyes turned heavenward. "Mama!" Bobby screamed until the filling sand stopped his voice. Tons of earth buried him and crashed to the waves below.

On the day of the memorial service for Bobby, Miss Bunton appeared without her notebook, but her frowzy manner remained intact. Joseph was not fooled by her apparent ineptness. His eyes slitted to narrow crescents as he watched her, watching them.

Miss Bunton's steady gaze noted everything: Delores as she wobbled in spiky heels. *But her only other black shoes are vinyl go-go boots!* Joseph's thoughts screamed. Miss Bunton read resentment in his eyes and her hope for an ally vanished.

The court needs only a little more evidence to prove Delores an unfit mother. *As if a dead child weren't enough!* She fumed to herself. "Circumstantial evidence, my eye!"

Joseph's eyes narrowed even further. Miss Bunton shook her head and thought, Better watch that one; he's too smart for his own good.

By the next week the world had started new again. Joseph led a wild gleeful pack of children. His destination: a holding lot by the harbor. His feelings teeter-tottered as he scrambled over the stack lumber:

Dangerous. Alive! Careful. Alive! Warning. Alive!

The fresh scent of cut pine underscored his belief.

"Olly, olly oxen free!" Joseph yelled. "Come on, Chloey, you are going to the store."

Puffed with pride, she clutched several paper bills and marched directly to Alden's Mercantile, located on the main strip that led into Taholah.

Decision making had never been a problem for Chloey Ann DuBois. "Ten sugar bears, twenny Bazooka bubble gums, Tootsie-Rolls, Tootsie-Pops, and one sugar beads necklace for me, please."

"I'm sorry, Chloey, but Monopoly money doesn't work here; it's only for play."

Chloey lay her head on the counter and sobbed. Joseph knew she would. He knew that she burned for a candy necklace. He figured even old penny-pincher Alden would melt after seeing those mournful green eyes.

Right again. Planning was everything.

"What day is it?" Joseph asked himself. He thought a moment, then his spine stiffened and his neck hairs bristled. *It's home visitation day again. Time to rally the troops or, more like, time to rally the trooper.* Bobby's absence cut again without warning.

"Come on. You don't want Miss Bunton to take us away, do you?" He glanced over the living room: mounds of dirty clothes, empty beer cans, a pizza box spilling over with ashes and butts. Not too bad. First, throw all the good stuff into the hall closet. Next, dump the garbage. Then, on to the kitchen.

"Chloey, let's play house, okay? I'll be the mommy. You can be the little girl. All right, here we go: 'Hello! I'm home! How's Mama's angel baby? Shall we clean up?' Chloey, NO! Put that back in the closet for now."

She protested and held overhead her treasure—a half-full box of Lucky Charms. She jumped onto the couch to elude Joseph's grasp.

"Chloey. Get off the furniture."

"Joseph, these my charms, *my* charms, mine." Her chin jutted out.

"Sure thing." Joseph relented and focused instead on closet cramming. Good enough.

He headed into the kitchen, looked back over his shoulder, and shrugged. "Okay, Chloey, just don't run on the couch when Miss Bunton gets here, all right? You remember her, don't you, that snoopy lady with her long looks at everything? Remember how we always play pretend when she comes? And it's a secret, right?"

"I 'member her. She was there when we tucked that box into the ground for Bobby. Was that pretend too, Joseph? With a box?"

"Miss Bunton made Bobby go away and now we got to stick together." He believed it himself.

"She smells like butterscotch Life Savers and writes my words down. Does that make me important? Can I wear my yellow pedal pushers with the blue tassels? What are my words again? No. Don't say." She paused then recited, " 'How are you? I am good. Yes, Mama stays home every night and reads me the Pooh-book.' That's the pretend part right, Joseph? I'm not lying, I'm playing the pretend game, right?"

"Good girl, you got it just right. Now go and change your clothes. You can wear those pants if they're clean. Then get a hot wash cloth and bring me Mama's hairbrush when you are done. I've got to get at that kitchen."

Stacks of dirty plates, cups, silver, and nearly every pan in the house covered the counter by the sink. In order to think, Joseph squinched up his forehead and squeezed shut his eyes. *How to make a Betty Crocker kitchen?* He opened his eyes and saw the oven.

"Nothing says lovin'," Joseph hummed and hid the dirty dishes. He threw out pop and beer cans, Chinese carry-out boxes, and frozen pot pie tins. He sprayed Lysol on the counters and left the back door open to air out the too-obvious scent.

He brightened as he thought of the finishing touch—he would be doing "homework" when she arrived. He sighed with relief. It would work.

"Good morning, Teena. How's our baby girl? Ready for some dry diapers?" Joseph laughed as she lurched toward him in her crib, as if in a daze. Tenderly he cupped her head in his hands; dark wavy hair spilled over his hands.

"Oh, no, no. God, please, no."

Her light brown eyes looked up, bruised and cross-eyed, but she could not focus on big brother. She saw a doubled image of Joseph peering into her face. Teena's damaged eyes watched as both faces of her brother contorted. Joseph wept. His sturdy shoulders sagged. He could no longer hide Mama's illness and protect his sisters at the same time.

"Operator, I need help and my baby sister is hurt bad. Could you get through for me to the Children's Services Division in Aberdeen?"

In a government office a telephone rang. A frazzled caseworker reached out to answer it, wondering if she could stand another day. "Miss Bunton speaking, how can I help?"

"You can come get us," whispered Joseph.

The driver in William Kitsap's car couldn't see through the shattered windshield. The rainbow web waited. Distance closed between car and web until two saplings bowed and thousands of strands of yarn cocooned their prey. Old Man Hall climbed out, red in the face and shaking his fist.

Hoots of laughter erupted on Tale's End Road as the rainbow children scattered on paths of their own making.

The road that reaches out of Taholah winds away from the coast toward Aberdeen. It passes by a plot of ground, now empty of secrets. We are free to leave. And we will always be returning, Chloey and I.

P ENNY OLSON is an Ojibway who lives with her husband and children on the Upper Peninsula of Michigan. She is completing a master's degree in English at Northern Michigan University, where she is a graduate teaching instructor. Olson is currently completing several short stories that she hopes to have published as a collection.

THE DREAM

Penny Olson

"Anne, wake up." Joe's voice broke into my dreams. "Babe, are you all right? You're shaking."

I shook my head. I had been sure the dream was gone. Positive it was over. I hadn't been bothered by it in what seemed like years. The plaid down-filled comforter, which was wrapped around our bodies, shook as I moved closer to Joe.

"What was it? A bad dream?"

"Uh-huh," I murmured, moving yet closer. I wanted to climb inside Joe. I started to tell him, but I couldn't talk, didn't want to talk; I just wanted to forget the dream.

"What was it about? It's okay. You can tell me. I won't think you're silly. Everyone has bad dreams."

"Just hold me," I answered as I pressed up against him. How could I tell him about the dream? How could I ever tell anyone about *the dream* ever again?

His arms tightened about me. The clock, next to the bed,

glowed 3:15 in fluorescent red numbers. Damn, I was going to be awake for the rest of the night.

I didn't have to wait long before I knew from the steady rise and fall of Joe's chest against my back that he had fallen asleep. I wiggled out from under his arm and stole out of bed. I tiptoed into the living room, sat down in the recliner, tapped a cigarette out of the pack, and flicked the lighter. As the small flame illuminated the end table, I picked up the TV remote control, and there was the obituary column staring me in the face. I furiously pushed buttons trying to find something to watch.

There isn't a whole lot on at three-thirty in the morning. Infomercials like *Fun with Phonics*, old Japanese horror movies, CNN news: Nothing I could focus on. Nothing that would make life seem less threatening, less like the dream.

How many times had I had that dream since I was seven? Mr. Walker's face suddenly looming in, leering at me, his hand wiping his mouth, yet that sick grin still plastered on his face. Kind of like the Cheshire cat's grin in *Alice in Wonderland*. Even if the rest of him disappeared the grin would still be there. His eyes glazed over. His face coming closer and closer; his breath on my neck. And then his hands crawling under the blanket, coming closer, like a tarantula capturing its prey.

I recognized the music for *One Day at a Time*. I stop punching the buttons on the remote. I need a laugh about now. I have always loved this sitcom about the young divorced mother with two teenage daughters. I always wanted a mom like Ann Romano —someone who would believe her children, no matter what— someone who stood by her family. We even had the same first name. Ann would have known what was bothering me; she would have made it better for me. I wouldn't have even needed to tell her. She would have known. If Ann was my mother, it would have never even happened.

The living room was cold. Or maybe I was still chilled. I grabbed the lap blanket that lay on the end of the couch and lay down on the couch, covering myself with the blanket. I curled my legs up to my chest, underneath the red flannel back of the blanket, trying to make it long enough to cover my whole body. I started tracing the flower patterns on the corduroy cover that was wearing thin with age. Gram gave me that blanket when I was six. Mine had these wild psychedelic flowers. Gram was always trying to turn me into a little lady. She had her work cut out for her; I was such a tomboy. She had made one for my little brother, Mike, too. His blanket had tiger stripes on it. I wanted the tiger-striped blanket. I had always been a tomboy and felt that the flowers were just too prissy for me. I would hide that blanket from Mike when we were little. I would pretend it was mine; play jungle safari with the tiger-striped blanket. I could be tough, just like a boy with that blanket, until it happened. Afterward I got in trouble for setting the blanket on fire. Nobody asked why I did it, they just punished me. I thought that if the blanket was gone it wouldn't happen anymore.

No, I'm not going to think about it. It was all just a bad dream. Adults don't do those things to children. Mother said they don't. She wouldn't lie. Remember when she read about the man in the newspaper, the one who had hurt those three children? She said then that only nasty people hurt children and that we're so lucky to have nice Mr. Walker living next door. Nice Mr. Walker. Mother said that Mr. Walker was the kind of man that you could trust with anything. She hoped that Mikie would be just like him when he grew up. After all, she trusted him to take care of us, and there wasn't anything more important to her than Michael and me.

Gram always said to respect your elders and to do what they tell you to do. If you want to be a good girl, you'll do everything they tell you to. Everything. Good adults protect and take care of good little children, and Mr. Walker is such a good man.

Did you and Mom really believe that, Gram? I trusted and believed in you. I thought you would never lie to me. I wanted to be a good girl for you. I wanted you to be proud of me. I did what Mr. Walker wanted, I didn't tell anyone. Now, according to the paper, he's dead. If I tell someone now, who would believe me?

They would want to know why I was bringing it up now. Why didn't I tell anyone then? It's been almost twenty years, surely it still isn't affecting my life.

You can't tell anyone because they won't believe you. You have to keep it a secret because they will blame you for it. You will be bad, dirty, and no one will love you anymore. If you say anything you won't be a good girl anymore. Isn't that what you made me believe, Mr. Walker? Well, Mr. Walker, I believed you. You might be dead, but I still believe you. I once told someone who said he loved me, and he left.

It was the episode of *One Day at a Time* where Ann's old boyfriend, David, meets Nick, her new boyfriend, and the two of them fight over her, and she doesn't know which one to choose. I knew I would find something to laugh at if I would just concentrate on the program. I needed to block everything but the TV out. If only it was that easy.

"Annie, you're such a pretty little girl, why don't you come and sit on my lap?" Mr. Walker patted his leg, motioning for me to come and sit down. I didn't like the way he looked at me. He was sitting in my dad's black vinyl recliner. He always sat in Daddy's chair when he came over. Even if Daddy was home he would sit there. Nobody else ever sat there but Daddy. It wasn't right, him sitting in Daddy's chair.

"No, I don't want to. I want to go and play with the kids." All my friends were outside playing kick the can. The reason I had come in was that the phone was ringing, and I wanted to find out how Gram was. Mom and Daddy said Gram was real sick and that she might even die. Every time I heard the phone I would hold my breath, until I found out that Gram was still alive.

"It won't hurt you to sit on my lap. I just want to play patty-cake with you." He grabbed my arm and pulled me onto his lap. "After we play pattycake, I'll tell you about your grandma."

There's a smell of pipe tobacco, not the sweet kind that Grandpa smoked, but a strong, bitter kind. His rough whiskers rub against my face, leaving little itches up and down my cheek.

His face too close to mine. I don't want to play pattycake; I'm too old to play pattycake. I want to go and play with the kids.

"Where's Mikie? He'll want to know about Gram. You can tell both of us at the same time about Gram. I want to go and play with my brother. Where is my brother? Let me go! Please?!" I try to pull away. I rub my cheek and my eyes. The smell of burning tobacco stings my eyes, and I don't want Mr. Walker to see the tears.

"Don't fight with me, Annie. You can play with Mike later. You have to stay here with me right now." He covers us with the nearest thing. Mike's tiger-striped blanket.

"It's too warm for a blanket. We don't need a blanket. Please let me go and play. Please . . ." I make a quick swipe at my eyes so he won't see the tears.

"Just in case anyone comes in," he whispers in my ear. His hands crawl over me, under the blanket, where no one can see.

I remember crying. Why didn't my mom come and save me? Ann Romano would have saved Barbara or Julie. She was always rescuing them from everything else. Ann would have never left them alone with Mr. Walker to begin with. She would have known what kind of man he really was. The kind of man that covered little girls with blankets and . . .

"What are you crying for? That didn't hurt. Just remember it's our secret. If you tell anyone they'll think you're bad. They'll blame you. They won't love you anymore. If you tell your parents they'll think you're lying, and only bad children lie. Do you want to be bad?"

I know, no one has to tell me, that I shouldn't have believed him. But I was only seven years old. I didn't even know where babies came from. I just knew that I didn't like Mr. Walker or what he did to me. But I never told, at least not until Jared.

For my eighth birthday, Mr. Walker gave me a string of pearls. He told my parents that they had belonged to his mother and he wanted someone special to have them. Mom said that I had to be very careful with them, and that I could wear them only on special occasions. Mom said that I could wear them when I got married someday. After she said that, I cut the string; she grounded me for three weeks. She told me that she couldn't believe how bad I had been lately. First Mike's blanket and now the pearls from Mr. Walker. She never asked me why, she just said that I shouldn't have done that after Mr. Walker had been so nice to me. Mr. Walker was right, she wouldn't believe me if I told her, not when she punished me for cutting a little string.

There is an old saying about how time heals all wounds. Maybe it's true. Now I'm engaged to a man that loves me. I manage a successful dress shop. I graduated from college. I have my whole future ahead of me. And now Mr. Walker is dead. His obituary is in the paper tonight. My mom called and asked me to go to his funeral; I refused. I almost told her that he deserved to die. When she started talking about how he had suffered the last few years, about how the cancer had eaten him away, I almost said good. Instead I gritted my teeth and said that it was too bad. Now I'm lying to protect a man who . . . Mom started talking about how wonderful Mr. Walker had been when Gram had her stroke. "I just don't know how we would have ever managed if it wasn't for him." She said, "He was always so good to you and your brother. Especially you, he would do anything for you."

I could never tell them what their friend, that really nice, good man, did to their daughter while taking care of her. They would never believe me. Not nice Mr. Walker. They would have thought I was lying. Even if I told them now, they wouldn't believe me. Sometimes I don't want to believe myself.

Before Joe and I started going together, I was in love with Jared Snyder. Jared had asked me to marry him when I was twenty. He was always telling me how much he loved me and how happy we were going to be together. He told me over and over that there was nothing that could ever change how he felt about me. We would be together always. We had known each other most of our lives. Jared had grown up on the next block, he was one of the boys that I played baseball and kick the can with when I was little. When my mom called three years ago and told me that Mr. Walker had cancer, Jared remembered him, and asked if I wanted to go and see Mr. Walker in the hospital. He was going to go with my brother Mike; they wanted me to go along. I said no at the time; that night the dream started again.

If someone stares at me for a long period of time, I can't help but wonder if they know what happened. At times I feel like there is this sign around my neck that only certain people can see. Those people stare at me, thinking "She doesn't look dirty, or strange, or bad." I feel this way especially after the dream. The dream follows me around for days. When I was little I would have other nightmares, that was before Gram had her stroke. I slept in the same room with Gram, and when I had a bad dream she would wake up and say, "Bad dreams, Babycakes? Want to crawl in bed with Gram?"

I would snuggle in her arms and she would tell me a story about when she was little and then everything would be okay. Then she got sick. She had that stroke, and Mr. Walker took care of us. Then she went to the nursing home and Mr. Walker always came over, and Gram wasn't there anymore to stop the nightmares. Especially the new bad dream, where there were no monsters, just Mr. Walker's face and hands and the blanket.

Sometimes after the dream I just want to go somewhere and hide, someplace where no one will ever find me. Other times I want to get in the bathtub and keep scrubbing until I come clean. One time after Mr. Walker came over, I filled the bathtub with the hottest water I could, then I took Daddy's Lava soap, the real gritty kind, and I scrubbed and scrubbed. My skin was lobster colored when I got out, but it didn't do any good. I can't believe how hard it is to come clean. I even went to confession, I thought that maybe if it was happening because I had been bad, if I was forgiven it would stop. But, the next time Mr. Walker came over, it happened again.

"If you tell anyone, they won't love you anymore," Mr. Walker said. For some reason I thought Jared would prove Mr. Walker wrong. I believed that he really loved me. Jared kept after me about going to see Mr. Walker. He said that Mr. Walker kept asking about me, wanting to know how I was doing. I kept coming up with excuses, until one afternoon . . .

"Sometimes a woman just asks for it," Jared said while we were watching *Donahue*. The show was about women who had been raped.

"That's ridiculous!" I told him. "Nobody asks to be raped."

"Come on, Annie, look at the clothes she was wearing, for heaven's sake. She was giving off the message 'Take me, I'm yours.' "

"Jared, you're wrong, dead wrong." I remember looking at him, feeling trapped, wanting to leave, yet I couldn't. "What about old ladies, small children, and little babies? What could they possibly wear that could be considered provocative?"

He didn't say anything; he just stared at me, the same way people do when I know that they know what Mr. Walker did. I couldn't stand him looking at me that way. Something snapped.

"I'm waiting for an answer. Just tell me what? You can't, can you? No one can. What child deserves to be touched or groped when they don't want to be? Nobody has the right to do that to a child! Nobody had the right to do it to me!" I started to pound on Jared. Half the blows probably didn't even touch him. I could see myself hitting him, but I couldn't stop, even if I wanted to. "It was your good old friend, Mr. Walker, the one you always want me to go and see. I was only seven years old, damn it! Only seven. It was when my grandma was sick. Everyone thought he was being so wonderful. While you were outside playing kick the can, he was . . ." Jared tried to put his arms around me. I pushed him away. "You understand what I'm saying? Nobody asks for it! Nobody ever asks for it. I certainly didn't ask for it."

I must have collapsed on the floor. I remember looking up at Jared's face. Utter disbelief, the shock never left his eyes. All of a sudden, I felt dirty. I could tell by the look in his eyes that I was bad. I had finally told someone, someone who supposedly loved me, and he looked at me like it was my fault. Like he didn't believe me. We broke up three weeks later; I told him to stop staring or get out. He said that I was crazy, that he didn't believe me because I couldn't tell anyone else. He did exactly what Mr. Walker said everyone would do if I ever told. He stopped loving me.

One Day at a Time is now over. Ann decided to stay with Nick, her new boyfriend. Maybe I can go back to sleep. I know Jared will be at the funeral; maybe now that Mr. Walker is dead I won't have the dream anymore. He can't hurt me anymore now that he's dead.

r ALPH SALISBURY was born on a farm in Iowa. His father was a Cherokee storyteller, with only two years of "reading, 'riting and 'rithmetic" to modernize the tellings. Salisbury has sought to follow the family oral tradition in five books of poems, available through Greenfield Review Press, and in a collection of short fiction published by Navajo Community College Press in 1992; the latter includes chapters of his just-completed novel, *The Raven Mocker Wars*. Salisbury's poetry and short stories have appeared in such anthologies as *I Tell You Now*, *The Clouds Threw This Light*, and *Songs of this Earth on Turtle's Back*. His work has also appeared in *Chariton Review*, *The New Yorker*, and *Transatlantic Review*. He teaches at the University of Oregon in Eugene.

SILVER BASS AND ALLIGATOR GAR

Ralph Salisbury

Farm work, plus school, then war—my brother and I hadn't learned to swim, but, despite our not having life preservers, and despite big logs shooting past aluminum, as thin as that of the plane I'd crashed in nine months back, my only concern, till near the end of the day, was which fish bobber dips were from shifting current, which from bass, scales bright as foil between wrapper and childhood treat. When our small boat lurched to the length of its anchor chain, struck by the first floodwaters from upstream, I said calmly, thinking of Cherokee forebears' "Trail of Tears" crossing, "Some of our people died in this river."

Short of breath from landing the big fish swimming in trickles of its own blood between his scuffed chore boots, another heart attack his worry, Dad ignored his "overeducated" only-chance-at-biological-survival's lamenting family long dead, but for my half brother, last beer downed, I'd parroted my Native American Studies prof in one tedious time too many.

"Don't piss your pants about some old book, Little Bro." I was nineteen, he was twenty-two. "My granddad's arm shot off fighting for the kaiser, the granddad that's yours and mine doing the shooting, my own dad, younger than I am now, with all them medals for getting killed by his Old Country cousins, your dad joining the army that drove his great-great-kinfolks to drown all soggy, by the dozens or hundreds, get shot or stuck with a bayonet, get sick, or starve, like I damned near did in prison camp—all that stuff that's dead and done for, it just don't signify. It's like you're in a helicopter, man, look down, see two, three dozen, three hundred corpses, who cares, 'cause you're up two hundred feet, three thousand, whatever, rotor blades like Mom's old eggbeater darned near busting your ears, vibrating the floor against your hip pockets and wind through those open doors blowing so hard you got to strain to snort every noseful like snorting coke. What's real, up there, man, is air, the air you never had to think about, your whole life, same stuff we are breathing in right now. But, on the goddamned ground, you see one corpse, rotting or bloody as a dog in the road, your buddy, or some other guy, or an enemy or a little kid got caught in the wrong place, wrong time—that gets your attention, Little Bro, that signifies."

Like rows of treetops lining sky, now red with sunset, over river, pointed rows of bloody teeth lined the gar's alligator-shape snout, and a crimson halo had dried to glue. Feet stuck, yellow bees beat wings into invisibility, boat aluminum echoing the desperate buzzing from my best friend's head, crushed by the same air-cargo crate that had broken my legs. Our radio signal fading in distant earphones, searchers only spotted the crash when sun had fallen low enough to send shattered Plexiglas reflections flashing through undergrowth. Medics reached us in time to save the pilot, the copilot, and me, my buddy's all-but-hollow skull, unstuck from its buzzing yellow halo, vanishing into a body bag.

One buddy, it "signified," as my half brother'd said. He was my "brother" really, though "half" in out-of-family speaking, as, later, I'd learn the name for half of my family was "Yunwiya," meaning "we the people," "Aniyunwiya" what other tribes called us, "they the people." All my life, my brother had been "Big Bro," and he was still though we threw the same length shadows out across swift water and though, having suffered nothing close to the malnutrition he'd endured as a prisoner of war, I added more pounds to the boat's sinking, a sinking we were slow to notice, my brother and I catching good-size silver bass, Dad getting strike after strike but, reflexes slow, failing to set his hook, then landing the alligator gar. Danger of starving in childhood more real than the fifty pounds his heart doctor had ordered him to lose, he said, "Because it's got no cholesterol, I'm supposed to eat a lot of fish, and this one weighs more than all of yours put together." Its meat tough and oily, most people would have thrown it back, but, relieved when he told us his heart had finally "quit acting up" after the excitement and strain, my brother and I let him gloat in the pleasure of a moment we knew might be his last.

Anchor set in river bottom stone cracked by a glacier eons and eons ago, our boat steadily rocked, like the chair in which Dad had told my half-German–American, half-English–American half brother and had told "school-book Indian," quarter-blood Cherokee, me, stories of tomahawk-and-bow-and-arrow resistance to invasion and of his own machine-gun-tank-battle-bomb-blast war. Between puffs on the pipe he'd been forbidden to smoke, leaned forward over the fish he'd killed and its halo of dead bees, Dad brought back to life brothers and sisters, whom I barely remembered as grinning teeth, startlingly white in dark faces. My brother and I brought back high school friends, from big city jobs, universities, or military graves, and I could picture my buddy's head whole again, hair and eyes as black and face as brown as my own, something from some old book or a letter from his girl back on the reservation spreading a grin all the way around to his two gold molars. Mended legs braced against the boat's lurches, mind anchored in words that had endured the erosion of time, I felt my friend's spirit, and the spirits of all our people, Caucasian and Indian, in wind surging past my ears and in waves surging past the prow, at this fork where tons of fish, generation after generation, found tons of food floating down the Yellow to join the Mississippi's massive surge of melted ice toward the Gulf.

Collided with log, hole gouged through hull, you notice, but rains causing flooding miles out of sight upstream, the river and the rear of our boat rising so gradually, we only knew that hours of remembered years had been moving, inexorable as the sun, toward death, when my brother, not able to admit I was stronger, tried to haul the anchor up, to obey Dad's "Let's call it a day." Dad still Dad, though my brother and I had commanded other soldiers.

"The damned thing's stuck," my brother said quietly, no fear in his voice, just impatience, his body—brutalized by malnutrition, illness, months of beatings and humiliation—tensed in anger, anger at his weakness, anger that the strength still real in his mind, and his due, after years of dawn-to-dusk farm work and rugged army training, was gone, gone as he'd sensed it would be, one day of thin soup and moldy rice too many, a foreshadowing of one day of aging too many.

"You give it a go, Little Bro," he finally said.

"I'm drunk, just too damned drunk," he'd mumbled last week, from the dark backseat of our father's old car, my date already taken home. "I'll drive, and you come on back here." Shocked, passed out, or waiting, the woman he'd picked up that night had said nothing. I'd kept on driving to an address earlier indicated and heard high heels, probably bought at the store where my girl worked, echoing like rapid-fire rifle shots off concrete walk.

Anchor chain pulled taut, thighs tensed, I lunged up, as my brother had done; then, prow dipping, water sloshing around my moccasins, I scrambled back amidships, failure summoning the man who was, as when his semen had surged, my chance at survival. "Crawl aft, boys." Though his words were from combat landings in France and though my brother had flown to war in Asia, myself to a crash in New Mexico, Dad spoke as if we were kids. "Lean from the stern till your hip pockets get wet."

We crawled past him and, sitting, outer hands gripping aluminum edge, inner gripping motor, stretched, our two weights scarcely equaling his, out behind the boat. Dad, shoulders strained against shirt, tugged inch after inch of wet chain to clank onto metal between crouched knees, the bow drawing, inch after inch, down, till, a wave drenching faded blue pant legs dark, he let the bow bob back up, just as I had done. Red tobacco tin in breast pocket jerking from gasped breaths or from the lurches of his heart, dark eyes like those of a conquered dog intent on its paws, he came, on all fours, through muddy water tinted by alligator gar blood and sunset, back amidships.

"To hell with this," my brother muttered, the same words he'd yelled a week ago when, two drunks eyeballing my short, new Cherokee braid and calling me "queer," he'd thrown his 130 pounds against the biggest of them, both fleeing before I could reach his side.

He started the motor and gunned it upstream, but the boat jolted to a careening, U-turn stop, almost flipping over, and, in Dad's muttered "Too damned rambunctious!" I heard the "Too damned timid" that had kept me lunging against the limits of my own nature through childhood and had made me enlist the day I turned eighteen and could legally sign my own name.

When a boat horn sounded from a mile or more away, in the main channel, Dad waved his black hat, though waving to a neighbor had caused his first heart attack. My brother, his hands pale in the dusk, tried semaphore signaling "S.O.S." and, my army jacket, as green as the water, I stripped to my white T-shirt. Something, maybe binoculars, gleamed a seeming answer, but, without even swerving, the boat sped downstream, stern lights dimming into mist.

The air force had taught me to use the edge of a dime gripped between two fingers as a screwdriver, but the chain bolt was rusted tight.

"The oars would float us some, and we could try that army trick of catching air in our knotted britches legs, so's I could swim you, one at a time, before it gets too dark to see shore," Dad said.

"They say it's better to stay with the boat," my brother said. The bow, snubbed to its chain, was only inches above the surface, and, after all our years of fishing here, he must have known that, as lock after lock opened upstream, floodwater would rise over the stern. I think he was asking himself, if only one can be saved, which one will it be? Guessing the answer, just as, a black guy wounded by the same grenade, and the only medic a black, he'd guessed who'd be dragged to safety and who'd be waiting as the enemy advanced.

When there was just my brother to save, Dad saved him, lifting adolescent body in arms brutalized—by day after dawn-to-sundown day of digging, pulling, carrying—into strength. Lifted and hugged, as if he were a little boy again, the son of my mother's dead husband had felt ribs, soon to be broken, expanding, at live-or-die moment, for war whoop, rebel yell, primal scream, or prayer. Dad leaped from toppling tons of hay bales about to become avalanche, landing, cushioning my half brother's fall, and crumpling, himself, shoulder and ribs banging against a huge boulder left by a glacier eons before Mother's father's father had found it beyond the strength of his Percheron horses, in erecting our barn.

"You wait while I swim with your brother."

I dreaded hearing Dad say it. For so many years, his well-loved wife's first child got a bike, got skates, got a beebee gun, the things my dad had not gotten as a child, and, in time, I got secondhand skates, bike, and gun.

"I ain't the swimmer I used to was," Dad said. "Fifty pounds of flab I can't seem to make myself take serious, not to mention a heart that ain't exactly what you'd hope. I reckon I'm better off trying to use what brain I got and just see how things work out. We won't be needing this, you done proved that," he said to my brother, and, unfastening clamps, let the motor, which he'd worked hard to buy, sink. The dark alligator gar slipped from his hands overboard, one bee unstuck and flying, legless, into the dark. Next to go were the glittering bass my brother and I had caught, Dad using the empty stringer chain to fasten one of his feet to the empty motor mount and to fasten my brother's pale foot beside his. Letting Dad noose my ankle with leather strips cut from his belt, I couldn't help muttering "The current's so strong, the stern will be driven under with us tied to it."

"Could be right," Dad said. It was the first time I'd ever contradicted him, without being told I was wrong. "But," he said, "undoing one pin frees the stringer chain, and my knife's tied to my wrist, ready to cut you loose if need be. Whatever happens, we won't be in any worse pickle than we are now."

I thought that after being spun around in the water, with not enough light to see whether he was swimming toward the near or the far shore, we could wind up a lot worse off.

The rear of the boat kept on rising, with the three of us perched on it, first sitting then kneeling, then half standing half swimming, and the bow sank deeper and deeper, snubbed to the same anchor chain length above the riverbed, while lock after lock opened, releasing more floodwater after a last cargo barge.

When the boat was floating nearly perpendicular, cold waves broke around our chests, and often we were spun, as I'd been in the plane the pilot had only controlled in time to level out and crash-land in treetops. The anchor chain, twisted to its limit, stopped us and, unwinding, spun us back the other way, leaving us as dizzy as kids on playground swings, one hand holding on to floating, lashed-together oars, other hand gripping air-filled pant legs.

Dad said, his voice shaky, his heartbeat erratic against my chest as I clung to his left side, "At least now your brother won't be the only one baptized, and, unless they shut the pearly gates on Indians, we just might all wind up keeping each other company."

It was the only time Dad spoke of our possibly dying, and the only time he mentioned my being raised to pray to the Four Sacred Directions of Creation while Mother raised my brother Christian, until he was too old to do what she said.

While fishing, we'd used the oars to deflect drift logs. Now, distant city lights faintly silhouetting a small tree about to float past us, Dad swam, towing the boat under our feet sideways, a branch, just inches beyond his hand when it twisted as the tail of the gar drowning in air had done, dark shape vanishing in dark water, then surfacing, white spray furrowing around another branch throttled in my brother's pale hand.

Often we went under and had to hold our breaths, but the tree, a better life preserver than our ballooned pant legs, brought us back up into air each time. Finally, dawn showing the silver arcs of bass leaping to strike insects, the river began to fall, flood crest subsiding into miles downstream and locks upstream closing for the first barge of the day.

Following my Big Bro's example, I'd quit blowing dope the day I left the army, luckily, because last night's speedboat rescued us, narcotics agents' binoculars spotting strangely bobbing shapes that could have been an anchored stash, dropped from an airplane.

"All Dad went through in the war," my brother said, less than a year later, the first time I'd heard him say "Dad" since we were both small. "And saving our asses from drowning in that hellishly cold river with his heart as bad as that."

"Well, at least he had another year, almost," I said.

"Yeah, another year," my older brother said, to himself, looking across the funeral home, to where our mother was sobbing in the arms of her sister.

"I guess, it's live it the best you can, while you can," I said, only able to console myself somewhat, years later, that it had been another year of family love, family stories, Dad and our people able to go on living a little longer in the memories of his sons and in stories we'd pass down to our kids.

"At least he caught that damned alligator gar, whatever that signifies," my brother said.

I was thinking of all the hard times our dad had endured for a few good times. The Great American Depression was my dad photographed in a little sailor suit, his brothers and sisters as emaciated as himself, as emaciated as European concentration camp children, for whom, history would say, a war was fought. My country was trying to pretend it had not just lost a war. My brother had lost friends. I'd lost a friend. We'd both lost our dad. My brother was crying. I was crying. Our mother sobbing between us, in the funeral parlor limousine as long and black as that of a diplomat, we didn't either of us speak on the way to the graveyard.

LeANNE HOWE is a Choctaw who has studied her tribe's traditional burial practices. She is currently working at the University of Iowa, where she is on a state commission that determines the repatriation of Native American remains. She has published two books, *Coyote Papers* and *A Stand Up Reader*. Her story "An American in New York" appeared in Paula Gunn Allen's award-winning *Spider Woman's Granddaughters*. Howe's work has been anthologized in *Reinventing the Enemy's Language*, edited by Joy Harjo; *American Indian Literature*, edited by Alan Velie; and *Looking Glass*, edited by Clifford E. Trafzer.

DANSE D'AMOUR, DANSE DE MORT

LeAnne Howe

As he climbed the burial scaffolding to the bony carcass, he thought of her sex and began growing an erection. He ached for her from the inside of his thighs to his testicles.

She was lying as her relatives had placed her on the burial mat. He raked the leaves that had blown over her remains and leaned down and touched the torn fragments of her hair. Shakbatina's small jawbone lay surrendering to the sun like gleaming pearls. Her skin had been turned inside out by some sharp-beaked, flesh-eating birds. What was left had dried to the bone and resembled snakeskin.

Over time, her exposed bones had taken on that stark, delicate beauty the Choctaws regard as chunk-ash ishi a-chuck-ma. The good bliss.

The Bone Picker examined his wife's decaying body. Some six months before, Imoshe Nitakechi had prepared her body in the

way of Choctaw People of the Eastern Sun; the preparation ceremony was as ritualized as the bone-picking ceremony.

Before being placed on her back upon the scaffold, the flesh
directly above both thighs had been sliced away in half-moon
shapes in order for the blood and body fluids to run out of the
buttocks. Choctaws had long ago learned that the blood of a dead
animal quickly gravitates to the lowest point of the body and if
an exit is provided, the decomposing process is enhanced. They
also pierced the stomach and bladder in order for the bloating
gases to escape in the wind. This was to announce to the animal
world the Bone Picker's woman was coming.

Shakbatina's head had been turned to face east so that she
would greet the rising sun each morning while she too waited for
the day of her rebirth. Her umbilical cord and medicine bag had
been tied around her neck as part of the ceremonial incubation.
A Choctaw's umbilical cord is their first toy; with them before
birth, it accompanies them into death. Many of her possessions
lay scattered around her body on the platform. The aging Bone
Picker looked over his wife's things: a corn hamper made of
swampcane; a smaller basket with a long lid that rolled doubly
over itself was filled with earrings, bracelets, and her favorite
embroidered sash made from the black-and-white skin of a porcupine that she had cut into thin threads and dyed different colors.
The threads had been carefully sewn into designs that represented the People of the Eastern Sun—the coiled Snake, the
Sunburst, and the Seven Grandmothers. For the most part,
Shakbatina's things were intact, even after the scavenger birds
had left her. After the bone-picking ceremony her relatives
would retrieve the goods and give them away.

The Bone Picker had also prepared himself for this moment.
Beginning with the cycle of the full moon, he started his ritual by
stripping naked and jumping into the river. Then he swam up
and down the shoreline until finally dragging himself onto the
bank, allowing the wind to dry him, only to return to the water
to repeat the exercise. It was a cold, dry November day and his
purpose was sacrifice. On the first day he denied himself warmth,

food, clothing, and shelter. The first day of discipline was for denial.

The second day the Bone Picker entered his sweat cabin to begin to smoke the leaves and purify his spirit for his visions. He drank water and black tea, a concoction that was used both as a narcotic and emetic to purify his scent. He inhaled more of the dreaming tobacco and searched his memories of Shakbatina. He thought of the day of her death, and of her shrunken body pock-marked by the sickness she had endured. He thought of her resolve to stand in her first daughter's place. He thought of the tormented wailing of his daughters at the death of their mother, and of Shakbatina's final words:

> This is the day when I will tear myself from your arms and follow my brother to the Nanih Waya. I have lived long enough with these scars. If I were to yield to your tears I would fail you and our iksa. I have done enough for you by bearing you inside my heart. Should you, who were formed of my blood and fed with my milk, be shedding tears? Heh-Hah-Heh! Rejoice because you are headwomen.
>
> I wish that my daughters live to be as old as I am, so that they may deliver all my relations to the Nanih Waya. This is why I am going to take my first daugh-ter's place in the blood revenge. It is a sacrifice that I am happy to make for Anoleta. Heh-Hah-Heh! Che pisa lauchi. I will see you.

When Shakbatina finished her speech, she sang her death song and walked over to the Chickasaws who were waiting po-litely outside her cabin. She offered her life in exchange for her daughter's life. This was to prevent the two families from engag-ing in a killing frenzy that would eventually spread to both tribes. The Chickasaws did not refuse Shakbatina's offer, because they had been told in advance that she was an Inholahta: the one who makes the peace.

In the presence of her husband, three daughters, twin brother, and extended family, she stretched out on a log and closed her eyes. As was the custom, a relative of the victim carried out the execution. The oldest brother of the murdered woman approached Shakbatina slowly. He said a long prayer aloud to the Choctaw and Chickasaw iksa members present, then with a swift callous motion, as if he were killing a gar fish coming up for air, he bashed in Shakbatina's head. Blood gurgled forth from Shakbatina's mouth.

Anoleta, in anguish, started to run toward her mother screaming "Alleh, alleh, alleh," an expression used by Choctaw children when they are in pain, but Nitakechi grabbed his niece and they both collapsed on the ground, sobbing.

As Shakbatina tried to raise her right hand to hold her head, she groaned loudly, and the Chickasaw clubbed her several times more. Now fragments of bloodied bone were strewn through her hair, and her body shook as all the remaining breath left her.

With her death, all iksa debts were paid. Everything was settled. After Shakbatina's body had been fastened to the frame, the Bone Picker returned to the place where his wife had stood to sing her death song. He looked across the oxbow river and heard the familiar whispering of the moody pines as they creaked in the wind. He watched a mated pair of fish crows scour the bank for sand crabs and carrion and tried to imagine the woman he loved. Exhausted by his suffering, he fell to the ground and tenderly traced her tiny footprints in the soft, black earth, and wept aloud.

The Bone Picker took another drag from his pipe and put away his memories. His ritual was not for endings but for beginnings. He continued to sing his personal songs until his throat was swollen sore. He gave himself sexual relief often, as the need in him arose. He prepared his clawlike nails with rose paint. His nails had grown purposefully long since Shakbatina's death. He smoked and refilled his pipe again. He was obsessive in his behavior and repeated the cycle until he was completely spent. Finally as his ritual peaked and he was fully in the grips of the black tea and dreaming leaves, the thing he sought came to him and he rejoiced in its nothingness.

As an aging bone picker, he had seen the nothingness many times before. It is that which separates itself from the known and that which cannot be known. As always, when it first arrived, the Bone Picker was terrified by it, seduced by it, and assured by it. And through his terror, he knew he was participating in the life mystery. On the evening of the second day the Bone Picker slipped into unconsciousness knowing he would live to die and that, through his ritual, he became his people's sacrament. The purpose of the second day was for indulgence in the sublime.

On the third day, the husband of Shakbatina emerged from the sweat, much thinner, still refusing food, and greatly introverted. He spoke to no one. No one spoke to him. He covered himself in bear grease and rubbed sage. He felt invigorated knowing he had succeeded in his purification. While no two ceremonies are alike, no two purifications are alike. Only the knower knows when the experience is complete. After two days with the pipe, the Bone Picker had seen his future in the seductive hallucinations of the smoke and black tea. He was ready to be with Shakbatina. He was ready to face his future and his fears. The purpose of the third day was for rebirth.

The people had also prepared for the bone-picking ceremony. Four weeks before the Bone Picker began his ritual, runners had gone out to the surrounding towns such as Chickasawhay, Yowanis, Conchas, Couechittos, in the eastern district, and as far away as Naniaba, a small town along the Mobile River, calling Choctaws together. The runners were also told to bring back the French traders from Mobile who had intermarried with iksa headwomen. Headwomen, as they were called, collected and traded the goods between iksas. Choctaw men did not own anything of their wife's iksa, rather they preferred that the women make the home and keep it. When a warrior took a wife he moved to her iksa and into her home. If he left her or was asked to leave, he moved out taking only his hunting tools and personal effects. This did not mean Choctaw men were paupers.

Their personal effects included clothes, knives, flints, blow gun, pottery, everything needed to live the complete life, and, as was the custom, women of the iksas shared everything. That way everyone had everything.

Because Shakbatina and her brother were the leaders of the dominant iksa at Yan'abe, the runners were told to extend an invitation to Father Baudouin. The Jesuit then sent an express messenger to the curate of Mobile, Sieur Denys Delage, and asked him to bring other priests to Yan'abe for this special ceremony.

Father Baudouin had been living in Chickasawhay for only one year and was not sure what to expect. All he knew was that something important was happening, and he wanted to be sure that this was not the beginning of another war.

During the three days the Bone Picker sought purification, his relatives had been busy preparing food. They began by cooking hundreds of pounds of pashofa, a corn mush, and deer stew that was heavily seasoned with sage. Adolescent girls prepared the corn flour dough and baked loaves of bread in hot oak ashes. They roasted hickory nuts and sweet yams and covered them with honey. Young children pounded pecans into bahpo, a chunky nut pudding, while their mothers roasted turkey hens over open fires. These were the foods for the day of the dead.

Iksa men stood around their own fires grilling deer tongues and alligator meat that would be eaten after the ceremony. Then the handgames and toli, a physically dangerous game in which two opposing teams of ballplayers attempt to move a small ball toward the goal of the opposing team. Each ballplayer uses a pair of long racketlike sticks to hit or carry the ball back and forth on a large playing field. Choctaws played toli with a vengeance, sometimes against enemy tribes to settle land disputes, sometimes merely for sport among themselves. Men and women of the iksas would come to gamble on their favorite ballplayers. The stakes would be high, and men and women would bring their best trade goods to bet on the games. Choctaws were incessant gamblers and the games would last as long as the food held out.

On the evening of the third day fires were set at dusk beside the burial scaffolding. When the Bone Picker ascended the scaffold, the host drum beat their cadence. Shakbatina's tribesman stopped singing as her man addressed the four directions then looked upon his wife's body.

Dressed only in a string cloth, the Bone Picker bent over the remains. He believed as all Choctaws believed that the spirit is related to the body as perfume is to the rose. Shakbatina's smell was erotic.

Once atop the frame, the tribal drums and the drumming of the forest became deafening. Their purpose was to wake the dead. In the Bone Picker's realm, under the mystic influence of the black tea and dreaming leaves, he could hear the internal drumming of the plants and trees. He could hear the collective prayers of his tribesmen, and if he concentrated, he could hear the thoughts of a single person. The combined noise was maddening and yet all-consuming. This special hearing was not new to the Bone Picker. The People of the Eastern Sun had learned to hear the internal drumming of the plant world eons ago. No Anoli, or Teller, had the knowledge of when this special hearing began, only that it existed and the ancestors had always used it as a tool of survival. The humming and vibrations of the trees and tall corn plants were a soothing comfort to Choctaws. When the musical sounds of the plants changed to a frantic drumming during the dry season, Choctaws helped the plants drum down the rains by imitating the plant rhythm.

The Choctaw drums helped bring the rains and the plants gave themselves willingly to the people as a gift for helping to call the rain. Thus began the stories that the Tellers told the young children of how Green Corn Woman seduced the rainmaker, Umbachechi.

In the Bone Picker's heightened sexual state, hearing the manic drumming of his wife's kinsman and the constant humming of the forest put him in an absolute state of panic and he called to the woman named Shakbatina.

At that moment, kinsmen from the Bone Picker's iksa joined

the chanting. Together the people of both iksas began chanting a different song and dancing the dance of the dead. The Bone Picker called again to the spirit of Shakbatina and yet, as he chanted for her, a memory of great uncertainty flashed in his head.

Before bone pickers, the Choctaw people merely left their dead to rot alone in the ground. Women would grieve over their brothers and husbands begging to stay with the body. Men, too, cried over their wives and sisters and could not be comforted. But still, the people would leave their beloved ones in the ground, never marking the spot where their relatives were buried.

Then an old Teller from Bokchitto named Atuk Lan Tubbee told a story one night that explained what had happened.

> Our ancestors were being punished because they left their beloved ones in the ground. One day a head-woman would not leave her brother. She told the people she would keep him with her and she cleaned his bones and put them in a box and Tchatak saw that this was good and they were happy again. A giant red-tailed hawk appeared to our people and told them to make their homes by the rivers. The rivers would be ours as long as we continued to honor our ancestors. A son and daughter were born to the headwoman and she taught them the ceremony of the bone picking. From then on, the people of the Eastern Sun live by the rivers.

The Bone Picker was born in the tradition of all Choctaw bone pickers. He knew as long as bone pickers called to the ancestors, as long as the people kept their covenant with the red-tailed hawk, they could stay near the rivers and the Nanih Waya. The husband of Shakbatina shook off the vision of the past. After all, the rules of bone picking would always be observed. There was no reason to be afraid. He would go on without fear.

Speaking his own name, which was held for special occasions, he began the ceremony.

"I am Koi Chitto, Foni Mingo of the People of the Eastern Sun, dancer of death, transformer of life, the one who brings sex, the one who brings rebirth. You must have death to have life. Tchatak people live by killing, by stripping the flesh from the animal corpse. Tchatak lives by dying. That which dies is reborn."

A shrill moan came from the belly of the Koi Chitto. He danced and rolled his eyes back in his head. He had again entered the center of the nothingness. The drums were vibrating his body and the platform shook as if it would break apart. Neshoba, the second daughter of Shakbatina, stopped dancing as the platform came to a standstill and Koi Chitto saw his wife coming toward him.

"Shakbatina is coming. She is here," he yelled.

She looked like the woman Koi Chitto had seen the first time he visited Yan'abe. She was beautiful and round. Slanting almond eyes explained the meaning of her name. Shakbatina: the wildcat. She was the headwoman of the Owl family, a daughter of the Inholahta, the Ones Who Make the Peace.

She came to her husband as a naked bride, her calf-length hair glistening in the evening moonlight. She put her hands on his penis and he put his hands around her hands and together they stroked him, facing one another on the platform, and he ejaculated on the body and screamed.

"Flesh of my flesh, I will be with you always. Flesh of my flesh, I will rest with you always. Until the nothingness becomes everything. Until everything becomes the nothingness. I am the Bone Picker, dancer of death, transformer of life, the one who brings sex, the one who brings rebirth."

Shakbatina continued to dance around the platform and Koi Chitto could hear her laughing and whispering to him as she had in life.

"Dance with me, the dance of death and rebirth. This is my body. You are my blood. Pull away my flesh, Koi Chitto, husband of Shakbatina, bone picker of the People of the Eastern Sun. I charge you to get inside me. Release me. Unlock me from my past so I can rest with our ancestors in Nanih Waya. Release me. Dance the dance that releases me."

Shakbatina smiled at her man and entreated him to touch her corpse and tear the remaining flesh from her bones. "I will come for you when your time is my time. Of this you know. For now, release me and dance the dance of death with me. Che pisa lauchi."

Hearing her promise that she would see him, that she would come for him when the time was right, Koi Chitto gathered his courage and tore Shakbatina's skull and spinal column from the rest of her bones and held them in both his hands above his head and again saluted the four directions. The aging bone picker knew when he finished his dance and Shakbatina's bones were painted and placed in the box he would not see her again until he too was strapped on the frame and released to join her in the place of the Nanih Waya. Until then, he let her fading scent engulf him. He closed his eyes. Together for the last time they were one, dancing the dance of death, both knowing that this was the ecstasy of life and rebirth.

From a distance of twenty yards, Sieur Delage watched the naked savage claw and tear the skull and spinal column from the decaying corpse fastened to the frame. In that moment of feral exhaustion, he vomited on the ground beside his shelter of palmetto leaves built for him by the Swiss mercenary, Critches.

Since he arrived in the province of Louisiana in 1725, he had never witnessed any pagan rituals. Before the turn of the century the Choctaws of the Lower Mississippi Valley had never allowed anyone not of the blood to witness their ceremonies. Even the early Canadian voyagers who'd been coming to the homelands since the 1690s for deer skins and trumpeter swan bellies had been forbidden to attend the rituals of the children they made with Choctaw headwomen. But that was before the English and Chickasaw slave raiders in 1702 took two thousand Choctaw warriors at gunpoint and marched them to the eastern sea for what the Choctaws called "the big die-up." That was before the French began exchanging muskets for scalps. That was before one of Delage's own predecessors, Catholic curate Henri Roulleaux de la Venter, tried to incite the Indians to make war on his French enemies.

Now after thirty-one winters of debate, whether to allow those on the outside to learn life from those on the inside, Hatak Holitopa, the Beloved Men, were trying something new. Because borderland wars, blood revenge, new diseases, and early death had come to be oke, or "as is," to all the people living in the eastern district, the leaders made a decision. Just as the people taught their children by example, they would teach Hashi's principles, Chunkash ishi fullo kachi, to the French. The Choctaw would adopt their puny, homeless Filanchi and teach them how to be ever-living, ever-dying, ever-alive in the universe.

Delage shifted his weight from one leg to another. He looked across the encampment. There were some fifteen temporary huts scattered across the cleared fields. Here and there greasy meat pots hung on poles outside of the huts. Iron vats of bear fat boiled over the open fires, which only added to the soured smell of burning hair, blood, and horse dung. The savages had at last set the scaffolds on fire. Some of the tribesmen started to dance. Others sat in circles and chewed on fried alligator meat and roasted sweet yams.

Delage wretched again. He grabbed his sides and sank to his knees. Someone would pay for this. Where is Critches? Why hadn't he brought the negress with him? He searched the encampment for Father Renoir. He looked down at his unwashed hands and bit a loose fingernail. His cassock was stained with grease and food. His body was covered in flea bites. He was not used to being degraded. As a curate, Delage was entitled to a cleric and ownership of slaves. Nothing in his early training, nothing he'd learned from his political manipulations in league with the Bishop of Quebec, had prepared him for what these savages called the dance of the dead.

Delage crawled inside his shelter and wretched again. Every-one had been vomiting for days after they drank kaf, the black drink of the savages. Now he reckoned that he had been poisoned by it. It was cold and dark inside his hut and his thoughts turned toward revenge. He would find a way to punish Father Baudouin for tricking him into taking this journey into the savage homelands. There were always threats of civil war between des Tchactas and des Chicachas. Violence is a constant between natural slaves. Everyone knows this. No one can pre-vent them from killing each other, just as no one can coerce them into killing each other. "The French are never practical," he said softly.

Delage closed his eyes. He wondered if Father Baudouin was always so uninhibited. A miserable year among des Tchactas was no doubt responsible for his rudeness. The curate smiled to him-self when he thought of Father Le Pen whom the savages referred to as "Rabbit Lips."

Then, without thinking, Delage drew up his blanket around his head savage style and yawned. "They all hate me."

When Jean-Marie Critches found Father Renoir slumped over next to a small fire, he first thought the Jesuit was sleeping.

"Father, it is time for the service," he said. Looking closer, the Swiss guard realized Renoir was bent over writing feverishly with his feather pen, covering page after page in his journal.

"A moment please," answered Renoir, and he continued writ-ing.

> . . . We traveled long hours, savage style for eight days until reaching the place they call Yan'abe. Four nights ago hundreds of des Tchactas, from twenty other villages arrived and built fires and shelters close to the site where the ceremony was to take place so they could participate in the ritual singing for a head-woman, her brother the medal chief and the chief's ticho-mingo, the dead leaders of Yan'abe. Many other

savages were scaffolded here as well who had died of old age or disease. While not knowing their ways, I observed more than three bone pickers among the villagers.

Before sunrise three days ago des Tchactas assembled together in small circles of twenty or thirty mourners, kneeling around drums of hollowed-out cypress and stretched skins. The beaters used wooden rods to make the drums sound dichotic and the clatter of wood was sometimes earsplitting. Both men and women then placed blankets over their heads and cried and sang with ten or twelve voices tracking each other in diaphonic tones, sustaining a timbre, a hundred times more powerful than the choirs at Notre Dame cathedral. I was hypnotized. Such feelings of loneliness, I have never known before. It was terribly mournful almost romantic, like the intermittent howling of mated wolves. I think I've learned the specific cries for the dead. Seated within proximity of the singers were pipe-smoking savages, harping to one another, their strident voices ripping through your very soul. For no matter what Father Baudouin says, des Tchacta's language is incredibly foreign, spit out of the mouth one syllable at a time.

Then there are the camp noises; barking dogs and clanging pony-bells on the horses and the high-pitched glee of the savage children. Child's play is not what one thinks of when you watch their games. Their games imitate all aspects of savage life. Hunting. Killing. Making war. Gambling. Giving birth; the savage child's version of playing house. I observed a tiny girl perhaps four or five pretending to be in labor. She was lying on her back, propped up by two young companions who were softly encouraging her in the delivery. The girl's legs were spread apart and she moaned and grunted as if this thing was happening to her. A truer imitation I have never seen. Another child was playing the role of a doctor waving a kind of feather fan over her. Two other small girls were helping pull the imaginary baby out from the child's legs. I watched in awe, thinking how at their young ages, they had probably all witnessed many such births. Extraordinary. All this childishness going on while in the background their parents sang for the dead.

Two more days and nights we waited. The wailing and hoarse quavering continuing, straining against our ears, ringing in unison with a thousand different sounds of the night forest.

Sieur Delage, Father Le Pen and Father Baudouin and I were huddled together for hours, sometimes roused at midnight by savages who shoved clay pots of food in our faces which we were forced to eat. Father Baudouin says it is considered a sin to refuse their food. Sometimes were overlooked entirely. Then this evening, 24th of November, when one of the bone pickers finally climbed the scaffold and began . . .

"Excuse me, Father, but the men are waiting and they will not be there long."

"They have not found the altar wine or brandy have they? They are expressly forbidden from giving it to the savages, do you understand, Critches?"

"No, Father. I have kept the brandy and the altar wine hidden."

"Good. I am almost finished writing in my journal. I will be with you shortly."

. . . Once the ritual was over many of des Tchactas carried fire in baskets to each other to signal the beginning of the feast which is continuing as I write. If I am correct, des Tchactas worship, among other things, "Hashi," the sun, and "Micha Luak," the fire. They set pine fires and burn cedar incense all around us. Whiffs of burnt honey drift in the air and mix with the aroma of roasted nuts, herbs, cooked meats and their special tobacco.

I am convinced now that des Tchactas pay more respect to their dead than any other race in the colonies of Louisiana. To them the bones of their relatives are holy. Proof that they existed in the past as they will exist forever. To them everything is "oke," as is. Life just is. One Tchacta who calls himself a diviner, and who is helping me to learn their language, told me a story. He said that Hashi, and Micha Luak, the sun's mate, are of the people. He said the Nanih Waya is their home. He ended by saying "Night begins with the setting sun. Oke." I don't know what that means, but must stop for service. I am a Jesuit after all . . .

Renoir finished his writing and carefully rolled his book and pen in his blanket. Before he arrived at Mobile he had descended the Mississippi with two Canadians and Critches. They were attacked by a small band of Doustionis, members of the Caddoan confederacy, at the confluence of the Red River and Mississippi River. Renoir's pirogue with all his belongings was turned over. Before he could retrieve any of his things, the priest was shot in the arm and shoulder with three small arrows. He and the Canadians escaped the Doustionis, only after Critches killed two of the warriors, but they were forced to leave the pirogue with the trade goods behind. It had taken the priest over a month to recover from his wounds when Regis du Roullet asked the priests and Sieur Delage to come to Yan'abe.

Each November the Choctaw celebrate the feast for the dead, and it was Regis du Roullet's hope that the French could instigate war between the Choctaws and the English-supported

Chickasaws. The latter nation was accused by factions of the Choctaws of using bad medicine to bring more deaths to iksa members.

As Renoir was about to stand and prepare himself for mass, a young woman walked up to him and smelled around his head and shoulders. She did not look into his eyes, but looked down at his feet. She walked around him three times, paying closest attention to his neck and ears.

Renoir had noticed her during the ceremonies. He had guessed she was directly related to the dead woman, whose body was the first to be prepared by one of the bone pickers. Father Baudouin explained that she was the old Bone Picker's daughter.

The woman stopped at his neck, breathed again deeply, and then walked away without looking back.

She was taller than many of the women, who were beginning to gather around the evening fire to dance. She had large, hooded brown eyes, full lips, and very dark skin. There was a two-inch, horizontal scar on her right cheek. Her dress was made of soft deerskin that hung loosely about her frame. She seemed to carry herself with an aloofness that other girls her age did not have. A strand of European glass beads hung down almost to her feet and tinkled softly as she walked. Such a great number of beads meant she was not without means. Her ears were cut and tiny bones and shells dangled from them. But when the priest looked into her face he realized she was still in youth. Still uncorrupted.

Renoir had not been contaminated with the closeness of the woman, white or savage, since he was fifteen. When she bent over to smell around his head and ears, her long black hair had fallen down around his face and smelled of sweet grass and cedar. The Choctaws never cut their hair and, for this reason, many other tribes in the region, especially the Alabimons, referred to them as "the Long Hairs." In turn the Choctaws called their cousins "the Bald Ones." Renoir thought their hair was extraordinary. Even though he was shocked at the woman's behavior, he felt his penis swell. He blushed, stood up, and walked away quickly with his back to Critches.

"Where did she come from?" asked the Swiss soldier.

"From God," answered Father Baudouin, who had the look of disgust as he approached the two men. "Let us not waste the evening. It is time for the service, is it not, Father?"

"Yes," answered Renoir. "I am ready."

The Choctaw woman walked straight from the Frenchmen to her relatives squatting by a rack of deer meat on a spit.

"He is well, Imoshe. He does not carry the illness."

She kept walking and did not stop until she reached her shelter. Neshoba glanced at the two Beloved Men who had begun to laugh, then she went inside.

"Heh-Hah-Heh! Pay up. You lose. I win," shouted Koi Chitto as he fingered a haunch a meat. "My daughter is never wrong about the sickness. She has the gift."

With a sweeping gesture, Nitakechi smacked his forehead with his palm and croaked, "This time you have fleshed this hen. Here! Take this knife. I am destitute and pitiful. And you, old man, can tell me nothing about my sister's daughter."

Koi Chitto shouted playfully at Nitakechi. "I told you Inki Sweets was not sick, just scratching to himself," he replied boldly. "But no, you said he was with the sickness. That we should take him out and kill him before he infected us. Heh-Hah-Heh! I told you. It is our Filanchi's way. They scratch because they cannot remember anything. They don't know where they are, so they scratch to remember where they've been."

"What for?" asked Nitakechi disapprovingly.

"For no reason at all," echoed Koi Chitto, gazing into the man's black eyes. "The Filanchi call it exrire. They scratch everything we say, so they can remember to nag us later. It makes me sad, but I must say it, our Filanchi have a trace of the Natchez in them," he said, tapping his forefinger to his temple.

Nitakechi was highly amused by the comparison between the

Natchez and the Filanchi. A clean-featured man of middle
height, he had long straight bones characteristic of his mother's
relatives. His black eyes were set in a broad face that was showing
signs of aging. His mouth was generous, with a kind of feminine
expressiveness that he could not help. He was Shakbatina's twin.
And, like her, he was a gift to the Inholahtas, something different they regarded.

As Nitakechi stood up, he winked at his sister's husband.
"And so, I guess you are fortunate that you didn't marry a Female
Sun of the Natchez, because when they die, the Natchez kill off
the Female Sun's husband," Nitakechi laughed.

Koi Chitto was reduced to speechlessness. He reached for the
knife, but Nitakechi put out his hand to make another speech,
drawing out his words like a great Teller.

"Yes, the knife of Filanchi, the one I gave them fifty deer skins
for. The man-killer that has ended the lives of twenty of my
enemies . . . the Stone Poker . . . who can hold up the sky
with his thing." Nitakechi paused solemnly, then laughed out
loud. "Well, of course, no one will ever call you that again."

The Bone Picker thought for a moment. His eyes crinkled and
he turned his head from Nitakechi. Finally he let out a whoop
and laughed at himself.

"Yes, yes, Waya Talifoni, the Stone Poker, that is what
Shakbatina called me. Hah! It has been so long, I had forgotten."
Koi Chitto laughed.

Sighing, Nitakechi opened his eyes wide, and as he whispered,
he gazed at the moon. "This night, Koi Chitto, you have sin-
cerely fleshed this innocent hen."

Both men were laughing now. "I remember exactly how her
voice sounded. It was fairly low and soft, and I always had the
impression that when she wanted, she could make it echo," said
Koi Chitto with a smile.

"At times, even I felt jealousy of her life mysteries," confessed
Nitakechi.

"No," murmured Koi Chitto. "You, who sing with the lo-
custs?"

Both men continued telling stories and remembering Shakba-tina. Now that the ceremony was over they could think of her and sing the fire songs. She was at the Nanih Waya and her life was complete.

"Yes," said Nitakechi. "It is good to gamble again."

Koi Chitto looked at the knife a second time, but waited politely for Nitakechi to make his last speech.

"Hekano. I am fleshed," said Nitakechi, grabbing his chest as if his heart were breaking. "Please take this knife, my friend."

Koi Chitto picked up the knife of his wife's twin and threw it in a pile of things next to the fire.

The two men laughed again and began talking in old code, slinging insults at one another. Eventually Koi Chitto lost his black horse to Nitakechi who belly-laughed so hard he fell down. Then together, arm in arm, they walked to Koi Chitto's iksa where his sister was cooking more meat before she went to the big fire dance.

During the service, Jean-Marie Critches shuffled his feet and tried to keep from wincing in pain. Each time he knelt in prayer he thought he could not get up again. His feet were swollen and bleeding in his boots. At first only his toes itched, then blisters appeared, then hot fever came into his feet. Now, when he took a step, the open sores oozed blood. The condition began right after the Doustionis incident at the Mississippi, and the Swiss merce-nary was positive the infection came as payment for the killings he committed. It wasn't the deaths of the two savages that both-ered him. He was a soldier in the service of the company and the king. What bothered Jean-Marie was not the job, but that he enjoyed it, even the killing.

He had confessed to Father Le Pen before the service in order to partake of communion, but his mind wandered. He heard very few lines of the liturgies. The habits of twenty years served him when his concentration wavered. Heads bowed in unison. The chants. The crossings. Alter prayers and beads.

Hoc est corpus. Sanctus, sanctus, sanctus. He floated in and out of the service. Jean-Marie was not only born Catholic, he was born into the Swiss Guard. His grandfather and father had been in Swiss regiments that served French kings Louis XIII and Louis XIV. For him Catholicism was his only experience. His faith and his father's Swiss Guard were his life. But now something new was bothering him. Devouring him.

Closing his eyes, he began, O Holy Mother of God, hear my cries. I ask for your help in my weakness that has affected my feet. I know I am here for a purpose and I will continue to believe that purpose is to march in the service of the King of France and for my faith, and to help the Jesuit Fathers. But unless the fever leaves my feet, I am afraid I will no longer be able to walk. I realize this is a lesson and I promise if . . .

Jean-Marie stopped in midsentence. Father Renoir's words broke his prayer.

"Remembering therefore his death and resurrection, we offer to Thee the loaf and the cup and give thanks to Thee that Thou has counted us worthy to stand before Thee and to do Thy priestly service. And we beseech Thee that Thou send down Thine Holy Spirit upon this offering of the church. Unite us and grant to all the saints who partake of it to their fulfilling with the Holy Spirit, to their strengthening of faith in truth, that we may praise and glorify Thee through Thy servant Jesus Christ, through whom to Thee be glory and honor in Thy holy church now and forever. Amen."

Renoir put the sliver of bread in Jean-Marie's mouth and tilted the cup. With him there were only three other Frenchmen and a Negro manservant whom Father Baudouin had instructed in the faith. As the priest was finishing the service, two young women standing in the shadows moved forward and stood next to Jean-Marie.

The priests were stunned. Renoir turned around and looked at Le Pen and Elage. No one moved. He looked back at the woman standing directly in front of him. She looked right through him, as if he wasn't there. Renoir stood silent waiting for something to happen.

Recognizing the women, Father Baudouin spoke up and tried to translate John's Gospel in her tongue.

"Anoleta, I tell you again most solemnly, that if you do not eat of the flesh of the Son of Man and drink his blood you will not have life in you. Anyone who does eat my flesh and drink my blood has eternal life and I shall raise him up on that day. For my flesh is real food, my blood is real drink. He who eats my flesh and drinks my blood lives in me and I live in him."

When the girl did not move, Father Baudouin spoke again.

"Anoleta, if you let Father Renoir instruct you, you too will have life everlasting. Please let us continue to honor our God our way. We can teach you about the one true God. He is your God also, but you must first believe in life ever-lasting."

The woman continued to look straight ahead, ignoring Father Baudouin. Then she looked briefly at Renoir, but did not make eye contact. Finally she began speaking her language in a lilting, almost magical whisper.

"Did you not see the one who was raised up from the frame this day? Did you know her flesh was food? Her blood was drink? Tchatak, the consumer. The animal, the consumed. Tchatak, the consumed. The animal, the consumer."

Pointing to herself she said, "This one lives. Chunkash ishi fullo kachi. We will pick your bones." Then the woman repeated a phrase of Father Baudouin's.

"Life everlasting. Ataha iksho. The People of the Eastern Sun are forever. Heh-Hah-Heh!"

She turned abruptly, but her young companion grabbed the cup from Father Renoir's hands and greedily swallowed the last bit of wine, then darted quickly into the crowd of women, tossing the cup as she ran. Anoleta never changed her expression of quiet dominance, but walked through the crowd and into the maze of temporary shelters.

"Blasphemy," cried Sieur Delage loudly. "Father Renoir, you let that savage grab the altar cup and drink the wine."

"Why was she whispering?" asked Renoir.

"It is known as the power that whispers. When they are deadly serious, they speak very softly. She is the first daughter of the headwoman, Shakbatina. The people of her iksa say she is a special kind of Teller, a Tchacta woman prophet, who is said to know the future. It was her mother who sacrificed herself as payment to avoid a blood feud when Anoleta was accused of murdering one of the Chicachas wives of Red Shoes. I was hoping that he alone would be caught in the middle and someone would murder him, but this was not to be."

Baudouin sighed.

"Since I arrived at Yan'abe, she has constantly spoken against me. Unfortunately she too has become a wife of Red Shoes. Since she has not met you formally, she addressed herself to you in this way. She hates all French, but she also hates the English. You will learn that des Tchacta women are different," said Baudouin. Then, exasperated, he began searching in the dark for the altar cup. Eventually a young boy brought it to the priest but would only trade it for a present of cheese.

Neshoba, the second daughter of Shakbatina, pulled the flap of her shelter back and walked into the night. She yawned and watched a fragile star blister, then burst and fall silently through the air.

The night smelled sweet with burning cedar's breath. The sky shown full moon white.

By midnight, every fire in the temporary encampment had burned an offering for protection from what the Choctaws call kon-wi anun-kasha, That Which Moves at Night.

Neshoba breathed in the burning fragrance. It reminded her of Imoshe Atokotubbee, her grandmother's brother, who always carried the crumbled leaves in his medicine bag. When she was a little girl she used to close her eyes, smell the cedar, and imagine it was winter and she was again snuggled up against her uncle's comfortable chest. Neshoba could never remember Atokotubbee coming to stay at her mother's house, except when the cold walks with you.

Atokotubbee's visits were a reassuring thing. The odor of tobacco was strong on his breath when he walked in the door of their cabin bringing gifts: deer meat and lots of gossip. Neshoba's grandmother would grab the old man's tobacco pouch and squeal thanks in a high-pitched voice.

As Neshoba started toward the center of the encampment to join the others for the Starting Dance Song, she took two steps, another, then stopped. A faint movement in the air, something from the west, startled her. The trees murmured, not enough to stir up the breeze, but enough to chill the sweat on the back of her neck. She looked behind her. Nothing.

"Intek aliha, Sisterhood," said Neshoba in a low voice as she bent over to pull out of the ground a small moist shell that gleamed like a silver lure in the moonlight. "I am growing stronger now." She looked back toward the woods with compassion.

Neshoba's world grew calm again. She glanced back toward the footsteps. There was nothing. The sound of the feet had vanished. She laughed, revealing her small white teeth, and said, "I am ready, Imoshe."

A group of Neshoba's relatives had been singing continuously since the bone-picking ceremony ended. When they stopped to eat, another iksa took their place and continued singing at the big fire in the center of the encampment.

Neshoba was glad she arrived in time to see her favorite uncle assemble everyone at the ahila, a plot of ground about a hundred yards away from the big fire prepared for the purpose of dancing. She loved the sounds of Atokotubbee's striking sticks. Despite his age, there remained something youthful about his playing and dancing. His eyes always held a kind of sweet mocking; full of so deep a knowledge that all the children of the iksa obeyed him without question.

When Atokotubbee saw Neshoba, he said, "Alla tek, a-chuk-ma taha che. The girl will be well."

The oldest member of the iksa danced all through the night singing his family's most ancient songs. The next day he burned a special plant and blew the smoke up the child's nose.

On that green morning, Haya, Anoleta, Nitakechi, and the tenderhearted Koi Chitto stood in the doorway of the cabin waiting to see if the girl would remember anything. Shakbatina placed her hand on Neshoba's head and caressed her lightly, so that she would not frighten the girl further.

"Try to remember what happened," she urged. "This is sometimes the way we are given things. Fight hard to remember, so you will know the meaning of this."

Shakbatina stepped aside with respect and motioned for Atokotubbee to come next to the girl. He took Neshoba's hand and patted it, but did not speak. At that moment, a fat buck ran in front of the door of their cabin and headed toward the woods. He had shown himself and several Choctaw hunters went after him.

While Neshoba's legs quickly healed, it was another year before she could use her voice. The wound on her cheek also healed, but left a scar. Some said, Shatanni Ohoyo, the Tick Woman, had kidnapped Neshoba and marked her for some purpose. Tick Woman was known to play tricks on the Choctaw: sometimes bringing sickness to them, sometimes to their enemies. Tick Woman could also be a helper.

As for Neshoba, she had never known what had happened to her, except that over the years, she had become an excellent tracker of wild game. She had a highly developed sense of smell. She was able always to lead her uncles directly to the animals they wanted to hunt. So tonight, Atokotubbee asked his niece to choose the Naholla with the young face and graying hair. "Teach that one to dance, alla tek," he said, motioning her toward the four white men seated apart of the Choctaws next to the fire.

Walking up to Father Renoir again, she was reminded of his scent, and she understood why her uncle sent her. She would teach Inki Sweets how to dance in her fire.

MICHAEL DORRIS is a well-known author who has published several books and stories. In 1985 he received the Indian Achievement Award. His novel *A Yellow Raft in Blue Water* (from which "Clara's Gift" is excerpted) was widely acclaimed, and his nonfiction work *The Broken Cord* won the National Book Critics Circle Award in 1989. He and his wife, Louise Erdrich, coauthored *The Crown of Columbus*. Dorris has recently finished his first children's book, *Morning Girl*, and a collection of his short stories, *Working Men*, is forthcoming. He is a Modoc Indian, living with his wife and children in New Hampshire.

CLARA'S GIFT

Michael Dorris

The nuns in Denver were enraptured when they heard the story of Clara's attack. She was a victim, they said, an innocent lamb, abused like a martyr by a rampaging beast of a man. For them, Clara fit into the stories of their saints, the tales of virgins pursued by pagan Roman soldiers, the legends of women who preferred death to surrender.

They overlooked the fact that Clara had not died.

With the nuns as her audience, the recounting of Clara's experience became more vivid and complicated: she had fought until she fainted or, occasionally, until she had been knocked unconscious by a large stone; she had sacrificed herself to save me, her sister, who had cowered in terror in a closet or behind a bush; she had tracked down her assailant and brought him to justice, the savior of her tribe. But even in this last version, even at the trial in which Clara courageously testified, the man's mask never came off. He remained nameless, without identifying marks, any man, every man. Each nun was free to see him with her own eye, in her own memory, in her own appallment.

As the tagalong sister I had no rights, no reason except Clara's companionship to be at the convent, and so I had to work for my board. I did the jobs reserved for novices—scrubbed floors and polished brass candlesticks and, with broom handles, turned laundry in large tubs. The bleach ruined my hands, burned lines off my palms as I lifted the heavy, scalding sheets from the water and fed them to the wringer. I slept on a cot in a bare room, watched by a crucifix and a window too high to see out. I was permitted to borrow one book at a time from the convent's library, but all the titles seemed to me the same.

Some days I didn't even meet Clara in the dining room. She was the only wayward girl in residence and had made friends among the younger nuns. I heard them whisper the hope that she would give her baby in adoption to a childless Catholic couple and join their order. They brought her along whenever they went about the city, took her to museums and public buildings, bought her five lunches at restaurants, found her practically new maternity clothes to wear.

Sitting alone between my jobs, waiting for the baby to be born, I realized that Pauline would have been a better mother for this baby than either Clara or me. She would have enjoyed my life at the convent and, more than that, she might have discovered a vocation. Me, I just backslid. I began to act as if I could barely speak English. I became difficult to awaken in the mornings, refused to kneel erect in the chapel but instead dropped my behind on the pew and buried my head in my arms. I gained weight on a diet of white bread and butter, sent a day-old by a devout Catholic dairy. I was everything those nuns expected an Indian to be, and after a while they hardly noticed I was there. Clara was the object of their prayers.

Still, I thought that when the baby came—when we returned home, when I saved Clara's name, provided Mama's care, took the burden off Papa, had stories of convent life to tell Pauline—

my life would be better than it had been. In our house I would once more be Clara's best company, and she, in my debt, would reopen her affections. I imagined a short vacation before returning for my last year of school, a flurry of scandal from which I would be saved in small ways by the truth Father Hurlburt guarded. I looked forward to the entertaining presence of a child, at once my brother or sister and my cousin, and to the resumption of my quest for Willard, who would return on leave from the army to see me in a new light.

I missed the smell of the reservation all that spring and early summer. Sometimes, in the breezes that blew through Denver from the north and west, I found the green scent of budding fields, the sharp catch of fresh dirt, the touch of air heated by the unshaded flow of sun. I missed the quiet, I missed easy talk. In my sleep, I dreamed conversations in which I made jokes and double meanings, in which I juggled words, weightless and fragile as abandoned mud dauber nests. In my dreams, I taught the baby to count.

I had one letter from Pauline, an assignment from her eighth-grade teacher, that was for the most part copied from a form in her schoolbook. On the front side of the page she said the winter had been mild, that everyone was well, that she had completed the nine First Fridays and received a large indulgence. She signed "Yours in Christ, your loving sister, Pauline George," and received a grade, recorded in thin red ink, of B+. On the back, far less carefully written, she added a note of her own creation.

> They fight all the time now. She is not better and he blames her for missing work. As soon as school is out he is going to hire on at a ranch and I have to take care of Mama. I hate this place. P.

I never answered.

I didn't hear that Clara had a girl until August 11, the day after the baby was born.

"Your brave sister bore a beautiful daughter," a young nun, Vivencia, told me when I came to breakfast.

I must have looked as if I didn't understand.

"An angel from heaven," she continued.

The child I had only vaguely imagined became female in my mind.

"Clara let us name her," Vivencia said. "We prayed over it and all agreed: Christine."

Like Christ, I thought. They had decided Clara was a virgin after all. Christine. I didn't mind it. I knew no Christines.

Vivencia was not satisfied that my English was sufficient to comprehend her news, so she spoke loud and slow, straight into my face.

"You are an *aunt*," she instructed. "You are Aunt Ida. That's you." She pointed her finger at my chest to make me see. Say that, *Aunt Ida*."

"Where is she?" I asked. "When can I see her?"

"Clara will rest in the infirmary for at least a week."

"No. The baby. Christine."

Vivencia pursed her lips. Her mouth was framed at each end with the wisps of a dark mustache. "Your sister has not yet de-cided what she will do. If she releases the child, it's best you not see it."

"She won't do that." I shook my head, stared her down. "Take me to Clara."

"She's resting now. She had a terrible time of it, she's so small. Perhaps tomorrow when she's stronger, when she has had more time to think clearly."

"Now," I insisted. "Now." I was bigger than Vivencia and frightened her. She stepped back from my determination, stroked the cross on her breast.

"Do not raise your voice to me," she hissed, but I could see she would do what I wanted. I was a mystery to her, a danger, a wild Indian not at all like her gentle Clara.

"I shall ask Mother. One of the sisters will accompany me to the hospital later. If you promise to behave, perhaps you may go too."

I promised nothing, but by afternoon I had ridden on a bus with a pair of nuns and followed them through brightly lit halls. I faced Clara in her white room. A picture of the Sacred Heart, framed in black wood, hung above her bed. I spoke to her in Indian so that only she could understand my words.

"Where is the baby?"

"Ida, don't be so loud. Why do you look at me like that?"

"You let them name her."

"You can always change it."

"They told me you might give her away." I expected her to laugh or be angry at the idea.

"They say it's for her own good, that someone else could take better care of her than a woman alone. Oh, my breasts hurt. You don't know the pain I suffered before I made them give me ether."

"You're not a woman alone."

"Well, they don't know that."

Her answers were so irrational that I wondered if her senses had been dulled by the gas the doctors had given her.

"Well, where is she, then," I said to change the subject. "Your breasts mean she's hungry."

"I'm not feeding her." Clara curled on her side, bunching the pillow under her head. "I'm too weak. They're giving her some other kind of milk."

I had never heard of such a thing, and Clara was not weak. I waited for her to go on. She took my hint.

"That way, if I should decide to let her go, there'd be no problem."

I raised my voice and shook the rungs at the foot of her bed. "What are you talking about? You can't give her away."

"I know, I know. That was our plan. But maybe not. I have to stay in the hospital for a while, then be near my doctor in Denver. What would I do with a baby?"

I realized that Clara had already decided that, for whatever reason, she would not keep Christine. Relief filled me like air. I had a vision of my life resumed intact, no gossip, no delays, no shame.

"So you understand?" Clara reposed in her white gown between clean white sheets. Sometime that day she had thought to draw lipstick on her mouth.

"No," I said. "I won't let you."

Clara's attention flew to my face.

"I can do what I want," she tried. "It's my baby."

"I'll tell them. They'll throw you out of here."

Her body froze in its spread position, flat as a centipede when you lift its rock. I saw her as I never wanted to see her, as what she was: moon-faced, whining, puny-limbed. My spine jerked as if awakened from a sound sleep. She was the other side of beautiful, and my love bore deep inside of me, leaving only a hole of passage to show it had ever existed.

"What do you want?" Clara's eyes, unaware, stared into the pillow beside her face.

"I'll take her home. You can come when you're well."

"She isn't even *pretty*," Clara whispered. "She's all nose."

"Where is she? Have them bring her here." I sat on the blue wood chair and looked at the cars parked along the street. I waited while Clara sighed, fussed, while she rang for the nurse and did as I had ordered. It was a hot day with almost no breeze. The leaves on the short trees looked heavy as tin. I wasn't pretty either. People would believe my story.

I did not turn my glance when the door opened or when I heard a nurse, moving softly in the room, say to Clara, "Here she is." I waited until we were alone again, and then I swiveled, rose, approached the bed. Only then, standing next to Clara's covered legs, did I extend my arms and see the child. One slanted eye was open, the other closed. Her lips were white from whatever she drank, her face was round as a yellow pear. On the very crown of her head was one thick patch of dark red hair, but otherwise she was bald. Her small hands pushed at her mother's uncomfortable grip. While I watched, her nostrils flared as if she smelled something alarming. I hesitated one last time, panicked to touch her, afraid to feel the bones beneath her skin, but Clara convinced me.

"Well, take her," she said. "Or let me do the sensible thing and give her up."

So I took her.

She weighed less than the candlesticks I polished, less than rinse water in a bucket. The skin of her face against my cheek was warm and clean. I moved to the window for better light and she squeezed her eyes against the glare, pressed her face to my sweater. I fed her when the nurse brought a bottle, and I let her sleep along the slope of my forearm, the back of her head supported by the palm of my hand. I waited like that, tense in all my muscles, until finally Vivencia and her Superior came back from their visits to the sick, until Clara disappointed them by announcing she would keep Christine, until I heard her say Aunt Ida would bring the baby home.

I steamed over Clara, how she didn't come to the depot for a last look at her own baby and how she refused to specify when she expected to return to the reservation. "There's so much I haven't seen in this city," she told me. "It would be a waste to miss it, because you never know when I'll be back this way."

During the two weeks since she had checked out of the hospital and returned to the convent, she had let me do everything for Christine—feed her, bathe her, rock her to sleep. Clara claimed to be still recovering, yet she had energy for herself. Those stupid nuns hadn't given up on her coming in with them. They treated her like glass, but to Clara their house was just a cheap place to sleep, the only rent that she say what they wanted to hear.

I wasn't afraid to travel alone. I was big and looked older than my years and had a baby to protect me. I took a Greyhound bus and transferred in Cheyenne for Billings. I arrived in early afternoon and sat on a bench in front of the station and waited for Father Hurlburt, my suitcase between my knees and Christine on my lap. By staying in Denver, Clara had made her design fool-proof. In my dress and in the way I carried myself, in my sullen-ness and in my exhaustion, I was the picture of a girl who had borne a child in shame.

I had left six months ago with only promises in my pocket, and, except for Pauline's note, I had no idea what to expect. A part of me imagined everything remained the same, but another part knew better. I didn't calculate what my presence had added or subtracted to that house in the past, but in my absence, what-ever poles I had held erect would have collapsed.

After an hour, Father Hurlburt arrived in old Father Gephardt's green Ford. When he saw me, he parked in the lane and got out to help.

"I hope you haven't been waiting long," he said. "I was later than I planned in departing."

I lifted the blanket away from Christine's face, and he gave a long look.

"My, my. A little girl?"

"Christine."

"Christine. And where's her mother? Inside?"

"I'm her mother," I reminded him. "Clara stayed in Denver extra time. She'll be back when she's feeling better."

"She's not ill?" he asked, worried.

"No." With my foot, I pushed my suitcase toward the curb, but Father Hurlburt excused himself and put it into the backseat.

Inside the car he seemed smaller, almost thin. He drove two-handed, and slowed down long before he reached each red light. I watched his movements from the corner of my eye, followed the line of his profile from his brown hair to his white priest's collar. At one stop, something slid from under the seat and brushed my foot. I reached down and landed an empty pint of Old Crow.

A blush rose beneath Father Hurlburt's skin. His ear turned bright rose and his teeth clamped together. I set the bottle on the floor where I found it, and adjusted Christine's blanket. I was glad to have a secret back on him, even not a very surprising one.

Christine could never sleep when she was in motion, but she

was content to consider my face. I wondered what she saw. In Denver I had grown taller and heavier. The muscles of my shoulders and back, already powerful from helping Papa in the fields, had thickened with my hard work at the convent. I wore one of Clara's maternity dresses to travel, since none of her regular clothes would fit me.

"When is she returning?" Father Hurlburt asked his question in Indian. I was impressed but didn't know how to show it, so I pretended it was as natural as day to hear a priest talk right.

"She doesn't know." I had to say something. "You've learned a lot."

He laughed, switched back to English. "I rehearsed that line for the last five miles. I'm not a good student."

It was not my place to contradict, so I looked out my window. Bales already dotted the fields.

"One reason I wanted to learn," Father Hurlburt said, "is that, well, you know I'm part Indian myself."

I turned to scrutinize him. I could see it.

"I don't know much about that branch of my family. My father's mother from New York State was a Seneca, but I only vaguely remember her."

"I've heard of them," I said, but I didn't know what.

"That's how I got interested in Indians, I guess. It must be in my blood." Father Hurlburt laughed at his own joke, and when I failed to join in, he didn't speak again for forty miles.

I closed my eyes and let my mind wander. I couldn't quite think of him as Indian, but knowing about that grandmother changed something. It made me less surprised about the night when he came to our house and listened to Clara's plan, when I noticed him as more than a priest. Now I had an explanation.

As we came closer to home, as I began to recognize the roll of the land, the familiar pattern of mountain ridges on the horizon, I could no longer avoid the anticipation of what awaited me. It occurred to me that with every mile we traveled, Christine was more my baby.

Father Hurlburt spoke again when we drove onto the reservation.

"Did you hear Pauline is no longer living with your parents?"

I tightened my hold on Christine, unwilling to admit my ignorance.

"She has not been happy there since . . . since your father has been out of work, so the good sisters found her a place with a family at the Agency."

"Mama?" I asked.

"I'm afraid her condition is no better. I, we, thought with the warm weather she would improve. He raised his shoulders and his eyebrows and glanced at me in puzzlement. "Perhaps with your return."

"Is he drinking?" This was not something I would normally ask a priest, but I had no one else.

"That has been a problem," Father Hurlburt admitted, nodding as if the idea had not struck him before. "Yes, a problem."

A few miles later I saw the roof of the house, obscured by the low hills that built toward the canyon close to our land. No smoke rose from the chimney. Christine squirmed in restlessness. Even with the windows open, the car was musty and close, as if the air somehow blew past us without touching.

"Do they know I'm coming today?" The nuns in Denver had written directly to Father Hurlburt with my bus schedule.

"I did stop by on the way to Billings, to make sure," he said uncertainly. "I'm sure they are preparing for you."

However, it was Clara's return that had captured Papa.

When the car stopped, he burst from the house, his hair slicked back with water, the sleeves of his shirt rolled over his long johns. Papa's face was eager, his eyes scanned the front seat. He pulled open the door next to me, but looked beyond my shoulder at nothing but my suitcase.

"Where is Clara?" he demanded, as if I were hiding her for a mean joke. I crouched over Christine at his tone, and Father Hurlburt answered for me.

"She was not quite well enough to leave Denver yet, Lecon," he explained. "She'll be back soon. But look who *is* here."

Papa observed me, then the baby in my arms. I held her for him to see. I answered the only question in his eyes.

"Christine."

"It's in their family," he said, almost to himself. "Nothing but girls."

Those next two and a half years blur in my memory in chunks large as seasons. A winter of shoveling snow, a summer in which Christine learned to walk, a long damp fall in which Papa worked in town and came home only on weekends. On Friday nights he'd sit in the washtub filled with water I had heated on the stove, drinking the bottle he had bought before he crossed the reservation line. He'd sing at first, splash Christine, and ask after Pauline, but by midnight he would turn evil, yell for another bottle, curse Mama for her illness, cry for Clara who never came back, assail me for the shame he said I brought him. It was as if he forgot the truth. He slept through Saturdays, all of us tiptoeing not to wake him, keeping Christine amused and quiet, and on Sundays he'd rise, purged and proper, to walk to church for a sight of Pauline, to show everyone they were still father and daughter. Sometimes he came home for an hour after that, other times he went immediately back to his job. By Sunday night our house of women could breathe easier.

Mama faded like a plant without sun. These days, they'd say it was a new stroke that stiffened her arm and slurred her speech, but, back then, it was as if she was breaking a part at a time. She never forgave me either. In her weakness she said I had chosen Clara and all that followed was my doing. But she saved her greatest recriminations for herself. "What possessed me?" she demanded almost daily. "Why did I send for her?"

I had no answer.

I nursed her as best I could, yet there were nights I lay quiet until her calls for water or company, for a person or a moment in time to blame, had passed. I had Christine to think of, and if I missed too much sleep, she overwhelmed me the next morning with her questions and wants.

Christine had not been pretty at birth and she wasn't a pretty child, but there was a quality she had, a way of standing, that made you look at her twice. She had no fear. She would wake from a bad dream and want to tell it, hampered only by how few words she knew. She would stray from the house and sit content until I found her, watching ants build a nest or a cloud patch glide across the sky. She tried to climb anything she found in her path.

When the time came, I had Christine call me "Aunt Ida," both at home and when we went out among people who assumed I was ashamed to claim her. And every time she said it, the feelings for her I couldn't help, the feelings that came from being the one she came to when she was hurt and the one who heard her prayers, the feelings I fought against, got flaked away. That was as I intended. Someday Clara would arrive at the door and might steal Christine back.

*L*ESLIE MARMON SILKO, the acclaimed author of *Ceremony*, *Storyteller*, and *Almanac of the Dead*, is from Laguna Pueblo in New Mexico, and much of her writing draws on the rich heritage of her people. The recent recipient of a MacArthur Foundation Grant, Silko lives and writes in Tucson, Arizona.

THE RETURN OF THE BUFFALO

Leslie Marmon Silko

Wilson Weasel Tail strode up to the podium and whipped out two sheets of paper. Weasel Tail had abandoned his polyester leisure suits for army camouflage fatigues; he wore his hair in long braids carefully wrapped in red satin ribbon. Weasel Tail's voice boomed throughout the main ballroom. Today he wanted to begin his lecture by reading two fragments of famous Native American documents. "First, I read to you from Pontiac's manuscript:

" 'You cry the white man has stolen everything, killed all your animals and food, but where were you when the people first discussed the Europeans? Tell the truth. You forgot everything you were ever told. You forgot the stories with warnings. You took what was easy to swallow, what you never had to chew. You were like a baby suddenly helpless in the white man's hands because the white man feeds your greed until it swells up your belly and chest to your head. You steal from your neighbors. You can't be trusted!' "

Weasel Tail had paused dramatically and gazed at the audience before he continued:

"Treachery has turned back upon itself. Brother has betrayed brother. Step back from envy, from sorcery and poisoning. Reclaim these continents which belong to us."

Weasel Tail paused, took a deep breath, and read the Paiute prophet Wovoka's letter to President Grant:

> You are hated
> You are not wanted here
> Go away,
> Go back where you came from.
> You white people are cursed!

The audience in the main ballroom had become completely still, as if in shock from Weasel Tail's presentation. But Weasel Tail seemed not to notice and had immediately launched into his lecture.

"Today I wish to address the question as to whether the spirits of the ancestors in some way failed our people when the prophets called them to the Ghost Dance," Weasel Tail began.

"Moody and other anthropologists alleged the Ghost Dance disappeared because the people became disillusioned when the ghost shirts did not stop bullets and the Europeans did not vanish overnight. But it was the Europeans, not the Native Americans, who had expected results overnight; the anthropologists, who feverishly sought magic objects to postpone their own deaths, had misunderstood the power of the ghost shirts. Bullets of lead belong to the everyday world; ghost shirts belong to the realm of spirits and dreams. The ghost shirts gave the dancers spiritual protection while the white men dreamed of shirts that repelled bullets because they feared death."

Moody and the others had never understood the Ghost Dance was to reunite living people with spirits of beloved ancestors lost in the five-hundred-year war. The longer Wilson Weasel Tail talked, the more animated and energized he became; Lecha could see he was about to launch into a poem:

We dance to remember,
we dance to remember all our beloved ones,
to remember how each passed
to the spirit world.
We dance because the dead love us,
they continue to speak to us,
they tell our hearts what must be done to survive.
We dance and we do not forget all the others before us,
the little children and the old women who fought and who
    died
resisting the invaders and destroyers of Mother Earth!
Spirits! Ancestors!
we have been counting the days, watching the signs.
You are with us every minute,
you whisper to us in our dreams,
you whisper in our waking moments.
You are more powerful than memory!

Weasel Tail paused to take a sip of water. Lecha was impressed with the silence Weasel Tail had created in the main ballroom. "Naturopaths," holistic healers, herbalists, the guys with the orgone boxes and pyramids—all of them had locked up their cashboxes and closed their booths to listen to Weasel Tail talk. "The spirits are outraged! They demand justice! The spirits are furious! To all those humans too weak or too lazy to fight to protect Mother Earth, the spirits say, 'Too bad you did not die fighting the destroyers of the earth because now *we* will kill you for being so weak, for wringing your hands and whimpering while the invaders committed outrages against the forests and the mountains.' The spirits will harangue you, they will taunt you until you are forced to silence the voices with whiskey day after day. The spirits allow you no rest. The spirits say die fighting the invaders or die drunk."

The enraged spirits haunted the dreams of society matrons in the suburbs of Houston and Chicago. The spirits had directed mothers from country club neighborhoods to pack the children in the car and drive off hundred-foot cliffs or into flooding rivers, leaving no note for the husbands. A message to the psychiatrist says only, "It is no use any longer." They see no reason for their children or them to continue. The spirits whisper in the brains of loners, the crazed young white men with automatic rifles who slaughter crowds in shopping malls or school yards as casually as hunters shoot buffalo. All day the miner labors in tunnels underground, hacking out ore with a sharp steel hand-pick; he returns home to his wife and family each night. Then suddenly the miner slaughters his wife and children. The "authorities" call it "mental strain" because he has used his miner's hand-pick to chop deep into the mother lode to reach their hearts and their brains.

Weasel Tail cleared his throat, then went on, "How many dead souls are we talking about? Computer projections place the populations of the Americas at more than seventy million when the Europeans arrived; one hundred years later, only ten million people had survived. Sixty million dead souls howl for justice in the Americas! They howl to retake the land as the black Africans have retaken their land!

"You think there is no hope for indigenous tribal people here to prevail against the violence and greed of the destroyers? But you forget the inestimable power of the earth and all the forces of the universe. You forget the colliding meteors. You forget the earth's outrage and the trembling that will not stop. Overnight the wealth of nations will be reclaimed by the Earth. The trembling does not stop and the rain clouds no longer gather; the sun burns the earth until the plants and animals disappear and die.

"The truth is the Ghost Dance did not end with the murder of Big Foot and one hundred and forty-four Ghost Dance worshipers at Wounded Knee. The Ghost Dance has never ended, it has continued, and the people have never stopped dancing; they may call it by other names, but when they dance, their hearts are reunited with the spirits of beloved ancestors and the loved ones recently lost in the struggle. Throughout the Americas, from Chile to Canada, the people have never stopped dancing; as the living dance, they are joined again with all our ancestors before them, who cry out, who demand justice, and who call the people to take back the Americas!"

Weasel Tail threw back his shoulders and puffed out his chest; he was going to read poetry:

The spirit army is approaching,
The spirit army is approaching,
The whole world is moving onward,
The whole world is moving onward.
See! Everybody is standing watching.
See! Everybody is standing watching.

The whole world is coming,
A nation is coming, a nation is coming,
The Eagle has brought the message to the tribe.
The father says so, the father says so.

Over the whole earth they are coming.
The buffalo are coming, the buffalo are coming,

The Crow has brought the message to the tribe,
The father says so, the father says so.

I'yche'! ana'nisa'na'—Uhi'yeye'heye'!
I'yche'! ana'nisa'na'—Uhi'yeye'heye'!
I'yehe'! ha'dawu'hana'—Eye'ae'yuhe'yu!
I'yehe'! ha'dawu'hana'—Eye'ae'yuhe'yu!
Ni'athu'-a-u'a'haka'nith'ii—Ahe'yuhe'yu!

(Translation)
I'yehe'! my children—Uhi'yeye'heye'!
I'yehe'! my children—Uhi'yeye'heye'!
I'yehe'! we have rendered them
desolate—Eye'ae'yuhe'yu!
I'yehe'!—we have rendered them
desolate—Eye'ae'yuhe'yu!
The whites are crazy—Ahe'yuhe'yu!

Again when Weasel Tail had finished, the ballroom was hushed; then the audience had given Weasel Tail a standing ovation.

"Have the spirits let us down? Listen to the prophecies! Next to thirty thousand years, five hundred years look like nothing. The buffalo are returning. They roam off federal land in Montana and Wyoming. Fences can't hold them. Irrigation water for the Great Plains is disappearing, and so are the farmers, and their plows. Farmers' children retreat to the cities. Year by year the range of the buffalo grows a mile or two larger."

Weasel Tail had them eating out of his hand; he let his voice trail off dramatically to a stage whisper that had resonated throughout the ballroom speaker system. The audience leapt to its feet with a great ovation. Lecha had to hand it to Wilson

Weasel Tail; he'd learned a thing or two. Still, Weasel Tail was a lawyer at heart; Lecha noted that he had made the invaders an offer that couldn't be refused. Weasel Tail had said to the U.S. government, "Give us back what you have stolen or else as a people you will continue your self-destruction."